PASSION IN BONDAGE

"How can you endure Marmarus?" Ilbaya whispered.

Lyra's voice was brittle with restrained anger. "By remembering I'll survive. Many women have had to trade their bodies to survive. I'm a thing to Marmarus because I have no choice. I'm not a woman with him."

Ilbaya brushed a golden curl back from her forehead. "You are a woman to me."

"If Marmarus should come upon us . . ." Her voice trailed off. Then, with a ferocity that surprised him, she said, "I don't care. If he killed me, I would die a woman—not a slave-thing. I'd chance kissing you and whatever follows. What would your decision be?"

Ilbaya looked into her eyes with an intensity that made her tremble. And then, forsaking caution, his mouth was upon hers. . . .

Fawcett Gold Medal Books
by Joyce Verrette:

SUNRISE OF SPLENDOR

WINGED PRIESTESS

WINGED PRIESTESS

Joyce Verrette

FAWCETT GOLD MEDAL • NEW YORK

WINGED PRIESTESS

Published by Fawcett Gold Medal Books, a unit of CBS
Publications, the Consumer Publishing Division of CBS Inc.

ISBN: 0-449-14329-5

Printed in the United States of America

First Fawcett Gold Medal printing: April 1980

10   9   8   7   6   5   4   3   2   1

WINGED PRIESTESS

One

The snow on the mountaintops of Minoa had become a fiery orange glow in the late-afternoon sun, and the lush, green hills below were washed with a rich, golden sheen. At the foot of the hills, the beach was burnished with the shimmering gilt reflected by the sea.

Through the glowing light a horse came thundering, his streaming mane and tail the same bright copper as the hair of his youthful rider, which was whipping in the wind like orange flames. Horse and rider appeared almost as if they were one being, the wild pace they shared as effortless as the flight of the hunting falcon that followed close by. Horse, man and bird joyously sped through the golden light as if their reckless freedom were as necessary as the air they breathed—and just as carelessly accepted. But when they approached a curve in the beach that would expose them to the sight of the house halfway up the slope of the next hill, the rider reluctantly slowed his horse to a more sedate pace, lest one of his younger sisters or even his brother report his breakneck speed to their mother. Ilbaya had resigned himself long ago to his mother's fear of his love for racing. Turning, he whistled to his falcon, which obediently folded its wings and glided in to perch on his shoulder.

As he approached the terraced lawns before the house, Ilbaya was surprised to notice that no workers were tending the neatly ordered flower beds. He lifted his eyes to the distant columned portico and saw a number of wagons and a crowd of men gathered at the house's entrance.

If his father had returned from his latest voyage, he wondered why he hadn't seen the masts of his father's ship in the bay by Knossos. He had been riding high enough in the hills to view the city. Then he decided he hadn't noticed the ship or the approaching caravan of wagons because he had been thinking about Kandia, the slave girl his mother had recently bought as an additional maid for his sisters. Remembering Kandia's many furtive glances in his direction, Ilbaya wondered if she would welcome him should he visit her quarters some night soon.

His thoughts turned from Kandia as he swerved his horse onto the winding road leading up the slope to the house. His hazel eyes filled with dancing green lights when he recalled his father's promise to bring him a hunting chariot from Tamera. Whenever Seres returned from a successful voyage— and he was a very prosperous merchant, so most trading voyages he made were successful—he brought a lavish array of gifts for his family. Ilbaya wondered if the gifts and his father's homingcoming would soften his mother's opposition to his accompanying his father on the next voyage.

Ilbaya had been arguing for several years that he must learn this phase of Seres' business as well as the management of his shop and warehouses in Knossos, a feat he felt he had already accomplished. Although he did want to learn every aspect of the business he would eventually inherit, he also desperately wanted to visit the lands his father had so vividly described. Each time the sea wind touched his face he could almost smell the mysterious perfumes, hear the strange languages of the exotic kingdoms that lay beyond the shores of his island homeland—Mycenae, Akkad, Retenu, Shekel, Kinanu, Tamera.

His mother opposed his traveling not only because she feared the dangers they would meet, but also because she knew once Ilbaya had tasted adventure, he, like his father, would be anxious to go again. She wanted at least one of them to stay at home until his brother, Nerou, was old enough to act as the man of the house.

As Ilbaya approached the entrance hall, he frowned. The workers were carrying items of furniture *out* of the house rather than taking them inside. He wondered if his father had brought all new furniture and was having the old shipped away. He dismounted, still frowning, as he untied his hunting bow and arrow case from his saddle. Running up the few stairs before the entrance, he ducked around a worker who was bowed under the burden of a large chest and stepped into the courtyard. There he stared in amazement.

All the household slaves had been herded into a corner of the courtyard, and Ilbaya saw that Kandia was cowering in a corner, looking very frightened. Then he realized that the slaves were being separated, the females being pushed into the shade of the stoa, the males against another wall. And the men separating them were *not* workers. They were soldiers. Ilbaya spun around to hurry through the house in search of his mother. He was so lost in conflicting thoughts he didn't notice that his falcon had left his shoulder and found a perch on the roof, carefully avoiding the strangers.

As Ilbaya entered the vestibule, he heard a sharp cry and whirled to catch a glimpse of his sisters being pushed and pulled by two soldiers into a doorway down the hall.

"Stop! What are you doing?" he called as he ran after them.

He passed a sitting room and, seeing his mother lying on a divan with her back toward him, came to an abrupt halt. "Mother, what's happening here? What are these soldiers doing?" he asked as he hurried into the room.

His mother neither moved nor spoke.

"Mother, do you know the king's soldiers are taking Chani and Mallia somewhere? Where's Father? I thought he was here!"

Ilbaya received no answer. He couldn't understand how she could be napping in such commotion, but any other possibility was beyond his imagining, so he shook her shoulder. The movement caused her body to roll over on its back. Her eyes were closed, her face as serene as when she slept; but on the front of her robe between her breasts was a great red splotch. Too shocked to grasp the situation fully, Ilbaya stared silently down on her.

Lord Chaon, the king's agent, heard Ilbaya's calls and, following the sound of his voice, turned into the room. He paused just inside the doorway. Observing Ilbaya's costly embroidered tunic, and his distinctive fiery hair, Lord Chaon knew he had found the oldest son of the house.

"She did it to herself," Chaon said warily. "Don't think, as your brother did, that she was murdered. It was a mistake he paid for, much to my regret."

Ilbaya straightened slowly and turned to face Lord Chaon, whom he recognized as one of King Velchanos' men; but Chaon wasn't looking at him. Ilbaya's eyes followed the direction of Chaon's gaze and fell on Nerou's body lying nearby on the floor. Ilbaya rushed to his brother and knelt wordlessly at his side. He gasped when he saw that Nerou had been nearly decapitated. He shut his eyes tightly, as if denying the sight would deny its reality.

After a moment, Ilbaya whispered, "Nerou was only a boy, barely thirteen. Why has this been done? Why any of this?"

"When Nerou saw your mother, he thought I'd murdered her. He took the dagger she'd used and rushed at me. Commander Kingu had to stop him," Lord Chaon answered. "As for the rest, your father was in debt to King Velchanos and his majesty is seizing your property to recover the debt."

Ilbaya slowly opened his eyes, but still didn't move. "My father is Seres the merchant. He's of a noble family, in debt to no one," he muttered brokenly.

"His majesty entrusted Seres with a great deal of gold to buy furnishings and decorative objects for the new palace that's being constructed, but the king received a message that Seres' ship had sunk in a storm near Troy. So, to compensate the royal treasury for the gold that was lost, all your father's possessions are being seized and sold—his house, his slaves, his family as well. Rather than submit to slavery, your mother stabbed herself to death."

Ilbaya couldn't speak. He just continued staring down at his brother's body. His brain seemed unable to acknowledge that his mother, father and brother were dead, that his sisters were being dragged away to be sold as slaves, that he would be enslaved also, that his world was smashed. A terrible pain filling him had grown into an agony that made it difficult for him to think at all.

"A healthy young slave like your brother would have brought a good price. I'm sorry he acted so foolishly," Lord Chaon was saying. "I understand you can read and know mathematics, even the decimal system. Those skills will make you a valued slave. Your life won't be too bad if you accept your lot and behave prudently."

"What about my sisters, who know nothing of mathematics or anything but being well-loved daughters in a happy household?" Ilbaya managed to ask.

10

"Pretty young female slaves always are valuable. They need know nothing." Lord Chaon paused, and a sneer crept into his tone as he added, "In some matters, the less they know, the higher their value."

Ilbaya's anguish overcame his reason. His fingers crept toward Nerou's dagger that still lay near the boy's body. With his back yet toward Chaon, Ilbaya was able to conceal his action.

"Your name is Ilbaya, is it not?" Lord Chaon asked quietly. As Ilbaya's bright head slowly nodded, Chaon moved closer to him and said, "Get up then, Ilbaya. We must be going. You can do your grieving anywhere."

Ilbaya sprang to his feet and turned almost in one motion.

Lord Chaon paled at the sight of the dagger Ilbaya held. "Don't be as foolish as your brother. Life for an intelligent slave can be comfortable and worth living."

"I care nothing for a lifetime of slavery however comfortable," Ilbaya snarled. He gripped Chaon's wrist and stepped around him, twisting Chaon's arm behind his back. "Now," he said in a voice full of menace, "you will go ahead of me out that door and down the hall."

"What do you think you can do against all those soldiers?"

"You will walk with me to where my sisters are being held. You will order their release. Then you'll supply us with horses," Ilbaya directed.

"Where could you go on this island—if you get even three paces away from the front stairs?" Chaon asked. "Have the good sense to give me the dagger and accept the destiny your father gave you."

"What happened wasn't my father's fault," Ilbaya snapped. "It's King Velchanos' greed that causes this. It will also put this dagger into your body if you struggle."

"You're mad," Lord Chaon said, but he began to walk toward the door.

Ilbaya concentrating so intently on guarding Lord Chaon he didn't notice, as he stepped into the hall, Commander Kingu flattened against the door they were approaching.

"I think your sisters have already been taken away," Lord Chaon said, hoping to keep Ilbaya distracted with conversation. "They wouldn't have been put with the household slaves, after all. They're probably halfway to Knossos by now."

"If necessary, you and I will follow them all the way to the palace," Ilbaya muttered.

11

"They aren't going to the palace," Chaon replied. "They'll be put aboard a ship bound for Tyre—a ship which you'll join. You won't escape."

"If I don't, you won't know it, because you'll be dead before I'm captured," Ilbaya threatened.

When they approached the doorway that concealed Commander Kingu, Lord Chaon made a sudden move, as if trying to twist himself out of Ilbaya's grasp, but his intention was to get Ilbaya to turn his back to Kingu. Struggling to hold Chaon, Ilbaya turned exactly as the man wished.

Commander Kingu tore Ilbaya from Chaon and pushed him away, slamming him against the wall, sending the dagger spinning along the floor down the corridor. Kingu drew his sword ominously.

"Don't kill him!" cried Lord Chaon. "He's too valuable!"

Ilbaya stepped away from the wall to face Commander Kingu levelly. "You do not have a choice. I prefer to die," Ilbaya said softly, then asked, "How can you hold a sword in position to defend yourself, Commander Kingu, and yet prevent a man from throwing himself on it?" He tensed his muscles as he spoke, and poised to leap on the blade, but a pair of arms reached from behind, pinning his arms down, holding him back.

Infuriated, Ilbaya twisted the soldier's grasp, stamped on the man's feet, and tried to kick him, but Kingu's fist smashed into his face. Ilbaya's head snapped back from the blow, and Kingu's fist slammed into his stomach caused his breath to explode from him. Another blow to his chin sent the world spinning around him; his legs sagged and he fell.

Dimly, as if from a distance, Ilbaya heard Kingu snap, "Carry him out to the courtyard. Dump him in with the male slaves and make sure he's watched closely."

Ilbaya felt his shoulders being lifted, his heels dragging along the floor, bouncing against the step down into the courtyard. When the soldier dropped him, the back of his head struck the paving stones. Slowly Ilbaya turned to lie on his side, still gasping for breath.

After a time, when his vision had cleared and he could breathe, he opened his eyes to see one of his father's slaves—one he had never liked—bending over him, peering into his face.

"Get away from me," Ilbaya mumbled and slowly sat up.

"You can't give me orders any more," the slave said

smugly, but he moved back before adding, "You're one of us now."

Ilbaya struggled to his feet, and although his stomach felt as if a horse had kicked him, he turned away from the slave and lifted his head defiantly.

Nearby Commander Kingu stopped to address Lord Chaon. "We've taken everything, my lord."

"Then load the slaves into the wagons," Chaon ordered. "I want them on the ship and safely in chains before dark so we can sail when the tide goes out."

"Yes, my lord," Kingu replied.

At the mention of chains, Ilbaya shuddered with revulsion. He raised his eyes to the sky to measure the time he had left before he was shackled. High in the blue, he saw his falcon circling the house. Envying the bird its wings, he vowed he would find a way to escape and rescue his sisters.

Two

Night crept toward the edge of the desert until the sky was the deepest of blue. There were no sounds from the desert's emptiness, though the beginning song of night insects rose from the fertile area. No sign of life was apparent among the desert's growing shadows save one small fire winking cheerfully at the approaching darkness.

Lying on his side on a blanket spread over the sand, Amenemhet leaned comfortably on an elbow. His dark-gold eyes occasionally lit to brighter streaks reflecting the dancing flames of the campfire. The corners of his mouth turned up slightly as he watched Nefrytatanen's suprisingly deft motions while she packed away the scraps left from their evening meal. Such menial chores weren't part of her training; but she was managing well, he observed.

Nefrytatanen turned to Amenemhet with a triumphant smile. She thought he might tease her about the unaccustomed chores, but he said nothing.

"Would you like more wine?" Her voice was low on the hushed desert air.

"Not that of the grape." He sat up and stretched luxuriously. "Come and kiss me, little sand-dweller."

Nefrytatanen came to sit beside Amenemhet, enjoying his

15

pretense that she was a sand-dweller. She kissed him lightly on the cheek and withdrew.

Amenemhet smiled and asked softly, "You're shy, girl? You aren't used to spending a night on the desert with a man?"

The firelight in her loose hair made a shining web of the strands as she turned to face him. "Is the night not pleasant?"

"It will become even more pleasant, I suspect, as the air cools." His eyes gleamed wickedly.

Nefrytatanen lowered her eyes in a pretense of modesty. "Does it become very cool?"

"As cold as those stars appear," Amenemhet replied softly, "at which time one blanket each won't be enough to keep warm."

Nefrytatanen continued to stare at the sand as if she were embarrassed. "What will we do then?"

A breeze brought her perfume like a gift to Amenemhet, and he smiled. "Come closer and I'll keep the chill from you while I consider the problem."

"Moving nearer the fire would warm me," she said drily, "and you're farther from it than I."

"I have my own fire," Amenemhet whispered, "which will warm you more thoroughly than that one." He reached for her, but felt only the strands of her black hair brush his hands, because she had suddenly gotten to her feet.

"You're not yet tired enough to sleep?" Amenemhet asked. He put his arms around his knees and rested his chin on them to regard her calmly. "If you need exercise, you might dance for me. I have heard the dances of sand-dwellers are entertaining. When you've tired, we can discuss a solution to our shortage of blankets."

"I have no music," she answered.

"The breeze can be your melody," he replied, then softly added, "and my heart will keep the beat."

Nefrytatanen stood motionless, as if she were deciding whether to dance. But Amenemhet knew she would, and his pulse quickened in anticipation. She would play the part of a sand-dweller girl and pretend reluctance, but she would make certain her dance would further arouse the desire he already felt growing in him. Their lovemaking often began with a game of pretense, of teasing each other and flirting like strangers contemplating love.

Nefrytatanen began to hum a melody, she raised her arms, and her hips began swaying in the slow, rhythmic movement

16

of the sand-dwellers' provocative dance. Her motions stirred Amenemhet exactly as she knew they would. The only sounds came from the nameless little song she hummed, the soft movements of her feet in the sand and the gentle clinking of her bracelets, but he felt as if a small drum were beating in his temples. She moved a little closer, and he reached playfully for her ankle, but she moved away, a look of reproach on her face.

Amenemhet sat waiting for another chance. She shook her shoulders in a manner that produced a most interesting effect, and he reached for her more seriously. Again, she moved out of reach.

"Would you lure me to you, sand-dweller?" he whispered. "You seem to promise many things, but you stay just outside my reach." He tilted his head slightly as he regarded her with a faint smile.

She gave no answer, and kept her distance. Suddenly she began to spin in a series of turns, first one way then another, again and again, making a sparkling blur in the firelight.

"Come closer in your dance." His voice had lost its joking lightness, though he spoke quietly. The distance between them promptly widened. He stood up and said clearly, "You've extended an invitation I would answer now!"

Nefrytatanen stopped humming, her feet pausing in her steps.

A few long strides took Amenemhet to her. He said, "I answer yes."

Her eyes darkened to blue smoke as she stared up at him, saying nothing, panting slightly from her dance. He slid his arms around her, drawing her close to his warm, hard body.

"Come," he murmured. "Can you not feel my heart already beating like a timbrel to your steps?"

Pulling her on to the blanket, he sat close to her and began to kiss her softly and lingeringly, his restless lips moving over her face and throat, until his shoulders pressed her back and she lay down, her breath quickening. His fingers began to explore her body, sensitively, carefully, as if she were new to him and his caresses made discoveries. His touch ignited small fires in her being, which grew, showering golden sparks lighting the desert's shadows. Overcome with pleasure, she closed her eyes.

Lying there, she felt as if the coals of their campfire glowed within her. But suddenly his hand left her. Opening her eyes, she looked up at him. He had moved away to kneel beside her.

"Are you not warmer?" he teased. "I promised to find a solution."

Nefrytatanen was already beyond teasing. She didn't answer. She looked up at him. Waiting.

He didn't move.

Finally, her arms reached out to him. A little breathlessly she asked, "You said you have your own fire?"

"I am a man of truth."

Her eyes stared at him in challenge. "Why did you stop?"

"So you would ask." He loosened his tunic quickly and dropped it on the sand, his hands trembling slightly. "Will you ask?" he said quietly.

Although Nefrytatanen's voice was low, he heard her sharpened desire speak clearly. "Soon I'll become angry."

He unfastened her simple robe and flung it aside. Still he knelt over her, a fingertip lightly tracing small unseeable circles on her skin, smiling enigmatically.

"Beloved," she whispered urgently, "soon I will beg!"

Amenemhet awakened with the sky's first hint of approaching dawn. The air was cool, but Nefrytatanen's back was warm against him. He drew closer, tucking the blanket carefully over her naked shoulder. He watched the sky grow lighter, while the stars paled; and when the rim of the sun appeared in the east, Nefrytatanen's eyes opened. She turned slowly to rest her face against the curve of his throat.

"Did my solution keep you warm?" Amenemhet asked softly. He felt, not saw, Nefrytatanen's nod. The warm, sweet scent of her was a subtle invitation, but he merely smoothed her hair from her eyes. "Are you still shy, sand-dweller?" he whispered. "I would think you'd have forgotten such things by now. You were most unshy last night." He could feel her arms winding their way around him, and he smiled. After lying quietly for a time, he said seriously, "I'm glad you thought of leaving the palace to spend the night alone out here."

"No gladder than I," she murmured. She moved a little away and looked into his eyes, which were becoming a brighter gold with the growing sunlight. "I'm afraid I underestimated our supplies or our appetites. We have little left for our morning meal."

18

"I have you," he said, his tilted eyes rekindling. "What more do I need?"

"Beloved," she whispered, "you still act as if you're trying to win a sand-dweller girl."

"Could that girl be won again?"

Nefrytatanen ran a finger lightly over his cheekbone, continuing to look intently at him. "Your eyes have always made shivers run down my spine."

"That's no reason to love me," he declared.

"Maybe not in itself," she murmured, "but added to all the rest, it isn't harmful to have such eyes to look into."

"Even though I teased you and made you wait last night?"

"Looking into those eyes filled with fire at such a time aroused me greatly," she admitted.

"Would you have begged?" he asked softly.

"Would you have waited so long?" she murmured.

Amenemhet smiled. "I might have done other things to further tempt you."

"Those other things would have tempted you as well as me," she reminded him. She looked at the sky beyond his shoulder, then moved again to him. He wondered what she was thinking—he knew she was planning something. Then she said, "Will we love once more before we go?"

His eyebrows lifted. "Are you asking?"

"Yes," she whispered. "Yes, beloved, I'm asking."

Nefrytatanen's eyes had again darkened; and seeing their warm shadows, Amenemhet knew she certainly was asking. He touched her hair, thinking there still was some time before the sand got too hot and deciding he would use that time very carefully. He wondered whether to kiss her mouth—it looked so soft waiting for him—or the base of her throat—its hollow seemed inviting—or begin elsewhere. While Amenemhet considered these possibilities, the glow in Nefrytatanen's eyes intensified. He wondered if the look in his own eyes was now the kind that sent shivers down her spine. He thought this might be true and decided to kiss those shivers.

"Turn over, beloved," he said softly.

As they rode slowly toward Ithtawe's walls, Amenemhet waved to people in the fields who had paused from their work to stare in amazement at their king and queen's casual passing.

"They're surprised to see us unguarded," Nefrytatanen remarked, "but they're smiling all the same."

"They'd be even more surprised if they knew how we've passed the night," Amenemhet replied with a grin.

Unconcerned with the gaping of the sentinels, King Amenemhet and Queen Nefrytatanen rode slowly through Ithtawe's outer entrance, then paused at the palace gates. The sun flashed on the copper surfaces of the great doors as they swung silently open.

After Amenemhet and Nefrytatanen had dismounted and were strolling through the courtyard, Commander Nessumontu walked quickly toward them, a worried and reproachful look on his face.

"I was concerned when Yazid told me you had gone out during the night," he said softly.

Amenemhet smiled. "That's why I didn't tell you we were going and ordered Yazid and Dedjet to be silent. I knew you'd send someone to guard us, and we wanted to be alone."

Nessumontu fell in step with them, not sure what to say. Finally, he remarked, "I hope your night was worth the risk."

"It was," Amenemhet answered calmly. "Every so often, my friend, even a king and queen would like uninterrupted privacy. Had you sent someone to follow us, that guard would have made a very short report when he returned, provided he was able to return and make a report."

Nessumontu sighed. "I suppose everything is peaceful enough, but you can never tell what might happen. There have recently been a lot of rumors about spies being in Tamera."

"There always are rumors about Hyksos spies posing as merchants or travelers," Amenemhet insisted. "Did anything important happen in our absence?"

"Ambassador Nakht returned," Nessumontu replied.

"Send a message to his house," Amenemhet directed. "I'll hear his report after I've bathed and had something to eat." A sudden noise from the direction of the palace distracted him. "Here come the children," he said.

The prince and princess raced down the stone walk toward them and plummeted into Amenemhet and Nefrytatanen's legs like missiles from a catapult. Amenemhet looked down into gold eyes that matched his own.

"Why did you go away last night?" Prince Senwadjet asked.

Amenemhet bent to pick up his son. "Your mother and I wanted to be alone."

"Alone even from us?" Senwadjet persisted.

"Sometimes men and women want to be alone together," Amenemhet replied. Senwadjet gazed at him a moment, decided this seemed logical and solemnly nodded. "It isn't that we don't like being with you," Amenemhet carefully added, "but sometimes we want to be away from everyone."

Maeti said impatiently, "Oh, Senwadjet, it's like having to always knock on a closed door before you open it."

"Oh," Senwadjet said.

Amenemhet put Senwadjet down and turned to Nefrytatanen with raised eyebrows. "They're precocious," he remarked.

"What's that?" Maeti asked, her blue eyes narrowed against the sun.

"Smart," Nefrytatanen answered, then motioned them toward the doors to cut off further questions.

The children willingly ran ahead, hopping and skipping in patterns of their own imagining on the paving stones, and Amenemhet and Nefrytatanen followed. When they reached the doors, it was necessary to urge Senwadjet and Maeti ahead once more, for a disagreement had delayed them in the doorway. Dedjet hurried to meet the group and, drawing the prince and princess to the side, led them off, while the king and queen went to have their breakfast.

Later, word came that Ambassador Nakht had arrived, and Amenemhet ordered that Nakht be told to wait in the garden while he dressed. Finally, robed in a short tunic, Amenemhet stepped onto the terrace. The heat was oppressive, and he paused on the stairs to enjoy the touch of the wind from the north, which was like a balm on his hot skin. As he reached the base of the steps, he recognized in the distance Nessumontu's lean silhouette standing with Nakht under the rose pavilion.

"How was your trip, Nakht?" the king asked his ambassador.

Nakht's wide mouth curved in welcome as he turned. "As always, I'm glad to be home again."

Amenemhet's eyes took on a gleam of humor. "Are you merely happy to be home, or did you think, in your absence, Nessumontu had lured away your collection of women with his charms?"

"What charms?" Nakht asked smoothly. "All he knows how to do is fight."

"It seems he finds a number of women who like his man-

21

ner of battle," Amenemhet replied. "His reputation is beginning to rival his legendary sword."

"In peace a soldier finds time on his hands," Nessumontu said softly.

"And women are impressed with his uniform," Nakht added.

Noticing the shadows in Nakht's dark eyes, for the first time, Amenemhet asked, "What happened in your travels, Nakht?"

Setting a sandaled foot on a bench, Nakht replied, "I was received with a great show of hospitality by most of the kings I visited, but beneath their smiles their eyes held fear."

"Fear of what?" Nessumontu asked.

"They all have enemies, as we do," Nakht replied, turning a grim face to Nessumontu. "Just as the Hyksos constantly eye Tamera but are too afraid of our strength to begin a war, others watch these kings and their lands' prosperity with greed held in check only by caution." Nakht's eyes shifted to regard Amenemhet.

"How strong are their enemies?" Amenemhet asked quietly.

"Strong enough to frighten the kings friendly to us," Nakht answered, then observed, "It might not be beneficial for Tamera to deal with new regimes."

"True," Amenemhet agreed. "Who is being most threatened?"

"At the moment, King Ami-enshi of Retenu is most uneasy," Nakht answered, "but Retenu isn't alone in its fear. Punt, Minoa and even Ur have their troubles."

Amenemhet grew grave. "These kings talked of this freely?"

"King Ami-enshi has enlarged his defenses and makes no secret of it," Nakht replied. "Other kings hinted, some subtly and others not so subtly, that they hoped for treaties of friendship with us."

"I have no desire to get drawn into their wars," Amenemhet said firmly. "The Hyksos are only waiting for a weakness in us. I'll allow none."

"Ami-enshi wants Retenu's friendship with Tamera confirmed by a trade treaty, which he hopes will intimidate his enemies," Nakht said quickly.

"They fear us more than I'd thought," Amenemhet commented.

Nessumontu smiled grimly. "Their spies see an army of our citizens, well equipped and disciplined, who have volun-

teered for military careers, not an army of foreign mercenaries. They see our officers of noble blood going to train
with their men in the field, not men giving orders while reclining in their comfortable houses."

"The day we use foreign mercenaries to defend our homes
is the day Tamera will begin its decline," Amenemhet said
with sudden vehemence. "It won't come while I rule; and it
won't come when Senwadjet reigns after me, if my teachings
have effect."

Then Amenemhet looked at Nakht with a more cheerful
expression. "I'll need time to consider what we should do.
But meanwhile, L advise you to busy yourself retrieving the
women you lost to Nessumontu in your absence."

"If I lost anyone," Nakht said coolly, "he can keep her. I
can find a replacement."

Amenemhet smiled and turned to leave them. As he started
toward the palace, he heard Nessumontu say quietly, "I bothered none of your old crones with crooked legs and flat
chests."

"Crooked legs! Flat chests!" Nakht exploded in mock anger. Amenemhet heard his voice fading in the distance: "Let
me describe a certain lovely blossom I plucked in Minoa . . ."

Amenemhet stepped into the shady corridor still smiling. It
was evident Nakht was unaware of Nessumontu's bouquet in
Tamera. He continued through the halls until he reached his
study.

He sat in the chair by his desk, which was piled high with
scrolls waiting to be read. His chin sank to his chest as he
contemplated Nakht's information. Would a series of treaties
embroil Tamera in the troubles of others? Would it be wise?
He considered the life of one Tameran to be worth more
than all the cedar, spice and precious stones Retenu could
provide. Yet he wouldn't like to see King Ami-enshi or others
beaten by invaders. The thirst for conquest was never satisfied when it was fed by victims.

Although Tamera was far from defenseless, if several
greedy kings summoned the courage to align themselves
against the Two Lands . . . Amenemhet shuddered at the
thought. Even if Tamera emerged from such a conflict victorious, the king didn't wish to see the land ravaged by war, its
cities in ashes, and hear the lamentations of those grieving for
lost loved ones. Would a treaty for trade sufficiently impress
possible aggressors to keep them within their own borders?

23

Amenemhet weighed the possibilities until his head began to ache.

So involved was he that he didn't hear Senwadjet and Maeti enter the room. They stood silently gazing up at him until Senwadjet finally tugged at his elbow. Startled, Amenemhet turned to look down at them. The two children had such solemn expressions that he had to struggle to compose his face before he could ask as solemnly, "What is it?"

Senwadjet cleared his throat. "We have a question, father."

"Then sit upon my knees," Amenemhet suggested, "so we need not cause cramps in our necks." He reached down for them and placed one on each knee. "What is your question?" he asked.

Maeti looked at Senwadjet, and he nodded. Amenemhet brushed Maeti's hair aside while Nefrytatanen's eyes looked up at him from the child's face.

"Father, if there's only one god, the One Alone, why do we speak of other divine beings like Ra, Tehuti, Asar and Aset?" Senwadjet asked.

Amenemhet leaned back in the chair. "That is a difficult question," he said slowly. "The One Alone, Whom we call Tem, is the beginning of everything, the life we all have. Every living creature has a soul, which is part of this force. We're all part of what we call Tem because we're alive." He smiled at them. "Do you understand?"

"Yes." They answered without hesitation.

"Are you certain?" Amenemhet was surprised. "This is a very complicated idea."

"Yes," Senwadjet replied. "We understand that."

Amenemhet's eyebrows rose as he regarded their upturned faces. They seemed certain.

"What about Ra, Tehuti and the rest of them?" Senwadjet persisted.

"They govern the laws and patterns of nature and are lesser forces," Amenemhet said slowly, waiting for more questions.

"And Ptah?" asked Senwadjet. "And Khepra?"

"Ptah and Khepra are really the same. . . ." Amenemhet stopped. How could he explain Infinity and its many names to children?

Seeing Amenemhet's hesitation, Maeti said, "I know the answer you're about to give. We're too young to understand that yet."

Amenemhet smiled. "*I* am too young to understand it yet," he said.

They looked at him for a moment before sliding off his lap.

"Father?" Senwadjet pulled Amenemhet's fingers. Amenemhet looked down. "Perhaps when you understand that one, you'll remember to explain it to us?"

"Yes," Amenemhet slowly agreed, "I will." He stood up to walk with them to the door. "Have you no other questions about what I did tell you?"

"No," Senwadjet answered and looked at Maeti.

"No," she said. "Thank you, Father."

Amenemhet watched the children as they walked down the corridor. Although they were constantly curious about something, he was surprised at their questions and wondered if other children considered philosophy and religion at their age. He decided he would soon need some advisers to help answer their questions. Finally he stepped back into his room and closed the door to the hall, then hesitated. Today, he decided, he didn't want the door closed. Although it would be more difficult to concentrate on the reports, the sounds of the household were too pleasant to shut out.

Amenemhet returned to his chair, but his eyes were on the windows. He watched the movement of the trees and the curve of the fountain's spray for a moment. Then, even though it would further distract him from business, he got up and opened the doors to the garden. On the rush of sun-warmed air came the scent of flowers and the bright songs of birds.

Reluctantly, he returned his attention to his reports. The delicious odor of meat roasting for the evening meal crept into the room. The scroll rolled shut with a rustle and a click. He rested his chin in his hands, thinking of Nefrytatanen, wishing she would visit him and rescue him from the dreary reports. The thought of her filled him with a pleasing warmth, but he reopened the scroll and, fixing his eyes on the characters, determined that he would read the reports.

A faint sound in the hall gradually became clearer, and his head raised in pleased recognition. As the light, rhythmic sound came nearer, he smiled hopefully. It was Nefrytatanen's soft step. She seemed to be hurrying to some task. As she came closer, her steps slowed, then stopped. His hopes began to fade, but he continued listening. Her steps resumed, but she slowed her pace as she approached. Finally,

Nefrytatanen appeared in the doorway. She glanced in, turned briefly to smile and throw him a kiss, then went on.

After more than six years of marriage, the rush of warmth that still suffused him at her appearance made him shake his head with wonder.

The grass in the distance rustled, and Amenemhet knew it was Nefrytatanen returning from her solitary walk. The rustle came closer until it stopped beside him. Her shadow made a cool spot on his chest, and he realized she was wondering if he was asleep. Then the soft whisper of her robe told him she had knelt by his side. Her shadow moved to his face, her warm breath touched his cheek; and as he was enveloped in a perfumed veil of hair, her lips brushed his.

Her kiss was hesitant, as if she were unsure whether he slept. A sweet warmth swept through him, banishing his drowsiness. Her lips began to move softly against his mouth, fondling him with delicate sensuality, arousing him to piquant urges. But when his lips reached up, wanting to possess her mouth more surely, she withdrew.

"I wasn't certain if you were awake, but your kiss gave you away," she whispered.

Amenemhet opened his eyes and murmured, "If I had been asleep, I would have awakened at your touch. I think if I were dead, I'd respond to such a kiss."

"You were frowning when I approached. I'd thought if you were lying here worrying about whether to sign a treaty with Retenu, I would distract you." Her fingers smoothed his brow, then lightly slid down his temple to caress the line of his jaw.

Amenemhet turned his head to nuzzle her hand with his cheek. "No, the brightness of the sun shining through my eyelids caused my frown. I thought about that treaty all yesterday and the better part of last night. Just now I was thinking of nothing."

"I'm sorry I reminded you of the treaty," she said softly.

"I'm not sorry, because now you must distract me," he replied.

"And if someone should come?" she whispered, leaning closer yet.

"I told Nessumontu we wanted to be alone and don't need anyone to guard us in our own park." He closed his eyes, and his hands reached up to grasp the back of her head and draw her to him.

Again Nefrytatanen put her mouth to his, tasting his kiss, savoring its flavor. She nibbled at his mouth, stroked his lips with the tip of her tongue, coaxing the eager firmness from them, persuading them to soft fullness before covering his mouth with hers. She knew he was aroused, but she didn't realize that he already seethed with hunger until he made a soft sound, little more than a slowly escaping breath. But it was like a spark unexpectedly flaring among her banked embers. She moved to lie over him, and the hard warmth of his body, the tremor that ran through him, was a flame igniting her answering fire. Amenemhet's arms tightened around Nefrytatanen, clasping her to him with sudden power, and she closed her eyes to lose herself in the passion about to engulf them.

The impulses that ran through Amenemhet were like a current racing along his nerves, feeding the urges that were rapidly eroding his reason. He felt Nefrytatanen's body moving against him more insistently. He released her and reached for the opening of her robe, running his fingers between its folds, seeking the soft velvet of her warm skin. Aware that she slowly was guiding his tunic up his hips, he became even more intoxicated with desire, whispering to her, softly telling her of his love.

Suddenly, Amenemhet's eyes flew open. The ground was trembling beneath him and the branches overhead were shaking violently. He leaped to is feet, and Nefrytatanen sat up, staring fearfully at the nearby pond, which was splashing as if it were a cup being tapped with a finger.

"It's an earth tremor," he said grimly. "We must get away from these trees." He took a few steps away to scan the clearing and decide which path through the forest would be safest. Alarm shot through him when he heard a sharp, ominous crack. He whirled around just in time to see a blur of plunging green. Nefrytatanen screamed and disappeared under the fallen tree.

"Beloved!" he cried and staggered across the writhing grass to the tangle of leaves covering Nefrytatanen. He dropped to his knees beside her shoulders just as the earth's convulsions stopped. "Beloved . . ." he whispered, then stopped, speechless with fear.

"I don't think I'm injured," she gasped. "At least, nothing seems to hurt me."

Amenemhet touched her cheek and wondered if she truly wasn't injured or if she was too shocked to know it. "I'll try to raise this tree," he said and got to his feet.

Although Amenemhet pushed his way through the outer branches in an effort to reach the trunk, he found he couldn't get close enough to grasp it. He moved away and looked speculatively at the tree, then at Nefrytatanen. She was pinned at its center. He wondered if he could move the tree far enough by raising either end of the trunk. The top of the tree, he decided, was too fragile and would simply bend. He measured the splintered base of the trunk with his eyes. To lift that, if he could, would shift more of its weight on her.

"What I need is a rope and a horse," he muttered through clenched teeth.

"Try pulling me out by my shoulders," Nefrytatanen said anxiously. "I think most of the trunk's weight is resting on the tree's inner branches."

"I'll try what you suggest only because I can see no other way," he said tensely. He bent to grasp her shoulders, adding, "If you feel any pain, say so immediately, and I'll go back to the palace to get help."

Nefrytatanen nodded, and he began cautiously to tug at her shoulders. He could feel her body beginning to move slowly from under the trunk; but when she cried out in pain, he froze.

"The branches are sharp as teeth," she gasped. "I think you must go for help."

Amenemhet frowned. "I don't like to leave you here alone."

"There's nothing to harm me. Just hurry. I don't want to get so cut up by these branches that Horemheb will wrap me in bandages and we won't be able to continue what we started before the tremor."

"I won't be long," he promised, then turned and walked quickly into the forest. As soon as he was out of her sight, he broke into a run.

Nefrytatanen breathed shallowly, because the branches were tearing at her chest more painfully than she had allowed Amenemhet to guess. Although there were no large animals in the forest to worry her, visions of poisonous serpents floated menacingly through her mind until she became so terrified she tried squirming her own way out from under the branches. They slashed at her skin like fangs, and she immediately stopped moving.

Realizing she must distract herself, she turned her thoughts to the earthquake. Although it had been a relatively mild tremor, she hoped it wasn't the forerunner of a new series of quakes like those she remembered from her childhood. She

28

recalled vividly how for months the populace of Noph had been terrified by a succession of earthquakes that had toppled obelisks, torn the temple walls, smashed houses and crushed their occupants, and had even opened cracks in the earth swallowing people and animals. Remembering, she closed her eyes and prayed to Ptah for the earth's stability.

"I didn't have to go to the palace for help."

Nefrytatanen's eyes sprang open at Amenemhet's voice. She turned her head, trying to see him, but couldn't until he stood over her. Accompanying him was a girl, whose dark eyes stared down at Nefrytatanen in awe.

The girl immediately dropped the coil of rope she carried and went to her knees in homage to her helpless queen. "My name is Ani, divine lady," she whispered. "I live at the edge of the park with my parents. Although they weren't home when his majesty came, I brought our horse to help you."

"I'm grateful, Ani," Nefrytatanen replied. "Now please hurry. Get up and do whatever the king tells you."

"Yes, divine lady, of course," Ani whispered and scrambled to her feet.

Amenemhet had picked up the rope and was tossing one end of it over the branch of a sturdy tree nearby. He handed the coil to Ani, saying, "Tie this end to the horse's harness."

While Ani set about that task, he pushed through the outer branches as far as possible. Then he leaned over, stretching until he could wrap the rope around the tree trunk. Knotting it firmly, he struggled back through the branches. After he had placed himself at Nefrytatanen's shoulders, he called, "Ani, lead your horse away so the tree will be raised."

"Yes, majesty!" she answered and obeyed.

Amenemhet watched the tree slowly moving off Nefrytatanen. When he judged it high enough, he tightened his grip on her shoulders and carefully pulled her out. As his lips parted to warn Nefrytatanen not to move, she slowly sat up and carefully inspected herself.

"I'm soiled, cut and scratched, but no more."

He sighed with relief, took her hands and helped her to her feet. Then he pulled her into his arms and said fervently, "For that I am grateful." After a moment he released her and, sliding one arm around her waist, turned to face Ani. "What would you have as reward, Ani?" he asked.

"I'm glad I could help, sire," Ani stammered. Reward had never occurred to her.

29

Amenemhet looked down at Nefrytatanen. "Could you use another personal servant?"

"Would you like to come to the palace, Ani?" Nefrytatanen inquired. Ani was speechless with surprise, so Nefrytatanen added, "Would your family object to your taking such a station?"

"If they would, say so, Ani, and we'll think of another way to reward you," Amenemhet prompted.

"Majesties, my family would be honored if I went to the palace, and I would be happy to serve you," Ani whispered.

"Then a decan from today a messenger will come to tell your parents you've been chosen to attend the queen," Amenemhet said.

"Yes, sire, thank you," Ani breathed.

Realizing that Ani was too stunned by their offer to move, Nefrytatanen prompted, "You must return home before your family misses you and worries."

"Yes, divine lady," Ani whispered and, dipping in a hasty bow, turned to hurry home.

As Amenemhet and Nefrytatanen made their way back toward the palace, halfway through the park they met Nessumontu and several palace guards searching for them. Amenemhet and Nefrytatanen behaved as if they were surprised by the lateness of the hour. They commented about the tremor, but not wanting to have royal guards follow them everywhere in the future, they said nothing of the accident.

It wasn't Nessumontu's place to ask questions, yet his eyes observed the soil and tears on Nefrytatanen's robe with suspicion.

Three

Dedjet had just wrapped Nefrytatanen in a towel and was unpinning her damp hair when Ineni thrust her head into the bath chamber and asked hurriedly, "Did Prince Senwadjet enter? I thought I saw him come this way."

Nefrytatanen had ordered that Senwadjet and Maeti be bathed and fed while she dressed for the banquet. Slowly she turned. "He got away?" When Ineni nodded, Nefrytatanen asked, "And Maeti?"

"The princess obediently awaits her brother's coming," the servant answered.

Nefrytatanen unwound the towel and dropped it. "Give me a robe, Dedjet," she directed. "I'll see to this myself."

"But, my lady, soon the king will come!" the servant reminded her.

Nefrytatanen's voice was muffled as she hurriedly pulled the robe over her head, "Throw him in any muddy pond and he swims like a fish, but even think of bathing him and he vanishes." She turned to Ineni. "You search every corner of this room, and I'll look into the bedchamber."

"My lady, what shall I do?" Dedjet pleaded.

"Search the hall," Nefrytatanen called over her shoulder.

Opening the door to the royal bedchamber, Nefrytatanen

paused to calculate where a small boy could secrete himself. A drape brushing the floor seemed to move slightly, and she crept silently forward. She was mistaken. Senwadjet darted from another direction, and she heard his light footsteps escaping with surprising speed down the hall.

As Nefrytatanen approached the door opening into the garden, her bare feet skidded to a stop on the polished stone floor. She stood behind a sheltering column by the door and cautiously looked outside. A crowd of richly dressed noblemen and their ladies were already milling about. She shrank farther behind the column, her eyes scanning the crowd.

"They've already begun to arrive," Dedjet panted at her side. "There he is!"

Senwadjet's triumphant figure was on an unswerving course to the group of guests. Nefrytatanen squinted at the sun-bright garden. "If Amenemhet isn't there, he'll wander around as he pleases," she muttered.

"The king is there. See where the women are looking," Dedjet suggested. "They always look at the king when their husbands aren't watching."

Nefrytatanen followed the direction of several feminine glances and discovered Dedjet was right. Amenemhet was engaged in conversation with Kheti, the governor of Orynz Province. She breathed a sigh of relief, because Amenemhet stopped Lord Kheti a moment, bent to lift the prince to his shoulders, then continued the conversation.

"The women always look to the king that way, my lady. He need not wear the crown to attract their eyes," Dedjet whispered.

Nefrytatanen watched Amenemhet begin to walk slowly through the garden, still talking with Kheti and carrying Senwadjet, who was quiet and obedient in his father's grasp. "Let us go back to my chamber," she said.

Dedjet smiled. "Those women would throw themselves at his feet and beg like puppies but for you," she said smugly.

"Think about how you'll dress my hair, not about the king," Nefrytatanen said coolly.

"Yes, my lady."

Dedjet had just removed the last snarl from Nefrytatanen's hair when Amenemhet entered the room. "I've placed Senwadjet in Yazid's hands," he said. "I saw you hiding behind the column."

Nefrytatanen looked up in alarm. "Do you think anyone else did?"

Amenemhet smiled and dropped onto a couch. "I looked up in time only to see your figure move into the shadows. I recognized it, although no one else would have," he answered. He continued watching her appraisingly as he pulled off his sash and loosened his tunic. "Have you decided what you'll wear?" he asked, leaning back comfortably.

"I was too busy chasing Senwadjet," Nefrytatanen answered. "When are you going to bathe?"

His eyes traveled over the sheer robe, with penetrating slowness. "We have time to spare," he said softly.

At the tone of his voice, Dedjet stopped combing.

Nefrytatanen turned slowly to face him. "We will be late."

Amenemhet drew his legs onto the couch and smiled. "It is one of the advantages of being king that others can occasionally wait."

Appraising the look in his eyes, Nefrytatanen said quietly, "That's enough for now, Dedjet. I'll call you later to finish it."

"Yes, my lady," Dedjet murmured and put down the comb. Suppressing a smile, the maid bobbed her head and left hastily.

When the door had closed, Amenemhet patted the couch beside him, but Nefrytatanen didn't move. Instead, her eyes traveled over his reclining figure in the same way as he had looked at her. She said quietly, "When we were searching for you in the garden, Dedjet told me to follow the other women's eyes, and she was right. They were all watching you."

Amenemhet smiled.

"I watched how straight you stood, how you walked, and I was filled with pride." She came a step closer. "Watching you when you were unaware of my presence gave my heart a strange flutter."

Amenemhet swung his legs from the couch and stood up. "I've felt that way at times when I've watched you from a distance."

"Yet, to see how those other women wanted you was a pain in me as sharp as a lance."

Amenemhet extended his arms to her. "There is no need for such a pain when you are the only woman I open these arms to."

Nefrytatanen stepped into his embrace and laid her cheek against his chest. "Still, I knew what those women were

33

thinking, and I would have liked to tear those thoughts from out their minds."

Turning her face up to his, Amenemhet put his smile against her lips. Warmth flowed through her and the familiar sweet aching began. He kissed her again, still softly, then again, lingering this time to caress her lips with his, pausing in his kisses to nibble gently at her mouth, until her lips, no longer content with caresses, hungrily sought his. Her fingers slid down his back to his hips and held him more tightly to her. She heard his soft intake of breath; but with his hard body clasped to hers, she already knew what she did to him.

She closed her eyes, absorbing the desire that radiated from him like a light, and she felt his hands drawing aside the folds of her robe. Without opening her eyes, she reached for his tunic and brushed it away. As his hands slid behind her hips, swirls of sparks seemed to rise around them, and as he moved her slowly, carefully backward toward the couch, their bodies had already become one being, moving together.

She opened her eyes and absorbed the desire that glowed from his eyes like a golden flame, until the fire they fed engulfed them both. They sank slowly to the cushions, which one by one slipped gently to the floor.

The sensation of his skin was like life to her, the scent of him as necessary as the air she breathed, his warmth, the texture of his hair, as vital as her heartbeat. With his touch, reason left her, and she became like a primitive creature, surrendering all sanity to the mouth whose kisses seemed to draw her soul from her body. She was filled with a new life force, and she moaned softly at this merging of the two fiery streams of energy they had become. The seal that was forever stamped on their souls was renewed.

Amenemhet was in a pleasantly languid mood as Yazid dressed him for the banquet, and the sound of Nefrytatanen's light laughter coming from the next room was as pleasing as perfumed smoke floating in the air, so when the guard tapped on the door, Amenemhet signaled him to enter without a thought. But his serenity began to fade when the guard announced that Lord Petamen from Thes-Hertu Province begged a private conversation before the party.

Petamen entered the room cautiously, and Amenemhet could smell the wine from where he stood. Petamen's steps were slow, obviously those of a man who controlled his movements with an effort. Yet Petamen sank to his knees and

34

arose at Amenemhet's order without incident. When Amenemhet signaled for him to speak, Petamen cleared his throat nervously.

"Majesty, I wouldn't bother you at this moment if my problem wasn't important, but I foresee no way to discuss this once you join the banquet."

Afraid that Petamen would soon find it difficult to form coherent sentences, Amenemhet asked coldly, "What is the problem?"

"Sire, my sorrow is great for what I must tell you," Petamen began. "At the time of cultivation, there was no hint of such a thing, but when the crops began to come up, my farmers found root worms. As they made these discoveries, the worms were destroyed, but lately other creatures have been found. Before I left my province to travel here, I received a report that a strange variety of voracious insects have been appearing in scattered areas of my province, and although the farmers are doing steady battle with them, I fear I'll have little produce at harvest time."

Amenemhet stared intently at Petamen's upturned face and finally deemed his story to be truth. "What crops have been attacked?"

"The staples and, so, the most valuable," Petamen whispered.

"You are hoping for a promise of a decrease in your taxes?" Nefrytatanen asked as she suddenly entered from the adjoining room.

Again Petamen lowered himself to his knees. "My queen, if the situation continues, I will have little with which to feed my peasants."

"What of the provinces adjoining yours?" Nefrytatanen inquired. "Are they having such problems?"

Petamen looked chagrined. "None have spoken of it to me," he answered carefully.

"Stand up, Lord Petamen," Amenemhet directed.

"Thank you, sire," Petamen whispered, struggling to his feet. He stood with his head bowed for a moment, then said, "If I may suggest it, maybe the governors of the adjoining provinces are afraid to mention such problems."

Amenemhet replied with a hint of sarcasm, "They are, unlike you, not afraid of me—because those men were handpicked by me to replace governors less than trustworthy."

"Now that you mention it, sire, I remember you appointing them," Petamen murmured.

"I'm sure you do," Nefrytatanen commented, recalling that Petamen had almost been replaced along with the others and only a lack of evidence had saved his title. Turning to Amenemhet, she said, "Beloved, I think the question of the taxes will be resolved at harvest time when we send out inspectors to make the assessment." She regarded Petamen with a stern expression. "In the meanwhile, Petamen, you know what to do to fight these pests."

"Yes, majesties, I know," Petamen conceded.

"You may return to the party," Nefrytatanen directed.

He looked at Amenemhet, who nodded. Bowing his head, Petamen backed toward the door.

"I'm not surprised he would see a great variety of crawling things in his state," Nefrytatanen remarked lightly.

Amenemhet said nothing, but he had a feeling of foreboding about the matter. As they entered the banquet room, though he smiled and made all the appropriate gestures, his mind was still on Petamen's report.

After they had finished their meal, many guests rose from their places and, carrying wine goblets, clustered with friends and acquaintances in the flower-garlanded room where pale-gold alabaster walls reflected the light of many lamps. Servants moved among the guests offering cakes, fruits and more wine.

In a corner, five girls sat on cushions on the floor playing instruments. Their soft music was pleasantly unobtrusive as it wound through the conversations.

Lakma, the young man who was Amenemhet's personal scribe, had sufficient status to attend the party, but his place was far from the front of the room where the king and queen sat. It wasn't his lowly place that caused his mouth to turn down at its corners as if in perpetual pout. His enthusiasm for parties had waned of late. He had really attended out of courtesy. Lakma sat in his place at the table turning his wine goblet around and around, his eyes narrowed, amusing himself by listening to nearby conversations, and without intending to, observing Ani, the queen's new attendant.

Involuntarily, his dark eyes had followed Ani's graceful movements all evening, and although when she came his way he dropped his eyes, he was aware of her passing close by, her delicate perfume bringing visions of shady forest paths and quiet, cool ponds.

Standing near Lakma's chair with Ambassador Nakht and Commander Nessumontu, Lord Kheti was also following

36

Ani's progress with appreciative eyes. Though not really wanting to hear their comments, Lakma still found himself listening.

"That new maid is most pleasantly formed," Kheti remarked.

"Yes," Nakht murmured, "especially the softly rounded area best viewed when she walks away." He took a sip of wine, considering Ani's attributes as he continued watching. "In fact, she seems nicely formed from all angles." Nakht turned to Nessumontu and asked, "What do you think?"

Nessumontu shrugged, saying nothing.

"Your eyes gleam suspiciously." Kheti smiled. "Are you already planning some strategy?"

"I was merely looking," Nessumontu responded.

"He'll say nothing—one way or the other," Nakht commented. "But someone will see her creeping out of his quarters early one morning anyway."

Nessumontu's gaze shifted to his goblet. "Speak when you do see a woman leaving my room at any hour."

Nakht laughed softly. "He never admits to anything."

"Women appreciate discretion," Nessumontu murmured, not really disturbed by his friend's teasing. To distract Nakht from further questions, Nessumontu turned to gaze at the dancer who was now entertaining the party.

Nakht wasn't distracted; he laughed and said to Kheti, "Then it must be the women who talk."

Lakma glared at Nakht and Nessumontu, though neither noticed, and resolved to warn the girl about them. Ani seemed to be innocent and might be taken in by their charming manners and overimpressed by their rank. Lakma's concern for Ani was confusing to him, because he had no personal interest in Ani or any other woman.

His last involvement had caused him enough humiliation to last a lifetime, he reflected. The object of his attention had sent him warm looks enough to turn any man's head, and when he had finally managed to gain an invitation to visit the lady, she had been even warmer. But then she had begun to make excuses to turn him away, and sometimes, after inviting him to her house, she would make him wait for hours, then charm and tease him out of anger. Finally, one night when he arrived at her house, he was told by a servant to go away because the son of a lord was visiting her. Lakma still squirmed with embarrassment to remember how he had felt. Recently he had passed her in the street, and she had ignored even his casual greeting.

His concern about Ani was different, Lakma decided. He felt sympathy for her. The palace was a new and exciting world for a farmer's daughter. It would be sad to see her hurt for someone else's amusement.

Lakma had also observed that in her zeal to make a favorable impression, Ani was far too humble in her attitude toward some people. He thought he might later tactfully tell her about this. Being a personal attendant of the queen wasn't the same as being a mere servant. The position demanded a certain amount of respect from others.

"Nakht is once again teasing Nessumontu about women," Kheti said, settling into a chair between his wife, Neferset, and the queen.

Neferset smiled up at her husband. "I wonder, sometimes, at Nessumontu's patience."

"They're too good friends for Nessumontu to take offense," Nefrytatanen commented. "It's been going on a long time. Nakht may tease Nessumontu, but when Nessumontu's had enough, he retaliates by stealing the woman Nakht is currently trying to win."

"How do you know that?" Kheti asked, taking a sip of wine.

"Yazid is an unfailing source of gossip," Nefrytatanen answered. "He talks to Dedjet and Dedjet tells me." With that, the queen turned to Amenemhet but he was looking into space as if he had heard none of their conversation. She asked softly, "What's troubling you, beloved? You've been silent all evening, and I know something is wrong."

Amenemhet sat back in his chair and sighed. "I've had my mind on trade treaties and worms."

"There's a fascinating variety of things to think about," Kheti remarked. "What treaties are worrying you?"

"Treaties supposedly made for mutual trade concessions, but which I wonder might lead us into wars," Amenemhet answered. "As for the worms, Lord Petamen has discovered a peculiar assortment of pests nibbling on his crops."

"His province is the farthest south, isn't it?" Neferset asked. When Kheti nodded, she looked thoughtful a moment before adding, "Maybe the pests are coming from Kenset's jungles."

Amenemhet turned to look at her in surprise. "You have a good point."

"Maybe they came from a wine jar," Nefrytatanen remarked sarcastically.

"I have noticed him drinking heavily all evening," Neferset agreed.

Kheti laughed briefly and without humor. "Petamen always drinks too much. There hasn't been a party he's attended these last few years that his servants did not have to carry him away from."

"I've sometimes wondered if it's wise to allow him to continue governing a province," Nefrytatanen mused.

"You aren't alone in your doubts," Amenemhet agreed. "I've often found myself considering his removal."

"He never does anything serious enough to warrant so harsh a step, but he is often embarrassing." Nefrytatanen frowned as her eyes found Petamen in the crowd. "Now Semerkhet is trying to avoid him."

Amenemhet looked up, hoping to be distracted from his troubles by Petamen's antics, but what he saw made his forehead crease with furrows of irritation.

Lord Semerkhet had deliberately turned from Petamen and moved a few steps away. It was clear he wished to cause no scene, but it was also clear that Petamen was blissfully ignorant of Semerkhet's growing anger.

When Petamen put his hand on Semerkhet's shoulder, Semerkhet turned to look into Petamen's bulgy, red-streaked eyes and said in a tone filled with menace, "Lord Petamen, you're becoming far too familiar with my person." He brushed Petamen's hand from his robe and said softly, "If you persist in your discussion with me, which I have tried so patiently to avoid, I'll soon lose my temper." Semerkhet's black eyes were glittering with anger, an emotion he seldom displayed.

Petamen blinked, wavering where he stood, making an effort to gather his befuddled wits, but he continued to bar Semerkhet's way. Several people nearby had stopped their conversations and were watching curiously.

Amenemhet beckoned Nessumontu grimly.

When Nessumontu approached the royal table, Amenemhet said in a cold tone, "Get Petamen out of here as quietly as possible. Put him in some room out of sight and hearing, and bolt the door. When he's sufficiently recovered to understand what I have to say, send him to me."

Nessumontu nodded and turned, waving for two guards to follow. As Nessumontu stepped between Petamen and Semerkhet, the guards moved to Petamen's sides and Semerkhet gratefully withdrew.

"Lord Petamen," Nessumontu said in a low voice, "King Amenemhet suggests you retire to a quiet room for a rest." Nessumontu's tactful request was given courteously because Amenemhet had asked for discretion, but the commander privately wished he could drag the nobleman out in disgrace as he deserved.

Lord Petamen looked at Nessumontu with unfocused eyes, his shaking hand tipping his goblet. Nessumontu watched the red wine trickle onto his immaculate white uniform and fervently wished Petamen would refuse to go. Then he could treat the boor as he was personally inclined.

Petamen opened his mouth, whether to apologize or protest Nessumontu didn't learn, because despite the wine fogging his brain, Petamen saw the gleam in the commander's eyes and understood Nessumontu's intention. He followed Nessumontu quietly, the guards pacing at his sides.

Having safely deposited the unresisting Petamen in a room and closed the door, Nessumontu stationed a guard in the hall to keep Petamen quiet. Then Nessumontu found another unoccupied room where he could examine the stain on his uniform. He was staring at it helplessly and had about resigned himself to going to his quarters to change when he heard a soft voice behind him.

"Commander Nessumontu?"

He turned to see Ani standing in the doorway holding a jar and a length of cloth. "May I help you remove the stain?"

Her eyes, Nessumontu silently observed, seemed the largest and darkest he had ever seen.

"If I have your permission," Ani murmured, "the sooner I attend to the task, the more likely the stain can be removed."

"Yes, thank you," Nessumontu said softly. "Please proceed."

Ani wet the cloth and began blotting the stain, which was already almost dry. Nessumontu stared down at the top of the girl's head. Her hair looked like silk, he decided, and the light perfume she wore was pleasant. He forgave Petamen's drunkenness and hoped the stain would take her some time to remove.

"You're very considerate," Nessumontu said softly. "I was going to leave the party to change my uniform, but you've saved me the trouble."

"I'm not sure I can remove it all, but I'll try," she said, continuing to work diligently on the stain.

40

"I'm not in a hurry."

The tone of his voice caused Ani to glance up at him. When she saw the speculative look in his eyes, she blushed and turned quickly to her work again.

"Your perfume is very pleasing," Nessumontu murmured.

Ani whispered her thanks without looking up.

"I think I've suceeded," she finally said. "If you'll wait a moment while it dries, I believe the stain won't show at all." She straightened and backed away.

"You did that very quickly, which is commendable," Nessumontu remarked, then added, "Perhaps you'll wait with me to see if the stain truly has been conquered."

"If you wish, commander," Ani said softly. She didn't know how to refuse gracefully and wasn't sure she wanted to refuse. The prospect was more than a little heady.

Nessumontu moved toward the door, intending to close it and talk to Ani in privacy, but he found Lakma's tall frame suddenly barring the doorway. Lakma was frowning.

"The king is asking for you, commander," Lakma said quietly.

"Then I must leave," Nessumontu replied and turned to Ani. "Thank you for your assistance. If I ever find myself in another such predicament, I'll know whose help to seek." Although he spoke the words casually, his eyes said considerably more, and Ani blushed again.

"I am pleased I could help you," she answered.

Once he was alone with Ani, Lakma said. "Can you spare a moment before returning to the banquet?" A little sharply he added, "I have some advice for you."

Surprised by his tone, Ani looked up at him.

"Why do you behave so humbly?" Lakma asked gruffly. He was irritated at her—and at himself, for being concerned with her welfare at all.

"I'm a servant!" Ani stared at him. "How else does a servant behave?"

"There are many ranks of servants," Lakma muttered. "You'll never raise your status if you act as if you're too dull to entertain any dreams."

Ani's eyes, black as a lotus pond on a moonless night, softened when she recognized his concern. "Chance is all that brought me to the palace," she said. "What other prospects can a farmer's daughter possibly have?"

"You seem intelligent and have a certain charm," Lakma

answered slowly, certain now that he had blundered, but determined to see it out. "You're attractive, and these qualities can be a formidable combination. Conduct yourself with wisdom and who can foretell what match you'll make? I heard Ambassador Nakht and Commander Nessumontu discussing your physical attributes with favorable enthusiasm; but if I were you, I wouldn't think of either of them with marriage in mind."

"If I were interested in making an ambitious marriage, why shouldn't I think of the ambassador or commander?" Ani couldn't resist asking.

"They aren't interested in marriage. Nessumontu's reputation as a womanizer is known from one end of Tamera to the other. Nakht's adventures are told beyond our borders. For a lady who merely wants to enjoy a lover, I'm sure either of them would be satisfactory; but a woman interested in a more permanent situation would be wise to look elsewhere."

Ani decided she liked Lakma despite his stiffness. Deliberately baiting him, she asked, "How do you know I'm interested in a permanent situation?"

Lakma gave her so black a look that she was hard put not to giggle. "I already said I thought you had intelligence."

"Maybe I could use some practice in the art of love before I look for a serious prospect," Ani goaded.

Lakma glared at her. "You're free to do whatever you choose, Ani. When you're ready to think seriously about your future, look around carefully and see where you would set your aim before you let loose your arrow, for I think you could strike a very desirable quarry."

To Lakma's consternation Ani said, "I would make my marriage for love, not for gold or a title—even if such a thing could be possible for me."

"You're a silly little dreamer," Lakma said sharply. "You'll learn how foolish that idea is if you marry some poor peasant. Then you'll see wiser women wearing beautiful jewels with servants caring for them, and you'll be envious."

Ani shook her head, wondering why Lakma looked at her with soft eyes and advised her to marry for wealth. She raised her head slowly to gaze up at him through her long eyelashes. He might be confusing, but he was also attractive, she decided. "I don't think jewels would warm my bed."

Lakma watched Ani walk away, bewildered at himself for

42

talking to her that way. He wondered if she already had a man in mind. He was certain that if she looked at that man the way she had just looked at him, Ani would get whomever she chose.

Four

Amenemhet sat on the riverbank watching the shadows of the palm fronds weave designs on the sand.

"What are you thinking about?" Nefrytatanen asked. "You seem far away."

Amenemhet turned to her. "I'm here."

"Perhaps. But your thoughts are somewhere else," she persisted. "I can see it in your eyes."

"That's true." Amenemhet sighed. He lay back to rest his head in her lap and said nothing for a while. Finally he asked quietly, "What would you do if I had to leave you for a time?" He felt her body tense.

"I would die of loneliness. Why do you ask?"

"I was thinking of traveling to Retenu."

She bent to kiss his forehead. "Why?"

Amenemhet closed his eyes. "To negotiate a treaty. I've decided to make treaties with all the lands where we trade."

"Would you travel to all those places to make the treaties personally?"

"Some of them."

"How long would a journey to Retenu take?"

"I would guess several months," he replied slowly. He was silent a long moment, then added, "It would be lonely for me, though, with only Yazid, Nakht and soldiers for company."

Nefrytatanen gazed at Amenemhet's closed eyes and considered how she would feel if he were gone three months— ninety days, also ninety nights. Amenemhet was a man of powerful instincts and not used to an empty bed. Their marriage contract didn't forbid him other women. Wondering what the women of Retenu looked like, she thought of Nakht and the adventures he had enjoyed on his travels. "I wish I could go with you."

"You wouldn't mind my going?" He looked at her through his lashes. Her eyes were tightly closed, as if she were on the brink of weeping, and her face was tight with tension.

She answered quickly, "Each day you're gone will be a torment of worry. During the nights I'll be a dead thing."

Amenemhet again imagined the loneliness of such a journey and reached up to touch her cheek. She opened her eyes to look down at him, and he saw the moist sheen of them.

"I'd prefer you to come with me," he said softly. "If I left you behind, my mind would be on you all the while and I'd accomplish little. As for the nights—if I could sleep—I'm sure the hours would be filled with dreams tormenting me all the more." He sat up and regarded her solemnly. "Tamera is at peace, and I see no reason we can't both go. Senwadjet and Maeti would be well cared for in our absence."

Nefrytatanen brightened at the idea. "When I think of us traveling to a new place together, I feel it would be an adventure, not a diplomatic task."

"Thinking of the journey in that way will make it pleasant to anticipate," he agreed, laying his head back in her lap. "I'll have to remind myself we have a serious reason for going."

"One reason I'd go would be to assure you keep your mind on the treaty," she said bluntly.

"You think my eyes would wander?" Amenemhet asked.

"It's not your eyes, but other parts, that would worry me," Nefrytatanen said tartly. "Three months is a long time."

Amenemhet chuckled and sat up. "I'll get the arrangements started. A courier should be sent as soon as possible to King Ami-enshi. We needn't wait for his permission to come. According to Nakht, Ami-enshi would welcome a treaty." Amenemhet stood up. "It should be easy to negotiate."

Nefrytatanen put out her hands and he helped her to her feet. Shaking the grass off her robe, she remarked, "I'm sure King Ami-enshi wouldn't mind an official confirmation of Ta-

46

mera and Retenu's friendship. Neither would other neighboring countries. They all wish to enjoy continued prosperity."

Amenemhet took Nefrytatanen's hand as they walked back to the palace. "They also have enemies who would be impressed by their signing treaties with us."

"I thought we spoke of trade treaties, not defense!" She stopped walking and looked at him in surprise.

"I do," Amenemhet said and resumed walking. "According to Nakht, a mere show of friendship with us is enough to strike fear into their enemies." He was silent for a time, then suddenly asked, "Have you noticed how strangely Lakma's been behaving the last week?"

Nefrytatenen smiled. "He's had a peculiar look in his eyes ever since Ani came to the palace. I suspect he has more than a passing interest in her."

Amenemhet considered a moment, then asked, "Shall we take both of them with us to Retenu? If what you say is true, such a journey could bring pleasant results."

"I'll need Ani with me, as I'm sure you'll need your scribe." Nefrytatanen smiled conspiratorially.

Ani emerged from the shadows of the trees carrying an armful of wildflowers. She had recently found a place in the royal reserve where tall, orange-colored lilies flourished, and her mistress had a particular fondness for these flowers. Ani rubbed her nose against the satin petals as she walked. When Ani had learned Nefrytatanen loved flowers, she had taken it upon herself to tramp daily into the garden, into the forest's cool depths, or through sunny meadows on a mission of equal delight to her and her queen.

Stopping to add a handful of ferns to the bouquet, Ani knelt in the cool, moist earth. She paused from her task to close her eyes for a moment and breathe the green scent of the forest:

"You look like another flower," Lakma said, coming up behind Ani. Startled, she turned quickly. "Don't be frightened." Lakma smiled and extended a hand to help her up. "I, too, enjoy walking in the forest when I have free time and the king and queen aren't here."

Ani smiled. "The queen likes my bouquets, so I get new ones daily."

"I've noticed them. They are beautiful, and I've been enjoying them too." He bent to retrieve a flower she had dropped. "Let me help you carry them," he offered. "It seems you must be planning a generous arrangement with this load."

Ani laughed lightly. "I had no plan. I just couldn't resist once I started gathering them."

Lakma rubbed orange powder from her nose. "I see you can't resist putting your face in them either. I know they have no scent, but I do it all the same!" He took some of the flowers and began walking with her on the path to the palace. "Have you heard about the journey to Retenu?"

"Yes," Ani replied. "I am surprised the queen wishes me to come along."

"I didn't know that," Lakma said. "I thought she'd take Dedjet and Senet."

"She is, also Yunet and Ineni. I expect she'll need a lot of help."

"Queen Nefrytatanen isn't one to need scores of servants," Lakma said thoughtfully. "I'd say she has it in mind to impress King Ami-enshi."

"She'd impress him if she arrived in rags."

"You like her," Lakma observed.

"I like both of them—and the children," Ani answered. Fixing her eyes on the forest, she asked casually, "Are you going on this journey, Lakma?"

"Yes, of course," he answered quickly. "As the king's scribe, I must record the treaty." He fell silent, thinking of Ani traveling with them. Turning his mind from his fancies, he became more serious. "It will be a long and uncomfortable journey."

"I don't mind," Ani said. "I'm looking forward to it. I've never been anywhere else before."

"The prospect of a new adventure excites you?"

"Oh yes!" The dark depths of her eyes were brilliant with pleasure. "Each day brings a new adventure now."

"Does it?" Lakma wondered what adventures she was experiencing in the palace.

Ani studied Lakma's expression carefully from the corner of her eye. Finding it to her satisfaction, she murmured, "I've decided to follow your advice, Lakma."

"What advice?"

"I've chosen the man I'll aim my arrow of love at."

"Who is it?"

"I'd rather not say. I'd be embarrassed if I were unsuccessful," she murmured, revealing only a trace of the smile she

48

felt. "When I think I've won him, I'll tell you. I think you'll approve of my choice."

Lakma didn't comment. He wondered whom Ani had chosen. He tried to ignore the sad feeling the news gave him.

Amenemhet's courier to king Ami-enshi and his escort had not even passed Ithtawe's outer gates before preparations for the royal journey began. Most of the decisions about assembling the caravan fell to Nefrytatanen, and she constantly gave instructions to the servants about what they must do while she was gone from the palace. Her greatest worry had been preparing Senwadjet and Maeti for their parents' extended absence, but there seemed little sign of the separation's causing concern—other than the fact that the children followed their parents about even more regularly than before.

Amenemhet conferred with his ministers daily regarding their various areas of authority and discussed decisions to be made during his absence. He was especially careful to reinforce the boundaries of authority between Meri, the prime minister, and Nessumontu, the military commander, because in the absence of Amenemhet and Nefrytatanen, these two men held the kingdom in their hands.

Everyone concerned with the journey worked far into the night on the eve of the caravan's departure, and well before the dawn the crush of people and animals crowded inside Ithtawe's walls was confusing to the eyes, though everyone knew exactly where to fall in line when the signal was given.

The darkness was silent with the serenity of its deepest moment. The sun leaped over the earth's edge, and in Ra's golden flaring, the night began to die. Ra had won a new day, and the stars faded as if in homage.

Nefrytatanen, who had already embraced her children, looked down at them and could say nothing. They weren't crying, though their eyes were moist and shining; Nefrytatanen resolved she wouldn't weep in their sight. She tried to turn her thoughts to the caravan, but found she couldn't drag her gaze from the small figures standing on the steps with Nessumontu.

Before he mounted his horse, Amenemhet spoke briefly to Lord Meri and several lesser officials standing in a nearby group. Then he gestured to Nessumontu to walk with him to his horse. Taking his reins in one hand, Amenemhet turned to the commander, putting his other hand on his friend's shoulder.

"I need give you no further instructions," Amenemhet said softly, "for you know well enough what to do without guidance."

Nessumontu nodded, but said nothing.

Amenemhet said, "You are as a brother to me, Nessumontu. It's well I can feel this for you, for I trust my kingdom to you while we're gone."

"Your confidence gives me pride," Nessumontu answered.

"May your days be fair and peaceful and your nights filled with dreamless slumber." Amenemhet patted Nessumontu's shoulder and added, "Not necessarily every night."

As Amenemhet mounted his horse, Nessumontu said quietly, "Go with the protection of all the divine beings and return safely."

Amenemhet pressed Nessumontu's shoulder once again, sent one last kiss to Senwadjet and Maeti and signaled that he was ready.

The caravan began to move slowly, forming a long, straggling column that gradually straightened into an orderly line.

Nessumontu glanced around to see Maeti smiling brightly as she waved, tears running down her cheeks, but Senwadjet's face was stiff from holding back his tears. The commander stopped beside Senwadjet. "Do not hide your tears, my prince," he said gently. "They are not tears of shame, but of love, and love should not be hidden."

After three hours of traveling, the caravan halted because a camel's load was rapidly loosening and had to be rearranged without delay.

Nefrytatanen turned to gaze at the long lines behind them. "It looks as if we're taking the whole population of Ithtawe with us," she remarked, wishing two more small travelers could have been with them.

The queen had been silent since they had left Ithtawe's gates, and Amenemhet wondered how to lighten her mood.

Amenemhet moved his horse close to hers and said, "We must look and act like Retenu's notion of royalty once we get to Yenoam, even if it's necessary to haul our thrones there." Nefrytatanen pushed back the hood of her cloak, which had fallen too far over her forehead, as the king cautioned, "Be careful of the sun when we get into the desert, or you'll look like a sand-dweller when we arrive."

"I remember a certain night you seemed to think a sand-dweller suited you very well."

"The goddess Aset is beautiful in every guise," he said

50

softly, "but a queen should be dignified and aloof, untouched by the sun's beat, so well cared for she need not lift one finger."

"I'm not sure I'd want to be queen from that description," she said. "It would bore me to distraction to live so dull a life."

Amenemhet was about to reply when he saw the caravan was ready to resume moving. He pulled the hood again over her head. "You may at heart be a sand-dweller, but at the end of this trip you will pretend to be a queen," he said. "You must seem to be used to luxury, pampered and dignified."

Nefrytatanen sighed. "I'll remind myself of those things frequently—as I scramble among the rocks and crawl through the sand." She took his hand as they rode. "I can imagine Dedjet's face in Yenoam when I ask her to peel an apricot for me. Poor girl, I believe I'll have to teach her some of these new chores before we arrive at King Ami-enshi's palace, so she can behave like a proper royal attendant." Nefrytatanen turned her head to look at him and smile. "If I like that way of living, I may want to continue in the same fashion when we return."

"I doubt that," he replied. "You'd be bored, as you said."

"Maybe I wouldn't. You once told me the remedy if that problem occurs." Her eyes on him had renewed their old brightness. "You said you'd rescue me from such dullness with lovemaking."

As dusk approached, the caravan stopped. Amenemhet and Nefrytatanen stood outside their tent watching the others prepare the camp for the night. Ani and Lakma were sitting on a rug in a shadowy place talking quietly. Amenemhet turned to Nefrytatanen with raised eyebrows, tilting his head in their direction. Nefrytatanen turned and smiled knowingly.

Amenemhet looked at the black sky. "The stars are so low and bright in the heavens, they're enough to make anyone fall in love," he commented.

"Don't mention that word in Lakma's hearing," Nefrytatanen whispered. "He doesn't realize what's happening to him."

"How can he not know?"

"He thinks he can live without love, that he's shut his heart to love's entering his life."

"I wonder if I should have so foolish a man for my scribe," Amenemhet remarked. "He has much to learn."

"I think he'll learn it soon," Nefrytatanen said in a serious tone. "I would continue to observe him and see how his lessons are absorbed before I throw him to the jackals if I were you."

Amenemhet laughed, and putting his arm around Nefrytatanen's waist, led her into their tent.

The caravan approached the quarries of Hammamat when the sun was at its zenith the next day. The workmen had been called out of the excavations to rest while the pits shimmered with heat waves reflecting from the stone, but at the caravan's approach, the workers grew curious and rose from their resting places. When they realized whose caravan it was, they fell on their faces along both sides of the road.

Amenemhet drew his horse from the ranks of their escort and motioned Nefrytatanen to come with him. The officer in charge of the guards sent six of his men to follow them. Amenemhet rode closer to the quarry, taking care to remain a safe distance from the steep edge. Peering into the pit, he stopped the horse.

"There," he said, pointing, "is where we inscribed our names and an account of my first expedition."

"What expedition was that, beloved?" Nefrytatanen asked. "The sun is too bright and I can't read the carvings from so far away."

"When I was seventeen, my father sent me on a mission as a kind of test. He bestowed on me the honorary title of prime minister. It was only for the mission." Amenemhet's voice grew soft as he recalled the past. "I was young for such a task, but he entrusted me with an army of men to search out suitable blocks for his sarcophagus." Amenemhet paused.

"Go on, beloved," Nefrytatanen urged. "What happened?"

"Many things," he replied. "It was a happy day when I returned, for my search had been successful and my father was pleased with the stone I'd selected."

"How did you manage so large a group of men at so early an age?" she asked.

"How did you manage the north kingdom? You were ruling Tamehu at the same age," he reminded her.

Nefrytatanen shook her head. "I did the best I could, which turned out to be not enough. But since my failure led to our marriage, I'm satisfied with the results."

52

Amenemhet's smile faded as he continued to think about the past. "I'm still not quite sure how I managed the problems we had," he admitted. "Despite our troubles, we did return without loss." He turned to look at her, and she could see in his eyes the pride of that seventeen-year-old prince who had accomplished his mission. "Not one man died or was missing. Not one injury was sustained. Not even an animal died."

"You must have been an excellent leader even then," she said proudly.

"The men said the expedition was well managed," he continued. "The people of this region said Amen-Min granted us good fortune. We did run out of water. The area was very dry at the time and our supplies hadn't lasted."

"What did you do?"

He shook his head. "I prayed. I prayed the most enthusiastic prayer I ever prayed." His eyes returned to the quarry. "I was concerned not only for my own life, but for all those I had in my charge. It would have been an ignominious end to my career to die of thirst while procuring my father's sarcophagus lid." He paused, remembering the strange way his prayers had been answered. "A gazelle, one of the shyest of all creatures, ran right into our midst while we stood too surprised by her appearance to move. On the very block of stone I'd chosen, she stopped and gave birth to her young." He looked at Nefrytatanen and smiled. "The men called it a marvelous omen of good fortune. It seemed so, because after the gazelle left us, there was a rainstorm. The rain filled a neighboring well and we were saved." He gestured in the direction of the inscription. "The men were so excited they insisted the story be recorded, and so I ordered the tale to be carved on the quarry's face." He turned his horse back toward the caravan, and she followed.

"Your father must have been very proud when you returned," Nefrytatanen remarked.

"Yes, he was satisfied. I was more grateful to be alive than I was proud. It had been a close thing." He laughed softly and remarked, "I did learn from that experience."

"Why do you laugh?"

Amenemhet turned into the caravan's column and resumed his place. "It's nothing," he said softly, a smile lingering in his eyes.

"It is a nothing I'd like to hear," she said.

"There was a girl," he replied uneasily. "Had I been less

53

absorbed in her and paid more attention to our supplies, we might not have suffered the water problem."

Nefrytatanen tried to imagine Amenemhet as he would have acted at that age. She wondered who the girl had been, and later during the day often found herself imagining amorous scenes. Realizing each time that she was wildly jealous, she turned her mind from further imaginings.

The caravan traveled east and deeper into the drier regions. The sparse vegetation dwindled to almost nothing, and the heat grew to rival the desert's. The caravan reduced its former brisk pace to save the energy of both people and animals.

Amenemhet resigned himself to the discomfort with as much patience as he could summon. The sun beat on his skin until he felt as if it shriveled. He longed for a bath and one of Yazid's skillful oil massages to make his skin again fit properly. By the time Amenemhet felt he could no longer endure the grit of sand in his teeth, they had come upon a small oasis. Although it was early to stop for the day, Amenemhet called a halt and gave orders to make camp. Nefrytatanen gave him a look of gratitude.

While camp was being established, Amenemhet and Nefrytatanen stood beneath a small group of swaying palm trees and waited silently. The trees afforded scant shade, but it was preferable to the blazing sun.

"May I join you?"

Amenemhet and Nefrytatanen turned to see the priest Senbi approaching. "There's little shelter here," Amnemhet warned, "but you may share it with us. It's a good thing you came instead of Ankhneferu. Although he neither looks nor acts it, I believe this journey would have been too difficult at his age."

Senbi agreed quietly. "I too thought it best for the high priest to remain in Tamera. Besides, I have to admit I'm selfish. During our journey to Atalan, I learned I like traveling. I seldom get a chance to do it."

"Maybe you should have been a soldier or a sailor instead of a priest," Amenemhet remarked.

"Never a soldier," Senbi declared. "I have no temperament for that work. But a sailor—yes. That might have been appealing."

"Talking about occupations reminds me of something I must discuss with my attendants," Nefrytatanen said. "I'll do it now while they're temporarily without chores." Observing

54

Senbi's confused expression, the queen added, "It seems that royalty in Retenu live more indolent lives than we're used to, and I must instruct my servants not to look surprised at some of the strange requests I'll make in Yenoam."

Senbi watched as Nefrytatanen gestured to her attendants to gather under another group of palm trees, and he said, "I'm not sure I understood that."

Amenemhet replied, "If Nakht has described the life of King Ami-enshi and his court accurately, we're going to have to be very formal, Senbi."

Seating herself on a rock in the shade, Nefrytatanen regarded the servants, who had settled themselves at her feet. "Ambassador Nakht has told me some interesting things about King Ami-enshi's household," she began. "The servants in his palace are slaves, the king is very strict, and his household very formal. King Amenemhet and I have chosen to lead more active lives and behave more casually with those close to us than is usually done in most kingdoms. If we continue this practice in Yenoam, it will seem to King Ami-enshi that we have too little control. He would probably conclude, that we aren't properly respected."

The girls stared at Nefrytatanen in amazement as she continued, "We will have to be very formal at Yenoam when we're in sight of others. We'll have to make requests of you that we haven't bothered with at Ithtawe."

"My lady, what would you have us do?" Dedjet asked. "I'm willing to be a slave, if you wish."

"No!" Nefrytatanen said firmly. "Although we've had slaves from time to time, you know very well slaves in Tamera are in that undesirable state for different reasons than are those of other lands. You aren't slaves and you won't pretend to be. But, to impress King Ami-enshi, we will—"

"My lady!" Dedjet exclaimed. "You're the divine rulers of Tamera! Is it necessary to impress—"

"Dedjet," Nefrytatanen stopped her, "there's an example of what I mean." Dedjet looked chagrined as Nefrytatanen continued, "You interrupted me, and that cannot be allowed. If you do that in Yenoam, I'll have to make a great and unpleasant noise over it. Please spare me that chore." She sighed in resignation and explained, "Sparing the king and the ambassador additional chores is what I'm talking about. I want no disrespect, however misguided, from Retenu's king and ambassadors to hamper the negotiations or make it unpleasant for King Amenemhet." Nefrytatanen frowned as she instructed, "When you come into the king's or my presence, you will prostrate yourself at our feet. You will not speak until first addressed. Once you have been told to rise, you will stand unless we give permission to do otherwise. You will not touch our persons without permission. You will run to and fro making us comfortable. Not even by a glance will you show less than absolute obedience. If I sigh, someone will rush for a fan, someone else will hurry for a goblet of wine and someone else will throw herself at my feet for orders. You must use formal titles at all times." Nefrytatanen finished, "The king will speak to Yazid and his attendants about this same matter."

"Then, we'll race to you with perfumed handkerchiefs, and if you wish, I'll act as your food taster," Yunet said with a smile. "I'll practice prostrating myself with grace so I won't offend your divine eyes with clumsiness."

"You're getting the idea," Nefrytatanen said. "But through all this pomposity, never forget you are free women. Show every respect to King Ami-enshi and the others of his palace in accordance with their rank, but remember they aren't your masters. Use your own intelligence during any situations you might face; but if at any time you think you need advice, don't hesitate to speak privately with me about it. If I'm present in an awkward situation, I'll handle it without your doing anything." Nefrytatanen paused, then said bluntly, "You're all pretty and well-formed. If this causes you problems with men, tell me."

The girls looked speculatively at each other, not knowing what to say about this.

Nefrytatanen laughed softly. "I'm not saying anyone is likely to carry you off by force, but if any man takes liberties you haven't invited and don't wish to enjoy, you needn't suffer in silence."

Ani stepped out of the tent and moved to a shadowy area a little distance from the fire. She leaned against the curve of a palm tree's trunk and thought over the plans she had made.

Lakma had been right about her attitude. When she had first come to the palace, she was so grateful she had been more than courteous. She had been so eager to be of service, that she realized now, she'd been too humble. She was a servant; but as Lakma had said, she was handmaiden to the queen, a place deserving respect.

Ani no longer dressed so plainly as to become invisible.

Now she wore the pieces of jewelry Nefrytatanen had given her. Her robes were simple, but she made sure they were carefully cut and fitted. In every way she could think of, she had improved her manners and appearance to achieve a subtle, understated elegance that wiped away the last traces of her humble beginnings.

The man she had chosen was not yet aware of her ambitions, but she had planned that too. He would know she wanted him only when he was ready to accept her. By that time, she was sure his defenses would have been demolished.

"Being in the queen's service has been good for you," a voice behind her said.

Nakht had come quite close before speaking, and when Ani turned, her shoulder almost brushed his chest.

"I'm sorry if I startled you," he said. "Your perfume is most elusive, but very pleasing. It has the quality of making one want to come a little nearer to see if it can be defined. You've changed, Ani, and the change becomes you."

"Thank you, my lord," Ani said calmly. She turned her back to him—a thing she never would have done before—to gaze at the shadowy horizon. "I came out to think."

"The stars are beautiful," Nakht offered softly.

"Do you often take walks after dark?" she asked.

"From time to time," Nakht replied. "Maybe now I'll make a more regular habit of it."

He had a very engaging smile, Ani decided, but she said, "It's a little cool. I think I'll go nearer the fire."

Nakht said nothing as he walked with her, but thought that this little maid wasn't simple, and that it would be best not to hurry her. Finally he spoke. "I believe I'm too tired to stay out, and so bid you a pleasant night. Don't wander away from camp," he warned. "I wouldn't like you to get lost or injured."

"I'll stay out only a moment longer," Ani replied. "Then I'll be on my way to my own bed." She smiled at Nakht. "Have a pleasant night, my lord."

Before he entered his tent, Nakht glanced back at Ani. She was looking his way and made no effort to conceal it.

Ani watched Nakht close his tent flap and wondered at the truth of the rumors she had heard of his prowess. She couldn't help but feel complimented at receiving such a sophisticated man's attention. She was smiling at the thought when Lakma approached.

"Is it Ambassador Nakht, after all?" Lakma asked. Ani's

face was bright when she looked at him, and he wondered if her eyes glowed from the fire or from Nakht's attention.

"You warned me he isn't interested in marriage," Ani reminded him. Her smile held a secret Lakma couldn't read, as she added, "I listened most carefully to your advice."

"I've noticed the change in you." Lakma faltered, dropped his eyes, then admitted, "You are beautiful."

"Your approval pleases me," Ani whispered. "After all, wasn't it you who led me to wisdom?"

"Yes." He sighed, looking away. "You learn quickly."

Ani was almost ready to comment that he didn't seem overjoyed with this, when she realized Lakma's attention was no longer on her.

"By all that's sacred!" he exclaimed softly, looking beyond her shoulder.

The expression on Lakma's face frightened Ani, and she turned at the very moment he rushed past her. Smoke was curling from the flap of one of the tents. Ani stood rooted to her place as she watched Lakma race toward the tent. In the few seconds he took to reach it, the smoke had increased to an ominous billowing. Suddenly, flames rushed out from the sides to reach toward the roof with greedy fingers.

"Fire!" Ani found her voice at last. "Fire, fire!" she screamed, but couldn't move. As she stared at the tent, she realized it was Senbi's, and watched in horror as Lakma tore open the flap and billows of smoke engulfed him. She heard him begin to cough, and he disappeared inside.

"By Sutekh!" Amenemhet roared as he ran past Ani. The tent was now a torch.

"Lakma went after Senbi!" Ani cried, following Amenemhet.

From all directions, others came running with containers to throw water onto the flames, even though they knew the tent was already beyond saving.

Lakma staggered through the opening, carrying Senbi over his shoulder like a grain sack. Coughing raggedly, Lakma lay Senbi on the sand and looked wordlessly at Amenemhet with streaming eyes.

"Never mind Senbi's tent!" Amenemhet called. "Wet the others!" Watching the hurrying figures outlined by the flames and satisfied that they had heard him, Amenemhet turned to Lakma. "Is Senbi alive?"

"I am not an apparition." Senbi sat up slowly, still gasping for air. "It was close enough." He wiped his eyes and groped

58

for Lakma's hand, then struggled to his feet. "I wanted to read awhile," he gasped. "I must have fallen asleep with my lamp still burning and somehow knocked it over." He looked at Lakma. "I would have died if you hadn't taken me out. I was already unconscious."

Lakma's face was grim. "It was only by chance I saw the smoke in time."

Again wiping his eyes, Senbi said, "It wasn't by chance you came in after me. I can say little enough to express my gratitude, Lakma, but if there's ever anything I can do for you—other than offer many prayers in your behalf—name it." Lakma shook his head, but Senbi insisted, "Perhaps not today or tomorrow; but someday, if there's anything, don't hesitate to ask."

Nefrytatanen looked at Lakma's smudged face, then at Ani's great eyes staring anxiously at him. "Ani," she said clearly, "get the ointment I carry in my case. Lakma's hands are burned. Attend to them for him. Are you burned, Senbi?"

"I think not," Senbi answered. "Thanks to Lakma's speed, I was only overcome by smoke. All I need now is to cleanse myself of this soot."

"Then do so and share Nakht's tent," Nefrytatanen suggested. "Let us all get some rest for tomorrow's traveling." She looked at Ani. "What are you waiting for, Ani? Get the ointment and care for Lakma's burns." The queen watched Ani hurry away, then said to Amenemhet, "Come, beloved. Let us get some sleep."

"It has been an eventful night." Amenemhet commented. "Don't worry about anything, Lakma. You'll ride in a litter tomorrow and rest. We'll make Ani available to apply fresh ointment to your burns and watch so they don't get infected."

Alone in their tent, Nefrytatanen settled close to Amenemhet and whispered, "You did that very tactfully, beloved. You're a marvel of diplomacy and cunning."

"I thought I did it well myself," he said smugly.

The flat, sandy land began to rise in gentle hills of green broken by cliffs, and when camp was made the next night, it was beside a rushing stream near a partially wooded ridge where the cedar was a heady perfume in the air.

Although Lakma's burns were minor, Nefrytatanen had insisted on Ani's continuing to attend them, and after the evening meal, Ani went again to Lakma to apply the ointment.

As the girl bent over his arm, absorbed with wrapping a

59

bandage around his wrist, Lakma said, "Ani, I appreciate your help, but I don't think you have to bother yourself further."

Ani glanced up as she worked. "The queen is very concerned about you—and it's no bother for me." She finished bandaging and straightened. "You must remember you have a job to do in Yenoam requiring the use of your hands."

Lakma hadn't thought about that. He was quiet a moment, then said, "Still, Ani, you've been very gentle in attending me, and I appreciate it."

"Well, didn't you do me a favor?"

"What did I do?" Lakma dropped his eyes. He knew what she meant, but he couldn't tell her he had repeatedly wished since then that he could take back his advice. He hadn't known he would be caught in the enchantment she would weave. The arrow of love she had loosed at someone, he reflected, seemed to have done himself some damage.

"You gave me excellent advice," Ani said.

"I only related my observations. It was nothing."

"It was an idea that's changed my life!" Ani exclaimed. "Don't say it's nothing. Of course I'm grateful."

When Lakma finally looked at her, his face was solemn, and he said quietly, "I only planted a seed, Ani. You grew the flower."

Ani was exasperated. Scribes were educated and supposedly intelligent, but the king's own scribe seemed so dense he couldn't understand her—a simple farm girl. Ani composed her thoughts. If Lakma didn't understand hints, glances and subtle gestures, she decided she would have to be blunt.

"Have you no sense?" Ani asked sharply. Lakma stared at her. "It's you I want, Lakma. It was for you I did those things. Must I write it on my forehead so your scribe's eyes will read it and your scribe's mind will finally understand?" Lakma's mouth fell open. Ani continued, "Perhaps I must write it elsewhere on my person so my meaning will be unmistakable."

He stared at her a long moment, a light growing in his eyes. "Yes, why don't you do that?" he said slowly. He looked at her another long moment, then added, "Maybe I can meet you somewhere alone to read this message."

Ani was dizzy with happiness, but she retorted, "You'd better bring a lamp, because I would meet you in a place too dark to read without one." She turned to leave the tent. It took great effort on her part to walk to the opening with dignity, because in her delight she felt like hopping and skipping.

Lakma's bandaged hands on Ani's shoulders stopped her. She was surprised at their strength as he turned her to face him.

"Ani, let us waste no more precious time," he whispered. "I have spent weeks longing for you while I stubbornly refused to speak of it. I thought you wanted someone else, so instead of trying to win you, I hid like a mouse. When you turned just now to go, I resolved I would finally tell you exactly how I feel." He grinned, relieved to be telling her at last. "My feelings for you aren't merely physical, although I admit that sensation is ever present. I love you, and if you also love me, I'll seek out Senbi this very night and take him up on his offer to do me a favor by asking him to marry us now."

Ani stared at Lakma a moment. Then, closing her eyes, she swayed toward him to lay her head against his shoulder.

Lakma wondered at her silence. Did she say nothing because it wasn't marriage she sought? A chill ran through him, but when she drew away and looked up at him, he breathed with relief at the expression on her face.

"No, Lakma," she said softly. "After all my patience, I can wait one more night. Let poor Senbi sleep peacefully. Tomorrow, Lakma, go to him early in the morning." She smiled and whispered, "At first light tell him that this was our last night alone."

Lakma's arms slid around her as he tried to convince himself he wasn't dreaming. Reality answered him by shining in his mind like a rainbow, by singing in his heart like a bird.

Amenemhet awoke as the first gray light of dawn crept into the tent. The day before, he had witnessed Lakma and Ani's marriage and the caravan had celebrated late into the night. He wondered why he was awake so early, since he had had only a couple of hours of sleep. His lips curved in a smile as Nefrytatanen turned in her slumber and moved closer. The celebrating had gone on so long, that everyone would surely still be tired. Was their journey so hurried they couldn't spend this day resting and sleeping late? Amenemhet decided Ami-enshi and his treaty could wait one day more. The travelers would rest and Lakma and Ani would have a day of solitude.

Having made this decision, Amenemhet moved carefully

away from Nefrytatanen so he wouldn't awaken her. He would inform the keeper-of-the-time not to sound the morning signal and awaken the camp. Nefrytatanen moved and Amenemhet waited motionlessly, but her eyes opened.

"I didn't want to disturb you," Amenemhet whispered. "I was going to give orders not to awaken the camp this morning so we all could sleep late and rest a day before continuing the journey."

Nefrytatanen sat up and slowly stretched. "You're thinking of Lakma and Ani."

"Now that we've finally gotten them together, it seems unfair to give them so short a time."

Nefrytatanen yawned. "If you'll wait while I put on a robe, I'll walk with you."

"You don't have to," he whispered, kissing her lightly. "I'll be right back."

"I want to see how the new day looks," she replied, already getting to her feet.

The air was beginning to turn softly pink as the sun's edge appeared on the horizon. Although a cool breeze spread the cedar's perfume over the camp, the air was comfortably warm and slightly moist. The mornings were different from Tamera's mornings, which were cool and dry. The strange fragrance of the region's forest was pleasing, and Amenemhet and Nefrytatanen breathed deeply of it as they quietly walked toward the keeper-of-the-time.

The man was sitting beside his water clock with his back against a tree trunk, head slumped to his chest. Smiling, Amenemhet touched him with his foot. The keeper-of-the-time grunted, looked up, then leaped to his feet.

"Quietly, my friend," Amenemhet whispered. "I've only come to tell you we'll travel nowhere this day. Go to bed and let the others awaken when each will."

Amenemhet and Nefrytatanen left him gathering up his blanket as they strolled, hand in hand, beyond the rock ridge where the camp's guards were posted. Starting down the rocky slope, they were careful not to loosen stones and cause a clatter.

The sky was still deep purple in the west and they paused to watch the sun's ascent, and to look below.

Down the slope halfway to the rim of shadowy trees, like a cup scooped out of the ridge, nestled a tiny valley. A cloud of haze, golden in the light, rose like billows of sheer veilings, and the rising sun sparkled like beads caught in its silk. Nefrytatanen led Amenemhet toward the mist.

They entered the haze as if they passed into another world, through a curtain that dissolved when they stepped into it. Shimmering vapor caught softly at their arms and the hems of their garments, following briefly like clinging cobwebs to disappear and merge again with the rest. Nefrytatanen's hair became part of the floating misty veils. When she stepped into the light, her robe became gold gossamer, her form a part of the magic of the unearthly valley. Her skin glowed translucently from the moisture, and her eyes were darkly blue in the shadows of the place. The scent of the cool, damp earth combined with her perfume until the whole cup of the valley seemed filled with her spirit as if she had merged with the morning.

The soft murmur of a nearby stream became part of her whisper, "This place seems like Tuat."

Amenemhet put an arm around her waist and they walked silently toward the stream, but she slipped from his grasp to lift her robe, floating with vapor, and glide alone to the edge of the water. A shred of topaz mist drifted by, threatening to conceal her, but she held out her open arms so the cloud veils were drawn aside one by one at his advance.

He stood before her and said quietly, "For a moment you seemed one with the morning's spirits, a creature separate from me." His voice was absorbed by the valley's hush.

Nefrytatanen lifted her head and replied, "Never separate from you—one with you always."

Amenemhet laid his cheek on her forehead, inhaling her scent, which seemed to him sweeter than the perfume of the newly opened flowers. "When you stood alone by the stream, you appeared to have come from the haze, as if the dawn was brightened by your presence."

She moved a little away to gaze wonderingly up at him. "I'm but a woman looking into my love's eyes," she said quietly. "What I see in them is what gives my dawn its warmth."

"To me you are a goddess."

"Come with this goddess then," she invited and turned away. He followed through the drifting clouds of luminous vapor until she stopped in a place where the grass was dotted with small starlike flowers. When she turned, she looked up at him, the thoughts in her heart a message he understood without words.

Five

Ilbaya dreamed of racing along the beach, the surging muscles of his horse blending with his own body. The dream was so vivid he could feel the wind blowing through his hair, smell the sweet, clean scent of the sea air, and his heart sang with the exhilaration of freedom. Then he turned over on his back and was awakened by a sharp pain from the network of half-healed welts in his skin. Immediately recognizing the odorous darkness of the slaves' tent, he turned to lie on his stomach, and his eyes filled with bitter tears for the loss of his dream.

The small space between the tent's bottom and the ground told Ilbaya the darkness was beginning to lighten. He remembered that when morning came he would have to get up and work. It was the first day he had had to work in a week because of his beating. He was glad he had awakened early and would avoid the slave master's stick; he would soon enter the tent to rouse the men, wielding his stick on the soles of those who hesitated rising. Ilbaya didn't think he could endure one more humiliation.

How many beatings had he suffered in the six months since he had been dragged onto Lord Chaon's ship, he wondered. He had had as many masters as the months, and several of them had administered more than one punishment before they grew disgusted with his attempts to escape and offered him for sale. Now he was owned by Bemen, a slave dealer. Once again he had tried to run away, and Bemen had had him beaten so thoroughly he hadn't been able to get on his feet afterward. How, he wondered, could they expect him not to try to escape?

Ilbaya thought of his sisters. His last sight of them had been when they were led off the ship still shackled to the other female slaves. They hadn't seen him or even heard his cries. Not that he had been able to call out much before the guard standing nearby had knocked him to the deck and kicked him several times. Ilbaya realized then that he would never see Chani and Mallia again. Seething with fury to think of what their lives had become, he clenched his teeth and deliberately turned over on his back so his pain would distract him from the memories he could no longer endure.

The one thought that made his life bearable was that of escape. He hungered so ravenously for freedom it had become an obsession with him. Thinking over the many futile attempts he had already made, he wondered why they hadn't succeeded. The answer shimmered before his eyes as if it was wreathed in flames—all his attempts at escape had been either hastily planned, or not planned at all. The next try, he decided, must be carefully thought out and it must succeed.

As painful as it was to stir up memories of his former life, he forced himself to remember the slaves his father had owned, to think of those who had escaped. There had been only a few who had even tried. Their life in his father's house had been a different thing from the kind of life he now led—his father had been a just and kind man. Yet there was one, Ilbaya reflected, who must have felt the same as he— one that wanted freedom no matter how well he was treated as a slave.

That slave had appeared to be no more interested in freedom than a milk cow, but Ilbaya had been alerted by the expression in his eyes. His eyes reminded Ilbaya too much of the eyes of his falcon. The slave had unknowingly become a specimen for Ilbaya's idle curiosity. The man was good-natured and always seemed ready to do whatever task was given him. He had been ingratiating in an unsophisticated way that had amused Ilbaya until he realized the slave was far from simple. Everyone in the household had grown to like and trust the man, and eventually he was given more freedom than any of the other slaves. When the man finally disappeared, Ilbaya was the only one who wasn't surprised.

Ilbaya wondered if he could behave like that slave, who probably was now peacefully tending his own flock of sheep somewhere in Minoa's mountains. Although it was too late for Bemen to be deceived by Ilbaya's plan, Ilbaya realized Bemen would try to sell him as soon as his back was healed, rather than risk his trying another escape. Ilbaya only hoped his back wouldn't heal until after they had left Zahi. To be sold to a Hyksos master was a fate dreaded by all slaves, for the Hyksos didn't punish a slave by simple beatings. If he healed too fast, Ilbaya decided he would reopen the wounds in his back to avoid being offered for sale.

Ilbaya closed his eyes and planned how he would behave to deceive his future master into trusting him and decided he could practice the new role he would assume while Bemen still owned him. If he appeared to be resigned to his status, it might even save him a few beatings before he was sold.

When the slave master entered the tent and roared that it was morning, Ilbaya was the first man to rise from his mat, although he flinched with pain. The slave master, who expected rebellion from Ilbaya on the first work day, looked suspiciously at him, but Ilbaya's hazel eyes appeared to hold no rancor.

When he was handed his morning meal, which was a cold, stringy-looking fish laid limply on a mound of sticky gruel, Ilbaya forced himself to remain silent, though he wondered how he would manage to eat it. Because Bemen thought slaves who didn't work didn't need much food, Ilbaya had lived with constant hunger during the last week. So he forced himself to eat what they gave him—though he carefully rinsed the lingering taste from his mouth with the water that accompanied the meal.

Ilbaya said nothing when he was told that his work for the day would be constructing the platform to be used for displaying the slaves for sale that week. Although he knew working in the hot sun would make his back blaze with pain, he controlled his anger with an ease that surprised him. He concluded he was able to do so because he now had a plan of his own to fulfill. Reminding himself not to take off his tunic and bare his back to the scorching sun and stinging insects, he picked up his ax and trudged away.

As he contemplated the task Zahi's Ambassador Gobryas had given him, Marmarus smiled with satisfaction. He was to go to Tamera, a land he had never visited but had heard from others was very prosperous, to complete the assignment Zahi's former agent had failed to finish. The other man had been exposed as a Hyksos spy and expelled. Marmarus was to sell slaves to conceal his true purpose. He would be paid by Zahi and, at the same time, would make a good profit from the slave trade. Who in Tamera would suspect a Babylonian slave trader of sabotaging their crops and plunging them into famine? He had to agree with Ambassador Gobryas that it was a perfect disguise even while he privately rejoiced over the double profits he would make. More than double. Gobryas had given him a pouch generously filled with gold to outfit his caravan and obtain slaves.

Marmarus had spent the last two weeks organizing his caravan and purchasing choice slaves. He decided he would buy a few more and, at the same time, learn some of the finer points of being a slave trader from the dealers he confronted.

Morning was the best time to inspect slaves because it was when they were engaged in whatever chores the dealers had assigned. A man would then reveal limps or deformities that might otherwise be hidden when he was carefully dressed and merely standing on the sale platform. Marmarus left his tent, wearing garments he thought suitable for a slave trader, and entered the marketplace trailed by several helpers who would deliver the slaves back to his encampment.

Late in the morning, after Marmarus had made two purchases, the sun's heat grew so oppressive he was ready to go back to his camp when a slave working near Bemen's tent caught his attention. It was the slave's hair that first interested Marmarus; it was a bright orange-gold, shining like new copper in the sun, a rare color, highly decorative and eye-catching. Marmarus was sure the people of Tamera would be attracted by such a slave, since most of them had dark hair.

Marmarus moved into the shade of a building to study the slave further. The man wasn't tall, but he was lean and strong. He had a lightness to his step, and a quickness to his gestures that was seldom seen among slaves. He didn't talk to his companions or waste time as he worked. Nor did he pause to look at the passing women, Marmarus observed with satisfaction. The slave appeared to be intent on his job, efficiently setting up the display platform.

68

Ilbaya was aware of the Babylonian watching him, but he pretended not to be. Having learned volumes about slave dealers in the last six months, he judged Marmarus to be a trader discreetly investigating a slave that interested him before the owner interfered.

After a short time had passed, Marmarus approached slowly and commented, "It's very hot to work in the sun."

Ilbaya glanced at him as he industriously continued to fasten a pole. "The heat has never mattered too much to me," he replied in a pleasant tone.

"You speak my language," the Babylonian remarked. "What other languages do you speak?"

"Minoan, which is my mother tongue, and Latin, Zahi, a little Tameran," Ilbaya answered easily, still working on the pole.

"What else do you know?" Marmarus inquired.

"Very little, but sometimes it's better for a slave not to know too much—or want too much," Ilbaya answered cheerfully.

"Greetings, my friend." Bemen had come over to see what was going on. Hoping to sell Ilbaya immediately, if possible, Bemen seized on Marmarus' visit as an opportunity and asked, "Are you interested in buying Ilbaya?"

"I was just mentioning that the heat was getting oppressive," Marmarus replied cautiously. "But I was attracted by the unusual color of his hair. How much are you asking for him?"

"The price for such a worker can't be decided hastily," Bemen responded.

"I really have all the slaves I need, and I don't have much time to bargain for extras because I'm readying my caravan to leave soon," Marmarus said. "I only asked from curiosity."

When Ilbaya heard that Marmarus was leaving Zahi, he moved to where he had laid his ax and began to trim the next post. It would be the answer to his prayers to have not only a new owner, but one that would leave Zahi soon and not learn about Ilbaya's attempted escape.

"He's like an ox—not very smart—but he does whatever he's asked," Bemen was saying.

"Maybe I could examine him more closely."

"Ilbaya, come here!" Bemen shouted.

Ilbaya put down the wood and hurriedly got to his feet. One of the things he hated most about being a slave was being inspected like an animal. He took a deep breath and carefully fixed an indifferent expression on his face before he turned to approach them.

Marmarus raised a hand to tug at Ilbaya's hair and noted that it wasn't only luxuriant, but springy, which was a sign of his health. He pressed Ilbaya's arm to judge his muscles. Satisfied, he slowly walked around to poke at Ilbaya's back. Ilbaya stood quietly, though his eyes watered from the pain, but Marmarus didn't see because he had bent to squeeze the calf of Ilbaya's leg. Then he straightened and walked around Ilbaya to face him. He peered into Ilbaya's eyes, noting they were clear and uninfected.

"Open your mouth," he directed.

Ilbaya squashed the rebellion rising in him and obeyed.

"You see? His teeth are clean, without even a hint of rot," Bemen offered. "Not only is he healthy in every respect, but he has a talent for handling horses. I'd thought some nobleman might pay a good price for him to use as a stable master."

Ilbaya kept his face blank, though he was sorely tempted to smile at this reference to his skill at handling horses. It was his riding ability that helped him almost accomplish his last escape.

"If you've inspected him to your satisfaction, let us go into my tent away from this sun," Bemen suggested eagerly. "We can have a cup of wine while we discuss the price. It needn't take too long."

Marmarus wiped away the sweat that was prickling his forehead and nodded.

As they walked away, Ilbaya turned his back to them. Despite his resolution not to show his true feelings, he felt like laughing aloud when he heard Bemen say, "He's a docile slave and good-natured, never causing a problem."

Ilbaya trudged behind Marmarus through the dust feeling very smug, though his expression revealed nothing. He had acted his part so well Marmarus hadn't even dropped a loop of rope around his neck to lead him to the encampment.

"There is my tent," Marmarus said.

Ilbaya lifted his head to look at the tent and found his eyes instead fixed on the graceful figure of a golden-haired girl who had just stepped from its opening. Catching himself before Marmarus turned, he tilted his head innocently to inspect the tent's height. "You must be very successful to have so fine an encampment," he commented to Marmarus.

70

Marmarus shrugged. "Business is not too bad."

Ilbaya's eyes swept over the slaves that were engaged in various tasks nearby before he regarded Marmarus. "What would you have me do?" he asked.

Gratified that the slave was so eager to work, Marmarus replied, "Bemen said you were good with horses."

Ilbaya nodded. "I understand them," he said modestly.

"Then go to Shamash and assist him tending the animals," Marmarus directed.

Following the direction of Marmarus' pointing fingers, Ilbaya located Shamash, then nodded and turned away. Although he knew Shamash would only allow him to rake manure and mend harnesses until he proved he wouldn't try to leap on a horse and escape, Ilbaya resolved to do whatever was asked of him without complaint. Not even his eyes would reveal his distaste for whatever was required of him. He approached Shamash wearing a vacant expression.

Later, Marmarus ordered Ilbaya to bathe, lest he bring lice into the slave tent. Shamash accompanied Ilbaya to a large tub of water behind the tent. When Ilbaya pulled off his tunic, Shamash saw the welts on his back and moved closer to run his fingers over the raw paths they made.

"Where did you get those?" he asked suspiciously.

"Bemen's slavemaster," Ilbaya answered, wondering how he would explain the reason for his beating. He knew Shamash would report his answer to Marmarus. He immediately dipped his head into the container of water so he would have a moment to think of a lie.

After Ilbaya had straightened, Shamash asked him, "What did you do to earn them?"

Ilbaya shrugged. "Not so big a thing, I'd thought. It was the horse I was tending that kicked at Bemen—not I—but Bemen thought I should have foreseen it. I tried to explain that I'd already mentioned the danger of walking too close to the horse's hindquarters, but he wouldn't listen. Bemen wasn't hurt, but I think he was in a bad mood that day and found it convenient to blame me for all his problems."

"If you think you were unjustly punished, don't you bear him ill will?" Shamash asked carefully.

Ilbaya needed all his resolution to keep anger from his eyes, but he answered, "Bemen owned me and could do whatever he wished with me."

"Don't you think he was cruel?" Shamash prompted.

Ilbaya sighed. "Be grateful to the gods that Marmarus isn't

71

like him," he advised. "Bemen was little better than the Hyksos, who, I've heard, enjoy watching slaves suffer."

Shamash nodded and advised Ilbaya to finish preparing himself for the evening meal.

After Ilbaya had dressed and was bending to squeeze the last drops of water from his hair, he noticed the golden-haired girl again standing a little distance away watching him. He wondered how long she had been there, and his eyes filled with dancing green lights to think of her watching him when he was naked just a moment before. He lifted his head to give her an appraising look. Then, remembering that she was a slave Marmarus was using as his own concubine, Ilbaya turned his eyes away. He dared not show an interest in her. He'd be wise to reveal no interest in any woman if he wanted Marmarus to trust him.

Lyra was attracted to Ilbaya the moment she saw him walking down the street with Marmarus. She observed him at odd moments all through the day, and, at first, thought he was the sort of slave who obeyed his master like a dumb animal. Then she began to wonder at his background. He didn't walk like a slave who was used to having his ankles shackled, and he had a way of lifting his head and straightening his shoulders that made her think he was accustomed to giving orders, not taking them. She wondered if he had come from a noble or wealthy family that had fallen into misfortune. Yet when she overheard him talking to Shamash, his words revealed him as uneducated and his thoughts as simple. She wondered what had earned the bright-haired Minoan his beating, which she could see had been severe. When he finally noticed her watching him and lifted his eyes to meet hers, she had seen the brightness that momentarily lit them before he turned.

Lyra walked away slowly, her heart beating at an odd pace, still puzzling over the new slave.

Ilbaya accepted the bowl of food he was handed without seeing it. He found a place away from the other slaves and sat on the ground to eat. Although the stew had a sour taste and the bread was stale, he didn't notice it. His thoughts still were on the golden-haired girl, speculating on why she had paused to watch him bathe.

He was startled when a voice above him asked softly, "Perhaps you'd like to share a melon with me?"

He raised his eyes to follow the graceful lines of the form

72

the clinging robe revealed. He put down the desire that leaped in him and returned his attention to his food. "Won't Marmarus object?"

Lyra lowered herself to sit beside him. "He allows his slaves to converse together," she replied quietly.

Ilbaya put down his empty bowl and looked at her with a deliberately vacuous expression. "Would you like me to break open the melon?"

Lyra dropped the globe into his hands and smiled encouragingly. "You're from Minoa, I've heard," she commented. When he merely nodded in answer and started pounding the melon with a sharp stone, she said, "I'm from Thessalia. My name is Lyra."

"My name is Ilbaya," he muttered.

"I overheard you speaking to Shamash about your beating." Ilbaya said nothing. Sure now that she had watched him bathe, he wondered if she would try to seduce him. He was surprised at her next words.

"You speak Babylonian very well, far better than I," Lyra remarked, accepting the chunk of melon he offered. "It's very awkward for me to say even this little to you. Do you speak Greek?"

Ilbaya shook his head. Scraping away the seeds from his piece of fruit, he said, "Latin, Zahi and a little Tameran, which is similar in some ways to my own language."

"I can see you learn languages easily, but I'm not so fortunate."

Ilbaya looked at her from the corner of his eye. She was taking a bite of her melon. "It's the only thing I do learn easily," he lied, wanting her to think him dense in all other matters.

"No one else in this camp can speak Greek, and I have no one I can talk to easily," Lyra commented. She was silent a moment. Then, as if it was an idea that suddenly occurred to her, she said, "If you learn languages readily, maybe I could teach you Greek so I can speak it once more."

Ilbaya turned his head to look at her. "Why don't you teach one of the women?" he suggested. When she didn't answer, he turned his attention to his melon and added, "Doesn't Marmarus speak Greek?" Glancing at her from the corner of his eye, he noted that she was nervously biting her lip.

"He doesn't speak very much to me in any language," Lyra whispered. She put her hand on Ilbaya's arm. "I only want to

73

have someone to talk to now and again. I get lonely for the sound of my language sometimes."

Lyra's hand on his flesh caused a tingle to run through him, but he waited until it had passed before he looked at her. He studied the expression in her clear gray eyes and wondered at her motives.

"When we have time to spare from our tasks, if you wish to teach me Greek, I'll be willing to learn," he said carefully. The smile that lit her face filled him with a familiar warmth he didn't like to acknowledge even to himself, and he returned his attention to the melon.

Sure that Lyra's friendliness had been ordered by Marmarus and that after she had reported their conversation she wouldn't approach him too closely again, Ilbaya resolved he would never encourage her. Getting involved with any woman could ruin all his plans for escape, but being discovered with his owner's concubine could cost him his life. He sighed softly as he thought of the body he had glimpsed when she stood above him. But, he reminded himself, even if it were possible to possess her, slaves that accidentally bore children only made their masters richer—and Ilbaya had no intention of giving his sons a life of slavery.

Six

On the fourteenth day of their travels, knowing they neared Yenoam, Amenemhet sent a rider ahead to see exactly how far the city was. The rider returned in the afternoon to tell them Yenoam lay beyond the next ridge.

At dusk, after camp had been established at the base of the ridge, Amenemhet and Nefrytatanen met with the leaders of each group they had brought with them and gave instructions for the preparations to enter the city. When Amenemhet and Nefrytatanen were finally alone, he turned to her with a tense expression.

"This lavish display is annoying," he said. "I'll feel like a fool going through so prodigal an exhibition."

Nefrytatanen smiled sympathetically. "This show of wealth and its accompanying pomp has little favor with me also, but it should impress King Ami-enshi. As children of Ra, we must seem more than human."

"Perhaps," he replied dismally, "but I prefer to use my power to accomplish, rather than pose and posture as if my soul were so impoverished I must show the world by outward trappings instead of simply being what I am."

Nefrytatanen sighed. "When the negotiations begin, King

Ami-enshi and his advisers will learn soon enough this grand display disguises no weakness in you."

In the early morning, Amenemhet watched as the tents were taken down and folded, the royal platform trimmed, and the animals given a last-minute brushing. Finally, he stood up so that Yazid could inspect the back of his white robe for any trace of soil left by the rock he had used as a chair. Then, Amenemhet got into the vehicle, which held replicas of the thrones at Ithtawe, and watched while Nefrytatanen entered and seated herself beside him. The servants arranged themselves in appropriate places to complete the picture of luxury. The captain of the palace guards, who was in charge of the soldiers on this journey, approached the vehicle and waited for Amenemhet's signal to begin.

Finally, Amenemhet sighed and ordered, "Have them move forward. Remind those riding before us that their king and queen are now almost at the end of the procession so they stir up a minimum of dust."

The captain bowed his head briefly before disappearing into the crowd to warn those at the head of the lines.

Noting the expression on Amenemhet's face, Nefrytatanen said sweetly, "Remember, beloved. We aren't sand-dwellers and must appear regal and dignified."

He gave her a look of disgust. "I did say that, didn't I?"

"Those were the very words you chose." She slipped her hand under his and whispered, "Beloved?" He looked at her questioningly. "Will you find it so difficult if you know your sand-dweller girl awaits you each night when we're safe from prying eyes?"

Amenemhet squeezed her hand and murmured, "That thought will give me comfort."

As the royal caravan neared Yenoam's gates, a chorus of trumpets announced welcome in a series of lavish flourishes suitable for such visitors. Amenemhet and Nefrytatanen exchanged meaningful glances, then watched the tall gates ahead slowly open. Standards along the top of the high walls displayed a myriad of both Tamera's and Retenu's flags, and their bright colors fluttered cheerfully in the wind.

Crowds of King Ami-enshi's subjects lined the streets and were held back by many green-and-gold-uniformed guards. Their faces were open and friendly, welcoming the visitors;

but mostly the people of Yenoam were curious about Tamera's people.

The inhabitants of the sunny Nile Valley were rumored to be advanced in the sciences, but had peculiar religious beliefs. It was said the people of Tamera believed themselves to have descended from their divinities, while their king and queen were divine beings in the flesh. Products of rare quality and art objects and jewelry of exquisite design came from Tamera. These pieces were difficult to obtain, and the craftsmen of Tamera were loath to teach others their knowledge. Kings of other countries paid high fees to obtain the skills of Tamera's architects, mathematicians, physicians and artists, but few Tamerans could be persuaded to stay permanently in other lands—whatever riches they were promised.

So Retenu's people were very curious about Tamera; to have the rare opportunity to actually view the king and queen of the Two Lands was an occasion not to be missed.

The first of the caravan to pass through Yenoam's gates was a line of elite guards riding dancing, satin-coated horses and bearing banners representing Tamera's provinces. Lines of scarlet-uniformed cavalrymen followed, carrying lances and shields that gleamed in the sun. A squad of archers, and a phalanx of foot soldiers marched in. The faces of the soldiers were expressionless, though they carried themselves proudly and with formidable confidence. The people of Yenoam were doubly glad the countries were on friendly terms.

A buzz of whispers ran through the crowd as, under the banner of a serpent, a flat, awning-covered conveyance carried priests and sundry assistants, who wore inscrutable expressions and rich garments. Tamera's effective use of magic was well known in every land, and the crowds were awed that the very priests who practiced these secrets were before their eyes.

A long line of camels, six to a row, covered with red and gold tassels and fringes, came bearing huge jars, carved from polished stone selected for its particular beauty. They held precious oils and the perfumes and incense for which Tamera was famous. Other camels were laden with magnificent caskets of jewelry, containers of highly prized herbs and medicines, fine linen, bundles of papyrus and sumptuous silks from the east, ivory from the south. But of all the gifts, the promise of continued trade was the most welcome.

Female servants traveled in litters covered by sheer white curtains, from whose swaying folds drifted a variety of Tamera's perfumes—and more than one Yenoam woman envied these servants who traveled like highborn ladies.

A wide gap preceded the silent arrival of a single, haughty guard in crimson, riding a white horse and carrying the personal banner of the royal family, a white-and-red field on which the cobra and hawk blazed, heavily embroidered in gold. The personal guards of the royal household, wearing white uniforms, rode before, after and to the sides of the platform that carried the king and queen. The crowds pressed anxiously closer to view the couple seated inside.

At the palace, Princess Zaya, first daughter of King Amienshi's favorite wife, strained to see as the golden platform neared her chamber's shady balcony, eager to get a first glimpse of the royal couple.

Columns of lapis lazuli held the golden canopy that formed the royal vehicle's roof, and from slender gold standards bearing the hawk and cobra flew small red-and-white banners. Tamera's royal couple, sitting erect on replicas of their thrones, were fanned by white ostrich plumes on long gold handles.

King Amenemhet wore a white robe and the gold-and-white triple-striped hemhemet crown, with its stiff folds that fell to the tips of his broad shoulders and the golden cobra that stood out from his brow. He had a sullen expression, Princess Zaya noted, studying him with increased interest. His skin was bronzed from sun, his frame slim but muscular. He was not a man grown soft from the comforts of his rank, Zaya decided, and she smiled. He pleased her.

Zaya's gaze reluctantly passed to Queen Nefrytatanen, whose hair was hidden by an ornate gold headpiece. The queen wore a crimson robe made of a lightweight material that clung to her in the slight breeze. Her head was held high, her expression impenetrable. Zaya noted, with some regret, that she seemed a fitting consort for such a king.

"You are a most impressive sight, beloved," Nefrytatanen murmured, as she watched Amenemhet's eyes sweep over the crowd. He turned to her.

"People will think I do no more than pose and be fanned," Amenemhet muttered. "If we had had to travel like this all the way from Ithtawe, we would have been months on this one journey."

"Perhaps, but you are an awesome-looking king. And you do look unapproachable, scowling as you now are."

His frown softened. "You hardly resemble the little sand-

78

dweller I spent a delightful desert night with. A more regal queen has never worn that crown." His eyes slowly ran over her as he added, "But when that breeze influences the folds of your garment, I see hints of a form I remember well."

Amenemhet's eyes remained steadily on Nefrytatanen until she finally whispered, "Beloved, if you continue looking at me in that manner, the expression on my face will change to something less than regal."

"I make you feel that way now, truly?" he asked quietly.

"Yes, beloved."

Amenemhet said nothing more, because that pleasant thought occupied his mind for the rest of the ride.

When they arrived at the palace doors, Princess Zaya watched intently as Amenemhet and Nefrytatanen stepped carefully from their places. Rows of Tamera's servants prostrated themselves before their advance. As she watched Amenemhet walk toward her father and the welcoming officials, Zaya's heart beat a little faster, for he moved with the sensuous grace of a lion. How did he make love, she wondered. His expression was reserved, but no longer sullen, and his mouth looked as if he could be moved to a warm response. A hint of Nefrytatanen's perfume reached Zaya, and for a moment she enjoyed the strange fragrance until she realized what it was. Then, abruptly, she turned and went inside, eyes narrowed as she considered Amenemhet's attractive qualities.

King Ami-enshi was unusually tall and, although broadly built, seemed neither fat nor soft. His mane of hair was competely white and gave the impression of being slightly unruly. Brilliant blue eyes looked appraisingly at Amenemhet and Nefrytatanen from beneath bushy eyebrows. He said nothing but contemplated the visitors coldly.

Although Amenemhet hadn't expected King Ami-enshi to welcome him warmly, he was a little taken aback by his cool formality. Concluding that Ami-enshi had no intention of uttering a word until the lesser officials were introduced, Amenemhet grew irritated. Instead of speaking to Ami-enshi or Ambassador Anir, Amenemhet continued staring pointedly at Ami-enshi and merely nodded to Nakht in signal.

"King Amenemhet and Queen Nefrytatanen are pleased to visit your beautiful country," Nakht said smoothly. Having no need to introduce himself because he had often spoken to Ami-enshi in the past, Nakht smiled and addressed the monarch directly. "Your highness, may I present King Amenemhet and Queen Nefrytatanen, divine rulers of upper and lower Tamera."

Nakht had carefully maneuvered Ami-enshi into the necessity of speaking by the informality of the introduction, and Ami-enshi smiled at Amenemhet's refusal to be intimidated. He had, in that moment, decided Amenemhet lived up to his reputation. Ami-enshi was pleased.

"My house is honored," Ami-enshi said quietly. Looking at Nefrytatanen, he added, "Your queen's presence makes my house beautiful." He turned to lead the entourage into the palace, where two young men stood waiting. Their eyes lit when they saw Nefrytatanen, and Ami-enshi decided a word of caution with them later would be wise. Aloud, he said, "These are the sons of my first wife, Crown Prince Balul and Prince Mamum."

Until this moment, neither Amenemhet nor Nefrytatanen had spoken, so Ami-enshi was surprised when Amenemhet replied in Retenu's language, "The house of Retenu is doubly blessed with two sons."

"Our home is honored by your visit, King Amenemhet," Prince Balul said politely, "and enhanced by the beauty of your queen."

Prince Mamum smiled widely in agreement with his brother's statement, though he didn't understand it because Balul had spoken in Tamera's language. Balul's hazel eyes, however, had said much more to Nefrytatanen without words; and Mamum understood that, too.

"After so long and tiring a journey, perhaps you'd prefer going immediately to your chambers to refresh yourselves," Ami-enshi said in surprisingly fluent Tameran. As the words were spoken an army of servants appeared in the doorway. "If you'll permit my own slaves to assist your attendants, they're at your command," Ami-enshi added.

"You're very generous," Nefrytatanen said in a low voice and turned to follow the servants he had indicated. At Nefrytatanen's glance, Dedjet, Ani, Ineni, Senet and Yunet surrounded her with such a show of solicitous reverence that she found herself struggling not to smile.

Nefrytatanen was surprised to be led to a suite of rooms separate from Amenemhet's. She paused outside her door and watched in confusion as he continued farther down the hall and stopped at the door indicated to him. He turned to nod to her in signal, then went into his room. Nefrytatanen entered her quarters feeling uneasy.

Inside the door, she turned to the slaves King Ami-enshi had ordered to follow her and, wanting no spies about to carry back choice bits of conversation to Ami-enshi, she told them, "I won't require you now. Go about your usual duties until I call." They left quickly, and Nefrytatanen turned to her own attendants. "Dedjet, go immediately to the king's suite and ask when he can see me. I wish to know if he intends to continue this separate arrangement for our entire stay."

Dedjet returned in a few minutes. "My lady," she said, looking uncomfortable, "the king said he will see you at the evening meal."

Nefrytatanen could understand Amenemhet's reluctance to criticize Ami-enshi's hospitality, but she wasn't happy that Amenemhet seemed to have no interest in talking to her. She paced the floor for some time, her sandals clicking sharply on the polished stones. Then she sat on a chair and looked around the room.

Had King Ami-enshi thought for a hundred years about which room to give her, he couldn't have made a worse choice, Nefrytatanen decided. Although luxuriously appointed, the room was decorated in pale green that put a curse on her skin. It was the one shade of green that made her light-olive complexion look pallid. There were so many polished-copper mirrors paneling the walls that Nefrytatanen couldn't avoid seeing her reflection, which was subtly depressing.

Noting the queen's expression, Dedjet suggested, "Will you bathe, my lady? Perhaps you'll be refreshed and your spirits lifted by a bath and a nap?"

Nefrytatanen's mood wasn't lightened by bathing in a room equally green as her sleeping chamber, and long afterward, she lay awake staring at the ceiling wondering at Amenemhet's distant attitude. She was thinking about which garment she would wear for dinner to make Amenemhet less anxious to please Ami-enshi and more enthusiastic about staying in the same suite as she, when she felt Dedjet's hand on her shoulder. She looked at the maid.

"My lady," Dedjet said softly, "maybe it isn't for me to say this, but we all have decided we must."

"What is it?" Nefrytatanen sat up.

"Ani was walking down a corridor on her way to get flowers and wine for after you arose and she saw something. . . ." Dedjet faltered.

Nefrytatanen turned to Ani, who stood nearby, and saw anger in the girl's eyes. "What is it, Ani?" she asked.

"My lady," Ani began, then hesitated.

"Speak, Ani! Don't keep me wondering!" Nefrytatanen snapped.

"It would be best if I showed you what I saw," Ani whispered, trying to disguise the miserable look on her face.

Nefrytatanen got out of bed quickly and nodded to Dedjet, who helped her into her robe.

Ani peered into the hall and, waving to Nefrytatanen that the corridor was empty, stepped outside. Nefrytatanen silently followed Ani. When they approached a wall that had open latticework on their side with sheer drapes on the other side, Ani motioned for Nefrytatanen to look. The drapery didn't conceal what went on behind the lattice, and Nefrytatanen stared at the scene before her.

Amenemhet stood in the room with King Ami-enshi and Ambassador Anir looking at a lovely girl with long, curling hair the color of ripe wheat. Straining her ears, Nefrytatanen heard King Ami-enshi refer to the girl as Zaya, his first daughter. Nefrytatanen's eyes widened in shock when she realized Ami-enshi was offering the princess to Amenemhet for his harem. Nefrytatanen threw a grateful look at Ani, but her eyes burned with anger. Again she turned to stare at the princess, who was turning slowly for Amenemhet's inspection.

Zaya wore an almost transparent gown, and Nefrytatanen carefully studied her figure, which was slender, almost boyish. The girl's skin was the color of a peach, her pouty mouth pale pink, her eyes a mixture of green and hazel.

Nefrytatanen observed that Amenemhet was inspecting his prospective gift thoroughly. She concluded that negotiations for the treaty had begun without her presence, and that the princess was the reason. Ami-enshi would give Amenemhet his daughter as a reward for signing the treaty. They had no doubt put her in a separate suite so they could send the princess to Amenemhet in the night to further tempt him. Nefrytatanen turned from the wall and hurried away.

There would be a series of treaties, Amenemhet had said. Would he acquire a harem out of diplomatic courtesy? Nefrytatanen paused to stamp a foot, forgetting she was still in the corridor. He wouldn't do such a thing, she argued with herself as she resumed walking. At the same time she was shamed by her jealousy, she couldn't drive away the knowledge that Amenemhet was allowed by their marriage

82

contract to have a harem. She had not met him before the contract was written, and so had been happy to leave that clause in it. Then, delirious with love when, finally, she had met him just before their marriage, she had forgotten to order that clause taken out.

Inside her chambers again, Nefrytatanen scowled at the maids and said grimly, "Let us do all we can in this noxious room to make me as beautiful as possible." She walked to the window and tore open the drapery. "Paint my eyes now with the sun to light your work."

Later, Nefrytatanen marched to the cabinet and carefully inspected the garments she had brought, finally choosing the robe of her station as Aset incarnate. Not only would the robe remind Amenemhet that she had been queen in the north kingdom before their marriage, but the golden cloth clung to her like the skin of a cobra.

"This is the one," Nefrytatanen said, tossing the garment to Ani, who nodded approvingly at the choice. "If this causes no response in him, I might as well give up."

In the robe of Amset, her golden coronet, and a magnificent iridescent collar made from countless tiny jewels and intricately worked silver threads, Nefrytatanen caused a sensation at the evening meal. King Ami-enshi, as well as his sons, could hardly consider negotiations of any kind in Nefrytatanen's shining presence. Even Nakht remarked that he was intoxicated with her magic. Amenemhet was courteous, but he seemed cool; and although Nefrytatanen realized he might be avoiding any affectionate gestures, however small, because of Ami-enshi's presence, she wondered at it. His eyes seemed to avoid her all through the evening, and when he quietly suggested that she leave them early, she said nothing, but her eyes flashed with anger as she left, bidding them a pleasant evening rather coldly.

Watching Nefrytatanen's shimmering figure pass through the doors, Amenemhet took a deep breath of relief. King Ami-enshi and his sons had stared at Nefrytatanen long enough, he decided.

Nefrytatanen posted the invaluable Ani at the door outside the dining chamber to warn her when the party seemed to be coming to an end. Ani stared defiantly at Ami-enshi's guards, who stood outside the door, until they shrugged and resumed their stiff posture, wondering silently why the servant had stayed watching them.

In her own suite, Nefrytatanen changed into a nightdress

Amenemhet had never seen, while Dedjet combed her hair to a silken sheen. The other servants, having nothing to do, watched the queen nervously.

When Ani entered the chamber to tell Nefrytatanen that the party was ending, Nefrytatanen turned to her servants and said, "You will have no additional mistresses at Ithtawe, if I can prevent it."

As the door closed behind Nefrytatanen, the servants stared at each other, not knowing what to say.

Settling herself in her husband's suite, Nefrytatanen awaited him with a sinking feeling in her heart. She was ashamed of her suspicions, but at the same time, she couldn't dismiss the memory of how he had looked at the Princess Zaya. She heard voices outside the door then, and wondered what she would do if Amenemhet was not alone when he entered his chambers. But the door opened and only Yazid accompanied his master.

Amenemhet was startled to find Nefrytatanen waiting in his rooms, but he quickly observed the expression on her face and immediately dismissed Yazid.

Forcing herself to smile, the queen pivoted slowly for Amenemhet's approval. "Do you like it?" she whispered, afraid her voice would betray how near she was to tears.

"Purple is very beautiful on you," Amenemhet replied softly. His eyes were confused and he asked, "Why have you come with a gown to wear to bed? We've never worn them to sleep."

"To make you want me," she murmured, looking down. She could think of nothing else to say.

Amenemhet smiled. "I always want you, but you're especially beautiful without lengths of cloth wrapped around you, which I must remove during the night."

Before Nefrytatanen could reply, there was a soft tap on the door, and Amenemhet went to open it. Although he held the door so narrowly open Nefrytatanen couldn't see who was in the hall, she smelled perfume. Her heart constricted in new fear and anger.

Amenemhet said, "The queen is here, and separate rooms won't be required." He listened to a whisper Nefrytatanen couldn't understand, then said softly, "We prefer to share our quarters." He hesitated a moment, then closed the door.

She whirled around so that he couldn't see the angry tears threatening to tumble from her lashes. Struggling to keep her voice steady, she said bitterly, "It begins, beloved. You wished to make treaties with many lands, you said. But I see it beginning with the first king you approach."

"What begins?" he asked quietly.

"I see them coming," she grated. "Women of all kinds, of every exotic land, throwing themselves before you, their garments whispering strange fragrances, their skins glowing and well cared for, their hair in all colors flowing loose for your choice like shining straight ribbons and in coils of swaying curls."

Nefrytatanen sank slowly to the couch, eyes downcast in grief and humiliation. She knew if Amenemhet accepted this princess, she would move back to the north kingdom, back to her former palace in Noph. She couldn't stay at Ithtawe and watch such a thing.

Amenemhet stared speechlessly at Nefrytatanen. Finally recovering from his surprise, he sat beside her and tilted her face to his. He was silent for a moment as he looked at her. Then he wiped the tears with gentle fingers and said softly, "Such pain is in your eyes I cannot endure it." He gathered her into his arms and whispered, "I would go to war with Ami-enshi before signing a treaty that gave me that female." He smiled faintly into her hair and murmured, "What would I use her for? I give all my love to you. To have her wipe the dust from your sandals would be her only purpose in our house, and her father wouldn't like that." He held her away to look into her eyes. "Do not weep, beloved," he whispered. "I won't accept Zaya, nor any other." He held her tightly until she stopped trembling.

Finally, Amenemhet stood up and drew Nefrytatanen to her feet. He looked at her a moment, then began to unfasten the nightdress.

"Turn," he whispered. She turned, and the garment fell into a shimmering pool at her feet. "When I reach for you during the night, we will be spared bother and delay."

Then he unfastened the sash of his robe, removed it and dropped it over a chair. When he faced Nefrytatanen again, she stood silent and motionless, watching him cautiously.

"We can discuss this treaty in a moment," he said softly. "The air in Yenoam has a certain dampness that makes me want warming."

Encouraged, Nefrytatanen pulled the covers loose and got into bed. She whispered, "It's warm here."

"Where you are it is always warm," Amenemhet replied. He blew out the lamp, then got into bed and put his arms

85

around her. For a while, he merely held her close and said nothing. Finally, he whispered, "Ami-enshi isn't used to thinking of women as more than pretty playthings. He doesn't realize you're really the queen and this title isn't merely courtesy. He assumed that I have a harem, as most kings do. It wouldn't cross his mind that I'd have any other arrangement. He wants me to take his daughter to further assure friendship between Tamera and Retenu. I could think of no way to refuse without insulting him." Amenemhet sighed and added, "I'll think of something he can accept."

After a long moment Nefrytatanen murmured, "I think I don't care to supervise the signing of other treaties."

Amenemhet smiled into the darkness. "You have the right to sign treaties, if you wish. If you don't care to do it in the future, I would have you be included this time anyway. I think I may have to use your authority as the reason for not taking this princess with me." Amenemhet paused, then drew her closer and kissed her shoulder. "In the morning I'll make clear our intention to share one suite and have your belongings moved here or mine to your quarters. You've seen them both. Which do you prefer?"

Nefrytatanen thought of the ivory of Amenemhet's suite and the green walls of her own. "I like this suite better," she said. "The other I occupied in sadness, and its shadow still hangs in the atmosphere."

"Then we'll stay here," Amenemhet whispered into her hair. After a moment, he released her and moved away.

Wondering, she watched his shadowy form get out of bed and go to the window. He pulled the heavy drapes aside and returned to the bed. The moonlight now flooding the room revealed his face clearly.

He said, "I like to see you when we make love." Looking down at her, his eyes glowing, he whispered, "Or have you the desire to?"

"You need ask?" she said. "You look at me that way and ask if I prefer sleep?" She held her open arms up toward him. "For me to deny you would be my death."

Amenemhet leaned toward Nefrytatanen, a kiss ready on his lips, and she said no more. When his arms closed around her and his mouth covered hers, she welcomed his love and forgot Zaya and the threat of harems.

The windows faced north, and the morning brought not the direct warmth of the sun as Amenemhet and Nefrytatanen were used to in Ithtawe, but only deflected light. They

86

slept late, their senses deceived by the dimness, until Dedjet finally came with Yazid to awaken them.

Amenemhet smiled and turned to Nefrytatanen. "Would you like to have the morning meal here together?" he asked. Her eyes held her answer, and he turned to Yazid. "Inform whoever needs to be told that we'll be delayed in rising." Amenemhet then asked Dedjet, "Will you bring us the meal?" Dedjet nodded and began toward the door. "And, Dedjet"—Amenemhet raised his voice, and she paused at the door—"after we've finished the meal, we will bathe slowly."

"I'll instruct the others," Dedjet said softly, looking at Nefrytatanen with triumph in her eyes.

After Yazid and Dedjet left, Amenemhet put his arms around Nefrytatanen and murmured, "May I compliment you on the loyalty of your spies and the artfulness of your schemes?"

Nefrytatanen replied solemnly, "It does no harm to have a friend to warn of approaching danger."

Amenemhet laughed softly, then asked, "How long do you think it will take Dedjet to bring the meal?" He held Nefrytatanen tighter, and his meaning was unmistakable.

Although Amenemhet had taken the sharp edge from Nefrytatanen's fears, the queen was left with a feeling of uncertain triumph as well as a grudging curiosity about the Princess Zaya.

Looking into the pool, Nefrytatanen said, "I'm pleased you found flowers to float in the bath. It makes it seem as if we were at Ithtawe again."

"Ani found them," Ineni replied as she measured and poured soothing herbs into the water. "Somehow, Ani always knows where to find flowers—even here."

Ani blushed as the queen gave her a grateful smile. Nefrytatanen seemed soothed at last. Holding her robe together loosely, she sat on a bench to watch Ineni's deft motions. From a variety of containers, the servant chose and carefully measured quantities of herbs, following her own recipe for the mixture she put in the water. The queen wondered how Ineni remembered which herbs to use, and did not notice the visitor approaching.

Without an announcement to warn them, Princess Zaya walked into the bathing room, a malicious look in her eyes. Amazed, Nefrytatanen got to her feet, and the servants gaped, then turned away in silent wonder at this rudeness.

Noting the defiance in Zaya's bearing, Nefrytatanen decided to ignore the princess.

"You are the wife of King Amenemhet?" Zaya asked coldly. She strolled toward the group, now swinging her hips in an obvious attempt to intimidate Nefrytatanen. Nefrytatanen smiled.

"Why do you smile?" Zaya demanded.

The complete absence of any hint of respect angered Nefrytatanen, and she decided she would be only as courteous to Zaya as the princess seemed to deserve.

"Her manners are sadly lacking," Nefrytatanen said quietly to Dedjet in their own language. Nefrytatanen wasn't sure Zaya would understand and realized from her expression that she had not.

Dedjet turned to Zaya with a solemn face and bowed elegantly to say slowly in Retenu's tongue, "Princess, when you address the daughter of Ra, please acknowledge her royalty."

Zaya gave Dedjet a cold stare but was speechless only a moment. "I am Princess Zaya," she said haughtily.

"With all respect, Princess Zaya, my mistress is Queen Nefrytatanen," Dedjet whispered.

Nefrytatanen turned to watch Senet and Yunet arrange the preparations to be used for her bath, deliberately ignoring Zaya until the princess addressed her properly.

Zaya's eyes swept curiously over the collection of jars and bottles appearing from various niches and compartments in Nefrytatanen's cosmetic chest, which was fashioned from ebony, ivory and silver. When Zaya spoke, her words were ice being cracked into usable chips. "Queen Nefrytatanen."

"Yes?" Nefrytatanen was equally warm.

Zaya's eyes widened slightly as Ineni let down the heavy black coils of Nefrytatanen's shining hair. Recovering herself, Zaya asked, "Why did you smile at me? It was not a smile of friendliness."

Nefrytatanen remained silent, wondering what she could answer.

"She has no eyelashes," Ani remarked in Tamera's language, her dark eyes glowing with mischief.

"They're too pale to see," Yunet whispered. The other girls giggled and made several more uncomplimentary remarks until Nefrytatanen's glance silenced them.

"Why are they laughing? What did they say?" Zaya demanded.

"They're only chattering among themselves," Nefrytatanen

said coolly. She forced herself to smile as she regarded Zaya wearily. "Princess, is there some emergency that you have come now, or may this visit be delayed for another time?"

Zaya continued to stare malignantly at Nefrytatanen's attendants. "Why won't you answer me?" she demanded.

Nefrytatanen's patience with the rude intruder was swiftly dissipating. "Which question do you want answered?"

"All of them!" Zaya exploded.

Nefrytatanen stood up while Ani applied oil to her shoulders. The scent of lotuses filled the air. Finally, Nefrytatanen leveled her eyes on Zaya and began, "I am King Amenemhet's only wife, and—"

Zaya interrupted to sneer, "If King Amenemhet needs only you, he must be very occupied with business."

Dedjet's face grew pale, while Yunet turned red. Ani and Ineni gasped, and Senet glared at Zaya.

Nefrytatanen's expression didn't change except for her eyes. They shot blue fire at the princess. "The answers to your other questions," Nefrytatanen said, "are that I smiled because when you walked in swaying your hips that way, you reminded me of a Hyksos boy trying to attract a man. Ani said you have no eyelashes, but Yunet pointed out that they're pale in color. The other servants made several remarks I cannot accurately translate into your language."

Zaya turned to Ani, who was nearest, and slapped her face sharply. Ani stared at her in shock.

"You will not touch my attendants, Zaya," Nefrytatanen warned. "They're free women, not slaves. They have my permission to defend themselves if necessary."

Zaya was stunned at Nefrytatanen's statement that a lowly servant might touch and even strike her. She noted that Dedjet, removing Nefrytatanen's robe, was giving her a menacing look.

"You'd best leave us now," Nefrytatanen said calmly, watching Zaya's eyes, which now were appraising her naked figure. She murmured in a deliberately provocative tone, "My beloved soon will join me."

"He bathes with you?" Zaya was dismayed.

"Of course," Nefrytatanen replied in a suggestively low tone. "We bathe together, we sleep together, we do everything together." She turned to walk to the pool's edge, where she smiled over her shoulder and added, "King Amenemhet lacks nothing, Zaya, nothing at all." Then Nefrytatanen dove, cutting the water cleanly, coming to the surface a moment later.

She shook the water from her eyes, then smiled. "You'd better leave, Zaya," she warned. "He'll come very soon, and you may be embarrassed if you stay."

Zaya didn't move. She stared defiantly at Nefrytatanen, who shrugged and closed her eyes to float on her back, unconcerned.

Amenemhet's voice carried down the corridor linking the bath with the rest of their suite. "Dedjet, is she there?"

Ani and Senet laughed softly. Dedjet looked at Zaya, then at Nefrytatanen, who continued to float serenely with her eyes closed.

"My lady is here!"

Dedjet answered clearly, knowing Amenemhet was certain to undress in the bedroom and come to the pool already naked. It was common practice at Ithtawe, but Dedjet wondered what Zaya's reaction would be.

Nefrytatanen opened her eyes and called, "I'm waiting, beloved!"

"I'm hurrying! Be patient!" Amenemhet called.

Nefrytatanen smiled calmly. "He'll come naked," she remarked. When she saw Zaya's face flush, she asked innocently, "Does nakedness embarrass you?" Zaya said nothing. "If it does, you'd spend a large portion of your time in Tamera blushing." Nefrytatanen closed her eyes. "Maybe you'd get used to it—if you ever get to Tamera," she said pointedly.

The attendants glanced at each other as they heard Amenemhet's bare feet running down the hall. He ran to the edge of the pool and, looking neither right nor left, dove into the flower-covered water. As he swam toward Nefrytatanen, she stood up and extended her arms toward him.

Embracing Amenemhet, Nefrytatanen whispered in his ear, "Princess Zaya is here."

Amenemhet drew away to stare at Nefrytatanen in surprise and some confusion. He turned in time to glimpse Zaya's hurriedly departing figure, then said to Nefrytatanen, "It seems she's left. What was she doing here?"

"Getting acquainted," Nefrytatanen answered.

Amenemhet gave her a suspicious look. "Why did she run out that way?"

Nefrytatanen replied, "She assumed that we're going to make love, I think."

"Before the servants?" He stared at her and she shrugged. "What kind of people does she think we are?"

"I'm not really sure," she answered. "I think in Retenu

people don't remove their garments unless they're going to make love."

Amenemhet began to smile. "Do they bathe clothed?"

"I think they must always bathe separately."

Amenemhet frowned. "They waste time and water and miss a pleasant experience."

Nefrytatanen's eyes grew cold. "Zaya came to tell me your life is lacking with your having only me for a wife. She also slapped Ani."

Amenemhet turned to the girls, who were listening attentively. He noted Ani's reddened cheek. "Did Ani deserve slapping?" he asked.

Nefrytatanen replied, "Zaya deserved slapping."

"If anyone mistreats any of you, I want you to tell me," Amenemhet directed. He turned to Nefrytatanen with a worried look. "Did the princess go away angry?"

"Somewhat," Nefrytatanen said.

"Why did she come at all?"

"To intimidate me with insults." Nefrytatanen looked at Amenemhet with fiery eyes. "I hope that you will decide soon how to refuse her so that the matter can be resolved. It's going to be very difficult for me to endure her impudence."

The king shook his head and began to smile. "This is all very educational," he said. "It must be a complicated business to actually have a harem. It's no wonder Ami-enshi's hair is white."

Seven

King Ami-enshi was standing by his desk, trying to gauge how the negotiations with Tamera's ruler were going, when the door flew open.

Princess Zaya stalked into the room, and Ami-enshi, taking one look at his daughter's face, turned away with a grim expression. He said nothing, because he knew she would only too soon tell him what now infuriated her.

"That woman is hateful!" Zaya said, throwing herself into a chair.

"What woman?" Ami-enshi asked.

"That Nefer, Nefry, whatever her name is—that creature." Zaya tilted her nose toward the ceiling. "She insulted and humiliated me."

"When?" Ami-enshi turned to look calmly at his daughter.

"I just went to visit her," Zaya said faintly.

"When?" he demanded, his blue eyes becoming sharp.

"She was preparing to bathe, and I thought we might converse a moment. No one was around but her serving girls, at first." Zaya's eyes widened in emphasis. "Father, the king joined her in the bath. He ran right past me naked!"

Ami-enshi's eyes narrowed slightly in speculation. "They share their bath?"

"I fled in embarrassment. What happened after my departure was surely done before her serving girls!"

Ami-enshi smiled faintly. "You think King Amenemhet couples with Nefrytatanen in front of her servants?" He shook his head. "I think not." He sighed. He was well acquainted with his daughter's habit of making much from little. He suspected that she had gone to Nefrytatanen to make trouble, and, he admitted silently, even if she hadn't had that intention, it had been rude to interrupt her bath.

"She was most ungracious even before he came, and insisted on being addressed as a queen," Zaya said.

"Spare me the details," Ami-enshi muttered.

"You don't care even that her servants insulted me? I had to slap one of them," Zaya persisted.

"How did the servants insult you?" Ami-enshi couldn't allow such an incident to pass, if it was true. He stared at Zaya, knowing he could intimidate her into the truth.

"The girl said I have no eyelashes," Zaya said carefully, "and Nefrytatanen encouraged all of them by her attitude to make other remarks in their own language so I wouldn't understand." She lowered her voice and stared defiantly at her father.

Ami-enshi looked calmly at his daughter and reasoned, "You're unused to their ways of thinking, and they're unused to our language. Maybe Nefrytatanen didn't know how to translate their comments. Maybe this was a misunderstanding."

"Nefrytatanen seemed fluent enough," Zaya said coldly.

Before Zaya could say more, Ami-enshi turned away in exasperation. "If you don't learn to be more courteous and use better judgment, giving you to King Amenemhet will result in a war," he groaned. He turned to Zaya with a grim expression. "If Nefrytatanen puts on airs, humor her. She's his wife, and it's natural she resents you. If she wants to be called a queen, do so for a time as a gesture of courtesy. You can settle your problems with Nefrytatanen later. King Amenemhet may refuse the treaty if you anger him."

Zaya wondered if Amenemhet would refuse her. Although he had looked at her with some interest when she was presented to him, he obviously enjoyed Nefrytatanen. Zaya stood up and walked to the door, where she paused again and turned to her father.

"When I slapped the servant, Nefrytatanen all but told them to slap me back," Zaya said softly. Ami-enshi looked horrified at this, and she continued triumphantly, "Father, would it not be a proud day if your daughter were slapped by a servant?" She left, slamming the door after her.

Ami-enshi stared at the window silently for a time. He was sure, from Zaya's expression, that she had told the truth about that. In his opinion, every servant, slave or free, needed a slap from time to time, but he would permit no hand to strike his daughter, unless that hand were her husband's. Finally, he decided that he must speak to Balul and Mamum about Nefrytatanen. They were too open in their admiration of her, and he wouldn't welcome more trouble added to the negotiations.

Ami-enshi sent one of the guards to search for his two eldest sons. He had no intention of putting thoughts in Balul's and Mamum's minds if they weren't already seriously entertaining such ideas, and he wanted to be careful how he spoke to them.

When Balul and Mamum entered the room, Ami-enshi smiled at them.

Despite his father's smile, Balul's hazel eyes were alert. "What have we done that disturbs you?"

"It seems you've done nothing so far but look." Ami-enshi's smile vanished. "You will keep the treaty in mind, my sons. King Amenemhet has come to express and, I hope, confirm by this treaty the friendship between Retenu and Tamera."

"I wouldn't interfere with a lasting friendship with Tamera," Balul assured him. "I can easily find friendliness in my heart for a land producing such women as I've seen."

"Their men might feel less friendly if you did, and they're the ones who go to war," Mamum observed. His dark-blue eyes were as sharp as his father's.

"Still," persisted Balul, "Nefrytatanen would be worth an enemy or two, I think, provided we didn't have to think of the treaty."

"One enemy would be all you'd need—her husband," said Mamum. "I've noticed his eyes miss little, and he has observed your glances."

Balul sighed. "I don't blame him for watching her."

Mamum looked at his father and remarked, "I'm afraid Nefrytatanen won't welcome Zaya to Ithtawe."

"The situation is delicate," Ami-enshi agreed. "I don't want either of you to make it worse. Zaya gives me headaches enough."

"What has she done now, Father?" Balul asked.

"I'm unsure of the details, but from what I could sift out of Zaya's version, she was driven to slapping one of the queen's servants, which made no friends for her. Evidently the incident was prevented from becoming a disaster only by King Amenemhet's joining his wife in the pool before he knew of your sister's presence." The princes glanced at each other in surprise, but Ami-enshi continued, "Zaya was frightened off by what she thought was about to follow."

Balul looked at Mamum with lifted eyebrows. He turned to the king. "Father, may I visit Tamera sometime after this treaty has been signed?"

"I wouldn't mind sharing my bath with one of their women," Mamum agreed.

Ami-enshi couldn't entirely suppress his own smile. "It seems a pleasant experience, but the treaty comes first," he said. "If Zaya doesn't behave more prudently, she may cause enough trouble to prevent the treaty's being signed. Is there some way you can persuade her to be more peaceful?"

"You've had some influence on her in the past, Balul," Mamum reminded his brother.

"Yes," Ami-enshi said quickly. "Why don't you point out to her what her behavior can mean? If she wants this king, she'd better use her wits."

"I saw the way she looked at him," Mamum said. "I'm sure she wants him."

"All right, I'll talk to her," Balul agreed.

"Go now," Ami-enshi urged. "The banquet will be held soon, and it will be embarrassing if she behaves badly with so many to witness it."

"She could use this banquet to lure Amenemhet," Mamum suggested. "Women are usually at their most seductive during such events."

"Yes, yes, yes," Balul said impatiently. He turned and left them immediately.

"I don't know why Zaya can't be as docile as other women," Ami-enshi sighed.

When Balul was alone with Zaya, he asked gently, "Do you want to marry King Amenemhet, my sister?"

"You're the first who's bothered to ask my opinion," she said coldly. She stood up and walked to the window opening to gaze at the garden while she considered her answer. "Yes, Balul," she finally said. "I want him."

96

"Then you must outwit Nefrytatanen," he said firmly.

Zaya's eyes widened. "How?" she demanded. "She never leaves his side, and I have no opportunity to be alone with him."

"Being alone with him would help, but it isn't essential at this time. You'll have to begin by pretending friendliness toward her." At the look on Zaya's face, Balul added quickly, "Pretend, Zaya! A minimum of courtesy, anyway! No man would happily anticipate a warring harem! Think how Nefrtyatanen must feel. It's not easy for her to accept you. Be gracious to her in his presence. Do what you can—carefully, so that he doesn't suspect it—to make her look her worst. Be charming and smile. Don't let Amenemhet know you hate her. He'd have to take her side now. Instead, show him you'd be a happy addition to his palace." Balul could see Zaya's expression turning to thoughtfulness while he spoke and he was encouraged. "You have the advantage of being someone new to him and therefore intriguing," Balul pointed out. "If you use this advantage well, you may eventually win first place in his harem."

"It won't be easy to put Nefrytatanen in a bad light," Zaya said slowly. "She has great control over her temper."

"There's a limit to any woman's control when she thinks she's losing her man," he observed.

"That's true." Zaya picked up a strand of her hair and held it across her forehead, examining the effect. "Perhaps I can do it yet," she murmured, again remembering Amenemhet's eyes when she had first been presented to him. "Perhaps . . ."

During the next few days Nefrytatanen saw nothing of Princess Zaya, but she hadn't forgotten her. Although negotiations for the treaty continued, Nefrytatanen was never invited to the meetings; she knew it was because Ami-enshi never dreamed that a woman might participate in treaty signings, let alone in their negotiations. She said nothing about it but she was angered that Senwadjet and Maeti had more authority in Tamera than she was allowed in Yenoam.

Nefrytatanen spent her days in a cocoon of exquisite luxury so dull she thought she would die of boredom. She saw little of Amenemhet during the day and often wondered what he was doing. Each night she looked forward to his companionship and conversation like a butterfly waiting for its freedom.

During the afternoon preceding the party, Zaya practiced making her eyes seem wide with innocence, smiling sweetly and modestly dropping her lashes. She had her slave arrange her golden coils of hair many times before she decided how its effect would most befit her game. She had chosen a pale-green garment and planned to weave in her curls a string of the smallest creamy pearls, hoping to remind Amenemhet of spring—fresh and innocent—and make the older Nefrytatanen appear to be winter.

But when Nefrytatanen entered the banquet room on Amenemhet's arm, Zaya was dismayed to see her looking nothing at all like winter. Making no effort to copy or imitate any fashion of Retenu, Nefrytatanen had accepted looking alien and turned it into triumph. Zaya controlled her temper with a discipline her father wouldn't have believed she possessed.

Nefrytatanen's softly clinging shift was a fall of sheer deep-blue pleats matching her eyes, which seemed to hold the shadows of the mysterious pyramids. Her coronet gleamed coolly silver, its hawk staring proudly at the crowd, the serpent poised to strike, while the lotus pendant on her breast flashed the color of her eyes and gown. The sleek black of her hair shone with lapis-lazuli lights, and with each step she took, her bracelets jingled like a sistrum softly shaken in the temple, her distinctive perfume surrounding her with ancient secrets.

Wearing a robe of tawny gold color and a sunburst collar of many intricately embroidered gold threads, Amenemhet reminded his entourage of Tamera's imperial lion. Any gaze remaining long enough on his golden eyes as they confidently swept the crowd discovered in their depths the glow of the sun. Men making this discovery found themselves feeling uncomfortably insignificant, though they all were of the highest nobility. One of the men who felt diminished by Amenemhet's presence was the ambassador from Zahi, Gobryas.

Aware that Amenemhet had received a message that afternoon informing him that another Tameran province had been infected with worms, Gobryas was sure Amenemhet must be deeply concerned about the destruction of Tamera's crops. He knew such destruction could mean a severe loss of income from Tamera's exports to other lands as well as possible starvation of its own citizens. But Amenemhet's face seemed clothed with confidence, impervious and dignified.

Nefrytatanen too seemed untroubled. She had looked like a

goddess untouched by earthly problems the first time Gobryas had seen her when, at seventeen, she had assumed her father's throne. Her beauty coupled with her attitude had aroused a desire in Gobryas which had not only endured, but had grown into an obsession over the years. The Hyksos ambassador watched Amenemhet and Nefrytatanen and was flooded with such intense hatred and desire he turned away because his mind seemed it would fly apart with his conflicting passions.

Amenemhet was surprised by the presence of Ambassador Gobryas. It was a widely known fact that Amenemhet had had the Hyksos lord escorted smartly to Tamera's border when they had last met, but Amenemhet's thoughts remained secret behind his golden gaze. He watched Gobryas suddenly turn away and wondered what Gobryas would say to them, if he came near enough to speak at all.

Expecting hostility between Nefrytatanen and Zaya, Amenemhet was surprised when they exchanged greetings without showing a hint of their former problems. As he returned Zaya's greeting, the king felt uneasy at the long look she gave him, and began to think more intently about how he could avoid the girl until they left Yenoam.

He had assumed that Nefrytatanen would sit beside him, so Amenemhet was startled when Ami-enshi settled between them. Zaya sat on his other side, and Gobryas sat next to Nefrytatanen. Annoyed, Amenemhet wondered who had decided on that arrangement. He had wanted to avoid Zaya and was, instead, trapped with her; but it troubled him far more to see Nefrytatanen beside Gobryas, who was looking at her with a calculating expression. Though he knew Gobryas would never evoke more than an icy response from Nefrytatanen, Amenemhet still couldn't endure watching the ambassador's attentions to the queen.

Nefrytatanen stared straight ahead with unseeing eyes. She didn't want even to acknowledge Gobryas' presence. She could feel the hatred mixed with lust emanating from him, and she could barely restrain herself from shuddering. Without moving her eyes, she could see that Amenemhet was speaking to Zaya, and anger flooded her.

"Will you completely ignore me, Queen Nefrytatanen?" Gobryas whispered. "It will be an uncomfortably long meal, and such tension is bad for the digestion."

Nefrytatanen could smell the heavy odor of wine on his breath and considered a number of replies, but voiced none

99

of them. Finally, she turned to him, her eyes flashing warnings. "Gobryas, we are old enemies and I have no intention to pretend a cordiality I don't feel."

He drank deeply from his goblet, and a thin red trickle from the corner of his mouth ran into his beard. Wiping it with the back of his hand, he said, "The friction between Zahi and Tamera has long ago dwindled to nothing."

"It has?" Her voice was ice. She remembered too well the raids on the north kingdom, the murders, the abductions, the fires.

'We've had no quarrels for years," he replied smoothly. "When I came to Ithtawe after your children were born, my errand was on orders from my king. I had no personal feelings about you. It seems to me I am the one who should remain silent after the treatment I received then."

Nefrytatanen's glance at him was a streak of lightning.

Gobryas added quickly, "I don't blame you for having been upset at the time, and I hold no ill will for what King Amenemhet did. You had many problems on your minds. But what is past is past. Tamera prides itself on being a civilized nation, so let us behave as civilized people and make this evening at least endurable with a pleasant word or two."

"I distrust ingratiating former enemies," she said flatly.

"I meant not to be ingratiating," Gobryas said a little sharply. "I meant to be reasonable."

From the corner of her eye, Nefrytatanen could see Amenemhet's attention still fastened on Zaya, and she seethed with jealousy. How could he endure the girl's artificial smile? Couldn't he see through her facade? Zaya was smiling sweetly up at Amenemhet, leaning close to him. Making a graceful but practiced gesture, she brushed his chest with her hand, and Nefrytatanen felt like leaning over to slap her creamy hand. Nefrytatanen turned to Gobryas hoping to distract herself from Zaya.

"Maybe you're right, ambassador," she managed to say without revealing her disgust at his sour, wine-soaked breath. "We can try to be courteous."

Gobryas smiled, his black eyes glittering too brightly. "It's a waste so beautiful a mouth is so tightly pursed, although your eyes are enchanting even when filled with anger."

Nefrytatanen stared in chilly answer. In his half-drunk state, did he assume courtesy meant flirtation, she wondered.

Gobryas shrugged. "We'll speak of other things." He

drained his goblet and signaled for more wine. "Was your journey very difficult?"

"It was sometimes monotonous, as any long journey might be."

"Do you find Retenu appealing?" he asked.

"The land we traveled through had its charm." Who had so untactfully invited him to this banquet, she wondered.

"Are you comfortable in Ami-enshi's palace?" he asked.

"Yes." Her reply was cool.

He watched a servant refill his goblet, then mumbled, "The king seems captured by Zaya. I've already been through all that and am repelled by her true nature."

Nefrytatanen's eyes narrowed in anger.

"If Amenemhet must pay court to the princess, why waste your evening worrying about it?" Again he emptied his goblet, then whispered, "If at the end of this party it seems you'll be alone, tell me."

Zaya had been watching Gobryas and Nefrytatanen beyond Amenemhet's shoulder, and she could see that a dangerous situation was developing. She smiled at Amenemhet and settled herself more comfortably to enjoy the results. The possibilities were endless. She hadn't known Gobryas was Amenemhet's enemy and decided she would pay more attention to politics. How convenient it was that the ambassador from Zahi desired Nefrytatanen—and how fortunate for herself he drank so heavily.

"Don't be ridiculous," Nefrytatanen hissed, at the end of her temper.

"What's ridiculous about it?" Gobryas carelessly went on. "If Amenemhet has no more wit than to be charmed by Zaya, I would gladly distract you." He leaned closer to Nefrytatanen, who stared incredulously at him. "You might enjoy me."

"You are disgusting to me," Nefrytatanen said softly and stood up. All other sounds abruptly ceased. "Your ignorance is beyond belief," she whispered. "You are so utterly lacking in refinement your mere presence in this room is offensive."

Gobryas arose to face Nefrytatanen, forgetting in his sudden anger where he was. "I could teach you some refinements."

Amenemhet was suddenly at Nefrytatanen's side. He put his hand on her shoulder, applying pressure in signal to sit down. Though upset, she obeyed. Amenemhet turned to Gobryas.

"A woman of the streets would be more interested in your refinements than Queen Nefrytatanen." Amenemhet stared at Gobryas a moment, then added, "If you're too drunk to understand my meaning, it would give me pleasure to make myself clearer."

Gobryas said nothing. He was supremely outranked and could say or do no more. But he was humiliated that the situation had become a public spectacle.

Ami-enshi waved to Gobryas to approach him. When the Hyksos bent close, Ami-enshi whispered, "I have no wish to send you from Retenu, but I suggest you visit my governor at Nuges." Gobryas stared at Ami-enshi as if he did not understand, so Ami-enshi added more forcefully but still in a whisper, "Before you compel me to order you to leave Retenu altogether, go amiably to another city for a while. Go to Nuges, Herenkeru, anywhere! Return when King Amenemhet and his wife have left."

Gobryas took a deep breath, his black eyes strangely flat and expressionless, his forehead creased with a frown. He glanced once at Amenemhet and Nefrytatanen, then turned sharply and stalked out.

Ami-enshi turned to Amenemhet and Nefrytatanen and said softly, "I apologize for this situation. I had thought that by inviting the ambassador from Zahi, I might impress upon him how friendly Tamera and Retenu are. I never thought such circumstances would result."

Nefrytatanen nodded silently, then stared at the table. Amenemhet returned to his place beside Zaya. Nefrytatanen gave him a sharp look, but said nothing.

"Perhaps Prince Balul will provide more congenial company," Ami-enshi said to Nefrytatanen and motioned for his son to move into Gobryas' place.

Retenu's wine was good, but strong, and Nefrytatanen drank sparingly to avoid losing her wits. Prince Balul engaged her in constant conversation as if he were trying to blot out her encounter with Gobryas. She smiled at Balul until her face felt stiff. She noticed Princess Zaya was less careful with the wine she consumed; the girl's eyes were growing shinier and her lips more moist as she looked with open invitation into Amenemhet's eyes. Amenemhet seemed undisturbed, and Nefrytatanen wondered at his reaction. His smile seemed genuine, and he looked very seldom in Nefrytatanen's direction. Was he enjoying his conversation with Zaya? Or was he pretending, as she was with Balul? But Nefrytatanen thought that if the king was acting, she wasn't doing nearly half as good a job.

Amenemhet stared fixedly at Zaya's eyes, trying to focus his own. He wondered how Zaya could drink so much of the strong wine and be no more affected than she was. He dared not take another sip or the servant would refill his goblet, but he was hot and thirsty and far from interested in Zaya's conversation. He began to think about the destruction of Tamera's crops and wondered if the worms were coming from Kenset.

When Zaya's laughter aroused him, he wondered why she had laughed in the middle of her monologue—because he had surely said nothing. He was aware that Nefrytatanen was watching them. He could see no way to talk to her past Ami-enshi, who sat as solidly between them as a sphinx. He wished Nefrytatanen could know how this empty-eyed, decorative creature bored him. No, he corrected himself, Zaya's eyes were not empty. They were filled with stealth, which became increasingly apparent with each glass of wine she drank.

Amenemhet had smiled politely at Zaya until he wondered if his face would crack. His head was beginning to feel numb from the wine he had consumed. He put his hand over his goblet, watching with wonder as a slave filled Zaya's cup again. Hoping to begin a long and politically complicated conversation to avoid Zaya, Amenemhet turned to Ami-enshi, but Ami-enshi was engrossed with Nefrytatanen. Amenemhet stared at the acrobats, whose antics didn't interest him. He was frustrated. If Balul wasn't leering at Nefrytatanen, Ami-enshi was, and Amenemhet began to lose patience.

Watching her out of the corner of his eye, he saw Nefrytatanen, head high, eyes clear, looking cool and poised, but he recognized she was on the edge of desperation. Her pale face turned in his direction. Her eyes were wide and glowed with blue fire.

Nefrytatanen stood up, still staring at Amenemhet and Zaya. Then, hastily whispering excuses to Ami-enshi and Balul, she was gone.

Amenemhet half-rose, but Zaya tugged at his robe until he thought she would tear its fabric.

"She said she'd return shortly. Please don't be concerned," Ami-enshi said quickly.

Amenemhet slowly sank to his chair, noting that Ami-enshi had not even the grace to call Nefrytatanen by name, let

103

alone title. He turned to Zaya and quietly, but forcefully, removed her fingers from the sleeve of his garment.

Nefrytatanen's sigh joined with the wind's whisper in the cedar as she walked though Ami-enshi's garden wishing she were in her own garden. "Nothing of mine is here but what I brought with me," she whispered, "and the most precious of my possessions is with Zaya, his head becoming befuddled with wine, laughing with her, utterly forgetting me."

In a dark corner, she sank to the grass. Moonlight reflected from the silver diadem on her bowed head.

"Where are you sending your breath, O Shu?" she asked the god of the winds. "When it passes me, do you send it to touch the tearful faces of others such as I? And the kisses he so recently blew to me, do they drift away on your wings, O Shu? Where do the eyes of my beloved turn? If they travel, like your breath to another, what will I do? Must I silently watch him go to her? Must I watch him take her to his chamber while I lie alone to wonder what happens between them? I don't have to wonder. I know! Too well I know!"

Nefrytatanen wiped tears from her eyes and rose wearily. She looked once more at the moon. How serenely it followed its course, she thought, while her own path was filled with turmoil.

"I will cast no spell to hold him, Aset," she said softly. "I want his decision influenced by nothing but his own heart. He chooses me of his own will or not at all."

Nefrytatanen straightened her shoulders and forced herself to close her ears to the music and laughter drifting from the banquet room. She walked slowly back to her quarters and, without calling her servants, undressed alone in the dark. She put away her gown and sandals, her bracelets and coronet, with exaggerated care, touching the metal of her crown sadly.

Slipping into bed wearing only the pendant that was her amulet, she shivered in the chilly place and lay with eyes wide and heart thumping peculiarly out of rhythm as she considered the possibility of sleeping alone in the future.

After some time had passed and Nefrytatanen neither sent word nor returned, Amenemhet interrupted Balul in the middle of an observation and turned to Ami-enshi.

"King Ami-enshi, I believe Queen Nefrytatanen is ill, since she did not return. I must excuse myself and see to her."

"But one of the servants will care for her," Zaya said quickly.

104

Amenemhet gave her a look that silenced her and rose from his chair. "I will care for her."

Ami-enshi studied Amenemhet's expression and nodded. "I hope she is only tired."

"Perhaps she drank too much wine," Balul suggested.

Amenemhet turned his stare at Balul, who was immediately sorry he had spoken. "Queen Nefrytatanen doesn't drink to excess," Amenemhet said coldly and turned to leave.

When Nefrytatanen heard Amenemhet enter the room, she said nothing. She only listened to his movements as he undressed. Although she felt as if she had spent hours lying there, she realized he didn't sound too unsteady from the wine. When she felt his weight on the bed, she almost turned to throw her arms around him in welcome, but she restrained herself, afraid.

She felt his lips softly brush her shoulder, his body move warmly against her side, his arm slide carefully around her. She smelled no perfume on him. She sensed no hesitation in his manner, no embarrassment. Slowly she turned to face him.

"I could not sleep because the bed was cold until you came," she murmured.

Amenemhet whispered, "The banquet ended when you left, for the room was empty without you."

Nefrytatanen nestled closer and laid her cheek against his chest.

"Your face is wet," Amenemhet said softly. "Why are you weeping?"

Eight

Amenemhet approached the door to hear Nefrytatanen's voice through the window saying sharply, "What can I do? Poison her?" Amenemhet stopped in midstep and listened while she added more softly, "What needs to be done, he must do."

"Can you not speak to him again?" Dedjet's voice was sad, as if she were offering the last suggestion she had.

"No," Nefrytatanen almost whispered. "I cannot bother him about this again."

Amenemhet turned around and went back into the garden. He leaned his arms against the low wall guarding the perimeter of the cliff and gazed at the sparkling sea below while he wondered what he could do. He understood that Nefrytatanen felt she was being treated by Ami-enshi as if she were no more than a pet cat. He was also aware she was haunted by the knowledge that their marriage contract was open to his having a harem. Her nerves were growing thin by having nothing to occupy her hours—except worry about Zaya. Nothing would help but to get her away from this palace.

The wind shifted from the sea to swing over the cedar forests, and the scent it carried into the garden was intoxicating. Amenemhet thought about the nearby forest where the trees hid streams and possibly little valleys like the one they had found at dawn while traveling. Longingly, he thought of being alone again with Nefrytatanen in such a place.

Amenemhet stood away from the rail, inhaling the fragrance of cedar for a moment. Then he again turned toward the door. As he walked closer, he deliberately began to whistle to warn Nefrytatanen of his approach.

Nefrytatanen, who was sitting on a couch when he entered, smiled wanly at the sight of him. He sat beside her, still thinking about the forest. The more he considered his idea, the better he decided it was.

"I think it's time we got away from this place for a day by ourselves," he said. Her eyes widened with surprise as he continued, "I've made up my mind. While the morning is young, I'll give orders that we'll go riding in the cedar forest. We'll have food packed for us and spend the whole day alone, unbothered by negotiations, politics or problems of any kind."

"Can we truly do this?" Nefrytatanen whispered. "How will we tell King Ami-enshi without his sending an army of guards and servants with us?"

"Don't worry about that," Amenemhet said. "I'll tell him myself and allow no arguments. No threats of wild beasts will deter us—unless you're afraid of wild beasts."

"I would rather face wild beasts than stay here," she said firmly.

Amenemhet stood up. "Change your clothes and get ready then," he said. "I plan to waste no time debating with Ami-enshi, and I'll take only a moment to change my own garments." He turned to Dedjet. "Tell the household servant responsible to pack a meal for us." He thought a moment, then added, "Tell Yazid to get someone to prepare our horses—not theirs, Dedjet. We want our own for this journey."

Dedjet smiled happily and hurried into the hall. This was just what they needed, she was certain. She ran to complete her tasks.

Amenemhet returned so quickly from speaking to Ami-enshi that Nefrytatanen had only begun to change her garments. He looked smug.

"Ami-enshi gave you no argument?" she asked.

"He didn't." Amenemhet smiled widely. "I gave him no choice. He was in the midst of some squabble with Zaya, who looked unwell after last night's drinking. I merely put my

108

head in the doorway and told him, then left. He had no chance to protest."

"And his reaction?" Nefrytatanen asked.

"I'd judge the idea was startling to him and displeasing to Zaya." He turned to see Yazid standing on the threshold. "Are the horses being prepared?"

"King Ami-enshi's stableboys weren't happy about the orders, but they're obeying."

Amenemhet was struggling with a boot, and Yazid hurried to help him. "I don't know when we'll return, Yazid," he said, "but I think it won't be before nightfall." Amenemhet's eyes gleamed as he added, "If we aren't back by then and searchers are sent, make sure they're noisy."

Yazid struggled to hold back his smile at the same time he struggled with the other boot. "Is there anything else you'll need?"

"Only your promise that no one will follow us," Amenemhet said bluntly. "The methods you employ to prevent such treachery I'll leave to your own judgment. I only ask, if they're embarrassing, you leave no evidence."

Yazid nodded. "I need do nothing."

"How do you know that?" Nefrytatanen inquired.

"I won't need to take measures already taken," Yazid whispered, "most discreetly of course."

Amenemhet looked at Yazid a moment, wondering what he had done. He decided not to ask for details. Instead, he turned to Nefrytatanen. "Are you ready?"

"I've been ready since I first set foot through Yenoam's gates," she said eagerly.

Amenemhet again turned to Yazid and motioned for Dedjet to come nearer. "If there's any problem while we're gone, you will warn whoever causes it that we'll deal with them when we return. I mean this not only for servants, but for anyone who bothers any of our people." Yazid nodded in understanding.

Amenemhet and Nefrytatanen wore dignified expressions as they sedately walked their horses past the sentries at Yenoam's gates, but as soon as they were out of sight, they urged their horses into a gallop across a meadow and into the cedar forest's shadows.

In the forest, they slowed to a canter, then to a walk. The forest was unlike anything they had seen in Tamera.

The trees towered like giant cones toward the sky, their branches spiraling up the tapering trunks, spreading a per-

109

fume so rich it was almost visible to the eye. The ground was thickly covered with fragile lacelike leaves that hushed the horses' hooves. In the quiet, the wind caused a strange singing in the branches.

The trees nearby had a blue cast to their branches, making it seem as if part of the sky had melted and coated them. In other areas the trees took on a silvery tint, and the sun caressing their branches seemed cooled by the cedars' touch.

Amenemhet and Nefrytatanen's rare comments were spoken in lowered voices as if in deference to the mighty trees swaying over them. They were content to gaze at the cedar and inhale its perfume, while the stillness of the forest seeped into their souls and filled them with peace.

When the sun was high, they stopped in a golden-green glade to eat their meal. Then they lay on the grass watching the swaying of the branches against the sky, being quiet together, not needing sounds from one another to share their feelings.

While Nefrytatanen watched butterflies float lazily among the wild flowers, and the droning of the bees made a soft humming in the air, she closed her eyes and tipped from drowsiness to sleep without knowing it. Amenemhet's lips softly brushing hers awakened her to stare into his sun-shadowed eyes.

"Open your mouth and close your eyes," he said softly. "I have something for you."

Without hesitation, Nefrytatanen did as he asked and felt a small, soft, round object on her tongue. It was warm from the sun and sweet-scented. With her eyes still closed, she rolled the object around in her mouth experimentally, discovering it was a berry of some kind. She squashed it into a tangy rush of cool juice, wondering how the outside of it could be sun-warmed and the inside feel cool. She opened her eyes and smiled.

"I have more," Amenemhet said, giving her a handful of little red berries. He sat beside her and leaned his back against a tree, eating the handful of fruit he had reserved for himself.

A large orange bird stopped on a nearby swaying twig and watched them as if it wondered whether their fondness for the berries equaled his own. Amenemhet tossed a berry close to the shrub, and after a quick flip of its tail and a bright glance of its eye, the bird decided these creatures were friendly and hopped from its perch. He looked at them again

110

as he stood over the berry, reassuring himself there was no trap. Then, with a quick motion, he took the berry in his beak and whirred to a higher perch.

There was a sudden movement in the bushes, the sound of the horses' agitated stamping. Amenemhet was instantly alert, staring in the direction of the noises as if his eyes could penetrate the foliage. The horses snorted fearfully. One of them screamed in protest. The bird dropped its berry and, screeching alarm, disappeared into the trees.

Amenemhet leaped up. "An animal must be nearby."

"Does anything dangerous live in this area?" Nefrytatanen asked, quickly getting to her feet.

"I don't know," Amenemhet replied as he put out his hand in warning. "Stay here. Whatever it is, I can't let it frighten away our horses."

He started purposefully toward the bushes, but as he went closer, his movements became lighter, more alert, like those of a hunting cat. The horses snorted and stamped more insistently, and as he silently slipped into the foliage Amenemhet loosened the dagger he carried in a case at his hip. Seeing him touch the dagger, Nefrytatanen's fear was heightened, and she hesitantly stepped forward. But she could see nothing through the tangle of leaves, and the only sounds were those of the horses.

Expecting to find an animal slinking near the horses, Amenemhet was surprised when he discovered two men, one of them already in Nefrytatanen's saddle, the other struggling with Amenemhet's horse, which stamped, reared and turned to try to bite the man. Confident that Sekhmet couldn't be mounted by a stranger, Amenemhet raced to Nefrytatanen's horse.

Using the momentum he had gathered in his run, he sprang up to grip the thief's shoulder. Amenemhet's weight, added to the wrench he gave the man, tore him from the saddle, and he tumbled awkwardly to the grass.

Amenemhet didn't wait for him to regain his feet, but while he was still on his knees, Amenemhet clasped both hands together, forming a double fist, drew them over his shoulder, then swung them forward to smash the thief's face. The man's head snapped backward, and he crashed to the ground. Amenemhet followed and, pulling the man up by his tunic's front, delivered several more blows in quick succession. Dropping the unconscious thief, he turned to the other man,

111

who was still frantically trying to mount Sekhmet without success.

Amenemhet ran toward the thief, but as he neared the man, he stopped abruptly. The thief had drawn a knife.

"If you must do this, step away from my horse," Amenemhet said coldly, reaching for his own dagger.

Suddenly the thief sprang at Amenemhet, holding the shining blade low, driving it toward Amenemhet's stomach. Amenemhet leaped backward, whirling away from the knife. As he turned, he whipped his arm around, giving the thief's shoulder a sharp push. The man slammed forward, stumbling before he caught his balance, then spun around to face Amenemhet, looking as desperate as a wild animal at bay. Amenemhet approached slowly, his eyes on the blade that glimmered menacingly in the sun. The thief lowered his head and shoulders, and, carefully watching Amenemhet, he began to circle around him.

Amenemhet didn't see Nefrytatanen cautiously making her way through the foliage until she stepped out midway between him and the thief. The surprised man hesitated only an instant before rushing toward her, but that moment was all Amenemhet needed to leap out and push Nefrytatanen away. Already half-crouching, Amenemhet continued forward. The thief's hip took the full force of Amenemhet's shoulder, and he staggered backward to fall against Sekhmet's flank. The horse shied away, blowing fearfully, his eyes rolling.

Regaining his balance, the thief sprang at Amenemhet, but the king turned the man's blade aside and drove his own dagger between the thief's ribs.

Amenemhet glimpsed a movement at the edge of his vision, and he whirled to face the second thief. The hesitating man stared for an instant at Amenemhet's eyes, which shone with the gold fire of battle, and quickly backed away. When he was near the edge of the clearing, he spun on his heel and ran into the forest.

The air was heavy with the smell of violence and when the shifting breeze brought the scent of the fallen thief's blood to the already excited horses, they screamed with renewed fear, rearing and plunging and tossing their heads until they freed their loosely knotted reins. Amenemhet dropped his dagger and dashed forward to stop them, but before he could catch the reins, the terrified horses raced wildly into the forest.

Amenemhet ran to the edge of the clearing, then stopped.

Sighing with disgust, he bent to retrieve his dagger and turned to face Nefrytatanen. She hurried into his arms.

"Did you get . . ." she began anxiously.

Amenemhet shook his head. "Only my knuckles are gashed from hitting the thief who escaped." He slipped one arm around her waist and turned to again gaze in the direction the horses had taken. "They'll eventually stop somewhere."

"It would be a long walk to the palace," Nefrytatanen commented.

They returned to the place where they had been lying, and he bent to pick up their cloaks and the bundle that had held their food.

Nefrytatanen knew Amenemhet was trying not to reveal his worry, so she said reassuringly, "I can walk as far as the palace if necessary."

Amenemhet smiled, pretending to share her light mood, but he was worried. He wasn't used to finding his way through large wooded areas. He hoped that by following the horses' tracks he would find not only them but the way to the palace before darkness fell. He realized how easily they could wander in circles in the forest.

When a dead branch fell with a crash, Nefrytatanen was startled out of proportion to how she would normally react, and Amenemhet saw it. He realized she was afraid and pretending for his sake. He squeezed her hand reassuringly as they trudged into the gloom.

They walked steadily after the tracks of the horses through a place filled with swaying ferns and green moss. Their feet sank soundlessly in soft layers of damp mold, and the air was filled with the smell of rotting wood. A cloud of gnats rose in the pale light to shine like dust specks, to be replaced by a swarm of mosquitoes that bit Amenemhet and Nefrytatanen mercilessly. They slapped and waved at the insects in a futile effort to drive them away.

When Amenemhet broke through a tangle of bushes to emerge burning with scratches and insect bites, he knew he had finally lost the horses' trail. He also knew they, too, were lost, but he remained silent and continued to slosh through a shallow marsh.

Nefrytatanen said nothing, though she was getting tired and falling behind Amenemhet's pace. Thinking to save herself the effort of struggling through some tall weeds, she turned to skirt them but when she hesitated for a moment, she discovered she couldn't lift her feet. Alarm flashed through her.

"Beloved, this place isn't ordinary mud!" she called.

Amenemhet quickly turned. Nefrytatanen's feet had disappeared in the mud. Fear chilled him as he realized that the mud was quicksand. He glanced around, looking for something to use to help pull her out. "Don't struggle," he said quietly. "Stand very still."

Nefrytatanen seemed paralyzed, and her eyes were purple with terror.

Amenemhet dropped the bundle he had been carrying and hurried to a tree whose limb was dead. Hacking at it with his dagger, frantically twisting and pulling at it, he finally broke the branch loose. With caution he started toward Nefrytatanen, measuring how near her he dared go. She had sunk halfway to her knees when he extended one end of the branch toward her.

"Hold tight," he directed. "Try to move toward me."

Nefrytatanen struggled to lift a foot and found it so difficult she could do no more than drag it through the mud.

Amenemhet could feel through the branch how she was struggling and he said quietly, "Keep trying and I'll pull you forward at the same time. If you slip and fall, roll over on your back. Just don't let go of the branch." He saw her shudder at the thought of being pulled through the mud, and added, "Don't be afraid, beloved. As long as you hold this branch, I'll pull you in." He was glad his voice sounded steadier than he felt.

With a strength she hadn't known she possessed, Nefrytatanen drew herself through the sucking mud until he clasped her wrists. Acutely aware of his firm grip and looking into his eyes all the while, she dragged herself forward and, with a last burst of effort, was free.

Amenemhet hastily pulled her with him as he backed away until they reached rocky ground. Once there he released her wrists and stood looking at her a moment, panting, his own fear at last clearly revealed.

"I lost the horses' trail long ago," he said quietly.

"I know."

"We're far from the place where they were frightened."

"We're also probably far from the palace," she observed calmly.

Amenemhet looked helplessly at the trees surrounding them and said in disgust, "How could I find my way on the

114

trackless desert and get lost here? There are any number of landmarks I might have used to find our way back."

"There are too many for your desert-trained eyes, and one tree looks much like the next," she said. "I could have paid more attention to what we passed, but I didn't. I'm as much to blame as you. You're angry with yourself because you're afraid for me. I'm not afraid."

"How can you say that after almost being swallowed by that mud?" he cried.

"I looked into your eyes and my fears fled."

Amenemhet was awed by her trust. He swallowed and said, "It will be getting dark soon."

Before long, Amenemhet and Nefrytatanen entered a part of the forest where the trees towered so high above the earth that the sunlight only sparingly filtered through the leaves. Nothing but grass was able to grow along the ground. Amenemhet and Nefrytatanen walked holding hands along a green-shadowed path, looking at the sun forming slender columns of gold dust.

"Do you realize, if we accidentally came upon a village, we appear enough like beggars they'd never guess who we are?" Amenemhet asked.

Nefrytatanen smiled and said gaily, "I won't tell them."

"We don't even have a coin to buy a loaf of bread," he reminded.

"We have a forest filled with things to sustain us," she replied. "I'm content living on roasted birds and fresh berries."

"Surely you must feel weakened by now with only love for the morning meal," he said.

"I'd wager I have more energy than you," she promptly answered.

He laughed softly. "Wager? Wager with what?"

"There's no point in searching my garments," she replied. "They're all torn out."

"If you wish to gamble, let the next fire be the stakes," Amenemhet suggested. "Whoever loses must start the fire."

Nefrytatanen shook her head. "You'd have to pay even if you won. I probably couldn't make a fire." She stopped walking and looked up at him. "Why are we betting?"

"You'll learn," he answered softly, raising an eyebrow suggestively.

Nefrytatanen stared at him in mock dismay. "Are you never satisfied?"

"I was thinking of the same thing as you," he teased.

115

"Oh." The word was a small cool raindrop sliding from her lips.

"It's you, it seems, who's never satisfied," Amenemhet commented. "Ami-enshi thinks I need a harem, but I wonder if he shouldn't be concerned about you. Maybe I should suggest he offer you Prince Balul or Prince Mamum."

Nefrytatanen looked startled at the idea. "Do you mean I should . . ." Her words trailed off when she realized he was joking. "That might be an idea. Balul does have a charming smile."

Amenemhet reached for her, but she anticipated his move and ran from him, laughing aloud. He watched her run into the meadow and walk among the clusters of swaying blossoms.

Admiring the variety of flowers, she bent to sniff their fragrance. Finally she could not resist and began to gather them, choosing carefully, inspecting each flower's perfection before she plucked it. She returned with a handful of red, orange and yellow blossoms and sat beside him cross-legged like a scribe while she plaited them into a chain. Closing the chain's ends, she dropped the ring of flowers around his neck.

"I award you this garland," she began with exaggerated solemnity, "as a gesture of my appreciation for your many outstanding services to your queen"—she began to smile—"and, therefore, to the Two Lands—" Her smile broke into laughter and she couldn't finish the pronouncement.

"What do you call this award?" Amenemhet asked, grinning at the flowers.

"It's so new an award it hasn't been named."

"I doubt it will ever be." He picked up the loop hanging on his chest and, throwing it over her head, put his hands at her waist. "In accepting this award, I must say I couldn't have accomplished what I have without your inspiration," he said.

"You're generous to share your triumph with me," she replied in a soft tone.

"I'm really very selfish," Amenemhet whispered. He kissed her cheek and put his face against hers as his hands slid around her back. "That's why I won't allow any prince to join our household."

"Why would I want a prince? I have all I desire in a king," Nefrytatanen murmured.

The hoarse shout struck them like a blow. They drew away from each other, their eyes wide with surprise. More shouts and the sound of running horses assailed their ears, and they turned their heads slowly in anticipation. Galloping toward them from the forest's shadows was a group of horsemen with King Ami-enshi and his sons leading them.

Amenemhet silently turned to look at Nefrytatanen, and slowly removed their flower garland, dropping it to the grass. Then he stood up and took her hand to help her to her feet. He was frowning when Ami-enshi and his sons dismounted and hurried to them.

"You're safe!" Balul exclaimed. "We've found you at last!"

"Yes," Amenemhet said in a flat tone, still holding Nefrytatanen's hand.

"Have you been injured in any way?" Ami-enshi asked anxiously. "You must be exhausted."

"We're all right," Amenemhet answered quietly. "Did our horses return?"

"We found them along the way," Mamum answered, wondering at their lack of enthusiasm at being rescued. "What happened, if I may ask?"

"Two thieves tried to take our horses. The horses were frightened off by the struggle," Amenemhet replied tersely. "One of the thieves escaped. The other lies in a clearing."

"You killed him?" Balul exclaimed.

Amenemhet nodded. "Yazid, bring our horses."

The servant came forward to give Amenemhet the reins. After everyone had mounted, instead of riding alongside Ami-enshi, Amenemhet wordlessly took Nefrytatanen's hand and turned his horse in behind Ami-enshi and his sons. Ami-enshi was surprised that Amenemhet was ignoring them, and he turned in his saddle to regard him curiously.

"It's a wonder we found you so quickly," Ami-enshi said. "This forest is very dense."

Amenemhet nodded in agreement.

Ami-enshi looked at him a moment, then turned to face forward, softly muttering under his breath, "You'd think they'd show some gratitude."

"If I were in his place, I'm not sure I'd be happy to be found," Balul commented.

"What do you mean?" Ami-enshi asked.

"I think we interrupted something," Balul whispered.

Ami-enshi turned to take a second, longer look at Amenemhet and Nefrytatanen, who were still holding hands as they rode. He rode the rest of the way thoughtful and silent.

When the riders entered the palace gates, neither Amen-

117

emhet nor Nefrytatanen looked to the right or left, but continued to look only at each other. Zaya, watching from her balcony, remembered how they had appeared when they had first entered Yenoam, and grudgingly noted that they were holding hands like new lovers even though they were as dusty as beggars. She turned quickly and left the balcony.

Yazid came to help Amenemhet from his horse, but the king leaped off, scorning assistance, and brushed past Balul, who was standing alongside Nefrytatanen's horse. When he came up to her, she put her hands on Amenemhet's shoulders and slid off the horse into his arms. He held her a moment longer than seemed necessary, Balul observed with some envy.

"Thank you for searching for us," Amenemhet said, turning to Ami-enshi. "If you'll excuse us, we'll go to our chambers to bathe," he added. Amenemhet didn't wait for Ami-enshi's reply, but took Nefrytatanen's hand and, nodding at Yazid to follow, left their rescuers in the courtyard feeling slightly guilty for having accomplished their mission.

Nine

Amenemhet awoke before Nefrytatanen and lay quietly staring at the ceiling. He once again determined to sign the treaty immediately so that he could take his queen away from Yenoam.

A violent pounding at the door made Amenemhet start in surprise. Nefrytatanen, too, sat up quickly, her eyes wide open with shock.

Amenemhet swung his legs from the bed. "Stay there, beloved," he said. "I don't know what the disturbance is, but I'll deal with it. Lie back and rest a little longer." He threw a robe around himself and, running his fingers through his rumpled hair, went to open the door. He found Yazid and a courier from Ithtawe standing in the corridor.

"What can be so important that you come beating at the door when the sun is barely risen?" Amenemhet demanded.

"Sire, I've brought an urgent message from Prime Minister Meri," the courier stammered.

"What is it?" Amenemhet inquired a little less sternly.

"There was no time for the message to be written, sire, so I'll tell you as well as I can," the courier said. "Lord Petamen of Thes-Hertu Province came to Ithtawe to report that his

119

people have found a new variety of insects attacking his crops."

"Surely Meri didn't send you all this way to tell me such a thing!" Amenemhet exclaimed.

"Sire, there's more," the messenger warned, then continued, "During Lord Petamen's journey back to his province, he lost control of his horse and was killed."

Amenemhet stared at the courier a moment before disgust entered his face and he commented, "He probably was drunk."

"Maybe so, sire, but his bridle was also cut and clusters of thorns were found under his saddle." The messenger paused for a moment, then continued, "Two ships from Atalan arrived at Ithtawe ten days ago. That was why the prime minister dispatched me so hastily."

"What is that?" Nefrytatanen came to the door holding a blanket wrapped around her.

"Who was on these ships?" Amenemhet asked. His face became a mask of calm to hide his fear. He was sure Atalan must have finally sunk, because no one from there had visited Tamera in years. King Sahura had predicted the destruction of his island kingdom, and Neferset, his daughter, had related many dreams prophesying Atalan's catastrophe.

"Prince Sarenput commanded one ship." The courier took a deep breath and said, "Atalan is gone. Prince Sarenput and those with him were the only survivors."

Amenemhet said nothing. Nefrytatanen backed away and sank onto a couch still clutching the blanket.

"King Sahura? Queen Nesitaneb?" Amenemhet finally asked softly. The messenger shook his head. "Why did they stay?" Amenemhet asked.

"King Sahura would not have been able to survive the rigors of the journey and insisted on giving his place to someone who could. Queen Nesitaneb wouldn't leave him."

Amenemhet could hear Nefrytatanen's quiet weeping behind him. "The physician, Apuya?" he asked softly.

"Apuya was with them," the messenger answered. "I was told a hundred survived."

"One hundred," Nefrytatanen said faintly. "Only a hundred out of the whole population." She took a breath and looked up, quickly wiping her eyes.

"Prince Sarenput said the disaster was too suddenly upon

them. It began with an earthquake, which disturbed the resting volcanoes, and then it was over."

"Was Commander Semu on the ship?" Nefrytatanen asked quietly.

The messenger shook his head. "I know of no one named Semu who came."

"Had Lord Kheti and Lady Neferset been told before you left?" Amenemhet thought of Neferset's grief for her parents.

"They were at Ithtawe when the ships arrived," the courier answered. "I was present myself. Lord Kheti was shocked, but he immediately invited Prince Sarenput and some others to go to his house to stay for a while. Lady Neferset was, of course, greatly saddened." The messenger looked confused as he added, "I remember what Lady Neferset said when she heard the news, for I was standing near enough to hear her words. She said she'd known it from her dreams. She had already seen it all."

Amenemhet and Nefrytatanen exchanged glances. Then the king turned to the courier. "Take time to rest before you return," he directed. "Tell Prime Minister Meri we've almost concluded our business here, and I expect to leave Yenoam in a couple of days. Instruct him to make the visitors from Atalan comfortable. Remind him that Sarenput's a king, though he now has no kingdom, and he will be given all the respect shown a visiting monarch. I want you also to go to Lord Kheti and Lady Neferset and express our sorrow. Tell Sarenput we're thankful at least he and the others were saved. When we return to Ithtawe, we'll see what can be done to help their people build a new life in Tamera." Amenemhet turned to Nefrytatanen. "Is there anything more we can say?"

She shook her head slowly. "Only that we weep with them."

Amenemhet turned to Yazid. "Make this man comfortable, but see that he leaves for Ithtawe as soon as he rests."

After Amenemhet closed the door, he went to sit beside Nefrytatanen and held her hand. "Be thankful some of them survived."

"I cannot help but remember Sahura and Nesitaneb's kindness to us," Nefrytatanen whispered. "I think of how Semu helped us. I remember that beautiful, peaceful island and its people, and I am beyond weeping. Think of how Neferset and Sarenput must feel. It's too much—I cannot absorb it all at one time."

"Nor can I," Amenemhet said softly. "I wonder what we can do with those people now. Are they nobles, peasants, artists? What work will they do in Tamera? Sarenput was crown prince. What will he do?"

"I think it won't matter very much to him for a while."

"It must be considered sometime." Amenemhet's face was grim. "Sarenput was trained to govern his country. He's intelligent and could be of great value, but what could he do in Tamera that wouldn't be demeaning?"

Nefrytatanen wiped her eyes again and turned to Amenemhet. "Lord Petamen will have to be replaced. Perhaps after Sarenput has rested from his arduous journey, he could be made governor of Thes-Hertu."

Amenemhet's face grew a little less sad as he thought about that. "Thes-Hertu is a rich and important province," he ventured. "I would like to have a man I fully trust running affairs there—and I can think of nothing else for Sarenput now."

"We'll have to know who else came before we can make other decisions," Nefrytatanen said slowly. "I cannot believe the whole land is gone—I just can't believe it."

"Let us turn our thoughts away from it for now," Amenemhet said. "We must prepare for the treaty signing." Nefrytatanen looked at him in surprise. Getting to his feet, he added, "I do expect you to attend the signing, although I'm sure Ami-enshi doesn't." He took her hand. "Why do you look at me that way, beloved? Can you have doubts about my intentions?"

Nefrytatanen smiled wryly. "We won't drag Zaya home with us?"

"Not unless they sneak her into our caravan."

"My heart is so filled with love of you I sometimes think I will die from the strength of the emotion," she whispered. "I feel like a small bird that comes to sing over your head, then fly in dizzy circles in the sky, so happy I cannot endure sitting still and merely singing of it. If you sent me away, I would die for all time."

Amenemhet held Nefrytatanen close for moment. "Loving you is life to me," he said. "Will you dress now to attend the treaty signing? I don't doubt Zaya will contrive some way to be there, despite her lack of an invitation. I would have you wear your crown, beloved—not the double crown, but the silver coronet of my family that lies so lightly on your head. You are queen, and today Ami-enshi will know it."

Prince Balul and Prince Mamum sat a short distance from the table where the treaty was to be signed. Along with King Ami-enshi, Ambassador Anir, and Prime Minister Ketah, they waited for Amenemhet's arrival. Everyone was subdued and patient, because news of the Atalan disaster had run through the place like a fire.

"What do you suppose he'll say?" Balul whispered.

"About what?" Mamum asked.

"About Zaya," Balul snapped. "You know he's going to refuse her, but how do you suppose he'll do it?"

Mamum's eyes fell. "I don't know," he said softly. "Maybe he'll accept Zaya for the sake of the treaty. Who can tell what's on his mind?"

"When we found King Amenemhet and Nefrytatanen sitting in the meadow among the flowers, I knew what he'd decide." Balul looked at his brother. "You know it as well. He isn't going to accept Zaya. He wouldn't do it if the decision meant a war."

"I could understand starting wars over some women," Maum whispered, "but Zaya isn't one of them."

Balul agreed. "If a war would be fought, it would be over Nefrytatanen—not Zaya."

Mamum smiled. "Father should have offered King Amenemhet one of his other daughters."

Balul sighed. "One of the others might be more pliable, but to offer less than the first princess to a king would be insult. Also, Zaya's such a troublemaker father wanted to get her off his hands, and he'd hoped a strong man like King Amenemhet would control her."

Mamum glanced at the entrance and his eyes widened. "Look, Balul," he gasped.

Balul stared, too surprised to speak for a moment. "What is Zaya doing here?" he finally whispered.

Princess Zaya had calmly glided into the room as if it were the custom that she attend such meetings. She wore a bright-orange gown, and her hair, hanging loose in golden waves, rippled like wheat as she moved. As she walked past her brothers, her perfume spread like the wave from a passing ship.

"She looks neither innocent nor sweet today," Balul commented.

"I would say she's throwing one last net for her fish," Mamum whispered. "She looks very seductive. Did you notice, Balul, you can almost see through her garment?"

"I did."

A page stepped inside the room and announced the arrival of King Amenemhet and Queen Nefrytatanen, and Balul and Mamum glanced at each other again.

"Queen Nefrytatanen!" Balul breathed. Mamum jabbed him with an elbow and threw him a warning look. More softly Balul said, "This should be a fascinating meeting."

Nefrytatanen wore a simple white linen sheath, but once again she brought the mystery of Tamera's night with her. As if deliberately disdaining the formality of King Ami-enshi, Amenemhet was casually dressed in a short white tunic and, like Nefrytatanen, wore his family's personal diadem. His face was serene and he didn't even glance in Zaya's direction. They walked directly to the table where Ami-enshi and his council were waiting.

Ambassador Nakht followed, then the priest Senbi and the scribe Lakma and his assistants. A contingent of Ithtawe's royal guards marched on each side of the delegation, carrying their spears upright.

Lakma and his assistants placed themselves by their inkpots and rapidly copied the account of what had so far been agreed upon. They looked up expectantly when they finished, waiting to learn what additions might be made.

"King Amenemhet, do you agree with the treaty as it has been recorded?" Prime Minister Ketah asked. Amenemhet nodded agreemnt.

"King Ami-enshi and King Amenemhet are satisfied with the wording of the treaty," Ketah announced. "Bring forth Princess Zaya to further bind Tamera and Retenu with marriage."

The room was silent with tension as Zaya stood up, ready to come forward.

"No. don't bring her," Amenemhet said quietly.

Ami-enshi stared at Amenemhet. "You refuse my daughter?"

"I refuse her," Amenemhet replied calmly.

"Why?" Ami-enshi coldly asked.

Amenemhet was undisturbed. "For two most excellent reasons, King Ami-enshi," he replied. "In Tamera, the king is

124

the son of Ra. He's Asar reborn—Heru. In other words, according to our law, I am divine. If my word and seal were lies, I would be an excellent divinity, would I not? If I am a man so devious my word means nothing, what would marriage to your daughter mean? If I were such a man, she'd only be an excellent hostage." Amenemhet looked at Zaya, whose eyes flared with anger.

"You had two reasons?" Ami-enshi couldn't argue the logic of Amenemhet's thinking, but he was far from happy.

Amenemhet looked at Ami-enshi. "I'm not the only ruler of Tamera. I rule jointly with Queen Nefrytatanen, which is as our marriage contract decreed; for she was ruler of the north and I inheritor of the southern crown. She is as lawfully queen as I am king." Amenemhet smiled coolly. "Please don't offer Queen Nefrytatanen one of your sons to obtain a more binding treaty. I would not like that."

Ami-enshi coughed to hide his embarrassment and turned away as if to consider the matter. "This is a weighty crown you wear."

"It is sometimes that," Amenemhet solemnly agreed.

Princess Zaya turned and marched out, haughtily, her veils fluttering after her.

Nefrytatanen watched her go, then stepped forward and said, "Now shall we seal the treaty?"

Ami-enshi, unused to the idea of a woman who had authority, looked at her with a startled expression.

Nefrytatanen smiled calmly. "The daughter of Ra is as divine as his son. Surely the seal of a goddess may bind a treaty of peace." She looked expectantly at Ami-enshi.

Lakma had gotten to his feet and was waiting with copies of the treaties in his hands, as were Ami-enshi's scribes with their copies. At Amenemhet's nod, Lakma put the papyrus rolls on the table and stood ready with the brushes and wax.

"Pour it," Ami-enshi ordered his scribe.

Mamum watched the wax being poured and the three seals being placed on each copy. While Ami-enshi, Amenemhet and Nefrytatanen signed the treaty, he whispered to his brother, "It's too bad King Amenemhet objects to Queen Nefrytatanen having one of us."

"I would certainly volunteer," Balul agreed.

"But you are not eligible," his brother pointed out. "I am. I am not going to be king."

"True. But I would be willing to abdicate!"

The afternoon was filled with the complications of not appearing too anxious to leave, but at the same time, hurrying the servants to be ready to depart early the next morning.

Even as Nefrytatanen directed the servants with the packing of personal items, a second courier arrived with a message from the prime minister almost begging they return, saying a strange variety of insects and root-eating worms had attacked a second province on the southern border—Ta-Khent. Nefrytatanen instructed the courier to rest and refresh himself, and went to find Amenemhet to tell him this latest news herself.

It was difficult to locate anyone in Ami-enshi's palace, because many doorways—as well as solid walls—were covered with drapes and tapestries, and it was easy to pass a wall hanging without realizing it covered a door. As Nefrytatanen was passing one such doorway, she glimpsed Amenemhet on its other side, standing and facing someone.

Nefrytatanen stopped and took a step back to see if he was talking with a person she might easily interrupt. He was facing a girl Nefrytatanen hadn't seen before.

The girl was a tiny creature; the top of her jeweled head did not even reach Amenemhet's chest. The girl bowed low at her waist, her palms pressed together, long gold-painted nails pointed upward in a curious gesture of obeisance. She was no child, Nefrytatanen could see now. Her garment was a swirl of graceful draping, a deep-green silk the color of a peacock's tail, heavily woven with gold. When the girl moved, tiny golden bells at her ankles made soft music. Her skin was the color of light honey, and Nefrytatanen could see slanted, almond-shaped eyes of darkest brown filled with golden lights looking at Amenemhet. The expression in the girl's eyes made Nefrytatanen sigh. She looked at the straight black hair that hung smoothly to the girl's hips and inhaled the girl's warm and tangy perfume.

The girl's soft voice addressed Amenemhet. "Most high lord of the Two Lands, I am Princess Taji—Princess Zaya's half sister, and the child of King Ami-enshi by Pahjee, a lady of the highest-born family in her land. Forgive me, highness, for disturbing you, and grant me but a moment to speak." Amenemhet nodded and the girl continued, "Majesty, my nature is not like that of Princess Zaya. My mother taught me the virtues of obedience and serenity and, from childhood, how to serve a man." The almond eyes looked up at him knowingly. "Take me, great king, in Zaya's place, for I have no future here and I would bring you joy. Zaya would cause disruption in your house, and I would live only to give you pleasure. If I did not please you, highness, I would spare you even the nuisance of ridding yourself of me, for I would poison myself."

Amenemhet frowned as he gazed at the girl. He realized she hadn't heard the news of his refusal of all princesses. He wondered what she meant when she said she had no future here.

"Your name is Taji?" he asked. She nodded silently. "Did your father tell you to offer yourself to me?" Taji nodded hastily, but he decided she was lying. "And what, Taji, would be your choice, if you were allowed to choose? Would you stay or come with me?"

Taji's long black eyelashes swept down a moment. When she finally looked up at Amenemhet, her mouth curved in a smile. "I would go with you, great king, because I find the prospect of serving you most pleasing." Her eyes briefly swept over him in discreet appraisal.

Nefrytatanen turned away and left the scene, unable to listen to more. Amenemhet sounded as if he were actually seriously considering Taji. As Nefrytatanen walked briskly down the corridor, she wondered if she would ever be able to drag Amenemhet home without some woman trailing after him begging to share his bed.

"Curse them all," Nefrytatanen muttered. That little Asian was an enticing creature with her golden bells and perfume and obvious willingness to give Amenemhet so much pleasure. "What pleasure?" Nefrytatanen muttered, wondering what secrets this snip of a girl had been taught by her mother. Nefrytatanen entered their suite and slammed the door behind her.

Amenemhet looked into Taji's eyes and said, "You are lying, Taji. King Ami-enshi didn't tell you to offer yourself to me. Why have you come?"

Taji's eyes fell. "My father wouldn't care if I left Yenoam. He considers me a burden. Zaya has taken a particular dislike to me and makes my life a misery. If I left, I would escape this torment."

"And your mother? Would not Zaya's anger fall on her?" Amenemhet asked.

"My mother is dead," Taji answered. "I have no one here on whom Zaya could vent her anger."

Amenemhet smiled. "I might be able to take you with me, although your duties would be different than you described. Would you then wish to go? What other way might you serve me?"

"Great king, I have been told I sing well and dance gracefully, but I was trained for more than that." Suddenly, there was concern in her voice. "Do you find me ugly? Do you have no interest in me?"

"You are most beautiful, Taji," Amenemhet answered. "But as strange as it may seem to you, I have no harem. If you're sure you want to leave Retenu, I might take you to Ithtawe in some other capacity. You might discover that life in Tamera can be very pleasant for a free woman—because that's what you'd be. I'm sure some nobleman of my court would appreciate a wife possessing such beauty and knowledge as yours."

Taji glanced away. "I'm not sure I would be allowed to leave Yenoam in such a manner."

"Would you want to?"

"Majesty, it's a prospect I've never dreamed of," Taji answered softly. She thought about it, then looked up at him. "I have decided. I would go with you," she said firmly.

"I'll ask King Ami-enshi to send you with me," Amenemhet promised. "If I must take back a princess to make him smile, I'll take you. Perhaps this will satisfy everyone."

Taji's face lit with happiness. If King Amenemhet, Ambassador Nakht and the soldiers she had seen were examples of Tamera's men, Taji was certain she would find one pleasing to her. The idea of pleasing herself, as well as a man, made her head spin.

"Great king, if such an arrangement could be made, I'd be happier than I ever dreamed possible, but will my father agree?"

"Did you say Zaya hated you?" Amenemhet asked. "Don't worry about being allowed to go. I think your father won't mind eliminating a source of Zaya's displeasure." He looked down at Taji and warned, "Say nothing of this for now. I'll insist I want you as a lady-in-waiting to the queen."

Taji was sure this was a miracle. She smiled widely and turned to run down the corridor, her bells making happy sounds in rhythm with her steps.

Nefrytatanen sent for Nakht and told him about the latest province infested with insects. The ambassador suggested that

128

since most of the trouble occurred on Tamera's south border, the insects might have originated in Kenset. Nefrytatanen promptly instructed him to rush back to Ithtawe ahead of the caravan, have Kheti join him and travel immediately to Kenset. If the rulers of Kenset had kept the insects from attacking their crops, they might know a way Tamera could deal with the problem. Nakht left Nefrytatanen less than pleased with his assignment. King Balthazar shared Kenset's throne with his half sister, Queen Karomana, and they were always struggling for supremacy—making negotiations with them a tangle of diplomatic confusion.

Nefrytatanen decided that Amenemhet should be informed of her decision to dispatch Nakht on the mission to Kenset. She called Yazid and instructed him to inform the king of her plan. However, after an hour, the servant returned saying he couldn't locate Amenemhet. At once Nefrytatanen was overcome with jealousy of Taji, though she was shamed by her imaginings and tried to rid her mind of them. The afternoon slowly passed and still there was no word from the king. Silently, she prayed for strength to control her jealous streak.

When Amenemhet returned that evening, Nefrytatanen's greeting did not reveal her inner turmoil. She watched him walk to his bath, and her jealous demon wondered how he had spent all his time. She managed to keep herself from asking him about Taji, but hoped he would relate the incident himself.

Amenemhet came in from his bath yawning and went directly to the bed. Nefrytatanen sat on the bed waiting for him.

"I'll be glad to go home," he sighed as he lay down.

"No happier than I'll be," she said, blowing out the lamp. The darkness was a friend that hid her face, which was wet with tears of shame. She dared not lie beside him yet, because he'd surely kiss her and discover the tears. "Will you then decide which land you'll next approach for a treaty?" she ventured, thankful her voice sounded calm.

"After I learn what's attacking Tamera's crops," Amenemhet answered. Nefrytatanen could tell from the sound of his voice he was stretching. "I am weary," he said emphatically. Nefrytatanen's demon wondered why, but she put aside her thoughts and said nothing.

Amenemhet suspected something was wrong and felt a tension between them he couldn't ignore. He reached for her before he realized she was standing in the shadows. "Why are you over there?" he asked.

"I felt a chill," came her soft voice. "I wondered if the door to the garden was open." She was silent a moment, wondering how she could apologize to him, but the demon was still too close to her. She returned to the bed without speaking.

Amenemhet put his arm around Nefrytatanen and noticed that, although she didn't refuse, it was necessary to pull her closer. "I would kiss you before we sleep," he whispered. He found her lips not eager, but she kissed him. "What is troubling you?" he asked.

Nefrytatanen didn't know what to say. She felt foolish and guilty, and her lips remained mute.

"Are you planning to travel with me the next time to assure I return with no princess?"

"No," she murmured.

Amenemhet withdrew his arm in irritation and turned on his side away from her. "I'll send Nakht to negotiate the treaties," he said. "Fair dreams, beloved."

Through the darkness and from very far away he heard her whisper, "Fair dreams." He lay in silence, waiting for her to smooth away the doubts. If she would only put her arm over him, he'd know in that small gesture she was sorry. If she'd move closer to merely touch his back, he would know she had laid suspicion aside. He had conducted himself properly, and it wasn't his place to apologize. Only one small gesture on her part could take the place of words.

Amenemhet lay awake a long time thinking Nefrytatanen would yet make some move to show she trusted him, so he might sleep in peace. He didn't know it was shame that kept her from him. Finally his eyes closed despite his resolution, and he slept, unaware that Nefrytatanen lay silently weeping, too full of love and penitence to find the words to express it.

Ten

"**Good evening,**" Kheti said quietly.

At the sound of his voice, Kenset's Queen Karomana immediately turned and smiled warmly. "Lord Kheti," she said in a low husky tone. "How glad I am to see you." She noticed Nakht standing a pace behind Kheti. "And Ambassador Nakht," she added, waving her hand. Turning to a serving girl, she commanded, "Pour a little wine for my guests. Oh, and, Weni, bring my own goblet. I, too, would enjoy refreshment."

Nakht's dark eyes admired the bronze satin of Weni's almost naked body as she moved smoothly to get the wine jar. Observing Nakht with an amused expression, Kheti turned his attention to Queen Karomana. She had been studying Kheti, and when he unexpectedly turned, her face still held a hint of her thoughts, which startled him. He brushed aside his uneasiness and smiled pleasantly. "This isn't a dinner party," he remarked, "but a feast."

Pleased at the compliment, Karomana nodded. She tapped Weni's shoulder with a long nail. "I'm thirsty," she said emphatically.

The slave put down the tray and poured wine from Karomana's goblet into her own, wiping Karomana's cup with a bit of linen. She sipped the wine quickly. "It tastes a little strange, my queen," Weni said softly. "Perhaps the wine cask got pitch in it from the seal."

"Get another then," Karomana said impatiently. "Meanwhile, I'll beg a sip of your wine, Lord Kheti, if I may."

"Of course," Kheti murmured, but his eyes were fastened with growing concern on Weni, who had become very pale. "Is something wrong?" he asked.

"I don't . . ." Weni said faintly. Her knees sagged, and, still looking confused, she slowly crumpled at Karomana's feet.

Nakht stared at the girl, who lay twitching slightly. Suddenly, she was still. Nakht turned to Karomana, who calmly lifted her gaze from the body.

"It would seem the wine did contain something," Karomana said. "Perhaps it was spoiled."

"Spoiled wine may cause the stomach agonies or even nausea, but it doesn't kill so efficiently." Nakht shook his head. "This is the work of a fine poison. You have powerful enemies if they can get close enough to slip such mixtures in your goblet."

"That's why I have a slave to do what Weni did," Karomana stated. Her eyes scanned the shocked faces of the crowd. "When my enemy knows the poison reaches another's lips before mine, he may stop."

"How many slaves must die first?" Kheti asked coldly.

Karomana shrugged. "I would die only once."

"And if your enemy tries another way?"

"I take every precaution," Karomana replied, turning to face Kheti. Glancing disinterestedly at the slaves carrying Weni's body away, she said, "My guards are numerous, skilled, and loyal."

"It's unfortunate they were unable to protect Weni," Nakht commented.

"Yes. She was a cheerful girl and pleasant to have near." Karomana sighed. "It is too bad she is dead."

"In Tamera we would say she had gone to the afterlife to await her next journey." Kheti noted Karomana's startled look and added, "But there are many differences between Kenset and Tamera."

"Ah," Karomana said softly, "my dear brother comes to view his damage."

Lord Kheti and Ambassador Nakht exchanged uneasy glances at her tone.

132

Karomana asked, "It shocks you that I speak so of my brother? It's true nonetheless. His was the hand directing the poison. He wants the throne of Kenset for himself, though he's the son of my father by a low concubine."

As King Balthazar strode across the room, the guests bowed, and Nakht noticed Karomana lifted her chin a little higher while her eyes glared hotly at her brother.

Balthazar bore little resemblance to his half sister, and Nakht wondered which of them looked like their father. Karomana was as slender as the stem of a tall flower, but Balthazar had a large-boned and powerful frame. Karomana's features were sharply etched against a skin the color of dark honey and Balthazar's features, though not unattractive, were heavier and his complexion bronze. Karomana's dark eyes were wide and slanted; Balthazar's equally black eyes were set straight on his face, narrowed as if he always stared into the bright sunlight. His gaze was almost unnervingly direct. They shared an equal love of finery, Nakht observed, looking from Karomana's bright-orange robe to Balthazar's blue garment. Both robes were encrusted with gold embroidery and jewels.

Kheti moved closer to Nakht, his gray eyes glittering. "I feel like a peasant in my simple tunic."

Nakht's lips curved in a faint smile. "I'll have a suitably ornate garment made for you," he murmured. "What color would you like?"

"Perhaps red, to match my eyes after I leave this party."

Nakht smiled, and then turned his attention to Karomana and Balthazar.

"You're unharmed, Karomana?" Balthazar asked, taking her hands.

"Yes, are you not grieved?" Karomana answered softly, withdrawing her hands. "Weni was your victim, not I. I expect you to replace her."

"Choose another slave of your liking," Balthazar said curtly. He turned to Kheti and Nakht, saying, "I'm sorry our guests witnessed such unpleasantness."

"There are more pleasant sights than poisoned slaves falling at my feet," Nakht said coolly, "but I don't shock easily."

"I hope your appetite is undisturbed," Karomana commented, "for the meal has been specially prepared—if the stupid kitchen slaves have followed directions."

The dancers were ready to perform, and Balthazar invited the gathering to be seated.

A man who had entered beside Balthazar took Karomana's arm as if to guide her to her place, but she quickly pulled away. "Keep your hands from my person," she snapped. Turning to Balthazar, she said, "Order Hamu never to touch me!" The orange plumes in her headdress trembled with her anger.

Balthazar's thick eyebrows lifted slightly. "Hamu, you heard her majesty," he said brusquely. He tried to take her arm, but she moved away from him, too. He shrugged and said, "Shall we make ourselves comfortable?"

Again Nakht and Kheti exchanged looks, as they wondered how comfort would be possible. The evening had taken a disconcerting turn. Battle lines seemed to have been drawn early, and although Karomana was queen, Kheti and Nakht wished to stay in the king's favor as well—a task that was growing more difficult each moment.

"Thank you," Nakht said smoothly. "I look forward to this evening's entertainment."

When Karomana was comfortably seated, she smiled up at Kheti. "Will you sit at my side?"

"Of course," he replied, feeling uneasy at the tone of her voice. He didn't miss Nakht's cautious look as he was seated beside Balthazar. Kheti kept his face serious and his manner formal but he, too, was becoming alarmed at Karomana's attention.

"Has your investigation of our soil been progressing to your satisfaction?" Balthazar asked curiously.

"So satisfactorily that I believe I can bring my report to King Amenemhet very soon," Kheti answered. "I've found no evidence the insects threatening Tamera's crops came from Kenset."

"I hear your conclusion with mixed feelings," Balthazar said. "While I'm glad we're not the cause of your problems, I almost wish we were so you might at least know the source of your trouble. Then we could work together to solve it."

"It isn't too serious yet," Kheti confided. "We're trying to take all precautions before it becomes an emergency. These little worms are insidious because the eggs they lay are under the soil and are invisible from the surface. It's a big task to have the farmers test each field by hand."

"We'll regret your leaving Kenset so soon. Have you found your stay a little pleasant?"

134

Kheti forced himself to smile. "Your hospitality has been generous, but I miss my family, so my feelings are also mixed."

"You've never spoken of your family," Balthazar said. He decided to ask Kheti about his wife and children. Balthazar was aware of his sister's interest in this Tameran noble, and he knew, if it was allowed to develop further, the situation could become politically awkward. He smiled warmly at Kheti and asked, "Is your wife beautiful? Tell us about your children."

Kheti's gray eyes softened. "We have three children, two sons and a daughter. Our firstborn, a son, we had the honor of naming after our king, who is our friend. Bekhat, our daughter, promises to grow as beautiful as her mother. Nakht, whom we named after the ambassador, is yet an infant."

"And Lady Neferset?" Balthazar prompted.

"Neferset was a princess of Atalan," Nakht said slowly.

"The island kingdom that recently sank?" Karomana's eyes widened. She had heard some strange stories about Atalan, but she had thought the kingdom a fable until recently, when its survivors had come to Tamera for refuge.

"Yes, that is the place," Kheti said sadly. "Neferset's parents were lost. She has only her brother, who brought the rest of his people to Tamera." Kheti's eyes darkened at the memory of the day the ships had landed at Ithtawe.

"Your wife is close to your heart?" Balthazar asked softly.

"Neferset is my heart," Kheti replied.

"She's beautiful?" Balthazar was determined his sister hear it all.

Kheti smiled. "She's a goddess, with her cat's eyes so gray and serene; but when she's stirred, they become the color of the Great Green Sea."

"Is it true, as I have heard gossip, that her hair is white in color?" Karomana couldn't resist asking, and she leaned forward slightly, waiting curiously for Kheti's answer.

"Neferset has the most unusual hair I've seen," Nakht put in. "It isn't white, but silver as the moonlight."

"The lady Neferset sounds most beautiful," Balthazar noted. He was satisfied that this discussion of Kheti's wife affected Karomana. He knew she was agitated and trying to hide it. "Ah," Balthazar turned to face the room, "the dancers arrive."

"Azza!" Karomana said sharply. "Get my fan bearer. This room is very warm."

Azza bowed low and hurried away. She knew her mistress' mood and would warn the fan bearer to do his job efficiently.

Kheti glanced at Nakht, but he was engaged in conversation with Balthazar. Kheti's eyes narrowed as he studied them, wondering what they discussed. He sighed, concluding from the expression on his friend's face that he was now practicing his profession. Nakht had come to Kenset for more than a discussion of worms and insects. He was striving to lay the groundwork for a treaty, and he seemed to be pressing forward—at least with Balthazar.

Kheti wondered how much authority Balthazar really had, since Karomana seemed more powerful. If Balthazar had really tried to kill his half sister, why did she not bring open charges? Perhaps Balthazar had too many friends in court. Alas, he didn't really understand the workings of the court in Kenset—he barely understood the rudiments of protocol in Tamera. His nature wasn't inclined to love the rigidity of any court rules, but he resolved to be scrupulously formal in Kenset. With Karomana looking at him with desire in her eyes, he dared not be anything but cold. Drawing himself straighter, he turned his attention to the dancers.

A dozen girls wearing carefully draped but very abbreviated robes walked with short steps to the left, bent in a swooping movement, then gracefully straightened and turned. Kheti watched with growing interest. The dancers's garments were semitransparent, and he studied the moving shadows of their bodies. The dancers pivoted and swayed, their skirts floating like clouds in a gentle breeze. Noting Kheti's interest in the slaves, Karomana frowned.

When the last notes of the lyres faded, Balthazar told Nakht, "That dance is a favorite of mine. I arranged to have them perform it tonight."

Karomana lifted her plumed head and said coldly, "The layers of clothes they wear conceal whatever grace they possess. It seems to me their skills—if they have any—are few, for they merely walk and turn in rhythm."

"I thought our guests might find them most amusing," Balthazar said.

"I am not amused," she replied. "I'd wager they've seen more interesting dancers in Tamera." She turned to Kheti, who said nothing.

136

"Lord Kheti, what kind of dancers do you prefer?" she prodded.

Kheti smiled politely and replied, "It depends on the occasion." He lifted his goblet and sipped his wine, hoping Karomana wouldn't pursue the subject.

Balthazar leaned forward. "We're having an event early tomorrow morning," he announced. "Perhaps our guests would be interested in participating in it."

"What event is that?" Karomana asked quickly. She disliked being left out of any function, however insignificant.

"A hunt for an old lion, who has evidently grown too feeble to stalk his natural quarry. We're going to hunt him out because several villagers have been killed and others maimed." He turned to Karomana. "Would you like to hunt this lion, sister?"

Karomana's dark eyes were brilliant and cold as the jewels she wore. "I won't chance another accident," she answered curtly, then added in a threatening tone, "I will not *tolerate* another accident."

Balthazar seemed unconcerned by her implication. He looked at Lord Kheti.

"Will you come? It's an exciting sport, as well as being necessary."

Kheti smiled in anticipation. "I've never hunted a lion."

"How is the hunt conducted?" Nakht inquired.

"With dogs and slaves to drive the lion out with noise while we wait with spears in our chariots," Balthazar answered.

"I'd like to join this hunt," Kheti said, leaning forward to see past Karomana and Balthazar to ask, "And you, Nakht?"

"I'm not as addicted to dangerous sports as you," Nakht replied with a faint smile, "but it sounds interesting."

"Don't feel you must," Balthazar cautioned. "I don't want you to think you must if you don't wish to."

Kheti chuckled. "The ambassador is as fond of danger as I," he said. "The only risk he declines is that of marriage."

Nakht smiled. "Being unmarried is convenient for my profession."

Balthazar laughed easily. "You think as I do," he said. "Lion hunts I enjoy. Marriage still dismays me."

"Does marriage require such courage?" Karomana looked at Kheti as if she expected him to answer.

Kheti turned to meet her eyes and said solemnly, "Not if the lady concerned is Neferset."

137

Karomana dropped her eyes and turned away, not fully able to conceal the jealousy burning in their dark depths.

The slave Azza carefully removed Karomana's headdress, fearing her mistress' anger should she pull even one hair. When Karomana suddenly arose, Azza leaped away.

Karomana quickly walked across the room, throwing off her robe as she went. "I hate her!"

"Who, mistress?" Azza asked cautiously.

"That woman with her green eyes and silver hair," Karomana snapped, throwing herself into a chair. She tapped the fabric of a cushion with her long nails and added in a whisper, "I hate her!"

Azza said nothing, thinking it was safer to remain silent.

"But I have in mind a way to defeat her," Karomana added thoughtfully.

"Yes, mistress. I'm sure you have a plan that will work to your satisfaction," Azza agreed, wondering what Karomana had in mind.

"You will make it work to my satisfaction," Karomana said, looking at Azza appraisingly.

"I? But what can I do?"

"You will be the heart of the plan, my faithful Azza," Karomana replied. "Lord Kheti, it seems, will look at no woman—not even me—as long as his lady lives." She lifted her eyes to regard Azza and said, "You will go to Ithtawe with Lord Kheti as a gift for Lady Neferset. At your first opportunity, you'll kill her."

"Mistress . . ." Azza began reluctantly.

"You'll decide how to do it, but I'll make sure you have many choices." Karomana rose and took Azza's hands tightly in hers. She squeezed Azza's fingers painfully as she added in a sweet tone, "You *are* loyal to me, aren't you, Azza?"

Azza's eyes watered with pain, but that was nothing compared to Karomana's veiled threat. She knew of others sent to do Karomana's bidding who had failed, and though they were great distances from Kenset's borders, had died torturous deaths. Whether their ends had been caused by one of Karomana's network of agents or by a curse leveled on them by Urum, the sorcerer, who schemed for power with Karomana, she didn't know. She only knew they had died unexpectedly and horribly. Fear traced an icy finger down her spine to think of it.

Yes, mistress, I will do whatever you ask," Azza breathed.

Karomana gave Azza's fingers one more painful squeeze to emphasize her next words: "You know you must." Then she released Azza and reseated herself, gesturing that the slave might now remove her jewelry. As Azza went about her task, Karomana's eyes were thoughtful. When Azza had finished, Karomana stood up to let Azza undress her.

"Do you still think of that lover who was denied you when you were taken from your village and put in my service?" Karomana asked quietly.

Azza dared not reply that she was less than happy as Karomana's personal attendant. She remained silent while she wondered how to answer.

Karomana read the longing in her slave's eyes and heard Azza's silent answer. "If you succeed in killing Lady Neferset, I will reward you with freedom. You'll be able to return to your village, your family—and your lover," Karomana said softly.

Azza's heart struggled up from the depths of her fear. "Mistress, you would allow me to leave?" she asked incredulously.

Knowing that Azza would do anything to be reunited with her lover, Karomana replied, "You have everything to gain by accomplishing what I wish—and everything to lose if you fail. You won't fail, will you, Azza?"

"I won't fail, mistress," Azza whispered.

Kheti turned at the knock on his door. "Who's there?" he called. Hearing no answer, he shrugged. "Enter!"

Nakht came in, his lean body wrapped in a loose robe.

Kheti smiled. "Are you trying to tempt a woman into sharing your bed tonight?" Nakht looked confused, and Kheti explained, "You're walking through the corridors wearing only that?"

Nakht fastened his robe more securely. "Just thirty paces from my room to yours. And what assassin do you expect?"

Kheti glanced down at the lances he held. "I was deciding which ones would be most suitable for tomorrow's hunt." He laid down the weapons. "It's better for me to choose now while I'm alert rather than in the morning when I'm still drowsy."

"You'd better not be drowsy to hunt a lion," Nakht declared.

"I won't be," Kheti replied. He gestured to his servant and

indicated a small pile of lances. "I'll take these, Senti." Then he turned to Nakht. "Why have you come at this hour?"

"To warn you," Nakht replied. Seeing Kheti's surprised expression, he added, "Queen Karomana desires you, you know." Kheti began to protest, but Nakht held up a hand. "I don't know why she wants you when I'm here, but it appears she does. I advise you to stay away from her if you're tempted. The situation is precarious, and our treaty depends on a sensitive touch."

"Surely you know me better!" Kheti exclaimed. "I have no interest in Karomana."

Nakht sat on the edge of the bed and ran a hand through his thick black hair. "It's what I'd hoped you'd say, but I had to allow you to say it. The struggle between Karomana and Balthazar is deadly. I'm afraid to get involved, even accidentally, in some incident between them."

"I think you favor Karomana's survival."

Nakht's eyes didn't waver. "Her slenderness gives her an appearance of delicacy, but make no mistake, Kheti. Whips are also slender." As he watched Senti gathering the lances, he murmured, "Kenset's palace is beautiful, but these people have a long way to go from savagery." His eyes moved to Kheti. "If killing her brother worries Karomana not at all, how much do you think your marriage bothers her?

"Does none of this upset you?" Kheti asked. "You speak of possible murders as calmly as if we discuss tomorrow's weather."

"This steaming climate bothers me more than the morality of Kenset's rulers." Nakht stood up and walked to the window opening. "I'm not dismayed by Karomana and Balthazar because I've seen such struggles in other lands. And the treaty would be beneficial to Tamera whether it's signed by Karomana or by her brother. Personally, I think Balthazar would be easier to deal with. I want to get this treaty signed on my next visit to Kenset. Meanwhile, let us both be careful to avoid even the slightest indication that we are taking sides in their politics."

"Tamera is known for certain standards of conduct, which we will observe," Kheti replied.

Nakht stepped away and smiled grimly. "Be very careful tomorrow and we'll be on our way the following morning." He walked to the door, saying over his shoulder, "Will Senti come with you on the hunt?"

The servant paused, listening for Kheti's answer.

140

"Who else could handle Shemes if I need to throw a lance?" Kheti asked. "Would I place my trust in one of Balthazar's slaves?"

"Even if you could, I doubt one of them could control that horse," Nakht replied. "Sleep well, Kheti."

"Amid these plots and poisonous insects?"

"So far, we're outside the plots," Nakht said, his hand resting on the door handle. "Just make sure the net around your bed is in place to keep out the insects."

"Will the net keep out Karomana?"

"If she comes, refer her to me," Nakht replied with a grin. "I'll negotiate with her."

Kheti gave him a look of mock disgust. "Go to bed," he said sternly.

In the morning Kheti met Nakht as he walked to the courtyard from the stables, where he had inspected his chariot and left Senti overseeing the stableboys preparing his equipment. The air lay as heavily as a wet carpet over them, and Nakht coughed frequently.

"This climate is unendurable to me," he finally said. "I cannot adjust my body to it however I try. I feel as if my head has a bronze band tightening around it, and all my bones ache."

"If they didn't have this rain and damp, the place would be a desert," Kheti noted as he looked at the jungle waiting beyond the palace walls. "It's going to be hot today."

"In Kenset it's nothing but hot," Nakht grumbled.

"There's Balthazar and Karomana waiting for us," Kheti warned.

"Are your servants so lazy you must prepare your own chariots?" Balthazar asked as they approached.

Kheti took offense at this, but remained silent.

Nakht smiled and answered, "The servants are energetic enough. We merely like to personally check everything—especially for a lion hunt."

"We don't want anything going wrong at such a time," Kheti said grimly, "particularly since this lion enjoys human flesh."

"You're wise," Karomana conceded. "I wouldn't wish to see you carried back torn and bloody."

"Are you going to accompany us, after all?" Nakht asked, hoping she was not.

141

"No," Karomana answered. "I've come to wish you well, and I've brought Azza with some wine to enjoy before you leave. It's deliciously cool, and you'll find the memory of it refreshing when you're in the jungle with nothing but tepid water to drink."

Nakht accepted the goblet and looked at it suspiciously.

Karomana smiled. "Have no fear. The wine will be poured for all of us from the same jar. The poisoner would poison himself, if he'd tampered with this wine." Karomana watched the red liquid fill her cup, then lifting it high, said, "May your lances fly true and may you return safely." Without hesitation, she took several swallows. "You see, Balthazar?" she said. "I drink the same wine you have in your goblet."

Balthazar, who had been watching Karomana closely, shrugged and lifted his cup. "May we return with all but the lion uninjured."

They turned to watch the arrival of the other hunters, and Kheti wondered if they were preparing for a lion hunt or a war as he counted the chariots drawing into the courtyard. It seemed an army would accompany them.

Karomana made a remark, but her voice couldn't be understood in the noise, and after another attempt to make herself heard, she turned to a nearby slave and gave him a meaningful look. He leaped off the palace steps and raced between the chariots shouting for silence.

When the turmoil had ceased, Karomana said nothing, though her expression seemed satisfied.

Balthazar had been studying Kheti's chariot, and he turned to Kheti with a perplexed look. "You use only one horse for your chariot?" he asked. "We use a pair or sometimes even three."

Kheti smiled. "Sometimes Shemes is worth three other horses to me."

"That's no mere horse," Nakht declared. "He's the reincarnation of the messenger of Ra."

"Shemes is swift of foot, then?" Balthazar studied the animal with even more interest.

"Like a gazelle," Kheti said proudly. "What's even better, Shemes is easily controlled."

"By you and Senti, but no one else!" Nakht exclaimed.

"That can be a useful trait in a horse," Balthazar commented. "He's a fine animal."

"He should be," Kheti said. "He comes from King Amenemhet's own stable. Neferset had Commander Nessumontu choose him for me personally."

"Shemes was a gift to Neferset from the king?" Karomana wondered what Neferset had done for the king to earn such a prize.

"Actually, this chariot was my gift from my wife," Kheti said. "King Amenemhet and Queen Nefrytatanen gave Shemes to Neferset to pass on to me along with it."

A servant approached with a worried look. "Highness, everything is ready," he said bowing low.

"And the sun continues its ascent," Karomana added. She stepped away. "Bring back the lion," she said, climbing the steps to avoid the dust when they rode away.

Nakht got into his chariot beside his servant, Bak. Although it was customary to ride alone in a small chariot on a dangerous hunt, it was necessary to have an extra pair of hands ready to control the horse while the lance was being aimed. Lions seldom gave one an opportunity to use a second lance, and immediate flight was often required.

"It's a good thing I brought my light chariot along," Nakht said.

Bak agreed and added, "I wouldn't want to have to borrow one of theirs."

"Nor I," Nakht said vehemently. "I might choose one of Balthazar's and find my axle sawed through."

Bak chuckled and gripped the chariot's side tightly as they began their ride.

After an hour of traveling, they neared the area where the lion had been reported to sleep during the day's heat. It was a plain, waving with tall grass the tawny color of a lion, and studded with rocks.

"This is fine cover for a lion," Kheti remarked.

Senti nodded, scanning the concealing grasses with a sharp eye.

The chariots were arranged in a long, single line, and the drivers waited while boys with dogs and torches circled the far end of the plain. In the distance, the figures of the beaters had disappeared in the tall weeds, and their progress could be followed only by watching the movements of the grass.

The hunters spotted the torches being lit one by one. The flames were low, since the wood had been well coated with thick resin, which smoldered, giving up a heavy black smoke and a peculiar smell. It was an odor from which lions fled.

If the dogs and the smoke weren't sufficient, noisemakers

143

were depended upon to drive the lion from his hiding place. A swarm of slaves were employed for this task. They carried every conceivable instrument which could be rattled or pounded. To this they added their own wails and shrieks, which were inspired by fear and considerable in volume.

Kheti wiped his brow while he waited impatiently in the hot sun. He glanced at Nakht and saw the shine on his forehead; he wondered how Nakht could spend his life traveling from one land to another, joining impromptu hunts and whatever other activities the respective rulers enjoyed, however hazardous or even distasteful to him. Kheti's thoughts were interrupted by the sudden outbreak of screams, howls and drumming of the noisemakers. The dogs began to bark in earnest. The chariots started forward slowly. The hunt began.

They were almost to the center of the plain before the lion finally broke cover. A nervous charioteer, coming too close to a rock heap, ran one wheel over the stones and tilted his vehicle precariously. Hearing the others shout that the lion was charging, he panicked and tried to whip his horses forward, hoping his wheel would be freed by the sudden jerk. The wheel fell off instead, and the chariot dragged through the stones until the harness snapped and the chariot collapsed on its side in a cloud of dust.

The lion veered and rushed toward the wreck as the driver and his helper ran shrieking with fear. The lion raced after the driver, bringing him down in a leap. Kheti could see the rapid motion of the lion's hind legs as he clawed the man, then leaped away to rush after the other, who screamed in desperation.

Kheti grimaced and pulled his chariot from the line and motioned for Nakht to follow. They anticipated the others would soon be trapped in a tangle of disorganized turning. By the time Kheti had turned his chariot, the lion had pulled down his luckless quarry. Kheti noticed that Balthazar had also foreseen a traffic jam and had acted quickly. One other chariot had turned and begun toward the lion, while the remaining vehicles were trapped in a welter of confusion.

The lion might have escaped had he merely clawed the second man as he had done the first, but he delayed his flight to gnaw on the other victim. As the chariots approached, he dropped the man and turned to stare at his pursuers with yellow eyes. His attention was attracted by the bright-orange robe Balthazar wore.

When Kheti saw the lion swerve toward Balthazar, he gave

144

his reins to Senti and lifted a lance, intending to allow Balthazar the first chance.

Having given Hamu the reins, Balthazar poised his spear in readiness. Suddenly his face turned pale. The spear had no point! He dropped the weapon and reached for another. It too was useless!

Another chariot that had followed raced forward to cut between the lion and Kheti, who had drawn back his arm. Kheti cursed, halting his spear. The man in the intervening chariot let fly his lance with so feeble an effort Kheti's mouth fell open in amazement. The shaft struck the lion's flank harmlessly and fell away.

In the moment gained, Balthazar had searched frantically for a lance with a head and, finding none, held his lance case upside down in frustration, spilling the useless shafts in the weeds.

The double-harnessed horses of the other chariot ran over them, and several shafts were kicked up between their legs. One horse stumbled, and his hindquarters sank. The other horse, terrified by the beast, which crouched nearby in momentary indecision, screamed and reared. The chariot lurched and crashed on its side, and its occupants fell out the open back. In one motion, the lion rose, turned and sprang with a roar.

Unable to get around the empty chariot, Kheti watched, frustrated with helplessness. He spotted Nakht, who leaped from his chariot and ran straight toward the lion. The beast was so crazed with the excitement of finishing his victim he ignored Nakht, until Nakht's lance was deep into his shoulder.

Senti, Bak and Hamu dragged the lion off the man, who had become no more recognizable than the carcass of an ibex. Balthazar watched silently, looking pale and ill.

"It's unfortunate three men had to die before this lion met his end," Kheti said slowly.

Balthazar's black eyes lifted. "It was unfortunate," he agreed. His face held many emotions, but none of them was sympathetic. He said nothing about his lances, but instead turned to Nakht and said quietly, "If you hadn't interferred, I would be dead. It seemed as if all the gods were against me."

"You're alive," Nakht replied. "One of them was in your favor."

"The god of Tamera," Balthazar murmured and turned away.

145

Nakht settled back on the couch and sipped his wine while he watched Bak packing. He was relieved it was Bak who must make order from the confusion of the room. He was also relieved they were leaving Kenset early in the morning. He was weary from the pressure of watching his every word and controlling each expression and gesture. How he would welcome the freedom of Tamera, he thought, and sighed. Hearing a soft knock at his door, he moaned in disgust.

Bak looked up and, seeing his master nod, put down the garment he had been folding and went to the door.

Kheti entered the room, and Nakht's face brightened. "Have a cup of wine," he invited. "And sit down—unless tonight you are searching for a woman."

Kheti glanced down at his abbreviated tunic and grinned. "I walked very quickly from my room," he replied, taking the wine Bak offered. "Thank you, Bak." Observing the confusion of the room, Kheti chuckled. "You're a messy bachelor, Nakht."

Nakht laid his head back against a cushion. "You should have seen how it looked before Bak began packing!"

"It was worse?" Kheti's eyes widened.

Nakht laughed easily. "Have you come to inspect my quarters, or is something else on your mind?"

Kheti smiled sheepishly. "I thought to escape the mess in my own chamber." His smile faded as he said slowly, "I also wanted to learn what you thought about today's hunt. That man drove his chariot between me and the lion at a most opportune moment—for the lion."

"I noticed that," Nakht agreed, "and although Kenset may lack in many advantages to our thinking, every man here learns how to throw a lance with great skill while he's yet a child."

Kheti nodded. "But I've seen Prince Senwadjet throw a straighter lance than that man! Even Princess Maeti has a truer eye!"

"The prince and princess also have truer hearts, I suspect," Nakht remarked drily. "It's too bad that man got his head chewed off by the lion. I think Balthazar had many questions to ask him."

"Then you think as I do—that he was part of a plan?"

"If his had been the only questionable move, I'd be uncertain. But I'm sure all Balthazar's lance tips didn't fall off by accident." Nakht's eyes dropped to his arm, and he slapped it. "These accursed insects!" he exclaimed. "Pull down the

146

window hangings, Bak! The vicious creatures will strip our flesh from our bones as we converse." He watched Bak hurriedly secure the protective hangings, then again turned to Kheti. "I don't doubt somewhere in the palace at this very moment there's a lively discussion going on between Karomana and Balthazar. I was thankful to have my evening meal in my room."

"And I," Kheti agreed. "Last night Balthazar tried to poison Karomana, and today she schemed to kill him."

"I hope tomorrow's attempt will come after we've left." Nakht sighed. "I wonder which of them will survive for me to negotiate with. I prefer to deal with Balthazar, but I dislike seeing so beautiful a woman murdered." He looked up at Kheti. "It's difficult for me to plan my next visit."

"It's more difficult for them to plan their futures," Kheti observed. "I'm glad I won't have to return. The next time soil samples need to be taken in Kenset, I'll recommend sending Taka."

Nakht nodded in agreement. "I wish I could send someone in my place."

"I'm finished packing," Bak announced.

"You deserve congratulations," Kheti muttered.

"Never leave my employ," Nakht said fervently. "I would disappear under a mountain of soiled laundry. Prepare yourself for bed if you wish, Bak. I'll soon retire as well."

Kheti rose from his chair and set down his goblet. "I too am tired, so I'll leave now. Sleep well, Nakht."

"Secure the netting carefully," Nakht warned. "You don't want those ferocious insects assailing you during the night."

Kheti turned at the door. "I don't intend to carry a pestilence home." His gray eyes gleamed as he added, "I also want to be in excellent health when I return to Neferset."

Karomana's eyes narrowed in the morning sun, and she turned blinking from the window opening to face Azza. "The day will be a fine one to begin a journey. I consulted the star diviner, and he said anything begun today has an excellent chance for a successful conclusion."

"Yes, mistress," Azza murmured.

Thinking again of the task Karomana had set for her, Azza lowered her eyes. She had killed one of the soldiers who had dragged her from her home and raped her before she was put into slavery, but she had never contemplated murdering anyone. But remembering Karomana's far-reaching pun-

147

ishment of those who had failed to obey the queen's orders in the past, Azza again was plunged into fear.

Karomana came closer and lifted Azza's chin with a finger, giving her a long, silent stare. Finally she said, "Don't look so gloomy, Azza. Remember the reward I've promised. Think of how happy you'll be when you return to your family and your lover—as a free woman."

The thought of freedom helped lessen Azza's fear. The Tameran woman's life became less significant when it was placed on the scale beside Azza's own future. She thought of the alternative—a lingering death either by mutilation at the hands of one of Karomana's agents or because of her sorcerer Urum's curse. Karomana was right when she had said Azza had everything to gain—or lose.

"You said you would offer me some means to kill Lady Neferset, mistress?" Azza asked.

Karomana walked slowly to a cabinet and brought out a small ivory box. "In this container, Azza, I have assembled a number of items you could use. I prefer you not use the dagger unless necessary. I don't want to give a Tameran physician time to come to Neferset's aid. Since I have no more of the poison I used on Weni, I prefer you not to use the kind I've included. It takes too long and it may allow time for an antidote to be administered. I have put both methods in this box only to be used if no other way seems possible. My first choice is that Neferset's death appear to be accidental, so that Lord Kheti would have no reason to seek a murderer, and possibly discover your guilt and consequently my own."

Karomana took from around her own neck a necklace made of black stone beads and silver strips. "I've had this talisman made so the gods will arrange an opportunity for Neferset's 'accidental' death, a talisman that will keep your mission a secret," Karomana explained as she dropped the necklace over Azza's head. "Keep it under your garments so no one may see and, perhaps, suspect its purpose."

"Thank you, mistress," Azza replied.

Karomana put the ivory box into Azza's hands, then reached up to slip Azza's hood over her hair. "Lord Kheti and Ambassador Nakht should be almost ready to leave. We'd better go out now," she said.

Kheti and Nakht were already mounted when Karomana brought Azza into the courtyard. After appropriate good wishes and farewells had been exchanged, Karomana approached Kheti. The hard brightness in her eyes made him uneasy when she looked up at him.

"I was much impressed by what you told me of your land, and I hope to visit Tamera one day," Karomana said clearly. "So you don't forget this journey to Kenset, I wish to give you something to take home with you."

"That isn't necessary," Kheti said quickly. "I won't forget this visit."

"Truly, you have seen unpleasantness which you'll surely remember," Karomana admitted. "It's my desire to give you something which will be pleasant, so I offer Azza to bring back to your lady. Azza will serve me by serving you."

"You're too generous . . ." Kheti began.

"I'll hear no protest," Karomana insisted. "Azza is yours. Bring her back someday when you visit again." Karomana stepped away. "I wish you a pleasant and safe journey," she said firmly.

Kheti rode out of the courtyard at Nakht's side. "Farewell, Kenset," he whispered sarcastically. He turned to look at Azza, who rode behind them. "I think you'll like Tamera," he said cheerfully. "I *know* you'll like Lady Neferset," he added.

"Yes, master," Azza said, lowering her eyes.

Eleven

Ilbaya moved swiftly up a slope of a ridge. He stepped onto a tuft of grass and smiled at the pleasant sensation of its blades curling cool and damp against his toes. He glanced at the slowly brightening eastern sky. The growing golden light made a fiery sheen on his hair, but his eyes lost their shadows, becoming amber sprinkled with green flecks.

Dawn came to Tamera like the Nile's flood, Ilbaya observed. Even in the south, where the climate was comparable to the desert, the dawn was cool and the river generous. Both were like gifts from a benevolent god. The river god brought water and rich soil every year, and the sun god gave warmth and light each day as predictably as the stars rose and fell. Ilbaya sighed. Rainfall and sunshine had been more capricious in Minoa.

Recalling his home brought a bitterness to his mouth, and he made a deliberate effort to turn his mind from Minoa. He resumed his walk at a faster pace, hoping to dissipate his memories even as he expended energy.

At the end of the ridge, where it dropped abruptly into a steep slope, Ilbaya paused to gaze out over the valley. Although he was only a short distance from the caravan, he realized he might as well be alone. He inhaled the fresh, clean air, drinking deeply of the delicious feeling of freedom his solitude brought.

As the silent countryside waited patiently for its awakening, Ilbaya sat on the damp grass and drew his thin cloak more comfortably around his shoulders. He pondered the strange route Marmarus' caravan had taken to reach Tamera. After leaving Zahi, instead of continuing west to Tamera to enter by its north border, Marmarus had hired a ship to take the whole caravan of slaves south into the Narrow Sea almost to Kenset, an expensive and far more roundabout route, which required the slaves to walk across the eastern desert before even reaching a city where he could do business. Then he had finally turned them north to follow the Nile's many curvings. Ilbaya smiled with bittersweet triumph to remember how little business Marmarus had done in the cities where they had stopped. The Tamerans seemed reluctant to buy Marmarus' slaves, so he had made very little profit so far.

Idly, Ilbaya recalled a large house the caravan had paused at, Marmarus hoping to sell slaves to the prosperous nobleman living there, only to be turned away. The house had been similar in design to Ilbaya's father's house in Minoa; Ilbaya had stared through the partly opened gate to the garden, hungrily catching glimpses of the sparkle of a fountain, flashes of flowers, the rich fragrance of the evening meal being cooked. On a balcony, a white-robed girl had stood dreaming in the sun, and Ilbaya recalled her graceful form, the shadow of her long legs under the thin fabric of her garment. Her hair was long and black, gleaming like polished onyx in the light, and she wore a blue flower twined in its strands. Her face was a delicate profile as she looked toward the distant hills, and Ilbaya wondered absently if she, too, had dreams of escaping from something.

Ilbaya sighed. Tamerans—especially those who lived in such houses—had no need to escape. The stories he had heard of the fertility of the Two Lands had not been exaggerated, he had discovered as the caravan had traveled north. He doubted hunger was a problem here. Most of the crops were being harvested now, and he had noticed great heaps of produce waiting to be gathered. Lush green and gold seemed to be the colors of Tamera, all under a sky so blue it rivaled the Aegean Sea. It was ironic that Marmarus' near-starved slaves should have to pass through such a land and yet be so poorly fed.

Ilbaya's lips curved in another bitter smile. He had always

dreamed of traveling to other lands, had spent hours trying to imagine the adventure in exploring new places, but he had never thought his journeys would be forced.

So far, Ilbaya reflected, he had managed to hide his inner rebellion from Marmarus. Normally, he was an impulsive man and it hadn't been easy to control each expression that passed his face, to be careful of each word he said and the way he said it. But by pretending to be a good-natured, even sometimes simpleminded clown, he had earned Marmarus' trust. Now Marmarus allowed him a certain amount of freedom of movement, but Ilbaya never took advantage of it.

He was waiting for an opportunity to escape, and he was determined it would be a success this time. He couldn't endure again being hunted down, dragged back and punished. He hadn't been born to be beaten to his knees. He had been taught to stand upright, educated to think and make decisions. He had been trained to give orders.

"If I had a gold piece, I would offer it to know what you're thinking."

Ilbaya turned quickly. Lyra stood a few paces behind him. Although he knew that his feelings for her made even casual friendship dangerous and he was cautious to keep his facade intact when in her presence, he also felt sympathy for her because she was Marmarus' concubine. He knew she was very lonely, and each time he thought of his sisters, no doubt in the same situation, he knew he would want them to find a friend with whom to pass a moment of conversation now and again. Ilbaya smiled and waved for Lyra to approach.

"Your hair is gold enough for me," he replied softly in Greek.

"I've taught you my language well if you can compliment me so gracefully in it," Lyra replied, coming nearer.

Alarm flashed into his eyes, but was as quickly hidden.

"You don't have to be afraid of me. I've known for some time you pretend dullness." Ilbaya's face was tense and watchful as Lyra continued, "I never told you, but I'm also more than Marmarus knows. It's a part I play, looking stupid when I'm with him. You're a clown and I a harlot, and Marmarus believes our acting." She paused, her eyes cold with the necessary insult she lived. "I know what you are because I saw the intelligence in your eyes and recognized the way you carried yourself from the first. When you weren't yet used to humility, your disguise slipped in a relaxed moment.

153

But don't worry. Your acting has improved since then, and Marmarus never noticed your finer points."

Ilbaya sighed. "You're better at this pretense than I. I never guessed it of you."

"Maybe I've had more practice at humiliation. When my opportunity comes, I'll escape just as you plan to." She sat in the grass beside him, her chin on her knees, and, with her gray eyes staring at the golden hills, murmured, "It's easier for you to gain trust in your position. However stupid he thinks I am, my situation makes him more watchful."

Ilbaya was silent as he thought about Lyra's confession. Finally he asked, "What would you do if you could escape?"

"Go home if I can." Her clear eyes turned to him. "If that isn't possible, I'll do what is possible." She looked at the horizon again. The sun's rim had begun to show. "Tamera seems a more agreeable place than many I've been," she observed.

"I wouldn't mind staying here," Ilbaya said softly. "I would gain nothing by returning to Minoa. There's no way I can win back my place there."

"Home is a place you love, not necessarily where you were born," Lyra whispered. Seeing Ilbaya's mouth settle into a grim line, she was silent a moment. Wanting to change the subject, she suddenly said, "Tamera grows many lovely flowers."

Ilbaya followed Lyra's gaze to a bright-yellow bloom near his feet. He reached out and plucked the blossom carefully. He could feel her smile on him. The flower was translucently golden in the light, as if the sun were gathering in its cup. He offered its magic to her.

Looking into the bloom, Lyra saw its heart was filled with dew, and lifting the fragile goblet to her lips, she sipped the shining nectar, sweet with the taste of morning and spiced lightly with pollen. Its petals were cool, sheer silk brushing her face. She looked up at Ilbaya in delight, her cheeks sprinkled with droplets of shining dew.

"Ilbaya, you'll reveal your true nature by doing such things," she said softly.

"It's this beautiful sunrise and your company that made me do that. I think it unlikely I'll give Marmarus or one of his guards a flower." He leaned back on his elbows to gaze at the sky. "Did you know the people here worship the sun?"

"I could understand it," Lyra murmured. "It does seem like a benevolent spirit in this land."

"That was my very thought," Ilbaya said slowly. He was

silent for a moment. Then, with intensity, he whispered, "How can you endure Marmarus?"

Lyra's voice was brittle with restrained anger. "By remembering I'll survive. Many women have had to trade their bodies to survive, and I've seen those who called it marriage." She brushed a lock of unruly hair from her eyes and turned to him. "Do you think I enjoy it? I do not. My body remains unsatisfied." She lay back on the grass with a sigh. "That's the evil of such a life. The shame and humiliation is misery enough, but it's especially painful that my passion is never fulfilled. I'm a thing to Marmarus, because I have no choice. I'm not a woman with him."

Ilbaya nodded in understanding. "In a different way, I'm also a thing, not a man."

"You're more a man than Marmarus could dream of being," Lyra declared.

"I won't be a man until I'm free," Ilbaya said softly.

"I said I wanted to be able to choose. If I could, I would choose a man such as you."

Startled, Ilbaya turned to look at Lyra. She gave him no alluring glance. She lay looking at the brightening sky, her eyes as serene as a mountain lake. He leaned over her. Her eyes moved to meet his, and she smiled.

"Why are you so surprised, Ilbaya?" she asked calmly. "Has slavery so affected you that you no longer think of yourself as a lover?" He moved away and she sat up. "I'm not asking you for love, Ilbaya. Don't mistake my meaning. I'm only saying that if I could ask, I'd ask you."

Disconcerted, Ilbaya moved a little away and turned his gaze to the valley. "Slavery hasn't affected me that much. I understood your meaning, but you startled me." He continued to stare at the valley with unseeing eyes. "I haven't even touched a woman for a very long time." He paused, reflecting. "Surely you can see that such a statement—though it isn't an offer—would arouse my interest."

"Maybe I shouldn't have said it," she replied, her eyes dropping to the grass.

Ilbaya didn't know what to say. It was ironic that, though she was a concubine, she was too innocent to recognize just how deeply she stirred him.

Ilbaya brushed a golden curl back from her forehead. It felt like silk beneath his fingers, and when he moved his hand away, her perfume lingered on his fingertips.

"I tell you frankly, Lyra. My impulse to deny that interest

155

is fading quickly," he said softly. "Other feelings have come to me." He touched her arm experimentally and, running his fingertips lightly over her skin, discovered satin. "Maybe you're a thing in Marmarus' mind, but you've become a woman to me in this last moment." His face was tense as he added, "It isn't necessary for me to hurry back to the caravan."

Lyra stared at him, her breath quickening.

"Such things, I know, can't be decided by merely a glance and a few words," Ilbaya whispered. "Maybe a kiss would leave us both unmoved and settle the matter."

"I suspect it would accomplish the opposite," she murmured. She fell silent, watching him, considering. "If Marmarus should come upon us . . ." Her voice trailed off, leaving them with visions of their punishment. Then, with a ferocity that surprised him, she said, "I don't care what he'd do to me. If he killed me, I would die a woman—not a slave thing! I've decided, Ilbaya. I'd chance kissing you and whatever follows. What would your decision be?"

Ilbaya laid his hands on her shoulders, looking into her eyes with an intensity that made her tremble. His hands gripped her tightly, but she felt no discomfort, for his mouth on hers was warm and firm and she found herself pleasantly drowning in a flood of sensations she had never before known. When Ilbaya drew away, he was smiling.

"Do I have to ask what the kiss decided?" he whispered. Lyra shook her head. "You are certain, Lyra? I don't promise, even after only one more kiss, that I'll stop."

"I'm sure," she answered, eager to return to the warm circle of his arms.

Ilbaya took the golden flower from her fingers and glanced at it, surprised that she still held it. He laid the bloom carefully on the grass and lifted his eyes to hers. Then he put his arms around her, holding her close, doing nothing more than feeling her against him. In his firm, undemanding embrace, Lyra discovered a joy she had never before experienced.

"Lying with anyone would have angered me, but to find you in the weeds with this fool . . ." Marmarus' voice paralyzed them with fear. "Get up," he said harshly. "Untangle yourself from your lover. I have no intention of beating you as well. I'd only have to look at the scars on your body later." Marmarus' face twisted in a cruel smile. "But be assured, Lyra, that you'll regret this moment later." He ges-

156

tured to the men he had brought with him, and they dragged the stunned Ilbaya to his feet.

Lyra rose slowly. Beneath her lowered lashes gleamed a fury she dared not reveal. She wished that, if their discovery had been inevitable, the gods had delayed it for a longer time. Marmarus would never believe nothing more than a kiss had been shared. Ilbaya's punishment wouldn't be lessened, whatever she said. Her own punishment didn't occur to her.

"If I'd wanted to share you, I would have lent you to my friends," Marmarus said sharply, taking her arm in a painful grip. "Why do you think I've kept you? I could have gotten a high price for you in Avaris. If you're going to give me this kind of trouble, maybe after we leave Tamera, I'll sell you to a Hyksos."

Lyra's defiance ran out of her. Now she dared not raise her eyes—and reveal her terror. She could think of no worse fate than being owned by a man of Zahi, a Hyksos.

"You grow pale," Marmarus said softly. He turned to face Ilbaya, but spoke to the man holding him. "Take him back to our camp and bind him. If anyone else takes a liking to Lyra, I must give him cause for second thoughts."

Ilbaya knew there was no escape. If he managed to shake his guards loose, his flight would be permanently halted by an arrow or spear. The thought of being beaten again made his blood rise to violence, but he dared not show it.

Although Lyra walked quietly beside Marmarus, Ilbaya was aware of her silent fear, and he resolved to follow her example of courage. He restrained his fierce anger with a force that made him tremble, and in controlling this, his walk became stiff, his face flushed.

He watched while the stakes were being driven into the ground with an outward detachment that surprised him, but when a hand on his back forced him to his knees, he could no longer maintain his indifferent stance. His struggles were futile, though, for they already had his arms pinned uselessly, while someone tied his wrists and ankles to the stakes.

When the first blow came, Ilbaya turned his face to the side and, realizing there was no way to protect his eyes, silently prayed they'd be spared damage. Through his anguish he knew the added torment that his degradation was witnessed by Lyra. Marmarus, holding her tightly by the waist, forced her to watch.

Ilbaya stiffened his jaw, not allowing himself to cry out, although he couldn't prevent an occasional gasp escaping him. When he thought he would faint, the blows stopped, and Marmarus signaled that he be cut loose.

After Ilbaya had managed to drag himself to his knees, Marmarus waved the others aside, forcing Ilbaya to rise alone. For a moment, he remained crouching while he summoned the strength to finally rise swaying and dizzy to his feet. He held his head up, although his brain was swimming.

Lyra watched a line over Ilbaya's eyes drip blood. Hot tears began to run down her cheeks. She hated her weakness, because she knew it was her weeping Marmarus had sought.

Marmarus' soft laughter made Ilbaya glance in their direction. Focusing his eyes with an effort, Ilbaya saw Lyra weeping. Then his eyes dropped in shame and his head fell forward in surrender.

Lyra felt in herself the wrench of Ilbaya's pain. He had deliberately abandoned his own pride in the hope Marmarus, surfeited with triumph over him, would spare her. She wanted to tell Ilbaya she understood that the vile debasement hadn't touched his spirit, but she dared say nothing—for both their sakes.

When Ilbaya observed Marmarus' smug glance at the rest of the slaves, he knew his ruse had worked. Ilbaya was more angry, more defiant than he had ever been, but Marmarus saw only the droop of his shoulders, the shame and humiliation.

The guards were used to watching lines of slaves bound together by heavy ropes, but during the day's journey, even their sympathy was aroused by the sight of Ilbaya limping through dust clouds that choked men seated high up on the backs of camels.

Catching a glimpse of Ilbaya's dust-caked wounds, Lyra controlled her anger and continued to sit quietly beside Marmarus, staring at the road ahead. Although Ilbaya had behaved all day like a properly repentant slave, Lyra knew he was acting out a very difficult role. She watched him when they stopped to rest for brief intervals. His pain was openly reflected on his face. Although Lyra felt pity for his misery, she felt agony at his showing it. She knew he was so proud that the worst punishment of all was having to give Marmarus the satisfaction of seeing his pain.

Ilbaya avoided looking directly at anyone for more than a moment. He trudged along the dusty road, wincing with each step, his imagination playing vividly on the many things he would like to do to Marmarus. By the time the caravan halted for the night, Marmarus had suffered death in Ilbaya's thoughts a hundred times, and Ilbaya's temper had cooled sufficiently from his imagined satisfaction so that he could turn to more realistic plotting. He could not endure slavery for one more day, he decided.

Twelve

Amenemhet entered the golden room where he set his seal, and was surprised to find that the prime minister had not yet arrived. He wondered what could have delayed Meri. Walking slowly past the table that held his writing materials, he lifted his head to gaze at the garden beyond the door.

Ra was sending shafts of light through the date palms that stretched over the stone patio just ten paces from the door. The palms changed their shadows on the stone with whispering sounds which seemed to be luring him to share their shade.

Several workmen labored on the new pavilion Amenemhet had ordered, and they sang to distract themselves from the dull job of stacking limestone blocks. Their voices were a pleasant sound in the quiet air, and their song made Amenemhet smile, for the words concerned a man's hopes regarding a certain girl. Their song stopped abruptly, and was replaced by one of praise to Shesata, goddess of teachers and learning, surprising Amenemhet. It seemed more fitting for workmen to sing of girls and sweet wine, but as Senwadjet and Maeti came into view and headed straight for the workers, he understood the change.

The prince and princess were as curious as kittens, Amenemhet observed, as he watched them approach the unfinished pavilion. Now the workers would be plagued with questions. One of the men bent to pick up Maeti and set her on one of the blocks. Amenemhet noticed that her hair—which was supposed to hang in a single comfortable braid—was coming undone, and it wouldn't be long before she lost the ornament that held it together. He saw her shrug, as if she had read her father's thoughts, and raise a sun-browned arm to pull the ornament out in a gesture so like Nefrytatanen that Amenemhet chuckled aloud.

Senwadjet wasn't content merely to sit and watch. He leaped over a low pile of stones, ran a few cubits beyond, then turned to race and leap again. Amenemhet's heart lifted with pride. Senwadjet was strong and well coordinated for a child his age. When Senwadjet climbed to a slab of stone balanced precariously, Amenemhet watched intently, tempted to step outside and call to him, but he saw a worker put down his chisel and drag the protesting prince from his aerie, placing him safely on level ground.

Amenemhet's eyebrows rose. He could clearly hear Senwadjet's protest from across the garden. Did the child actually threaten the worker? Amenemhet pushed the door a little farther open. Senwadjet spoke of banishment? Amenemhet couldn't prevent his smile. Now Maeti slipped from her vantage place and drew Senwadjet a little away, perhaps advising him to show mercy to the worker, who was struggling to hide a smile. Senwadjet turned to the man, holding up his hand in an attitude of forgiveness, but Amenemhet could see the pardon carried a price. The worker ran a distracted hand through his hair, then brought Senwadjet a small stone tablet, a hammer and a chisel. Another workman painted figures on the stone, and when he was finished, Senwadjet studied the tablet and nodded reluctant approval. The prince waved in a gesture Amenemhet recognized as his own, and the workman dragged over a stone block. Another man spread a cloth on the stone, and Senwadjet sat down to chip solemnly at the stone with his hammer and chisel.

Amenemhet frowned. He was glad the children were healthy and had the intelligence to be curious and enterprising, but he was becoming concerned with Senwadjet's increasing arrogance. The boy was issuing orders a bit prematurely. Amenemhet had no wish to thwart Senwadjet's pride in his position, nor did he wish to smother Senwadjet's curiosity, but the prince needed discipline. Maeti usually seemed cooper-

162

ative and well-mannered, but Amenemhet knew that from behind those wide blue eyes, many a scheme was launched.

When Amenemhet heard the door behind him open, he turned slowly, his thoughts still lingering on his lively children, but his attention was caught by Prime Minister Meri's grim expression. Meri was accompanied by the minister of agriculture, and Taka's brown face appeared no happier then Meri's. This added to Amenemhet's dread, because Taka was a man who was in the habit of looking on the optimistic side.

"You enter with an expression that offers me little hope of cheer," Amenemhet remarked.

Taka's brown eyes met his king's without wavering. "Sire, I cannot yet be sure what to think," he said. "My face reflects a puzzled mind, not entirely pessimism. Will you hear Meri's report while I gather my thoughts?"

Amenemhet turned his attention to Meri, who looked worried. "What have you learned?"

Meri cleared his throat as he nervously looked at the scroll he carried but hadn't unrolled. "I can only relate what I've been told. According to the governors, we stand on the precipice of disaster, but, sire, I question if they exaggerate." Meri unrolled the papyrus and began to spread it on the table before the king.

"What is this?" Amenemhet muttered. Meri's information seemed always to have to come from various scrolls when it could be more quickly recited. Amenemhet closed his eyes. "Meri, can you not tell me? I place high value on a good memory."

Meri gave him a sideways look as he rerolled the papyrus. The king seemed unusually impatient this morning, he observed. He slipped the scroll neatly into its case. "It's curious that the complaints of crop failures come from provinces most distant from Ithtawe," Meri said slowly. "The governors claim they have worms and caterpillars as well as flying insects." Meri sighed. "Usually, we have one or two reports of this type, and such reports concern a particular kind of crop being attacked, usually where fields are close together. These reports are widely scattered. According to the minister of taxes, the governors say not only has barley been affected, but also wheat, flax, malt, vegetables—"

"Sire," Taka interrupted, ignoring Meri's glare, "it's not possible, or at least it's highly improbable, that these crops would all be affected at the same time."

"Why?" Amenemhet's eyes were like stones.

"What is enjoyed by one type of pest is ignored by another!" Taka exclaimed. "If all these crops truly are being attacked, we have hordes of as many kinds of creatures with which to contend."

"If that were true, what would we face?"

Taka went pale beneath his tan and said faintly, "Disaster, sire, of a magnitude Tamera has never before experienced."

Amenemhet sank into the chair behind his table and put his chin in his hands. "And these pests come from the borders of Tamera, it would seem, to work their way inward to the heart of the Two Lands." He stood up and paced impatiently before the window opening, striding stiffly like a lion trapped in a pit.

"If these reports are accurate, there will be nothing to harvest from these areas," Taka added. "Closer provinces will then be infested, and in two more seasons, we'll have nothing."

Amenemhet stopped pacing and looked out the doorway at Senwadjet and Maeti. "The governors have been silent for some time," he murmured. "I had hoped their ambition had been stifled. Now I wonder."

"Do you think some of them are trying to cause trouble?" Meri asked. "We must remember Governor Sarenput reported that the problems in his new province are as Petamen reported."

Amenemhet didn't answer. He turned to Taka. "How likely is it that these reports from provinces other than Sarenput's are true?"

"Such a thing is possible," Taka replied, lowering his eyes, "but I find it unlikely. Are you certain of Governor Sarenput?"

"Sarenput is one of the few governors I trust absolutely, which is one reason I named him in Petamen's place," Amenemhet snapped. He was silent a moment, then looked at Meri. "Say nothing of this trouble," he directed. Meri nodded, and Amenemhet turned to Taka. "I want you to take a journey, Taka.

"It will be said you go to confer with King Ami-enshi in Retenu as Kheti went to Kenset, but you will double back and quietly visit the troubled provinces—except Sarenput's—and inspect the fields," Amenemhet said. "You will not visit the houses of the governors unless someone recognizes you. Meri will give you a list of the provinces and crops affected. I wish you to return with your report before the beginning of Het-Hert. That gives you two months to learn what is happening."

"Yes, sire," Taka said immediately.

"Be ready to leave tomorrow night." Amenemhet's tone was sharp, and Taka bowed, then left quickly. Amenemhet faced Meri. "Queen Nefrytatanen has told me she's planning to take the test of Aset's high priestess. When she gains her wings, there will be a celebration, so you must start preparing for this event."

Meri's eyes widened. "Sire, you'll allow this?" he blurted.

"I cannot refuse her," Amenemhet admitted. The ivory handle of the brush in his hand snapped with a sharp sound. "Replace this with another," he said quietly.

Meri nodded and took the brush. He was stunned by the news that Nefrytatanen would risk her life and sanity in this test of her magical prowess, and Meri could see his king was much afraid.

"Sire," Meri said slowly, "Queen Nefrytatanen will surely win her wings in this test. Her power is awesome, and this achievement will bring her greater glory."

Amenemhet turned away. "She'll do it two decans hence. Send for the lords Sarenput, Semerkhet, Rakkor, Ankef, Hesyra, Nekhen, Saneha, and Setme. By the time they arrive, Kheti and Nakht should have returned from Kenset. The queen will then have finished her testing and they'll celebrate her victory with us."

"I'll send the messengers at once," Meri replied.

When Meri had gone, Amenemhet sank again into the chair and put his head in his hands. To think of what Nefrytatanen planned filled him with terror. He had tried many times to convince himself of her success; but he was chilled by the thought of Nefrytatanen's body lying in that coffinlike stone box in the pyramid's inner chamber as if she were dead for four days while her spirit flew to the afterworld.

Nefrytatanen's mother had been a worker-in-magic from Atalan, and Nefrytatanen might be even more powerful than her mother was, but Amenemhet wondered how she could bear to have the double stone doors of the pyramid close, leaving her alone in the silent black room without food or water, without light, for four days and nights. If Nefrytatanen couldn't make her body slow its processes almost to the point of death, if her body was somehow injured by her spirit's leaving, or if she couldn't reenter it, she would really die.

165

Amenemhet remembered vividly a priest he had once seen who had tried the same test and failed. The priest hadn't died, but death would have been merciful. He had emerged from the pyramid of Amenemhet's father with his mind shattered, his eyes blank with horror and his mouth loose and drooling. Amenemhet turned away from the memory. Nefrytatanen would succeed. She would return in triumph. Amenemhet arose from the chair slowly, his head aching.

In the garden he saw Nefrytatanen walking toward Senwadjet and Maeti. In her white garment, so light in weight that it floated on the breezes, she already seemed like a spirit. New fear chilled him. Perhaps the divine beings would love her too much to allow her to return from her test. No, the divine beings would be more compassionate than to steal her from the earth when the grass itself drew pleasure from the touch of her feet. Even the sky must become three shades deeper with the approach of night before it could match the color of her eyes. The sunlight seemed to caress her golden skin like a lover, and Amenemhet was startled that he felt jealous of even Amen-Ra.

Nefrytatanen stood for a moment on the terrace outside the royal bedchamber looking at the night sky. The moon sailed like a silver ship on the Nile. The clouds reached playfully toward it as if to catch its magic in their arms.

When Nefrytatanen returned to the room, she found Amenemhet sitting in a chair wearing a grim expression as he stared at the floor.

"Beloved, why are you frowning?" she asked softly, tracing the furrows on his brow with a fingertip, smoothing them as she went.

"I'm worried about ruined crops and scheming governors." His golden eyes lifted to meet hers briefly, and she saw the extent of his concern.

She sank to the floor at his feet and laid her cheek against his knee. "I have considered the problem from every angle I could think of, but found no suitable answer. I've decided I can come to no conclusion because we don't have all the parts to this puzzle. I've decided I'll remain alert until these missing parts come to light. Until then, I'll stop worrying. Worry accomplishes nothing but to steal the joy from my day, and I won't allow happiness to elude me."

Amenemhet said nothing but thought of her coming test. Did she surrender her life to this, he wondered.

"Your joy and your life are mine as well. Would you surrender my joy to your worry?" she asked.

"No," he answered sharply. "You're right. I waste my time—and yours."

"Let us stay awake and enjoy each other's presence," she suggested. "Let us leave the palace in the dawn and go swan hunting. We haven't done that for a long time, and we need to be alone together." Her eyes dropped. "Tomorrow night I must begin going to sleep early, and I'll have to spend my days in meditation, visiting the temple frequently, as I prepare for my test."

"You must do this?"

She was silent a moment as she considered her reasons for risking the test. First was her hope for personal spiritual fulfillment, which would give her the inner strength to control her jealous streak and even overcome it. And then the magical powers she would receive, which would help strengthen the throne. She replied, "This is the high place to which I've steadily climbed. A hawk is born to fly. He could choose not to take the chance of falling, but he has wings attached to his body, and according to the nature of a hawk, if he remains earthbound he'll never fulfill his nature and be a true hawk."

Raising her eyes to look at him, she whispered, "So it is with me, beloved. I must leap from safety or never fulfill my nature. I must attempt flight to confirm my own wings." She saw fear darken his eyes and answered the question he couldn't bear to ask. "When have you seen a hawk whose wings failed him? As these birds trust the Wisdom that fashioned them, so must I."

"Lately I have wished you weren't fashioned in this manner," Amenemhet said quietly.

"So, I'm sure, have you sometimes wished you weren't born to the crown. But if you'd had a choice, you wouldn't have refused the double crown though being a ruler brings responsibilities and sorrows men in lesser places can't imagine." She took his hands in hers and gazed up at his eyes. "So it is with magic. This training I've had brings painful insight others could never understand, but it's something I can't turn from. Even as ruling Tamera is the work of Heru, which you do in his place, so magic is Aset's work. I'm privileged to do it for her."

"Your reasoning is too excellent for me to argue," he said.

"Will we go tomorrow to hunt in the dawn?" she asked.

"If you wish it," he replied.

"And tonight? Will we remain awake?"

Amenemhet took a strand of Nefrytatanen's hair, curling it around his finger. "I can refuse you nothing," he answered.

At an hour when priests are dressed in preparation for their dawn rites saluting Ra's triumph over darkness, Amenemhet and Nefrytatanen left the palace. The trek of the king and queen along the Nile caused no comments, because they looked like peasants dressed in coarse-spun garments with their leather bow cases and quivers slung over their shoulders.

They paused on a hill to rest and look back at the fishermen's huts clustered near the river, from which the soft coral lights of solitary lamps glowed at windows. The sweet, rich smell of baking bread perfumed the air, mingling with the pungent scent of fires being stirred to life for breakfast cooking. The dark figures of two fishermen already inspecting their nets appeared in the haze by the river, and the murmur of their voices drifted to Amenemhet and Nefrytatanen's ears.

As they resumed their walk, Amenemhet shifted the sack he carried to his other hand so he could take Nefrytatanen's arm. The rocks they trod were darkened with slippery dew, but after a few steps Nefrytatanen paused. "Beloved," she whispered, conscious of her voice's loudness in the morning's hush, "I think it will be easier if you free my elbow when we cross this next patch of rocks. The place to walk is narrow and we cannot be together without a struggle."

Amenemhet smiled and released Nefrytatanen's arm, allowing her to go ahead of him. He watched her as she moved among the rocks softly as a deer, nimble and light. Could the royal sculptor capture such living grace in granite with his tools and wondrous hands? Never, Amenemhet decided. Iuti made poetry from stone, but never would he carve the song that was Nefrytatanen.

Turning into a crevice in the low cliff they'd followed, the queen climbed up through the canyon's shadows with Amenemhet a pace behind and stepped out onto a slope strewn with pebbles. Below a marshy meadow, filled with flowers just opened in the sun, spread gold before them. They paused to look at the glowing beauty of the scene.

They could also see below swans floating on a pond, and they watched silently for a time. Then something frightened the birds and they suddenly rose from the water in a white

168

cloud, the dim sound of their beating wings reaching Amenemhet and Nefrytatanen.

"Look at the beauty of those creatures!" Nefrytatanen exclaimed. "They form a living archway in the sky." She turned to Amenemhet and added more quietly, "I don't feel like putting an arrow through such birds."

Amenemhet smiled. "Then let us hunt ducks," he suggested. "Can you endure shooting a duck?" When Nefrytatanen nodded, he took her hand to lead her down the slope.

They sat for two hours in a clump of tall rushes waiting patiently for ducks while they watched the swans float placidly in the water.

From Amenemhet's midriff came a soft rumbling sound, and Nefrytatanen looked up at him and smiled. "It's well past time for our morning meal," she said, reaching for the sack he had carried. "My own stomach has been grumbling too."

"I haven't heard it," he said, gratefully accepting the loaf she offered.

"Really? My first reminder came as we were climbing through that crevice, and it seemed as if it echoed off the walls."

"I thought that was a fall of rocks," he commented humorously.

"Oh, listen!" she exclaimed. "The golden meadow bird is singing!"

Caught in the ripe sweetness of the bird's song, Amenemhet stopped chewing the crusty bread. He closed his eyes, wondering if the bird's heart was breaking to give up such beauty.

Watching Amenemhet, Nefrytatanen forgot the bird and wondered if other men came near to weeping from hearing a meadow bird's sweet melody. When the bird finished, Amenemhet opened his eyes to see Nefrytatanen watching him. "Was it not a glorious thing?" he asked.

"Yes," she agreed, "but watching you was even more glorious. You looked as if you absorbed the music, and I felt as if I could see your soul swelling with each note."

"The song gave my ears the gift of vision and caused my soul to hear," he said.

They were silent as they finished their loaves and fruit, but when they were sipping nectar from a skin provided in their sack, Amenemhet said, "I suspect we'll find no ducks this morning."

"Must we then go back?"

169

"No," he answered. "I have no wish to return to my problems. But I think we should find a drier place." He lifted his foot as he stood. His soft leather boots were dark with moisture.

Nefrytatanen examined her own boots, which were soaked through. "Let us go. I feel like finding a sandy place in the sun to dry my feet."

They left the meadow, the water squeezing up around their feet with every step, and were relieved to find firm ground again beneath them. Following a path lined by tall orange lilies swaying in the warm sun, they entered a forest. Ferns, which softly brushed their knees as they passed, gave off a cool green fragrance. Soon they reached a pond that sparkled in the sun and was ringed with cattails on one side and a length of golden sand on the other. They sank down to stretch out on the warm sand.

Nefrytatanen shut her eyes to the sun's glare and yawned. "You knew I wouldn't want to shoot the swans, didn't you?"

"Yes," Amenemhet answered.

"You aren't disappointed we'll return without game?"

"Being alone with you and escaping our problems is what made this excursion appealing to me," he murmured. He was silent a moment, then commented, "I'm glad you enjoy the same things I do and we can share such moments. You and I are much alike in many ways."

Nefrytatanen turned her face toward him. "When Ptah made us, he used the same clay on his potter's wheel, merely dividing it in half. We are two parts of the same soul."

Amenemhet leaned over her and whispered, "I believe that." He put his arms around her and rested his head on her breast. "I'm grateful to Ptah for making your half of the clay so agreeable to look upon."

"I find the other half pleasant to my eyes," she said, smoothing his black hair with her fingers.

The sun was high overhead before they left the bright pond. Nefrytatanen, thinking of the silence of the dark room waiting in the pyramid, was reluctant to leave the sunlit place behind.

Lords Nakht and Kheti entered Ithtawe's gates with the air of a victorious returning army. Their caravan had been accompanied by an escort of the royal army because they had brought rich offerings to Kenset and now returned with many gifts of great value. While Kheti was in Kenset, Neferset and the children had stayed at the palace with Amenemhet and Nefrytatanen. Neferset anxiously stood on tiptoe on the palace steps now, looking for Kheti. Amenemhet held Bekhat on his shoulder so the little girl could see over the crowd in the courtyard, and Nefrytatanen held the baby, Nakht. That left Neferset free to embrace her husband. Senwadjet and Maeti stood nearby under Yazid's and Dedjet's watchful eyes.

Bekhat wriggled and bounced excitedly on Amenemhet's shoulder, and her clenched fists held tufts of his hair. Nefrytatanen smiled, enduring her own burden with good humor, although the child was making an enthusiastic effort to eat her pendant.

Nakht dismounted with the dignity befitting an ambassador, but Kheti threw himself from his horse and ran up the steps to lock Neferset in his arms.

Azza watched quietly from her horse. She recognized Neferset because of the woman's silver hair shining in the sun. Nervously, she wondered which method of killing Neferset would be most convenient.

After warm greetings had been exchanged with Nakht and Kheti, Amenemhet was eager to discuss their findings.

"How did it go, Kheti?" the king asked. "Did you find anything?"

"No," Kheti answered promptly. "No crop problems."

Amenemhet turned to the ambassador. "Nakht, I don't mean to ignore the results of your negotiations, but I'm anxious to hear Kheti's report because of some new and serious developments."

"Let me carry my little namesake," Nakht offered, smiling. The queen handed over the child with obvious gratitude.

"Did you see any kind of insect at work on any crop in Kenset?" Amenemhet persisted.

"None," Kheti answered firmly. "They have an abundance of pests in Kenset, but they seem more interested in human blood than vegetable juice."

"The insects in Kenset are an abomination," Nakht declared, feeling itchy at their memory.

Kheti smiled. "If you don't bind nets tightly around your bed each night, the insects will carry you away, so they can feast on you in comfort in their own nests." His smile faded when he saw Amenemhet's grim expression. "What has happened in our absence?"

"I'll tell you in private." Amenemhet leaned forward to call Nefrytatanen. "Beloved?" She turned to him. "While you

171

and Neferset examine the gifts they've brought from Kenset, I'll hear the results of their journey." Amenemhet smiled and added, "Take your choice of what you find."

Nefrytatanen knew Amenemhet wished to inform the two men of the harvest troubles and to tell them discreetly of her coming test, but she said nothing. Instead, she smiled and took the baby back from Nakht, saying, "Come, Neferset. Let us be generous to ourselves with our choices."

Amenemhet turned to his servant, who had followed them from the entrance. "Yazid, will you supervise the unloading?" Yazid nodded, bowed slightly and left. Amenemhet took a deep breath and opened the door before them. He paused to instruct the sentry, "I don't wish to be interrupted."

The guard dropped his lance in an acknowledging salute, and Amenemhet, Kheti, and Nakht entered the room. The guard stepped in front of the closed door with a sharp sound, so the king would hear that he had moved into place.

Hours later, when the door reopened, Kheti and Nakht looked as grim as their king.

Glancing up, Amenemhet saw a woman in a red robe sitting on a bench in the corridor. "Who is that?" he asked. At his words, the woman immediately stood up, then sank to her knees before him.

"She's a gift from Queen Karomana for Neferset," Kheti replied.

Amenemhet looked at the woman thoughtfully, but said nothing.

"Her name is Azza," Nakht said. "She was Karomana's personal slave."

Amenemhet walked around Azza, examining her with an appreciative eye. "If Azza is a gift to Neferset, what did Karomana give you, Nakht?" he asked.

"Nothing nearly as warm and soft," Nakht replied.

"Where did Nefrytatanen and Neferset go?" Amenemhet asked Yazid, who had appeared so silently Nakht wondered where the servant had come from.

"They're in the garden, sire," Yazid answered.

"Get up, Azza," Amenemhet said. "Kheti will present you to your new mistress." Azza rose gracefully, the whisper of her silky garments the only noise she made.

Having sent the children for their midday nap, Nefrytatanen and Neferset came in from the garden and met the group still standing in the corridor.

"Azza is a gift for Neferset from Queen Karomana," Amenemhet told Nefrytatanen.

Neferset stared at Azza with large gray eyes.

"Karomana is generous," Nefrytatanen remarked.

"Azza was Karomana's personal slave," Kheti said slowly.

Neferset looked pleased, but she asked, "Why did she send Azza to me?"

"She was so impressed when Kheti spoke of you, she wished to send Azza to encourage you to visit Kenset one day," Nakht said smoothly.

Neferset looked embarrassed. "What did you tell her, Kheti?" she asked.

"If I may remark," Azza said softly, "my lord Kheti spoke only the truth. He told my queen of your beauty, which surpasses his description, and of your goodness, which is apparent in your eyes."

"Azza has graceful manners," Nefrytatanen observed, feeling uneasy about the woman and wondering why. Was it simply that she was unused to looking up at women—Azza was taller than Nefrytatanen by half a head. Nefrytatanen looked steadily at Azza's onyx eyes as if to see what lay behind them and at her mouth as if judging the sincerity of its smile. There was something about Azza that troubled Nefrytatanen, but she didn't know what it was.

Thirteen

Nefrytatanen spent hours in the temple, receiving instructions from the high priest to prepare for her test, praying and meditating. She spent many other hours walking alone in the garden or along the riverbank thinking about what she was about to do. Ankhneferu's instructions sharpened her mind and gave her necessary information, while the prayers and meditation strengthened her soul. Nights of deep, prolonged sleep gave her body fresh deposits of energy on which she later would draw.

It wasn't the customary schedule for an initiate, but Nefrytatanen wasn't an ordinary initiate. Anyone else preparing for the test was usually sequestered in special quarters in the temple and saw no one but a close relative or friend. Because of her past training from her mother, and her own special, already highly developed powers, Nefrytatanen continued to live in the palace and only visit the temple.

As Nefrytatanen's day of testing approached, the palace grew tense. No one escaped its shadow, except Senbi.

The young priest from Wast, whose swift rise through the stages of priesthood had brought him to a position second only to Ankhneferu's, was undisturbed and even looked forward to Nefrytatanen's testing. He was so confident of the results he had no qualms about speaking of the day she would have her wings. Nefrytatanen drew courage from his unwavering faith in her.

On the night before Nefrytatanen's test, Amenemhet stood silently on the terrace overlooking the garden. He dreaded the dawn, but he said nothing to Nefrytatanen about his fear. When he felt her standing very close behind him, he turned and saw that she was wearing a thin garment he could see through. A poignant sorrow went through him at the expectant expression on her face.

"Why did you dress so alluringly?" Amenemhet asked in a soft voice. "Surely this isn't a night to spend in love."

Nefrytatanen came closer, a kiss waiting on her lips; her perfume made his senses sing. "Why do you think love is forbidden on this night?"

"Is it not necessary that you sleep and gather strength?" he asked. He longed with every part of his being to take her in his arms this last night before she sealed herself in the pyramid, but he was fearful that memories of love would distract her from her task, thus endangering her even more.

"It's necessary to be strong," she whispered, "but I know of no better way to gather strength than by loving you. Let me travel to Tuat with your kiss yet warm on my lips. Let my body carry the sensation of you with me so remembrance will guide me back to Ithtawe."

Amenemhet stared at her, torn between longing and concern. "I don't want to endanger you in any way."

"Your love will never bring me danger," she replied. She took his hand and whispered, "Let us go into our chamber and confirm our love, for between us is so great a beauty it is a prayer to Aset."

Protesting no more, Amenemhet went with Nefrytatanen. He was drunk with his need of her, with wanting her for this, perhaps, last time. He tried to stop thinking of what the dawn would bring, but the fear would not go away. He sat on the edge of the bed for some moments while she lay waiting for him.

Finally Nefrytatanen said quietly, "Beloved, believe in what I do. Trust me."

Amenemhet turned to look at her but said nothing.

"Come to me. Give my soul strength," she urged. "Will you send me into the pyramid distracted by my body, which aches for you?"

Amenemhet leaned over Nefrytatanen, his golden eyes

176

looking intently into hers for a long moment, filled with a soft fire that made her shiver until she could endure it no longer. She pulled his face to hers, and his fears faded in the perfumed sweetness of her kiss.

Releasing his lips, she whispered, "Don't you know I would do nothing that might take me from you?" She didn't pause for an answer, but let her hands slide from his face down to his shoulders, her fingers tracing a warm path over his chest. He bent to take her lips again, and his kiss revealed the longing mingled with the shadows of the fears he struggled against, his mouth caressing hers as if, in his kiss, he would deny death its power.

"You bring me eternity while I am yet in my body," she whispered against his mouth.

"In this body is where I want you to stay."

"As you have your name engraved on all your possessions, let my body and soul be marked as yours. Not even the lord of eternity will take me from you then."

"Why should the divine beings bow at my command?" he asked.

"Because according to the ancient laws, you are one of them," she murmured. "Because I see Amen-Ra's fire burning in your eyes."

Her hands moved around his back and tightened as if to draw him to her, but reaching behind his back, he loosened her fingers and firmly placed her hands at her sides.

Stunned, she whispered, "You say no?"

Amenemhet shook his head and knelt beside her. "I would begin this sealing by placing my kisses on every part of your body," he murmured, and bent to begin at her feet.

Small points of white fire, like sparks flaring into life, lit each place the warmth of his lips touched, and as his caressing mouth moved over her, it seemed as if every cell of her body was alight with newly formed stars. She almost could not endure the sensations and wondered vaguely if her spirit was rising to the surface and preparing to leave her body now.

When his lips again met hers, she didn't know she was moaning softly, and when they were joined, she wasn't conscious of how her body writhed. Her eyes opened to gaze into the tilted eyes of Amen-Ra's image. From them came a golden light, shimmering like the reflections on a wave sweeping from the sea, spreading itself with the tide on her sun-warmed shore.

Amenemhet could not bear being in the same room with Nefrytatanen while she prepared herself. Instead, he stayed in bed until she began to dress, then hurried away for his own bath. It was a silent ritual, because Yazid said nothing to his master. When he looked into Amenemhet's tormented eyes, the servant could think of nothing to say that would comfort him.

Amenemhet and Nefrytatanen left the palace to face the double line of priests led by Ankhneferu and Senbi. Amenemhet's solemn face was offset by the cheerful yellow of his long garment. He wore no crown because he was today a man escorting his beloved to the pyramid.

Nefrytatanen wore a robe in the blue of Tehuti—that of the lapis stone—and she wore the silver pendant, Amenemhet's gift of long ago, a twin to the one he wore. She had refused to remove the pendant because she felt its power would help bring her back to him. On her head she wore a simple gold circlet, to show that Ra would protect her and lead her again into his light. She carried in her heart the promise given long ago of her mother's protection, and her whole being carried the stamp of Amenemhet's love.

A golden litter carried Nefrytatanen, and Amenemhet walked alone behind it. With each step toward the pyramid, Amenemhet prayed harder. At the pyramid's top a fire had been kindled, as was the custom when an initiate came for the test. The king gazed up at the white smoke curling from it and hated the pyramid his father's plan had created.

The procession was more silent than a funeral. Today, Nefrytatanen dared ask for Tem's decision. As the people watched the litter pass, they looked at their queen and wondered if her life would end in the pyramid, if she would survive in lunacy, or if she would emerge in triumph like a soldier from a battle.

Nefrytatanen looked at the faces she passed and knew their minds. She recalled that she must hold tightly to the thought of victory to avoid the insidious undermining of her resolve by fear. Her thoughts, therefore, flew to Amenemhet, lit upon his love as shelter, and stayed.

Once they arrived at the pyramid, Amenemhet walked behind Nefrytatanen, who was now escorted by Ankhneferu on one side and Senbi on the other. The temple seemed an alien thing today, and the king felt as if he were moving through an evil dream. He walked through the colonnaded court,

178

blind and deaf to the flowers and birds, the silver veil of the fountain's spray unnoticed as it drifted over him.

When the cool darkness of the pyramid's stones fell on Nefrytatanen, she felt panic suddenly grip her, and she began to doubt her readiness. Senbi glanced at her and, imagining her thoughts, he put his hand on her arm to steady her. Assured again by his confidence, the queen took a deep breath and continued up the gloomy passage. In order to keep Amenemhet from feeling worse, she resolved to reveal no fear or hint of doubt in her expression.

Even with the torches brightly burning, the black marble chamber was a cold and lonely place. Amenemhet stood aside, not daring to touch Nefrytatanen, knowing if he did, he would tear her from the hands of the priests who were helping her and carry her out of this place.

Nefrytatanen lay down in the black marble coffin, the stone chilling her skin through her garments. She was perspiring and hoped it couldn't be seen in the dim light, lest Amenemhet see it and his fear increase. She couldn't see beyond the sides of the coffin. She yearned to look at him one more time, but could understand his hesitancy to approach.

Having watched Nefrytatanen disappear into the stone sarcophagus, Amenemhet shivered. He knew he wouldn't have had the courage to undergo such a test. He felt as though every nerve in his body had been activated, until his skin crawled. Senbi turned from the coffin, his face serene with confidence. Finally, taking a deep breath, Amenemhet approached it.

As Amenemhet looked down, his first thought was how small Nefrytatanen seemed in that great black sarcophagus, how huge and darkly blue were her eyes. He wondered if he might touch her one more time, and she smiled and held out a hand to him. He gripped it tightly, not wanting to let go.

"Are you fearful of having for your wife so powerful a priestess as I will shortly be?" she teased. Her eyes looked anxiously at him, begging him not to be afraid.

Amenemhet forced himself to smile. "Not as long as she's on my side."

"On your side and at your side is where I'll always be," she promised. She touched his face with her free hand, then withdrew them both, saying softly, "I take your love with me."

Amenemhet stared at Nefrytatanen until his vision blurred. Then he turned away, lest he reveal the tears on his face, and left the chamber quickly.

"May Aset protect you," Ankhneferu said, putting his hands on the lid of the coffin, preparing to slide it in place.

Senbi smiled down at Nefrytatanen and whispered, "Your wings are ready. Triumph lies ahead."

Nefrytatanen smiled at his reassurance, and forced herself to continue smiling as they slid the stone lid over her, shutting off from her view the last mortal faces she would see for four days and nights.

She had never known a place could be so dark. She had never imagined such stillness. It was the silence of absolute solitude—not the quiet of night when there were myriad sounds of insects and soft bird calls, not the peace of the temple's vast chambers, where one heard the distant sounds of quiet footsteps or chanting priests, not the serenity of a lazy afternoon, when bees glided on the air currents. There were no air currents here and suddenly Nefrytatanen found herself longing for the things of sunlight.

It was dangerous to cling to such thoughts, she instantly reminded herself. She turned her mind to focus on one golden thing—Amenemhet's eyes. She wasn't so desperately alone when she thought of him. She clung to his memory, wishing she were once again in the warm circle of his arms.

She shivered, knowing such thinking unchecked would mean certain doom. It was difficult to deliberately put aside the thought of Amenemhet, so she thought of his gift, the pendant. Her fingers groped for it and, touching its silver, found it seemed as warm as a living thing. It was her link with him. Holding the pendant as if she held Amenemhet's hand, Nefrytatanen leashed her rebellious mind into submission and followed the instructions she had practiced so many times, feeling her body growing heavier and sinking, while her spirit grew lighter and more buoyant until, like a fledgling bird, she leaped from her bough into another plane of being.

A kaleidoscope of scenes flashed before Nefrytatanen's eyes, exchanging parts and moving colors, as if she glimpsed them through a haze she could see through, but might not yet enter. She wondered vaguely if it all was a dream.

Nefrytatanen stood at an opening looking at a landscape with colors similar to earth's, but so clear and bright they would have blinded earthbound eyes, and she knew at last this was no fantasy created by her sleeping mind. She had escaped her earth's body as well as its dull senses.

A thick gray fog swept over the source of light illuminating the landscape, and the place was obscured by shadows.

Before her was the path she must follow where dark shapes gathered. An unspeakably evil aura emanated from the shadowy figures, and she saw the glitter of colorless eyes.

Nefrytatanen stared at the things, horror coiling around her trembling heart, but she knew she must control her rising fear. She remembered Ankhneferu constantly repeating, "Things of darkness cannot resist a being of light. When you meet evil, you must find the courage to continue, and if you are resolute, darkness will fade before you." Nefrytatanen straightened to her full height, and lifting her chin, moved forward with a firm step, blue eyes glowing in the darkness that had fallen over the place.

"The spirit of the priestess who is queen has come," whispered one of the things.

"She shines," came another's hiss.

And Nefrytatanen continued forward, no longer afraid, because the dark things faded at her approach and disappeared as she passed.

The grayness became darker, until the atmosphere was that of a very clear night on earth. The night was lit by a full moon, which hung low over the horizon like a pale silver melon. The stars in the silken black of the sky were so large Nefrytatanen paused often to look at them in wonder. The path she followed led along a narrow stream of smoothly flowing white liquid. She thought, with surprise, that this part of Tuat seemed like an enchanted night in Tamera. She continued upstream until she saw cliffs rising before her. The stream continued through a crevice, and she followed it.

She came upon a grotto, open to the sky at its top, circled by curious cliffs, which shimmered in the moonlight. The white stream fell in an opaque cascade over what Nefrytatanen now recognized as crystal. She turned slowly to look at the cliffs. All of them were crystal, and from their glistening sides grew white grapes hanging in rich clusters among lavender vines. The floor of the place was covered with a lush carpet of wild mint exuding a cool, refreshing perfume. The blue-green mint was broken only by a silver pond, its surface covered with blue lotuses. It wasn't a place to fear, but a place in which Nefrytatanen felt a curious safety. She knew she was in the realm of Aset, her patron goddess.

A ring of shimmering ripples broke the silver pond's surface, and the lotuses were swept gently aside to permit a figure to rise, a gleaming silver statue that was alive.

"I am Female," the creature said softly, "but you know me

181

by many names." Nefrytatanen came closer, and the goddess smiled. "You are not afraid of me, Nefrytatanen? That is good, for you are part of me. Your people call me Hat-Hor, when they see me in the form of a girl, who is the giver of joy, lover of music and laughter. They call me Sekhmet, when they seek justice, and I give them reward or retribution—cooling water or fire. But, Nefrytatanen, you know me best as Aset, for that is what you are. You lost your girlhood and were never permitted to be Hat-Hor—you went from child to queen. You are she who loves and nurtures, giving peace and wisdom, strength and courage, she who smiles and weeps at once. You are also the enchantress, and nothing can be denied you."

The goddess fixed her eyes on Nefrytatanen, inspecting her soul. Nefrytatanen lifted her gaze, and two pairs of sapphire eyes met and blended, one pouring a luminous blue stream into the other, until the goddess said, "I have given you my sight and hearing so your eyes may see and your ears hear that which mortals can't. I have accepted you, Nefrytatanen. But there are other qualities you must also be given."

Nefrytatanen left the grotto reluctantly, for it was beautiful and she wished to linger. She found herself in a place where the substance beneath her feet was black and her steps made sharp sounds so she knew she walked on metal. From the metal grew sweet, dark-red flowers with pointed petals like flames. The sky had become topaz, burning with a dull-red sun. It was hot and dry, running with red light like blood, but Nefrytatanen felt no fear.

A hawk appeared in the smoky gold atmosphere overhead, circling lazily, its copper feathers shimmering with the sun's crimson. Nefrytatanen began to wonder if the hawk looked on her as prey. He swooped to land in a red sanders tree, under whose swaying branches she must pass. She brushed aside the evil thoughts, which had begun to encroach upon her peace, and walked steadily toward the hawk, who watched her with lonely eyes.

When Nefrytatanen reached the tree, the bird had vanished; under the tree stood a copper man. His eyes were as filled with loneliness as the hawk's.

"Being Male is a lonely thing," he said softly, "and being a man-king is lonelier yet. You know me as Heru, who is Mortal Man. I have three faces, Nefrytatanen, as do all men. Heru's is the face of that which is good in man. Sutekh is man's violent and bestial nature. I am also Asar, who fulfills

182

the promise of immortality. You have seen me in your temples as separate entities, but like all mankind, I am three beings in one." The divine being's sad eyes left her face to gaze at the winding path. "The path you have walked on is my gift to you. For, in advancing yourself despite your fears, you have been given the gift of moving on the winds at your will."

Nefrytatanen was standing in a colonnaded hall whose vast length seemed to stretch to infinity. She turned around to search for the copper man, but he was gone. The place of the topaz sky had vanished, and the majesty of the shining hall surrounded her. The air was filled with the sweet scent of blue iris, and sapphire pillars supported a roof of twining juniper branches from which light filtered as through an arbor. Luminous silver globes rolled like bubbles over the alabaster floor. She bent to pick up one large bubble in both arms, but when she straightened, it broke into many sparkling fragments, forming other silver balls that scattered around her feet.

"Those are thoughts," came a voice, "which multiply when they're grasped." A man stood before one of the columns. He was very tall and lean, and his eyes held the timeless look of the ancient. They were wiser than any eyes she had ever seen, and they were warm with humor.

"You are Tehuti. How many others are you also?" she asked.

The divine being smiled, pleased with her, and said, "You know me well. Knowledge is always preceded by courage, and because you had the courage to touch the unknown globe, I have found you worthy and given you secret knowledge you will draw upon later when you need it. I am Intelligence. I am the guardian of words, Nefrytatanen, and you understand the importance of words."

As Nefrytatanen thought about that, she felt as if a new light suddenly blazed in her mind.

Tehuti smiled with satisfaction. "Now you know why words are holy. With words men think thoughts too complicated to conceive with instincts. Through words men rise above mere instinct. Without Maet, which is the courage of truth, words grow meaningless in lies."

"The secret knowledge you gave me includes words of power," Nefrytatanen whispered in awe.

"Some you already had, but I have given you words beyond those you knew," Tehuti replied. "Now you will go to

183

the place where intelligence becomes more than an idea, where it is used and makes thoughts into reality."

In a cool dry cavern, pierced with amber shafts of light, Nefrytatanen stood among stalagtites and stalagmites which hung from the ceiling and pushed up from the black onyx floor. From dark corners, pure white jasmine spilled out, spreading its sweet scent to mingle with clouds of frankincense rising from a black censer in the center of the passage.

"You're in the hall of Anpu," said a voice behind Nefrytatanen. She turned quickly to face a figure wrapped in an amber cloak. A hood hid its face in shadows. It said, "Here is the place where knowledge creates."

"What is it that I am to receive from you?" she asked.

"You are receiving it now from the fumes of my censer with each breath you take," the figure said. "You are receiving the ability to make your will manifest in the world outside you, to make your thoughts into a living force."

Nefrytatanen considered this carefully, awed at the power this divine being so easily put in her hands. She began to wonder, then, why Anpu, unlike the others, hid his face.

Anpu knew her thoughts and said, "I am a being without a body, an energy you cannot see. But you will recognize me when you use my force."

Suddenly, Nefrytatanen found herself standing in a meadow, where the light was as bright as the sun on a white wall, where the sky was the color of ripe wheat, and tall orange lilies swayed in the perfumed breeze. A golden river ran through the meadow. Dipping her fingertips in it, she discovered it tasted like sweet fragrant wine. Forming a cup of her hands, she drank deeply of it before she arose.

Beside the river, beneath an almond-colored tree, stood a man. When he turned to look at her, his tilted eyes were the gold of dark honey lit by the sun. His smile welcomed her and he said, "You know who I am."

Nefrytatanen stared at his eyes, speechless with wonder, her heart pounding.

"Each day my warmth smiles on Tamera," he said quietly, walking toward her with the graceful movement of a lion. "Each morning I give the Two Lands light and nourishment. When you drank from the stream, I gave you a strength which will never diminish. When the world becomes a cold, barren place, infinitely dark, you will yet retain what I have given you."

184

Nefrytatanen felt like dropping to her knees in gratitude, and she sank slowly to the grass, reaching out to touch the god in thanks. But he stepped quickly back and warned, "Do not touch me. You cannot touch any of us without doing harm to yourself."

Amen-Ra smiled and gestured for her to rise. "We have revealed ourselves to you in forms easily recognized from the legends. For centuries those forms have been faithfully executed by your artists and written of by your scribes. These descriptions were given your people by Tehuti through what you call inspiration. Neither men nor women are we, but it's easier for you to think of us that way. And we surely aren't beings with the heads of animals, birds, or insects. We have allowed ourselves to be so depicted, because these are symbols easily remembered by your people."

Amen-Ra smiled and said, "Tuat surrounds you even in Tamera. You cannot see us with your mortal eyes, as you cannot see fragrance drifting on the air, but we are among you as surely as the flowers which give you their perfume. You cannot see the notes of a flute's music, but you hear its song."

Nefrytatanen was silent, overwhelmed by the knowledge that even on earth she walked among the beings of Tuat. She wondered about the things the One Alone had arranged.

"Now you are thinking about Tem," Amen-Ra said quietly. "You have given Him many names—Ptah, Tatanen, Kheper, Khnum. His face you can see only when you have left earth the final time, for Tem is the source of life. You see a part of Him each time you look at a living thing, when you look into your own mirror." Amen-Ra smiled at her expression, then said, "It's time for you to leave this dimension."

"I've been here so short a time!" Nefrytatanen whispered. "Has it been four days and nights?"

Amen-Ra nodded. "In Tamera that period has almost passed," he said softly, "but here there is nothing called time to measure. The earth travels around the sun as the moon circles the earth, and you count the revolutions, separating them into days and nights, months and years. This counting is a thing invented by men to order their mortal lives. We ignore it for its unimportance in a universe filled with countless shining stars and spinning worlds."

"It is so beautiful!" Nefrytatanen whispered.

Amen-Ra's golden eyes were sympathetic. "You will return one day, and that day you will not travel alone," he said

185

gently. "Return now to your present dwelling place in your journey toward perfection. A celebration awaits you." Amen-Ra smiled. "We are satisfied with you, Aset-Nefrytatanen."

Nefrytatanen wanted to speak longer with Amen-Ra, but, still smiling, he disappeared; the golden meadow faded with him.

Fourteen

As soon as he was allowed to rest, Ilbaya found a corner in the tent and lay on his mat. Turning his back to the other male slaves, he watched the crack of light between the ground and the tent wall fade and gradually darken. A soft hand on his shoulder startled him.

"Marmarus has allowed me to come to help you," Lyra whispered. Ilbaya turned his head to glance at her as she knelt next to him. "I suppose he wanted to impress upon me his power over us by having me see your wounds closer, but I wanted to come."

Ilbaya said nothing. Her touch was gentle and light, and the fire in his lacerated back gradually lessened as she applied cooling unguents. When she had finally wrapped his back in clean soft cotton, he mumbled his thanks, without looking at her, wondering if he dared. She hesitated before rising.

"I am grateful," he finally whispered.

She leaned closer. "Are you going tonight?" she murmured. When he nodded, she sighed and said, "I wish I could come with you."

"I'll leave after the others fall asleep," he replied. "If it's possible, meet me by the river in the papyrus rushes where that great sycamore stands."

"I'll be there, if I can," she agreed.

"Marmarus summons you." A guard's voice came from the tent's entrance. Lyra straightened stiffly at the sound.

"I'm coming," she said sharply. She turned to Ilbaya again. "It won't be possible if I must be with him," she whispered. "May Zeus protect you and may we meet again." She rose quickly and walked away before he could answer.

A flood of anger came over Ilbaya as he thought of Marmarus taking Lyra in his arms. Ilbaya longed to delay his flight to take her with him, but if he was to escape at all, he must try when it was least expected. The guards had been so deceived by his docile attitude they hadn't put him in chains for the night. He would never have a better chance. He could never steal Lyra from Marmarus' tent, he knew, but he thought about it until long after the camp had grown silent.

Though it was difficult for him to move once his limbs had grown stiff, he did so—silently. The guards had relaxed their vigilance, not anticipating that he would attempt to leave while he still ached from his beating, and Ilbaya crept into the night.

The night birds made soft sounds by calling, even as Ilbaya's own heart called to Lyra, while he waited by the sycamore near the river hoping without reason that she might have found some way to escape Marmarus. The north wind moved softly through the rushes, and Ilbaya's heart lifted a hundred times only to sink when he realized it was only the wind, not Lyra moving through the papyrus. The stars were vivid in the blackness, and he felt as if their winking lights mocked him. At last he could wait no more. With a heavy heart, Ilbaya left the river's soft murmurings and walked swiftly toward the south.

In the midst of a small wooded area, which compensated for its insignificant size with the ferocity of its brambles, Ilbaya stopped to disengage his tunic from a thorn-infested shrub. Its groping branches threatened to tear his garment from his body. Twisting and turning with impatience, Ilbaya was about to vent his anger by uttering a curse or two when he stopped his struggle and even hesitated to put down his foot. He heard voices ahead. Almost tearing his tunic from the bush, he crept toward the sounds.

Looking through the foliage into a small clearing, he peered out with surprise. What, he wondered, was a man of Tamera—and an obviously high-ranking one—doing in the middle of the night meeting with a Hyksos and Marmarus?

188

Ilbaya brushed his shaggy hair from his ears and listened carefully. They spoke so low the murmurings were almost impossible to understand.

The Hyksos seemed to be a courier who had orders from someone of importance, because he spoke with authority. The Tameran's posture and gestures indicated irritation with the Hyksos' lack of respect, which confirmed the Tameran's own high rank. Marmarus' attitude was one of solicitous concern, as if he were trying to please both men.

Ilbaya concentrated with such intensity on the whispers his head ached, but he could understand little. They spoke too softly and too quickly. He knew something of great importance was happening, but there was no way to get closer. Several other Tamerans, evidently in the nobleman's employ, stood on guard at the edge of the clearing.

Though Ilbaya dared not move a muscle, his eyes took in every detail of the shadowy figures, while his ears noted each rise and fall of their whispers. He couldn't hear the Tameran's name, but if he ever met the man again, he would recognize his gestures and manner of dress and even the spicy fragrance of the pomade he used in his hair.

Wishing he were more fluent in Tamera's language, Ilbaya struggled to catch a phrase or two, but the Tameran's words ran together so fast Ilbaya's unpracticed ears could distinguish none of it. He decided the softness of the language was perfectly suited for secrets. It was much easier to understand the clipped, hard accents of Zahi.

What could a Tameran nobleman have to discuss with a Hyksos messenger and a Babylonian slave dealer? Even when Tamera and Zahi weren't openly fighting, the peace was guarded. Ilbaya knew the Hyksos were always greedy for Tamera's wealth and were kept from the borders only by the unrelenting vigilance of King Amenemhet's army.

Remembering the stories he had heard of some governors who had tried to set themselves up in their own provinces as little kings, Ilbaya wondered if the man he saw was one who entertained such ambitions. King Amenemhet had once replaced several defiant noblemen with more trustworthy officials, Ilbaya recalled. Perhaps that was one of the noblemen, seeking aid from Zahi. Ilbaya took a deep breath. If such was the case, King Amenemhet might be grateful enough to reward the bearer of such news with freedom, especially if the messenger was owned by a man involved with the plot. But how was Marmarus involved? Ilbaya could think of no legiti-

189

mate reason for a night meeting between a courier from Zahi, a Tameran nobleman and Marmarus.

Ilbaya's attention was caught by the messenger's horse, which suddenly had become restless, throwing up its head, its nostrils flaring. Had it caught his scent? His concern quickly grew to alarm as the disturbed horse began to paw the ground nervously. Ilbaya tested the air currents and found that his scent couldn't have alerted the animal, but he wasn't anxious for the guards to begin a search, lest he accidentally be flushed from his hiding place.

The Hyksos spoke quickly to the horse to quiet it, but his words had little effect. The Tameran scanned the clearing's perimeter, running his eyes slowly over the shadowy circle of foliage, while Marmarus seemed frozen with fear. Ilbaya held his breath and squeezed behind a tree trunk.

The guard nearest Ilbaya began to walk toward the foliage, as did those on the other side of the clearing, and Ilbaya wondered if he should continue trying to conceal himself in the shrubbery or flee. The guard was approaching, but as Ilbaya made his decision to run, he heard a commotion from the other side of the clearing. The guard spun around and ran toward the sound, and Ilbaya edged around the tree to see what happened.

A guard ordered someone to halt. There was a violent threshing in the shadows. A man's voice shouted, and two of the guards dragged a struggling figure into the clearing.

"Ahsen!" The Tameran nobleman breathed.

Though Ilbaya sighed in relief for himself, he felt sympathy for the luckless Ahsen.

"I saw nothing!" Ahsen said distinctly. "I heard nothing!"

Ilbaya, who understood the words, shook his head in wonder at Ahsen's stupidity. Ahsen had proclaimed his guilt with his hasty denial. A chill went through Ilbaya when he saw the expression on the nobleman's face.

"Kill him," the nobleman said.

Ahsen begged for mercy. But the guards began to beat him, and his words grew inaudible. Ilbaya wondered why, if they must kill the poor peasant, they didn't simply run a sword through him.

The Hyksos asked, "How will you hide the body?"

"He'll be carried to the river field," the nobleman answered. "It wasn't used this season, and the flood water will cover him. When it recedes, there will be nothing recognizable left."

190

The noise of the blows and Ahsen's moans, which were fading into a pitiful weeping sound, were unendurable to Ilbaya. On impulse, Ilbaya bent to pick up a sizable stone and, straightening, threw it into the trees. It crashed through the branches like a charging army. Ilbaya stood quietly a moment, noting with satisfaction the abrupt halt in Ahsen's beating, while the man with the sword whirled around to peer into the shadows.

"Someone else is out there!" the nobleman exclaimed.

"This man is almost dead," a guard stooping over Ahsen observed.

"Leave him to die," the courier said harshly. "Get whoever else is there!"

Ilbaya had hoped they would rush in the direction of the stone he had thrown, but they looked around the clearing's perimeter, confused. Had their ears no sense of direction?

"There he is!" cried the nobleman, and at his words, the whole group started in Ilbaya's direction.

Ilbaya decided to do what he could to help Ahsen's rescue and, sure that they would follow him, he fled. He hoped to draw them far enough away to give Ahsen a chance to crawl away if he could move.

Ilbaya raced through the woods as nimbly as a deer—close enough for his pursuers to follow and far enough away to stay out of their hands. He heard them crashing through the underbrush behind him, while he slipped through the forest as silently as snow fell on the mountains of Minoa.

When Ilbaya judged them far enough from Ahsen, he turned into the denser foliage, where vines hung thickly among intertwining branches to form walls. It wasn't easy for Ilbaya to slither through the small open spaces he chose, but he knew it was more difficult for the group following him. His progress was slow, but their pursuit was slower. He wound his way in a confusingly intricate series of turns, following no pattern. His pursuers soon found themselves surrounded by a silent wall of anonymous shadows, not knowing which way to go, unaware of Ilbaya's watching eyes behind the waving ferns. Finally they turned away, grumbling uncomplimentary comments about his parentage, and Ilbaya smiled.

Sitting on a mound of mud and stone, Ilbaya thought over what he had witnessed and weighed the shaky freedom he had won against the chance of legal freedom awarded by King Amenemhet for the information he possessed. Lyra's

191

face rose before him. Was his knowledge worth enough to this king to buy the freedom of two slaves? Ilbaya made his decision and stood up. He would rejoin Marmarus' caravan and go to Ithtawe with it. Then he would contrive some way to get his message to the king.

Ilbaya hesitated only a moment before he struck out for Marmarus' camp. He had sufficient time to return before anyone would awake to discover his absence, but he intended to take no unnecessary chances, so he walked at a rapid pace.

Parting the protesting branches of a thorny bush, Ilbaya found a road. From its overgrown condition, it seemed seldom used, and he decided to follow it. Ilbaya wondered how harshly the laws of Tamera dealt with escaped slaves, but thrust the thought aside. It was useless to dwell on such things. Turning his mind to Lyra, he found he couldn't think of her without remembering her kiss, and he forgot to listen for other travelers.

Before Ilbaya was aware of it, a horseman was almost upon him. The sharp staccato of hoofbeats sent the slave leaping for the bushes, but a lance suddenly quivered in the road before him like a fencepost.

"Stop where you are!" The Hyksos courier commanded.

Ilbaya hesitated a moment, calculating his chances of escape. Then, shrugging, he turned. The courier had drawn his sword.

"I think you are the spy we chased," the Hyksos remarked, his thick accent spoiling the music of Tamera's language. He beckoned with a finger and said, "Come closer."

Ilbaya obeyed, careful to remain outside the sword's reach.

The Hyksos studied Ilbaya. "You risked your life for that peasant," he said. "Why did you do it?"

Still hoping to spare himself, Ilbaya asked several simple, suitable questions in Minoan. If the Hyksos could be satisfied that Ilbaya had understood nothing of what had been said in the clearing, he might be allowed to go.

"You aren't Tameran," the Hyksos said, lowering his sword, though he didn't sheathe it. "Why did you help the peasant?" he asked softly in Minoan.

Ilbaya realized the Hyksos intended to kill him—Minoan or Tameran. He drew himself straight and answered in the Hyksos tongue, "Because I am a man." Then he smiled coldly.

The Hyksos looked at Ilbaya with more curiosity. "Come closer," he directed. "Where are you from?"

192

Ilbaya knew the Hyksos meant only to draw him near enough to strike, so he slowly stepped back.

"Come here. I don't want to shout," the courier said in a friendly tone, but his eyes weren't friendly.

When Ilbaya reached the lance, which was still stuck in the road, he stopped his slow retreat. Anticipating trouble, the Hyksos dug his heels into the horse's side and rushed at Ilbaya. Ilbaya tore the lance from the loosely packed soil, but its point was broken. Quickly, he darted into the middle of the road on the opposite side of the horse, striking the animal's flank with the lance's handle as he passed. The horse squealed and reared, and the Hyksos cursed and struggled to control him.

Ilbaya dropped the lance and reached up to grasp the Hyksos' arm in a firm grip, then threw himself backward. The Hyksos fell from his saddle with a crash and a grunt.

Ilbaya rolled and rose quickly, picking up the lance just as the Hyksos got to his feet. Cursing softly, the man searched for his sword, which gleamed in the moonlight a few paces beyond Ilbaya. Again Ilbaya used the handle of the lance, swinging it with all his strength to land a mighty blow on the Hyksos' midriff. Gasping for breath, the Hyksos bent forward, and Ilbaya, holding the lance with both his hands, brought it down on the courier's head with a resounding crack. The Hyksos fell like a stone, his skull crushed.

Ilbaya picked up the sword and thrust it into its scabbard. Then he dragged the Hyksos some distance into the concealing foliage, carefully noting the place. If evidence was needed when he told his story, he would point out the location of the body.

Returning to the road, Ilbaya found the horse standing in the same place. Speaking softly to the animal, he approached cautiously. After sufficient soothing words accompanied by caresses, the horse allowed Ilbaya to mount it.

Riding through the night, Ilbaya wondered at how the stars of Tamera must gape at the sight of a Minoan riding a Hyksos horse in their land. He inhaled deeply of the clean, cool air and smiled. Tamera lacked nothing he could discern. It was no wonder the Hyksos sought to take this land by force.

Ilbaya thought of Lyra walking through a fragrant field at his side on such a night. He wondered if they might be allowed to stay in Tamera when they were free. As beautiful as

193

were his memories of Minoa, he thought this land could distract him from homesickness.

Ilbaya stopped the horse and dismounted. He freed the animal from his leather-and-metal burden, and giving the horse one more pat, released him. Then the slave walked quickly through the night, breathing the temporary air of freedom until he reached Marmarus' camp.

Everything in the camp was as it should be, and the guards were quietly pacing in their designated places. Ilbaya wiped some of the road's dust from himself with a large leaf. Then he crept silently through the shadows to the side of the tent and slipped through the crack he had used before. Everything was peaceful and quiet, except for the raucous snores of a couple of the sleeping slaves. Ilbaya lowered himself to his mat. Wincing from reopened wounds, he turned to rest on his side.

"Where did you go?" whispered Bacis, a Greek slave.

"For a walk," Ilbaya hissed. "Go back to sleep."

"If I could manage such a walk, I'd keep walking," Bacis grumbled.

In the darkness, Ilbaya smiled. He would gain his freedom, but it would be by other means, so that he wouldn't have to hide all the rest of his life.

Lyra awakened before dawn and, carefully untangling herself from Marmarus' grasp, got out of bed. With a look at him, she shuddered and resolutely turned to go to look at the brightening skies outside the tent.

Only yesterday morning she had shared the dawn with Ilbaya, and for that his back had been fired with pain. She thought of Ilbaya sitting beside her on the hill overlooking the green cup of the valley, his hair shining in the sun, his eyes on her filled with dancing green flecks. When he touched her hair, she had seen the look in his eyes. She closed her eyes, again reliving their kiss, and inevitably, she found herself recalling his beating. Her head ached at the memory.

When the time had come for her to meet him by the river, she had been held in Marmarus' arms, and she had wept. There had been no disturbance during the night, so she assumed Ilbaya's escape had succeeded. Watching the early-morning mist begin to drift away, she sighed. She wished Ilbaya a good journey and let the tent flap fall back into place.

And so, later in the day, Lyra was shocked to see Ilbaya's

copper hair in the straggling line of slaves. Her lips parted slightly, but she collected her wits and showed no other sign of surprise.

As she rode in the litter with the curtains drawn, she sat staring at the wall before her, wondering why Ilbaya hadn't left. He would never get another chance like last night. They wouldn't leave him unchained tonight. She couldn't understand it. Slowly, her amazement began to fade as a new idea crept into her mind. Had he waited for her by the river until he knew she couldn't come? Had he been unable to leave her with Marmarus? Despite her sorrow at Ilbaya's lost chance, she felt joy rise within her being. Did he love her? Her heart sang at the idea. She wasn't alone. She wouldn't have to find her freedom alone. They would find their way together. Lyra put her head back on the cushions while tears of joy ran freely down her cheeks. She was humbled at the thought of Ilbaya loving her even while he knew she was with Marmarus, and she thanked Aphrodite for his love.

"We've had some hard times," Marmarus was saying loudly to one of his guards, "but they've passed now." Marmarus chuckled. "When I leave Tamera, I'll be rich. The land is prosperous—look at it! A prosperous people wants servants and workers in the fields. I'll drive such bargains as I've never driven before. I'll leave the Two Lands with my purse filled with Tamera's gold." He turned to the guard with instructions. "Tie Ilbaya to my camel, for he will be most valuable. I'll set a high price on him in Ithtawe, and I'll get it. Make sure he walks beside me so I can supervise him myself."

The guard nodded and left to fetch Ilbaya, who stood with head hanging, while his rope was being fastened to the camel's harness.

"I see you've learned your lesson," Marmarus observed. "It's well for you, Ilbaya, that you've profited from the experience. Perhaps your next master will be grateful for your new humility and will treat you accordingly."

Ilbaya sighed. "Perhaps," he said. He dared not look at Marmarus, for fear his face would betray him. Instead he gazed at the rest of the slaves, who waited to walk behind the camel, a long straggling line in the dust.

Halfway through the morning, the caravan was stopped by a group of men standing in the road. Marmarus was afraid they might be soldiers, for they were well armed. Several of them approached, and Marmarus held his breath. Although they wore uniforms of a sort, it was not that of the royal army, he realized.

"We're in the employ of Lord Menkara, governor of Su-Sekhem Province," one man called. "Who owns this caravan?" He cast a critical eye over the slaves.

"I'm Marmarus of Babylonia," Marmarus answered, relieved at the mention of Lord Menkara, whose name was on the list of friendly Tameran nobles that Gobryas had given him. "I own this caravan."

The guard stopped beside Marmarus' camel. "Where are you going?" he asked quietly, his black eyes appraising Marmarus.

"Ithtawe, to trade," Marmarus replied. "Why have you stopped us?"

"Did you camp in this province last night?"

"I suppose we did," Marmarus answered impatiently. Menkara's guard was ignorant of both his employer and Marmarus' common affiliation, Marmarus surmised, and he decided to be cautious. "We have no way of knowing where this province's borders are. Did we trespass?"

"No," the guard answered curtly. "The road belongs to King Amenemhet and Queen Nefrytatanen. It's meant for public use." He looked up at Marmarus, his dark eyes narrowing in the sun. "Did anyone leave your camp during the night? Perhaps one of your men wandered?"

"No one left my camp," Marmarus declared. "My guards don't wander. My slaves are securely chained for the night. Do you think I'm a fool to let my merchandise walk freely?"

The guard gave him a black look and said, "I doubt you'd let your slaves loose at any time from the way they look now. Did you or anyone in your caravan see a stranger pass?"

"We saw no one," Marmarus insisted.

"Will you ask the others?" the guard pressed.

"I needn't ask," Marmarus replied. "I'm aware of everything that happens in my caravan." He was angry at the delay. "What is this about?" he demanded.

The guard shrugged. "There was some disturbance during the night, and Lord Menkara has commanded that anyone found in the area be questioned."

"I've answered your questions," Marmarus said sharply, knowing Menkara never intended that *his* caravan be stopped and he questioned. "Let me be on my way and about my business."

"In a moment." The guard seemed indifferent to Marmarus' demand. He turned to the other guards standing behind him. "Walk along the caravan's length and look it over," he directed.

"Look for what?" Marmarus snapped. "I've answered your questions. You're delaying me for nothing!" This persistent guard was going to discover a very unusual and puzzling cargo if he and his men searched too thoroughly, Marmarus feared. Although Menkara would do nothing about the discovery, all these guards would know. How could so many be silenced without causing questions?

"Lord Menkara regrets the delay and inconvenience," the guard replied in a sarcastic tone. "I have my orders."

The guard turned from Marmarus and walked closer to the line of slaves. His head was aching. He had stayed late at a party the night before because he had expected easy duty in the house today. He didn't know why he had to be in the sun on the dusty road asking questions for which he knew he would receive only lies as answers. He wished he could have pleaded illness, but his commander knew he had been carousing and wouldn't accept a bad head as excuse from duty. It pained him even to focus his eyes on these piteous slaves he passed.

Ilbaya stood quietly beside Marmarus' camel, partly turned away from the guard. He didn't recognize any of the guards from the meeting in the clearing last night, but if one of them had been there and had glimpsed his hair in the moonlight, it would be useless to plead innocence. There probably wasn't another head of red hair like his for miles.

The guard walked past the caravan in a disinterested fashion. When he reached Lyra's litter, he lifted the curtain with the tip of a short staff he carried, smiled, dropped the curtain and went on to join the rest of his men by the roadside. He waved the caravan to proceed.

Ilbaya took a deep breath, but he dropped his head as he paced past the Tamerans, appearing more subdued than ever. While he was watching the guard's inspection, he had noticed that several new camels had been added to the caravan since yesterday. He wondered what was contained in the boxes they carried. He was sure their cargo concerned the mysterious meeting of the night before.

Marmarus observed Ilbaya walking stiffly beside the camel he rode and noted the slave's stooped shoulders. "Don't walk so dejectedly when we reach Ithtawe," he directed.

Ilbaya winced as he glanced up at his master.

"You'll bring a low price if you appear sick and you'll be bought by a lower-class owner. You might think about that, Ilbaya. They tend to work slaves harder," Marmarus warned. Ilbaya's gaze returned to his feet. Marmarus continued, "Your value, Ilbaya, is in your health and excellent muscles. I intend to drive a hard bargain for you." He paused before adding softly, "Then we will be rid of each other."

Ilbaya stared at the dust rising in little clouds around his sandals each time he put down a foot. He might be rid of him, Ilbaya thought, but Marmarus could have greater problems by then. He wondered again what the strange camels were carrying. He wished he could sneak a look at the boxes, but doubted he would get the chance. At least now he knew the name of the nobleman, Lord Menkara, and the province, Su-Sekhem. Ilbaya hoped he would be able to contact someone of a high enough status to get his message to Tamera's ruler.

Fifteen

As the procession plodded slowly through the streets, Amenemhet stared blankly at his horse's mane. The turmoil of his thoughts had finally become a dullness, which was a mercy to him, for he had spent the last four days and nights in a torture beyond anguish.

Amenemhet had found it impossible to concentrate on the problems of his kingdom, and he had canceled all audiences during that time. His friends and servants had given up their efforts at distraction or consolation, for they could say little to his silence. He had taken long walks invariably ending at the temple, where he had spent hours unable to pray, his presence in itself a mutely eloquent prayer. .

Four sleepless nights had Amenemhet spent, haunted by visions of the black marble chamber where he had left Nefrytatanen. Four weary dawns had he paced the floor, afraid to sleep, because his dreams were filled with scenes of madness and suffocating death.

Looking up at the pyramid now, he watched the smoke at its apex curling into the blue sky. He wondered once again what they would find in the structure's chamber. The procession finally approached the gates to the courtyard. Amenemhet dismounted and glanced up once again at the massive pyramid as if it might fall on him.

A silent throng had accompanied the procession, and they followed the officials through the doors of the courtyard, until they flooded the enclosure from its outer walls to the pavement around the pyramid's base.

Senbi walked beside Amenemhet, his face shining with confidence. He glanced at his king, offering reassurance, but Amenemhet's face was as expressionless as a statue's, his eyes dark with dread.

Ankhneferu entered the pyramid first. Amenemhet and Senbi followed, and behind them came the physician Horemheb. The silent group climbed the incline of the ramp with white faces and shaking knees, except for Senbi, who smiled. The torches cast grotesque shadows on the walls and ceiling, filling the cool air with the smell of burning pitch.

When Ankhneferu unbolted the door, he wondered grimly if its opening would free Nefrytatanen's soul to fly invisibly through the corridor, like the royal hawk, to the sun.

The room was silent. Amenemhet breathed in relief, because at least Nefrytatanen didn't meet them raving from a disordered mind. Fixing his gaze on the coffin in the center of the room, Amenemhet forced his legs to propel him forward.

As Ankhneferu slid the cover to the side, Senbi held the torch nearer to give them light, and Amenemhet held his breath and looked down. Nefrytatanen's face was as peaceful as when she slept in their own bed, her fingers softly curled around her pendant.

Even before Ankhneferu touched Nefrytatanen, her eyes opened easily, as if she had been napping at the midday resting time. She lay staring up at them, unmoving.

"We must help her," Ankhneferu whispered, "for she's weary from her journey." He took Nefrytatanen's hands and drew her to a sitting position. Awkwardly, she stood up in the box. Senbi took one elbow and Ankhneferu the other to help her step out.

Nefrytatanen said nothing, but looked as dazed as a child awakened at midnight. Amenemhet stood aside, uncertain if she was tired or ill. Horemheb watched her carefully, but he didn't touch her.

With great care, the priests helped Nefrytatanen walk slowly to the door. Amenemhet hurried out ahead of them, so he could precede them down the ramp in case she slipped or fell. Walking backwards, he faced her all the way down the passage to the entrance. She did not speak, and her eyes retained their dazed look.

When the group stepped out of the passage, the wind caressed Nefrytatanen's hair in greeting, and she breathed deeply, lifting her eyes to the sun.

"I have wings," she whispered. She looked at Amenemhet and smiled weakly.

Amenemhet stared at her, his eyes shining with joy and bright with unshed tears.

"Beloved," she said softly, "you have eyes like Amen-Ra's."

The people filling the courtyard had watched tensely for Nefrytatanen to appear in the doorway, not knowing what to think when she did, since she looked pale and unsteady on her feet. Then they saw their king's solemn face become radiant with his smile. As he lifted the queen in his arms, her own arms moved around his neck and she laid her cheek against his and clung to him.

Ankhneferu's voice was lost in the roar of the crowd, because anticipating his declaration, they cried, "She has wings!"

The very air in the banquet room seemed luminous from the shimmering decorations. Garlands of lotuses were draped around the columns, and bouquets of white jasmine spilled from gold baskets on the tables. Cushions on the gilded chairs and couches were woven with silver, as were the linens on the tables. The bowls and platters were plated with gold.

From large golden censers on floor stands rose clouds of incense, filling the air with perfume. In a corner musicians in silver robes played instruments recently coated with gilt for the celebration, and palace servants in silver-trimmed white robes glided silently among the guests, carrying golden fans on long silver handles or pouring wine into gold goblets from silver urns.

On a platform at the far end of the room, intimates of the king and queen relaxed around the royal table, conversing as they awaited the entrance of their rulers, who were expected momentarily. A line of trumpeters stood along the wall by the entrance ready to give the signal when the king and queen arrived. The leader, who had been standing just outside the door, walked quickly in and, with an anxious expression, lifted his hands. From the throats of the golden horns came a soaring flourish to announce, at last, the entrance of the royal couple.

Everyone turned quickly, as if they were magnetized by the sound. Ithtawe's nobility had been awed by the afternoon's events, and they were very curious to see if Nefrytatanen's experience in the pyramid had changed her in some visible way.

When Nefrytatanen came through the doorway holding Amenemhet's arm, guests and servants sank into deep bows, although their eyes stared up through lashes in careful inspection.

Nefrytatanen's long straight black hair was in striking contrast to the silver crown of Aset and the silver robe she wore. Instead of ending at her ankles, as an ordinary garment would, the robe swept the floor behind her as she walked. Today she wore the formal robe of the highest rank of Aset's priestesses. Her eyes were darkened to blue smoke, matching exactly the stone in her pendant, and her silvered eyelids seemed to provide a setting for her eyes, as the silver pendant did for the jewel in its heart.

Amenemhet walked more slowly than Nefrytatanen wished, but he turned to her and whispered that he wanted her to slow her pace so she would be seen clearly by all those present. His crowned head held high, he walked with shining eyes sweeping proudly over the crowd.

When they reached the place reserved for them, Amenemhet and Nefrytatanen remained standing, since they were immediately surrounded by their friends in an excited tangle of congratulations and good wishes. Finally, Nefrytatanen begged for an end to it.

"Have mercy!" she said through her laughter, still grasping Nakht's hand. "This flesh I wear is as mortal as ever, and I must sit down and catch my breath!" She sank into a chair, still smiling widely, her eyes glowing with pleasure. "I love you all, my friends, but your reception is so enthusiastic that my wits are scattered."

"Then rest yourself," Nakht said, "and merely allow us to look at you. Aset herself surely can be no more beautiful."

Amenemhet cast Nakht a warning glance. "Release her hand, my friend," he teased, "or I'll send you back to Kenset."

"You'll send me anyway," Nakht declared, laughing.

"While I was in the pyramid, what happened in the kingdom?" Nefrytatanen asked.

202

"I must confess I paid little attention," Amenemhet whispered.

Nefrytatanen took his hand and squeezed it, knowing the torment he had suffered.

Nakht, sipping his wine, looked at them over his goblet and decided to change the conversation's direction. "I've heard there's a Babylonian slave trader in Tamera," he said.

"That trader is in Ithtawe," added Prince Sarenput, who had journeyed from Thes-Hertu to join the celebration. "From the stories I've heard, I think he may become a nuisance."

Amenemhet turned to Sarenput. "What did you hear?"

"His way of dealing is very shabby," Sarenput answered. "I've also heard he treats his slaves shamefully."

"Meri!" Amenemhet called. The prime minister made his way to Amenemhet's side. Amenemhet again turned to Sarenput. "Are you sure of this?"

Sarenput nodded. "Nessumontu is the one who told me. He witnessed some unpleasantness regarding this trader."

Amenemhet looked up at Meri. "Send a message to the Babylonian. Advise him that I've never approved of his profession. Advise him as well that I don't view his methods with a kindly eye, and if I continue to hear such reports, he'd be wise to leave Tamera."

"It will be done tonight," Meri said quickly.

"Tomorrow morning is sufficient," Amenemhet replied. He turned to Sarenput. "Did you see this Babylonian? Can you tell me how he looks? We had trouble with one of his kind two years ago, and I wonder if he's the same man."

"I haven't seen him," Sarenput answered. "Nessumontu could probably describe him."

"Where is Nessumontu?" Nefrytatanen asked, glancing over the room.

Nakht sighed. "I last saw him with Taji outside her door."

Amenemhet smiled. "I'll send Yazid for him or he'll find the way into Taji's room and she'll forget she's to entertain us." Amenemhet gave Yazid his instructions and the servant bowed and hurried away.

"Speaking of those who are missing," Nakht said, glancing over the room, "I haven't seen Lord Menkara. Does he avoid the queen's celebration?"

Amenemhet sighed. "Frankly, I don't mourn his absence. I wish to speak privately with some of you later; and when Menkara is around the palace, I find it difficult to exclude

203

him." He looked across the room and said, "Here is Nessumontu now."

Nessumontu's crimson uniform stood out in the crowd as he made his way toward the royal table. When he reached Amenemhet's side, he said softly, "You wish to speak to me?"

Amenemhet's eyes briefly examined him. "I'm pleased you came so quickly. I had thought you'd take longer."

Nessumontu's expression was solemn, but his eyes gleamed in understanding. "I was on my way when I met Yazid in the hall."

"Taji turned you out?" Nakht teased.

Nessumontu shrugged. "It sometimes happens."

"We were speaking of the Babylonian slave trader," Nefrytatanen said. "Sarenput told us you've seen him."

"Who is he?" Amenemhet inquired. "Is he the same one we had escorted to the border two years ago?"

Nessumontu shook his head. "No, he's a different one, but I suspect he's no improvement on the other."

"Why?"

"He treats his slaves as generously as most Babylonian slave merchants," Nessumontu answered, "which means he looks upon them with a greedy eye. He keeps them in reasonably good health because they're valuable, but I'm sure they aren't fond of him."

"Have you heard complaints regarding his dealing?" Amenemhet asked.

Nessumontu replied, "He's traveled almost the whole length of Tamera from the south, and his reputation for high prices has preceded him. He has only just arrived in Ithtawe, and although what I've heard about him so far is not exactly commendable, he's done nothing yet I could arrest him for."

"I wonder why a Babylonian would come from the south," Amenemhet speculated.

"Maybe he visited the lands on the other side of the Narrow Sea and thought to swing to the north through Tamera," Nessumontu reasoned.

Kheti, who had approached in time to hear the last of this conversation, asked, "Is he camped just north of the marketplace? I think I may have seen him."

Nessumontu nodded.

"He actually accosted Lord Semerkhet in an effort to make a sale," Kheti said. "You know how useless it would be to try to sell *him* a slave." Amenemhet smiled at the idea, but Kheti went on, "That trader never stopped trying. Even when Semerkhet walked away, the trader was persistent enough to follow him." Kheti's face reflected what must have been Semerkhet's expression of distaste, as he continued, "Finally Semerkhet turned around and gave him a look that should have made anyone cringe and told him to go away. When the Babylonian saw Semerkhet's anger, he merely lowered his price a little." Kheti shook his head. "I think that man has a tongue this long!" He gestured its extraordinary length with his hands, and they all laughed.

After they had quieted, Nessumontu asked, "When is Taji to dance?"

"Any moment, I would think," Nefrytatanen replied. "She's to perform before the meal so she can change from her costume and sit with us."

"I hope she dances soon," Kheti said. "I'm getting hungry."

"So am I," Nessumontu said softly.

Sarenput turned to look at Nessumontu, curious at the tone of voice he had used. Noting the gleam in Nessumontu's eyes, Sarenput concluded Nessumontu wasn't thinking of food. When it was announced that Taji was ready, Sarenput waited quietly, wondering about Taji, since Nessumontu wasn't easily impressed by women. He had never seen Nessumontu in the company of a woman who was less than dazzling.

Two musicians began a strange melody on their flutes, and one shook a sistrum very softly. Although the tune was alien to Sarenput's ears, it had a rhythm that affected him in a way no music had before. When he closed his eyes, he imagined spicy-scented flowers in the sun among vines that intertwined as the flutes intertwined their melodies.

Noticing that his brother-in-law had his eyes closed, Kheti nudged Sarenput's elbow and whispered, "Do you want to miss the dance?"

Sarenput opened his eyes in time to see a girl barely taller than a child finish a bow before Amenemhet and Nefrytatanen's place. She slowly backed away a few paces, her head still respectfully lowered behind hands pressed together at shoulder level. She wore a tight-fitting purple jacket of a strange design that ended at her ribs and bared her midriff, which Sarenput noted was the color of honey. Purple pantaloons, very loosely cut, were held tight around her ankles by red embroidered bands. The legs of the pantaloons were slit from her ankles almost to her hips. Her hair was drawn to the crown of her head and fell in a single fat braid to her hips. An intricate arrangement of tiny gold bells and amethyst beads threaded on gold wires somehow clung to the top of her head, shimmering and sparkling as she straightened. Her eyes were almond-shaped and black as dates, and Sarenput wondered from what land this diminutive creature had come.

Taji began to dance, a small golden figure swaying in impossibly supple arcs, her body bending as no one else's could, her tiny gold bells singing with the flutes.

The girl writhed in a slow, sinuous movement that brought her closer, almost to Sarenput's feet, and when her golden face lifted, their eyes met briefly. Sarenput felt the peculiar sensation that he would disappear in a flash of light if he gazed at those eyes too long, and he reluctantly turned away. Taji was the only person who had ever made him drop his eyes first, and he was surprised. At the same time, he recognized the pleasantly warm sensation that was coming over him.

Seeing Sarenput's gray eyes flash with fire like a storm gathering over the sea in Retenu, Taji felt her heart flutter strangely. Her dance grew slower, even more sinuous, as she thought of the look in the tall, quiet nobleman's eyes.

Noticing that Taji's steps had slowed, the musicians looked at each other and adjusted their music to her movements.

Sarenput realized that after each turn, Taji's gaze found him and she came near his table at every opportunity.

Amenemhet saw the looks passing between Taji and Sarenput, and his eyebrows rose slightly at the deliberate movements of Taji's dance. She had become almost maddeningly subtle in the provocative way she swayed, and her restraint added to her sensuality. Sarenput's face was alight as Amenemhet had never seen it.

After Taji's dance ended, she bowed low before the royal table, and Amenemhet gestured for her to come closer. She lifted her jeweled head, and as she approached her eyes were carefully fastened on Amenemhet's face, but he knew her attention was really on Sarenput.

"Your dances are always a pleasure to watch," Amenemhet said softly, "but tonight you were a special delight."

"Thank you, sire," Taji murmured. "It's a special occasion."

"You haven't met our Princess Taji from Retenu, Sarenput?" Amenemhet turned to face him.

Sarenput dragged his gaze from Taji and, realizing what Amenemhet had said, looked startled. "Retenu?" he asked.

"Taji is King Ami-enshi's daughter, and her mother was from a distant eastern land," Amenemhet explained. "It was, in my opinion, the best marriage Ami-enshi made." He smiled at Taji. "Princess Taji, this is Prince Sarenput of Atalan, now lord of Thes-Hertu Province."

Taji dipped gracefully before Sarenput. Her eyes moved to meet his and didn't turn away. When he smiled, Taji thought she might fall in a faint, but she managed to stand quietly.

Feeling as if a storm rocked him, Sarenput said, "While I watched your dance, I wondered if you were the goddess Wadjet come to life. But as you are still Taji, I compliment you on your extraordinary grace." Taji's golden face blushed the color of a ripe peach. Sarenput added smoothly, "Or perhaps you are Wadjet and have come to amuse yourself by pretending you're mortal."

Nessumontu and Nakht stared at Sarenput, and Neferset's eyes widened in amazement. She had always known her brother to be restrained with women and had thought him shy, so his sudden confident charm stunned her.

"You are most generous, Lord Sarenput," Taji said softly. The look in his eyes sent a trail of shivers down her spine. Reluctantly, she turned to Amenemhet.

"When you've changed, remember to join us for the meal," Amenemhet reminded her.

As Taji bobbed her head and hurried away, sharply aware of Sarenput's eyes on her, she had the feeling that her knees had no joints. She hoped she wouldn't have to sit near Sarenput, because in her present clumsy state, she couldn't trust herself to lift one morsel of food to her mouth.

Amenemhet watched Taji slip out the side door, then turned to Nefrytatanen and observed, "Taji's walk seems even more provocative than usual. Do you think we might arrange to have her placed beside Sarenput? It might give an interesting turn to this evening's events."

Nefrytatanen lifted her hand in gesture to the servant standing behind her. The girl moved to Nefrytatanen's side and bent close to hear Nefrytatanen whisper, "Make a place for Princess Taji at Lord Sarenput's left."

Neferset leaned forward, her green eyes gleaming, to ask, "What are you arranging?"

Amenemhet didn't answer. He smothered his smile and looked at Sarenput, who was still staring at the door through which Taji had disappeared. "Sarenput," he said clearly, "would you like more wine?"

207

Sarenput pulled his attention from the doorway to look at Amenemhet with a light in his gray eyes that startled even his host. "Yes, thank you," Sarenput replied, lifting his goblet to the waiting servant.

"I think Nessumontu has competition," Amenemhet remarked.

"No," Sarenput said firmly. "The contest is already finished."

Long after the torches in the banquet room had died, the light Taji had kindled in Sarenput remained burning brightly, and he sat in his chamber staring at the shadows, thinking of her. Every detail was vividly engraved on his memory, as he relived each moment of her presence. He could hear the soft, clear music her bells had made each time she had moved. Her laughter had seemed like golden bubbles in the sun. His nostrils were filled with the tangy spice of her perfume, and his mind feasted on dreams of the golden skin he had never touched. Her eyes haunted him, the black depths of them filled with his reflection as she stared into his face. He wondered if he would ever sleep again—or wish to.

Still dressed, Sarenput wandered into the silent corridor and followed the passages to the empty banquet room. There, on that moonlit cushion, was where she had sat. He touched its cloth in wonder; he regarded it almost as if it were a holy place. He looked at the shining floor, where she had danced, and heard echoes of the music.

When Taji had returned for the meal, Sarenput had discovered that he no longer had an appetite. Although the dishes placed before them were excellently prepared, neither had eaten. Instead, they had stared into each other's eys until it was too much to endure.

Sarenput smiled, recalling how he had compared Taji to every goddess in the firmament. He had lavished her with every poem that had ever touched his heart. Unabashedly, he had poured his soul out through his eyes, and by the time even the musicians had wearily dragged themselves away, he had revealed more of himself to Taji than even Neferset knew of him.

Sarenput grinned with satisfaction. His unrelenting pursuit of Taji had won her complete attention. After one prolonged effort to distract her from Sarenput, even Nessumontu had capitulated. He might as well have been invisible.

"Why are you smiling so smugly?"

Sarenput looked up quickly at the voice. Taji stood just inside the doorway in a spray of moonlight, still dressed in the crimson robe she had worn at dinner. Did she turn the silver moonlight to fire? "Now you are Hat-Hor," he said.

"I'm only myself," Taji said, coming closer slowly. "It was difficult to sleep this night."

"As it was for me," Sarenput replied. "Many times I closed my eyes, but I thought nothing of sleep, for I saw your image even on the inside of my eyelids."

Taji sat beside him. "Either you hide none of your feelings from me or you always speak so to impress a woman."

"Do you think I've lied?" Sarenput asked softly.

"I have heard praise from men's lips which much exaggerated their true feelings," she replied.

Sarenput placed his hand on hers, marveling at their softness. "Taji," he said quietly. "It has always seemed, from what I've observed in others, that love is a thing which develops slowly. Yet, when I looked at you, so powerful a sensation came over me, I cannot think it's merely desire—although that is part of it."

"I think I should return to my chambers now," Taji said suddenly.

Startled by her sudden rejection, Sarenput looked intently at her a moment. He slowly got to his feet, sighed and said, "I'll walk with you."

No further words passed between them until they stood by Taji's door.

"All evening I poured out my private self to you and wanted so much to touch you," Sarenput whispered. "Only a moment ago I merely held your hand, and this small thing made the earth rock beneath me. I'm not a child, Taji. Neither am I a man who roams from one woman to another. I would kiss you, Taji."

Praying she wouldn't move away, but bending closer very slowly to give her time to object if she wished, Sarenput pressed his lips to hers. At the touch of her lips, his being flared with desire unlike any he had ever known. His arms moved around her as if they were separate things over which he had no control, and holding her tightly to him, he kissed her until he wasn't sure he would survive the ecstasy of it.

Finally stepping away a little, Taji stared up at Sarenput, but she said nothing.

Sarenput took a deep ragged breath and, with a distracted

expression, whispered, "I will never again be a whole person when I'm away from you."

Taji continued to stare silently at Sarenput.

"Must I leave you now?" he asked softly. She said neither go nor stay. She only looked at him. "What have you done to me with one kiss?"

"What have you done to me!" Taji whispered. "Or is it that we've only obeyed what the divine beings planned?"

Sarenput smiled. "That may be the answer," he agreed. His face grew more solemn and he said, "When the One Alone made from emptiness what is, and fashioned Ra to give warmth and light to the earth, that was accomplished by His thought and a word. When I first looked at you, I think Tem said again, 'Let it be.'"

Taji leaned closer and rested her head on his chest. He could feel her trembling. He put his arms lightly around her and again desire shook him.

"You aren't backing away," he murmured. "I stand before your door and you know how I am, but you aren't wishing me fair dreams and telling me to go." Taji did not reply, but she slid her arms around him, holding him closer. Sarenput shivered. He silently prayed to Hat-Hor to be generous with him this one night, and he vowed that before another dawn, he would bind this golden creature to him forever. Softly, he said, "Your attitude invites me to linger."

Taji's breath was warm against his chest as she whispered, "And will you accept the invitation, Lord Sarenput?"

"I would choose death rather than leave you," he answered, "and I speak not only of this night."

Taji stepped away. "Then let it be forever," she replied, opening wide the door. "It will be forever, Sarenput. I'll make it so."

Nefrytatanen sat up in bed with a jerk. Through the halls was echoing a series of heart-stopping sobs. She turned to Amenemhet and shook him. He sat up quickly, his muscles rigid with tension.

"What is it?" he asked. Before Nefrytatanen could answer, the sobbing began again. They looked at each other in alarm. "By Heru, what is that?" Amenemhet exclaimed. Brushing his hair from his eyes, he got out of bed and pulled on a robe.

"It's the most piteous sound I've ever heard," she said quietly as she drew a light robe over her shoulders.

When they stepped into the corridor, the guard outside their door came smartly to attention.

"What's happening out here?" Amenemhet demanded.

"I'm not sure," the soldier answered. "The noise comes from Lord Kheti's room."

Other doors were opening, and the hall was quickly filling with disheveled noblemen and their wives. Senwadjet and Maeti came running from their rooms with their guardian, Senet, at their heels. Maeti's fearful eyes looked up at Nefrytatanen as she clung to her mother's knees. Nefrytatanen bent to soothe her daughter.

"Stop being a baby," Senwadjet said sharply. Nefrytatanen glanced at him, surprised at the coldness in his voice.

Amenemhet stooped before his son and their golden eyes met. "You will not speak to your sister that way," Amenemhet said coolly. Senwadjet stared defiantly at his father, and Amenemhet added, "Prince or not, you'll be considerate of others."

Neferset's serving woman, Amset, came to Nefrytatanen with a worried look. "Majesty, my mistress is very distressed," Amset said. "Can you help Lord Kheti soothe her?"

"Of course," Nefrytatanen answered, still wiping away Maeti's tears. "Don't be afraid," she whispered. "Neferset has had an evil dream, I think. Go with Senet and I'll stop to see you before I sleep." Nefrytatanen straightened. "Senet, keep a lamp lit and I'll come in later." Then, giving Senwadjet a look of disapproval, Nefrytatanen turned to hurry to Kheti and Neferset's room. She noted that Sarenput and Taji stood holding hands in Taji's doorway, but she said nothing as she passed.

Before she went into Kheti and Neferset's room, she called to Yazid, who was hurrying down the hall, "Yazid, get Horemheb!"

"I'm on my way now!" he called back over his shoulder and rushed around a corner out of sight.

Neferset was sitting up in bed with Kheti. She was clinging so tightly to him as she wept that her fingers were white from her grip.

"Can I help?" Nefrytatanen asked softly.

Kheti glanced up and said nothing.

Nefrytatanen stopped, wondering whether to go or stay, feeling awkward and helpless. "Amset came to me," she said feeling like an intruder.

Kheti gently smoothed Neferset's hair and continued to hold her close, although the violence of her weeping seemed to have lessened. Finally, she loosened her hold on him. Bidding her to lie down, Kheti arranged pillows and pulled the blanket closer around her.

"She's had a dream," Kheti whispered. "I can't leave her now to explain, but there is something you can do."

"What is it?" Nefrytatanen came a step nearer.

"Go to little Nakht's room and confirm that he's unharmed," Kheti said.

Nefrytatanen asked no questions, but hurried to her task. When she returned and assured them the baby slept peacefully despite the commotion, Kheti smiled.

"Thank you," he said. "That leaves no room for doubt in Neferset's mind. She knows you'd make no mistake."

"Neither would I allow anything to happen to Nakht," Nefrytatanen said firmly. "If you wish, I'll post Dedjet in his room."

"That isn't necessary," Kheti said softly. "It was merely a dream."

Nefrytatanen nodded and left them. Closing the door quietly behind her, she wondered if it was merely a nightmare or if Neferset had had another one of her prophetic dreams. At the thought, she shivered.

"Is she all right?" Horemheb asked.

Nefrytatanen looked up at the royal physician. "Yes. It was an evil dream, but Kheti soothed her. I'm sorry I had you awakened."

Horemheb yawned. "I don't mind," he said and went wearily down the hall, his bare feet making soft slapping sounds on the floor.

Nefrytatanen turned to Amenemhet, who was still standing in the hall. Amset stood with Azza a few steps behind him.

"Everything is all right now," Nefrytatanen advised. "You may go back to sleep, Amset." She glanced at Azza, again feeling an inexplicable dislike for the girl, who looked very concerned. Nefrytatanen said no more, but continued to Amenemhet's side.

"Queen Nefrytatanen doesn't like me," Azza whispered to Amset. Amset said nothing, but she, too, sensed Nefrytatanen's coolness toward Azza, and it confused her.

The sun was high when Sarenput opened his eyes and found himself in an unfamiliar room. Curtains of violet gauze moved softly in the gentle breeze. Across the foot of the bed lay a length of golden veiling. In a heap on the floor was a crimson gown and his own blue tunic. When a spicy and tangy perfume drifted to him, he finally realized where he was. He turned to find Taji's black eyes contemplating him.

"You have slept long," she observed.

"And you've been patiently waiting for me to wake up? You should have awakened me," he said.

"I've been looking at you and thinking."

"Thinking of what?" he asked.

"I've been admiring you and remembering the happiness of last night."

Sarenput held out his open arms, and she entered them to lay her cheek against his shoulder. "Your happiness couldn't have surpassed my own," he said softly. "Never did I know love could give such pleasure. I didn't know I was capable of feeling so much."

"There is even more," she murmured. "When I'm better acquainted with your heart and body, there will be more."

"How do you know such things?" Sarenput asked, suddenly suspicious. "Who taught you all this?"

"My mother," Taji replied.

Sarenput was silent, wondering how it was possible.

At his expression, Taji smiled and murmured, "In my mother's land, a woman makes her place in life by means of her skill in love. She made sure to teach me well, so I could win a high place—and keep it."

"You speak of the mechanics of sex," Sarenput said coolly, "not of the emotions inspiring lovemaking."

"So it was in my mother's land, and in Retenu as well." Taji looked at Sarenput, her smile fading. She again put her face against his shoulder. "Until King Amenemhet took me from my father's palace, it had been all I could expect of life—that my appearance would attract a man of high rank, that my skill would make him his favorite."

"And why did Amenemhet bring you here?" Sarenput asked suspiciously.

"He took pity on me." Her voice was muffled against Sarenput's shoulder. "King Amenemhet told me I would find a man of my own choosing in Tamera, which was an idea I could hardly believe, but found much favor in. Now I have found him."

"And how much have you searched?" Sarenput asked a little sharply.

Taji's head came up quickly. "Do you think I've lavished myself on others in experiment?" She sat up stiffly and stared at him. "Have I asked you about other women?" She swung her legs off the bed and stood up, pulling a robe around her. "I would never mention such things."

Sarenput reached out and took her hand in a firm grip. She tried to pull away, but couldn't. "Forgive me," he said urgently. "I've just now learned I'm jealous. It wasn't a thing I knew about myself before." He smiled sheepishly. "One night with you has taught me many things. I told you last night, when we stood outside your door, I wasn't a man to wander from woman to woman." He pulled her toward him. "Come back and teach me more about myself."

"We should go downstairs," Taji whispered. "Queen Nefrytatanen saw us standing together in my doorway last night."

"She'll say nothing," Sarenput assured, continuing to tug at Taji's hand.

"There were others who raised their eyebrows," Taji said.

"Their eyebrows will ascend no farther if we spend another hour here," Sarenput said. "We'll go out properly for the midday meal. It will, no doubt, be the first meal everyone will eat today anyhow." Taji looked uncertain and Sarenput coaxed, "Give me one kiss, then."

"One kiss from your lips seals my fate," Taji whispered, staring at the growing light in his eyes. He pulled her nearer. She stood unresisting as his free hand loosened the knot holding her robe. When the cloth slipped from her shoulders, she looked at him helplessly, saying nothing. He laid his hand on her waist.

The touch of him was fire to her, but she didn't move. "There's no law in Tamera that condemns lovers," he whispered. "Neither of us breaks a marriage contract." His hand slid slowly around her back, following the curve of her waist. "Yes?" he asked. She sank to the edge of the bed, staring at him. He finally released her and put both hands at the nape of her neck, pulling her face toward his.

Feeling her resistance, he asked, "Why do you fight me? You were born for love. You told me how carefully your mother taught you. Would you let it go to waste?" He saw the smile hovering at the corners of her lips. "Do you question my loving you?" he asked. "Look at my heart through

214

my eyes and confirm what you should already know. Later today, we'll go to the temple, and one of the priests will marry us. After all, Taji, you are a princess, and I would have been a king. I would have our heirs born in honor." Sarenput smiled. "Come to me," he whispered, and the hands at the back of her head drew her closer.

When their lips met, sweet hot desire poured through them both. There was no way to resist it. There was not even a thought of resisting.

Amenemhet glanced up from his food to see Sarenput and Taji come slowly through the door, looking self-conscious. He nodded and smiled at them, but turned to Neferset to continue their conversation. "Rich roasted meats and honeyed almond cakes with cream don't always sleep happily together. I had some peculiar dreams myself last night."

"I was afraid it was a prophecy," Neferset said slowly.

"Who would harm the baby?" Amenemhet reasoned. "Little Nakht has done no worse than dampen laps. No one would demand revenge for that indiscretion."

"I've sometimes felt like it," Kheti said humorously.

"It was merely a dream, but so vivid you couldn't easily awaken from it," Nefrytatanen said softly. "It's best put out of your mind."

"It will be difficult to forget," Neferset said slowly. "That woman watched him tumbling and rolling down the stairs, striking the stone with a sound that yet sickens me. And she laughed." Neferset's eyes were haunted with remembered horror.

"Your description of the woman sounded like no one I've seen here," Amenemhet reasoned. "Perhaps something Kheti mentioned about his journey stayed in your mind and combined with last night's mixture of food to conjure up the evil dream."

"Now that you say it, I admit the description of the woman in the dream reminds me of Queen Karomana—and I did tell you about her, Neferset," Kheti reminded his wife.

"Perhaps you're right," Neferset conceded.

"Did Nakht tell you of the military movements in Zahi?" Kheti asked, wishing to change the subject and spare Neferset.

"Yes," Amenemhet sighed. "Since Gobryas became prime minister, he has been urging King Shalmanesser to war."

"It isn't necessary for Gobryas to influence Shalmanesser,"

Nakht said bitterly. "Shalmanesser is sufficiently warlike on his own."

"That whole land is evil," Nefrytatanen said sharply.

"What makes them so?" Sarenput asked.

"Greed," Nakht replied.

"They have no respect for life," Kheti added.

"What would you expect of those who live as they do?" Nefrytatanen exclaimed. "The Hyksos are thoroughly evil. I know. I visited their capital city once with my father when I was a child. I remember it well."

"But you remember it with a child's eyes," Amenemhet reminded. "No one looks with more contempt on the people of Zahi than I, but you must remember that things influence a child differently."

"Human sacrifice would horrify me no less now than it did then," Nefrytatanen replied coldly.

"Human sacrifice?" Amenemhet stared at her. "Are you sure?"

"I'm sure." Nefrytatanen's eyes were purple ice. "My father signed a treaty of peace, which we later learned was worthless from the start. We went to the temple to honor the treaty in ceremony." Nefrytatanen shuddered at the memory. "They dragged a young girl into the temple—she was dressed in crimson and I remember the crown of scarlet flowers in her hair. Then, though she screamed and begged for her life, a giant slave lifted her and threw her into the flames." Nefrytatanen's eyes raised to meet Amenemhet's. "The stench of burning flesh filled their filthy temples then, and it fills their temples yet!"

Sixteen

Amenemhet turned and put his hands on Nakht's shoulder. "Don't look so grim, my friend," he said softly. "If Kenset is filled with women like Azza, your stay shouldn't be too unpleasant."

"The women in Kenset seem too interested in poisons and are adept at severing the heads of lances," Nakht replied with a grim smile. "If I took one to my bed, I wouldn't be sure I'd awaken in the morning."

"It can't be that bad," Nefrytatanen declared.

"Between the plots and insects, it's worse," Kheti said quickly. "If you survive all that, you never can be sure when a lion will attack you, and usually the climate is such you almost don't care."

"He speaks the truth," Nakht said. "I'm not happy to go. But being a loyal servant of the king, I'll face the dangers." He squared his shoulders in exaggerated dignity and solemnly stepped onto the gangplank. "But I'm happy to shorten the journey by sailing instead of tramping through the jungles on horseback."

"If you must leave Kenset suddenly, a horse is easier to saddle than a ship to load," Kheti reminded.

217

"That ship will be prepared to sail every moment I'm there," Nakht declared. "The crew will never disembark."

"You'll have a very surly crew," Amenemhet commented.

"I think you'll get the treaty signed more easily than you'd have us believe," Nefrytatanen said with a laugh. "I suspect you've told many women you're much endangered so they will weep all the while you're gone."

"That would inspire me to return quickly to soothe them," Nakht replied.

"Do you think you'll persuade Balthazar and Karomana to sign the treaty?" Nefrytatanen asked.

"By the time I arrive, there may be only one of them to deal with," Nakht replied. "That land is full to the top with treachery."

"Remind Karomana or Balthazar—whoever has survived—that friendship with Tamera would be as beneficial to Kenset as to us," Amenemhet said seriously. "If any treachery seems turned in your direction, you may hint that their border is not too long a march from Ithtawe."

"Knowing I have your support is balm to my soul."

"Was there a time you doubted it?" Amenemhet asked. He gripped Nakht's shoulder more tightly. "It isn't that I have reason to be suspicious, Nakht, but hear me anyway. Be careful."

Nakht felt Amenemhet's arm drop from his shoulders, then said softly, "I'll be careful. I have no desire to be carried back to Tamera and buried with the honors due a fallen ambassador. I much prefer the simple funeral of an obscure citizen, very old, of course."

"You'll die in peaceful circumstances," Nefrytatanen assured him.

"There is one way, though not exactly peaceful, in which I wouldn't mind dying! But it will require a great number of years before I get weak enough to die that way," Nakht said, grinning wickedly.

Kheti glanced beyond Nakht's shoulder at the ship's commander, who, with a look of resignation, leaned elbows on the ship's rail, waiting.

"The ship is ready to sail," Kheti reminded Nakht.

Nakht sighed and started up the gangplank, then turned and called, "I'll bring you back a robe like Balthazar's, only in red, as you requested."

Kheti rolled his eyes heavenward. "My prayer is granted at

last," he said sarcastically. Nakht laughed and hurried onto the ship.

Watching the lines being thrown onto the deck, Amenemhet asked, "Why do you want such a robe, Kheti?"

"They're a great help on lion hunts," Kheti replied. "They attract the eyes of the lion and ensure drawing him near enough to spear easily, provided no one has sawed off the point of your spear."

Neferset looked at Kheti with a confused expression. "Why would someone do that?"

Kheti smiled. "It's a long story and I'll relate it later—in the shade of our room, with a goblet of wine in my hand."

"I wish I could join you," Amenemhet said. "I'm going to meet with the province governors this afternoon, and I don't look forward to it. I've had nothing but complaints from them, and I suspect I'll have nothing more than that during this session." He looked at Kheti in surprise, as if something had just occurred to him. "You govern a province!"

Kheti's face fell. "I suppose I must attend this meeting?"

"I'd like to see a friendly face or two."

"My face won't be friendly," Kheti said in disgust. "I'll be wishing I were somewhere else."

"So will I," Amenemhet said, "but I can't be excused from such conferences."

"What a pleasure it will be for me to attend this discussion," Nefrytatanen observed. "I'll have nothing but cheerful faces to look upon."

"Do you see no way to solve the problem?" Neferset asked.

"I find myself in the same position with the governors as I was when Shera and his thieves harassed us. Only that time the food shortage was real. I'm still doubtful about it this time."

"You've heard nothing from Taka?" Kheti asked.

"I expect his return any day," Amenemhet answered. "I had hoped he would give me a definite answer before this meeting, but I can delay no longer. If I do nothing else, I'll command their cooperation."

"If you go into the meeting in your present mood, I think you'll have little patience with anything they say," Nefrytatanen observed.

"If I hear more whining, I'll have no patience," Amenemhet declared. "I wish Taka had returned so I could go into the meeting armed with truth."

Amenemhet sat, chin resting in his hands, no longer listening to the droning voices of the governors. Their stories were as he'd expected—lengthy accounts of crop failures and pleas for lowered taxes, with no suggestions about how the problems could be solved. Amenemhet could have accurately predicted which governors would complain, but offer no constructive ideas. He also knew which of them would sit through the meeting, even as he was, disgusted and bored. Of the latter, those who were in need of help would remain silent, trying every means possible to solve their own problems.

Amenemhet's golden eyes drifted over the faces to Kheti, who stared at the floor stifling a yawn. Beside Kheti, Lord Rakkor's massive bulk hunched in his chair like a mountain. Amenemhet noted that Rakkor was either resting his eyes or sleeping. Lord Semerkhet's eyes were definitely open, and they looked like pieces of onyx as he stared angrily at Lord Menkara, who was giving another full accounting of his monumental problems. Next to Semerkhet sat Sitah, his son, gazing in awe at Nessumontu. Amenemhet smiled. Sitah was almost ten years old, and far more interested in following a military career than in succeeding his father as lord of Uto Province.

Nefrytatanen startled Amenemhet by tugging his arm to draw his attention to Taka's entrance. Taka's brown face was grim as he walked swiftly to the front of the room to kneel before Amenemhet and Nefrytatanen.

"Rise, Taka," Amenemhet said. "How did you fare in Retenu?"

"Not badly, sire," Taka replied slowly as he stood up. "But there's a private matter I must discuss with you without delay."

"Then we'll step into the adjoining room," Amenemhet said, rising. "I'm sure Lord Menkara can use a few moments to rest his throat." Amenemhet turned and led Taka to the anteroom.

Nessumontu silently drifted over to post himself outside the door to the anteroom, thereby ensuring Amenemhet and Taka complete privacy. To the curious looks he received, Nessumontu smiled coldly.

Amenemhet walked to the far side of the room and looked through the doorway to the garden. Satisfied no one loitered nearby, he turned to Taka. "What have you learned?" he asked as he sat down, his eyes still on the garden.

"More than I'd dreamed," Taka replied. "I don't know where to begin."

"Sit down and begin where it suits you," Amenemhet said quietly. "Don't worry about delaying that meeting. They've complained for two hours and can wait awhile to resume."

Taka took a deep breath and settled wearily in a chair facing Amenemhet. "Some governors overtax their peasants, then hide the surplus when Meri sends your tax collectors, so they can plead a poor harvest and obtain a still-smaller assessment. They bring their peasants forward to demonstrate their lack of nourishment. The tax collectors take pity and lower the assessment, which benefits the governors, not the peasants. You may have noticed the girth of certain noblemen seems to indicate prosperity, not privation. The peasants are afraid to complain."

"Do the peasants fear me?" Amenemhet asked.

"Only the lords of the most distant provinces dare this particular scheme," Taka said shaking his head. "The journey their peasants would have to make to seek an audience with you is long, and during such a journey, a man can be more easily traced and caught."

"How did you learn all this?" Amenemhet leaned forward anxiously.

"I guessed much from studying the tax records before I left Ithtawe, and my own observations confirmed it." Taka's eyes lifted to meet Amenemhet's, and they were filled with anger. "One peasant almost escaped. He never reached a town or a garrison, because he was caught and left for dead in a large field, which hadn't been planted so it could rest this season. No one would have gone out there until after the spring flood. When the river went down, nothing would have been left of his body. I came upon him only by chance. I was out taking soil samples at random, searching for some pattern in this infestation of pests, and I went to the river for a drink. The peasant had crawled to the river and hidden himself in the weeds where he could be near the water. He hadn't the strength to go farther."

"This peasant told you of the governor's cheating?" Amenemhet asked.

"He had only enough strength to tell me something of what I already surmised. He did say something about a Hyksos in the province, but he fainted before he could say more. I wrapped him in my cloak, covered him with straw and carried him off secretly in my cart." Taka sighed. "But he never awakened."

"Where is this man's body?" Amenemhet demanded.

Taka looked as if he wished he could disappear. "Sire, I'm ashamed and even afraid to tell you."

"Tell me anyway," Amenemhet sighed.

"As I ferried myself across the river, the peasant's body rolled between the openings in the railing and fell in the water. The crocodiles made short work of him," Taka whispered.

Amenemhet was silent for a long moment, until he finally said, "How can I confront the governors with the story of a dead peasant whose corpse I can't produce, whose name I don't know?" Amenemhet looked up at Taka. "You didn't get the peasant's name? His governor's name?" Taka shook his head and Amenemhet asked, "Where, then, did you find him?"

"Su-Sekhem Province," Taka answered.

"That doesn't prove it's the province where he lived," Amenemhet reasoned. "Mention this incident to no one." Amenemhet sat back in the chair with a grim expression, "Did you find any insects?"

"I found some, but I'm confused. They're a strange mixture of parasites, not ordinarily found in each other's company. I don't understand it—but they are there," Taka said.

Amenemhet mutered in disgust, "Now we'll have to burn fields." He got to his feet and stalked to the door, Taka following dejectedly. Before Amenemhet opened the door, he turned to Taka. "Don't be so distressed. My anger isn't for you," he said quietly. "I'm grateful you learned as much as you did. Tomorrow we'll speak again."

Taka looked relieved. "Maybe we will find an answer yet."

"Not maybe," Amenemhet said quietly. "We must." He opened the door and stepped out.

When Amenemhet returned to the meeting, Nefrytatanen knew from his expression that he was disturbed by Taka's report.

"Sit down, Lord Menkara," Amenemhet said quietly.

Menkara stared at him in disbelief. "Sire, I haven't finished speaking. If you recall—"

"Sit down, Lord Menkara," Amenemhet repeated. Menkara sank into his chair, turning red with embarrassment. Amenemhet began, "I've heard of hardships, poor harvests,

222

starving peasants and insects, but I've heard no suggestions on how to solve these problems." Amenemhet looked at Menkara and asked, "When did you first discover the worms you claim ruined your barley?"

Nefrytatanen knew, from the tone of Amenemhet's voice, that Menkara had better have something worthwhile to say or he would be well advised to remain silent.

"Two seasons ago," Menkara replied faintly.

"What did you do about it?" Amenemhet inquired.

"There weren't enough pests to bother with then." Menkara sensed a trap, but there was no way he could think of to avoid it.

"You neither plowed nor burned the field?" Amenemhet asked. At Menkara's silence, Amenemhet went on, "Why are you amazed, Lord Menkara, that you find more worms this season? Aren't you aware of the laws of reproduction?"

Kheti laughed softly, but audibly. Menkara glared at Kheti, which seemed to disturb Kheti not at all.

"Haven't I always governed Su-Sekhem Province well?" Menkara asked angrily. "Why am I being questioned as if I'm on trial?"

"I won't remain at this meeting if it's becoming a trial," Lord Hesepti said, rising from his chair.

Nefrytatanen turned to look at Hesepti. She knew he was Menkara's friend, but she was surprised he acted so imprudently. She could almost feel the rising heat of Amenemhet's anger.

Amenemhet arose, his eyes hot with gold fire, and commanded, "Lord Hesepti, place your hindquarters again in your chair and move only when I look to you."

Amenemhet's sharp command surprised Menkara and, impulsively, he stood up.

"Menkara, you rise to depart?" Amenemhet's voice held the softness of distant thunder, and golden lightning lit his eyes. "Let me invite you to remain a little longer." His words were almost a caress as he added, "Or have you forgotten with whom you sit?"

Menkara sank back into his chair, visions of his future career passing through his mind. He had thought, since Amenemhet and Nefrytatanen's return from Retenu, that Amenemhet's temper had cooled, because they had seemed so friendly and informal. Now he wondered if the plans he had made with Zahi would be accomplished only after his own banishment.

"My temper is short today," Amenemhet said more quietly, "for I am weary of hearing complaints. I have decided the only proper action is to plow under and burn every field invaded by any destructive creatures whether they are beetles, worms or caterpillars. It must be done immediately, because the floods will soon begin. I will make sure this order is carried out by arranging with Taka to have inspectors travel to every province affected. The inspectors will make their reports directly to me. Make sure no misfortune befalls any of them, for I wouldn't be happy to suspect anyone of arranging an accident."

The governors stared at Amenemhet, wanting to deny even thinking about such things, but they were too frightened to speak.

"Regarding the reduction of taxes," Amenemhet added, "those already collected will not be returned in any part."

Amenemhet stood up abruptly, and Nefrytatanen followed. The governors got to their feet silently as Amenemhet and Nefrytatanen left the room.

Amenemhet stood in waist-deep water at the edge of the bathing pool watching Nefrytatanen, who floated on her back with her eyes closed. He plucked a nearby lotus from the water and, taking careful aim, tossed the flower so that it landed neatly on her navel.

She opened her eyes to examine the missile, then shut them, allowing the lotus to remain undisturbed.

Amenemhet approached her and asked, "Will you stand up?"

Nefrytatanen's legs promptly disappeared and she stood up, looking up at him questioningly through eyelashes sparkling with droplets of perfumed water.

Amenemhet leaned down, and his lips had just brushed Nefrytatanen's when the door of the bathing chamber opened and slammed loudly. He looked up, but neither released her nor stepped away.

Yazid and Dedjet hurried to the edge of the pool, carrying drying cloths and robes. Amenemhet glared at them.

"We left orders not to be disturbed until we called," he said.

"Sire, excuse us," Yazid quickly replied, his forehead wrinkled with a frown. "A messenger has come from King Naram of Akkad. He has ridden fast and hard and said the message is of great importance."

Amenemhet and Nefrytatanen exchanged looks of alarm and waded to the pool's edge.

"Get Nessumontu and Meri," Amenemhet ordered as he took the cloth Yazid offered. Yazid nodded and ran out.

Amenemhet and Nefrytatanen dried themselves and dressed quickly. Then, they hurried, still arranging their garments, to the chamber where Amenemhet received couriers. When they arrived, Nessumontu was already waiting with the Akkad messenger, and Meri followed them through the door.

"Where's the message?" Amenemhet asked immediately.

"Majesties, my king had no time to write it," the courier replied.

"Sit down," Amenemhet offered. "You look exhausted."

The messenger sank gratefully into a chair. "I haven't stopped since I left Agade," he said. "I fear my horse is dead." He looked up at Amenemhet, feeling embarrassed that the king and queen stood while he sat.

Amenemhet smiled faintly and seated himself. "Tell us the message," he directed.

Nefrytatanen remained standing, staring intently at the courier. Her mind reached out and touched his, and she learned his news by a method faster than words. She turned, walked to the window and looked out at the garden, her face stiff with anger.

"Sire," began the messenger. He stopped, appearing as if he would weep. He controlled himself, took a deep breath and continued, "Under the command of Sargon, the army of Zahi invaded Akkad. When I left our capital city, Agade was under steady fire from the catapults and seemed ready to fall. King Naram wished to warn you the Hyksos might march on Ithtawe next."

Amenemhet heard Nessumontu curse softly behind him, and he could find no words to say what was passing through his own mind. Finally, he leaned wearily back and said in a disgusted tone, "Tell me what happened, and embellish it not. I must know the exact situation so I may judge this accurately."

"Sire, I need not embellish it. The story is bloody enough," the courier replied. "By this time my people are slaves to Zahi—those still alive, anyway. Agade must already be razed." The messenger lifted anguished eyes to Amenemhet. "They marched through our country at night, killing any of our people they came upon so we couldn't be warned. They attacked Agade so suddenly and with such force none from

225

the surrounding countryside had a chance to seek the city's shelter." The messenger began to rise from his chair as he continued, "But we fought back with a similar fury. At one point, though we were bloody, we launched an assault on the invaders which threw them into retreat!" The courier sank back into his chair, his eyes filled with pain. "Sire, can you imagine the next command Sargon gave?" He stared at Amenemhet as if he couldn't believe it himself. "Sargon ordered the Hyksos archers to fire on their own men, thus forcing them to turn back to the walls of Agade!"

Again Nessumontu cursed and began to pace the floor in frustration. Finally, he stopped before the messenger. "Is there any hope at all?"

"Commander Nessumontu, none," the courier said. "If I return, I'll be killed or enslaved like the rest. I have no doubt of it." .

"You'll remain in Ithtawe until you can return to Akkad in safety," Amenemhet said quietly. "Go now. Refresh yourself. Food will be sent to you."

"Majesty, I cannot eat," the messenger said as he slowly got to his feet. "I'm like a dead man. I saw all my family killed before I left Agade's gates. A fiery bolt from a catapult landed on my house, and there was no way to save any of them." He turned and walked wearily to the door. "Thank you for asylum," he said, pausing a moment before he followed a waiting servant.

"What will we do?" Meri asked softly.

"For the moment we can do nothing more than give refuge to those who managed to escape," Amenemhet replied sadly. "Nessumontu, you will increase the ranks of the royal army and prepare for possible invasion. I don't think King Shalmanesser is so foolish that he'd actually try to invade our borders yet, but we'll try to dampen any such ambitions by being obvious with our readiness to defend Tamera."

"It's disgusting that Sargon would fire on his own men," Nessumontu declared. "I've never heard of so dishonorable a thing."

"What would you expect from the Hyksos?" Nefrytatanen turned from the window opening. "I told you what they are."

Amenemhet waved Meri and Nessumontu out, then turned to Nefrytatanen. He said, "Your eyes hold the heat of a blue flame."

Nefrytatanen's chin lifted a bit higher. "Zahi will look at

226

Tamera next. They wait, as always, for some hint of weakness in us."

Amenemhet took both her hands in his. They were cold.

"They're people who love war!" she exclaimed.

His golden eyes lifted to hers, and they were filled with anger. "As long as there's an army in Zahi, they'll look at Tamera and measure our strength."

"If they had any hope they could defeat us, they'd be at our throats," Nefrytatanen said. "Gobryas would come himself to kill you."

"As long as I'm alive, Gobryas will plot my death," Amenemhet agreed. "When our eyes met for the first time, there was in his glance so great a malice I knew he'd never stop until one of us is dead."

Nefrytatanen's eyes flashed up at her husband. "Beloved," she said, "it must be him."

Amenemhet nodded grimly. "I surely hope so."

She stared at him a moment. "Then we'll prepare fully for their coming?"

"It will be a strain on the land with these other problems we're having," Amenemhet reflected.

"The land will be united behind you as always, for it was your will and strength that made the Two Lands one," Nefrytatanen said quietly.

Two decans later, while Amenemhet and Nefrytatanen were holding court, a palace guard opened the tall copper doors and strode the length of the lapis-paneled throne room. A hush fell over the court, and his sandals seemed to echo ominously. The crowd watched closely as he stopped at the base of the dais and knelt before the golden thrones.

At his whispered message, the expressions on Amenemhet's and Nefrytatanen's faces changed, causing a tense murmur to run through the crowd like a moving drift of desert sand. The guard waited for a reply, but the king and queen said nothing. Their eyes were fixed on the great doors, and Meri silently motioned the petitioner standing before them to move aside.

When the doors again swung open, Amenemhet and Nefrytatanen stood up. Their expressions were forbidding and their bodies seemed stiff with tension. Heads turned and necks stretched as the crowd struggled to see who had entered. Now the throng became so still there was not even a whisper from the movement of their garments.

Amenemhet turned to Nefrytatanen and murmured, "I will step down and walk a few paces toward them." Nefrytatanen's nod indicated agreement; the gesture indicated that the delegation from Zahi was unfit even to approach the thrones of the Two Lands. Nefrytatanen remained on the dais watching Amenemhet walk slowly toward the Hyksos.

Ambassador Adadni's triumphant smirk faded to an uneasy look. Amenemhet's lips held no polite smile, and neither did his eyes indicate pretended welcome. When Amenemhet stopped, there were still several paces between him and Adadni, which forced Adadni to either speak loudly or come closer. He chose the latter.

"Greetings from King Shalmanesser, radiant son of Ra," Adadni said, dropping to his knees. Adadni noted his words brought a frown to Amenemhet's face. He paused, waiting for Amenemhet's returning salutation or at least permission to rise. Amenemhet remained silent. Adadni wondered what he should say next. He hadn't anticipated Amenemhet's cringing, but he thought the king of a country threated by an army that had already conquered its neighbor might show some measure of respect. Adadni didn't think King Shalmanesser would be happy to know his delegation was being deliberately insulted. Adadni got to his feet without Amenemhet's permission and decided to remind Amenemhet of Zahi's victory over Akkad.

"Will you not congratulate us on defeating our enemy?" Adadni said in a deliberately insinuating tone. Commander Nessumontu, who was standing nearby, moved closer to King Amenemhet. Adadni addressed him. "And you, commander, do you not appreciate the meaning of such a triumph?"

Nessumontu opened his mouth as if to answer, then looked at Amenemhet and remained silent.

Amenemhet turned to Adadni and observed, "The lilt of Tamera's language is coarsened by your Hyksos accents, or does the harshness of your tone reveal a threat the words themselves hide?" Amenemhet turned and returned to his throne, giving the impression that he had examined his enemy and found him too weak an adversary to trouble with.

Adadni remained where he stood for a moment, wondering what he might say. He glanced at Nessumontu. His gaze lingered curiously on Tamera's military commander, because Nessumontu's eyes glowed with a strange orange light.

"We heard of Zahi's victory at Agade," Nessumontu said contemptuously. "I congratulate Commander Sargon for his brilliant victory." Nessumontu gave Adadni one more hard look and turned to follow Amenemhet. "Sire, I feel unwell. May I be excused from court?"

Amenemhet nodded and turned to Nefrytatanen. "I doubt Nessumontu has ever been sick in his life," he remarked, "but I don't feel well myself." He took her hand and peered into her face. "Beloved, you appear pale," he said. He glanced at his councillors' angry faces. "It seems some strange malady has struck the whole court." Looking at Adadni, who finally approached the dais, Amenemhet said coldly, "We must delay the audience until we recover, ambassador."

Making no further explanation and not waiting for Adadni's reply, Amenemhet nodded to Nefrytatanen; they stepped off the dais and left the throne room.

When they were in their private corridor with the doors securely bolted behind them, Amenemhet said, "If I'd had to look at Adadni one moment longer, I'd have begun a war with Zahi by having their ambassador parted from his head."

"Do you think he actually wished to frighten us?" Nefrytatanen asked.

"He should know better," Amenemhet replied. "I think his mission is to observe our reaction and spy on our defenses."

"Can't we send him and the delegation away?" Nefrytatanen didn't like to think of Adadni's even being in the palace.

"We could," Amenemhet answered, "but I want him to see the royal army's strength. Let him carry back to Zahi descriptions of Nessumontu's preparations for war."

"They'd know they won't be able to take Tamera as they did Akkad."

"That's what I intend," Amenemhet agreed.

After Amenemhet and Nefrytatanen had given Yazid and Dedjet their heavy crowns and scepters, they went to their private apartment to relax, but they were told Kheti and Nessumontu wanted to speak with them.

When Kheti and Nessumontu entered, Amenemhet said, "I congratulate you on your swift recovery, Nessumontu."

Kheti smiled. "You should have seen Adadni's face when he marched out of the throne room! The comments of the rest of the court added to Adadni's anger, for many people chuckled openly as they filed out, making loud comments about their own fevered brows."

"I don't intend to give Adadni an audience," Amenemhet said. "We will make him and his delegation as uncomfortable as possible. But," he said, looking at Nessumontu, "I want him to see your preparations, so he'll bring Sargon a report of the royal army's strength."

"He'll see enough military might," Nessumontu said quietly.

"It's interesting that each time the governors begin to have some kind of trouble, Zahi also threats us," Kheti remarked.

"The nobility's struggle for personal power is like a weed with long roots," Amenemhet observed. "Each time I have pulled up this weed, and thought I was rid of it, it sprouts again in another place. I had begun to think present complaints were no more than stories, until Taka told me the insects are real. I think the insects, the Hyksos and the governors are somehow connected, but I need proof."

"It will be revealed eventually," Kheti assured him.

"In the meantime, it's most frustrating," Amenemhet said.

"I've found one of the best ways to relieve frustration of many kinds is to go to the exercise room and practice with my sword or shoot arrows," Nessumontu said. "Sometimes I picture a particular person as my target, which gives me a truer eye as well as some satisfaction."

"That idea has appeal." Amenemhet's face brightened. "I've had no practice for some time. What would you say to coming with me now?"

"I wouldn't mind sending an arrow or two through a target I imagine as Adadni," Kheti agreed.

Amenemhet stood up and smiled at Nefrytatanen. "With these two talking of imaginary revenge, I'm not sure it's safe to go with them," he said. "I hope they don't get too enthusiastic."

"Just be sure you don't lose your own head," she warned. "You were very angry in the throne room."

"I won't," Amenemhet replied, still smiling. "I'm so out of practice I think I'll be harmlessly clumsy."

A number of off-duty palace guards and some noblemen were in the room that was set aside for practice. The air rang with a clash of swords, shouts of encouragement and gibes. Amenemhet paused in the doorway a moment, taking in the lively scene. A feeling of exhilaration came over him. No one noticed him, because he had changed into a short tunic unidentifiable from the rest. He found himself enjoying one of his rare moments of anonymity.

"What do you wish to do?" Kheti asked.

"I didn't bring my sword for decoration," Amenemhet declared, then challenged, "Which of you want to taste defeat?"

Kheti smiled and shook his head. "I think I'll delay awhile. I think you're going to imagine your opponent as Adadni, and I fear your anger."

"I'll take you on," Nessumontu offered. He looked over at a small group of boys, who were watching the men enviously. "I see Sitah, Lord Semerkhet's son, standing there," Nessumontu noted. "His eyes seem ready to fall out of his head with wishing. I think I'll ask him to come and help me." Nessumontu grinned suddenly and added, "He's a fine boy and much interested in the military. He'll be pleased to join us."

"Ask him, then," Amenemhet said, taking his sword from Yazid and examining the sharpness of the blade. "From the way he stares at you, I think he'll be very honored."

Nessumontu nodded and walked over to Sitah, who looked up at him in amazement. Sitah nodded with such enthusiasm his black hair fell in his eyes. When Nessumontu returned with Sitah, the boy stared at Amenemhet with even more awe. His curious companions followed at a little distance, while their excited whispers attracted other glances. Soon a small group stood nearby, waiting to see what the king and the military commander would do.

Amenemhet glanced at the gathering crowd, not particularly pleased to have spectators. But he knew there was little he could ever do without attracting attention, and he sighed in resignation.

"Are you ready?" Nessumontu asked. Amenemhet nodded. "Don't be so gloomy. I'll go easy on you," Nessumontu teased.

Amenemhet said nothing. When he got into place, his eyes contained a light Nessumontu should have recognized and taken as a warning. But Nessumontu stood in position, unaware and confident.

Amenemhet attacked Nessumontu immediately, and Nessumontu, seldom surprised by any tactic, looked amazed. He found himself stepping back from Amenemhet's onslaught, knowing retreat was to his disadvantage, but having no choice.

Lord Semerkhet and several other noblemen came closer to watch with great interest.

"The king's arm is mighty, and he's as light-footed as a cat," Semerkhet commented.

Kheti was silent, absorbed in watching the combat. Nessumontu's defense was growing desperate, while Amenemhet pressed him even more fiercely. Kheti felt alarm rising within him.

"The king becomes so enthusiastic I wonder if he forgets this is but practice," Semerkhet said with an edge to his voice.

"I agree he goes after Nessumontu most vigorously," Kheti murmured.

Although Nessumontu's sword beat off Amenemhet's steady blows, the commander's forehead was beginning to shine. Each time Nessumontu stepped back, Amenemhet pushed relentlessly forward. The air vibrated with the sound of their clashing swords.

Catching a glimpse of Amenemhet's glowing eyes, Kheti and Semerkhet exchanged looks of shock. It seemed Amenemhet fought with deadly intent. Did he have some secret reason to defeat Nessumontu, they wondered, or had he actually lost his head in excitement? They dared not stop the king or even voice their rising fear. They watched helplessly, while Amenemhet continued his merciless attack and Nessumontu's defense steadily became more ragged.

Swords locked handguard to handguard, and Amenemhet and Nessumontu stood motionless for a second, until the king suddenly withdrew. As he did he hooked one foot around the back of Nessumontu's ankle. With a quick snap of his leg, Amenemhet sent Nessumontu sprawling on his back. Semerkhet gasped softly. The point of Amenemhet's sword was at Nessumontu's throat.

Nessumontu looked at Amenemhet, panting, wondering at the king's narrowed eyes, which glittered with a fierce golden heat. The fear that had been creeping at Nessumontu's heels during the fight now stared full into his face.

"By the war god, Montu," Kheti whispered, not knowing what to think. He held his breath, watching Nessumontu helplessly looking up at Amenemhet.

Slowly Amenemhet withdrew his sword and slid it into the scabbard Yazid had been holding out to him. Then he offered his hand to Nessumontu and pulled the commander to his feet.

"That was an excellent attack," Nessumontu breathed in relief.

"If we have to face Zahi's army, I must keep my strength and skill," Amenemhet replied.

232

Nessumontu accepted a towel from Sitah, who had watched the fight paralyzed with fear. Nessumontu smiled sheepishly and observed, "I must avail myself of more practice or my captains will lose respect for me."

"I doubt that," Amenemhet said. "It isn't necessary that you defeat your king."

"I think it would also be unwise to try," Kheti remarked.

"Except in practice." Amenemhet accepted a cloth from Yazid and began to wipe his brow and hands.

"If possible," Nessumontu added.

"I hope you don't want to try me now," Kheti said slowly. "I know I'd be humiliated."

Amenemhet laughed softly. "I think I'll watch the others for a while," he answered. "I haven't been here for some time and find I've missed it." He ran his fingers through his damp hair and admitted, "Besides, I could use a moment to rest."

Nessumontu approached Sitah, who had continued to stand a few feet away watching him. "Sitah," Nessumontu said, laying his hand affectionately on the boy's shoulder, "would you like to have a lesson or two from me?" Sitah stared incredulously up at him. "Or, perhaps, after what you've seen here, you'd prefer someone else as your teacher," Nessumontu added with a smile.

"No, Commander Nessumontu," Sitah recovered himself enough to say quickly. "I would be honored to have you teach me."

Nessumontu looked at Amenemhet. "I haven't completely lost face, after all," he said and, still grasping Sitah's shoulder, turned and led them.

Watching Nessumontu, who had drawn Sitah into a quiet corner of the room, Kheti said, "Semerkhet, I think you may have a future officer in Sitah."

Semerkhet smiled. "Sitah must decide on that," he said.

"Don't you think he'll follow you governing Uto Province?" Kheti asked.

Semerkhet nodded. "I do hope so. But even if he wants to try this other path, I'm sure he'll one day prefer to assume my title."

"Why?" Amenemhet asked.

"I think Sitah's character is such that he couldn't pursue a military career successfully. He'd manage for a time, but he's too gentle for it." Semerkhet looked thoughtful. "Such a career requires some hardness, a trait the boy doesn't have." Semerkhet paused, then quickly added, "It isn't that he lacks

233

courage or that I think a soldier like Nessumontu is insensitive, but I think Sitah is possibly too sensitive. Do you understand?"

"Yes, I understand," Kheti answered. "I think I wouldn't do well in a military career either." He grinned. "In my case, it would be a lack of discipline."

"You have self-discipline," Amenemhet pointed out, "but you wouldn't constantly follow someone else's orders over a long period of time. I think, if I'd had to, I wouldn't have risen very far through the ranks either." He smiled wryly. "I think too much and would rebel too often. Also, I truly dislike violence."

The others stared at Amenemhet in surprise, and he added, "I've done what was necessary in the past, but I don't enjoy conflict." He shook his head slowly. "If I were a more militant person, would I not order an attack on Zahi instead of always having them threatening our borders?" he asked. He smiled at their expressions and confessed, "I've never wanted to be known as a warrior-king. I'd rather be remembered as a builder."

"I, too, am a man who loves peace, and I understand," Semerkhet said.

"I would prefer the Hyksos to turn away because they're afraid to strike," Kheti admitted.

Semerkhet's dark eyes turned to Amenemhet. "You have the courage and strength to stand fast," he said. "For this you may be remembered as a warrior-king even though the wars are begun by others. You've chosen plans for temples with the eye of an artist, but these will, no doubt, crumble in time. What will be known is that King Amenemhet fought Zahi, he terrified Retenu into signing a treaty, and his garrisons kept Kenset and Djemeh outside Tamera's borders. Such is the fate of the kings who must fight."

Semerkhet's eyes briefly shifted to Sitah, to whom Nessumontu was demonstrating the finer points of a certain technique, then returned to Amenemhet.

"No wall paintings will be left to show King Amenemhet giving his wife a flower or holding his children on his knees. Nor can the records give an account of a joke you told to cheer a friend or relate how tears ran from your eyes when you walked among the pallets of those struck down in battle." Semerkhet smiled sadly. "Such moments are seldom recorded by men," he said softly. "They are only remembered by the gods."

Seventeen

"No man has a greater measure of my respect than Nessumontu," Amenemhet said, turning so Yazid could fasten his tunic, "but he's a strange man."

"In what way do you think he's strange?" Nefrytatanen lifted her hair so Dedjet could arrange the intricate gold feathers of a delicate necklace.

Amenemhet faced her. "When I held my sword at his throat, I could see in his eyes he wasn't sure what I'd do, but he lay there coolly looking at me. It gave me cause to reflect. I've seen him in battles when he fought with a composure that startled me. When we won, he never seemed elated by victory. He's always so calm I've wondered how he can be a soldier. Still, he's not only a superior soldier, but an excellent commander of our whole army. His temperament is so even it sometimes frightens me."

"Why should it frighten you?" Nefrytatanen asked.

"Because he's a man capable of incredible things."

"Nessumontu saw too much too early," Nefrytatanen said slowly. "We were barely past childhood when I took the throne of Tamehu and appointed him commander of my army." She walked across the room to gaze at the garden as

235

she recalled the past. "Nessumontu never was boisterous, but before then, he was much more lighthearted."

Amenemhet followed Nefrytatanen and put his arm around her waist. "Tell me more, beloved," he said quietly. "I want to understand him better."

"Nessumontu has good reasons to hate the Hyksos. They killed his parents in one of their raids. In the next raid, they killed the commander of Tamehu's army, whom Nessumontu regarded with a respect akin to adoration." She looked up at Amenemhet. "Had you seen Nessumontu then, the last thing you would have called him was calm. When Nessumontu, already grieving for his family, received news of the death of the commander, he looked like one of Sekhmet's avenging demons. After his victory, which was one of the bloodiest fights in Tamehu's history, he returned no more excited than if he'd been on the practice field. When I questioned him, he merely said he was satisfied to have won." Nefrytatanen sighed. "After that, he came back from every patrol triumphant, but unmoved by triumph. I asked again if he wasn't aroused by victory. He answered he felt neither joy nor sorrow. He said that if he mourned each soldier who fell, he would go mad, and if he thought too much about having to kill, he would be haunted by ghosts. He said that in any conflict he preferred to feel nothing."

"I wonder how he's able to do it," Amenemhet said softly.

"Beloved . . ." Nefrytatanen put her hands on Amenemhet's arms and looked into his eyes. "Nessumontu and I lost our youth in the course of events. Because of our positions, we were never childish enough to play, and he was yet too young to carouse. We understood each other very well, because the situation thrust upon us was a bond. Nessumontu stopped hating the Hyksos because in the depth of his hatred he was capable of something he couldn't endure living with." She released Amenemhet's arms and walked slowly toward the door. "We're going to be late for the review," she said, but her eyes were still in the past.

When Amenemhet stood beside her, she paused before opening the door. "Nessumontu handed me his victories like a gift, and I gave him decorations as rewards," she said thoughtfully. "The victories, like the decorations, were gestures. What we really exchanged was love."

"Nessumontu loved you?" Amenemhet asked slowly.

"Yes, he loved me," Nefrytatanen replied. "Not as a woman, but as his queen. I've always returned that love in the same fashion." She saw Amenemhet's expression, and the hint of a smile lit her eyes before she added, "He loves you in the same way."

Amenemhet made no comment, but as they walked through the corridors into the sunlit courtyard where the lines of soldiers awaited inspection, he wondered how much of Nessumontu's youthful heart had looked upon his girl-queen platonically and how much had regarded her in a far different manner than Nefrytatanen had ever realized.

Inspecting the troops with Nessumontu, walking between the rows of men standing smartly at attention, Amenemhet observed Nessumontu's attitude, and finally concluded that now Nessumontu's life was devoted to his men.

"I've never seen the army look more fit," Amenemhet finally said.

"Or more proud," Nefrytatanen noted.

The expressions on the sun-browned faces they passed never altered, but the men's pleasure at this exchange was tangible.

"It's reassuring to know such men protect Tamera," Amenemhet remarked. "How much better it is to have an army of citizens who love their land than to buy foreign mercenaries."

"They're well paid," Nessumontu noted, "but you're right—their loyalty isn't bought."

Nefrytatanen studied the face of the man who stood before her and said, "The light in his eyes wasn't paid for in gold." She looked up at Amenemhet, adding in a whisper, "Your people love you."

Amenemhet made no comment.

As they turned from the last line of men, Nessumontu glanced in the direction of the palace's entrance and observed, "Adadni and some of their delegation watch us. It should be Gobryas and Sargon who stand there."

"These soldiers are an impressive sight," Amenemhet agreed.

Nefrytatanen looked at the straight, lean bodies and the proud set of the shoulders in the lines they passed. "They're more than impressive."

Nessumontu's eyes scanned his men with satisfaction. "If these soldiers saw the Hyksos archers firing on their own men to drive them to attack Ithtawe's walls, they'd know we had won the battle." He turned his gaze to Adadni and the other Hyksos. "Look at them," he said under his breath. "There's a glimmer of fear in their faces, I think."

"There should be," Nefrytatanen said.

"They're ambassadors, and not hardened to the sight of bloody battles," Amenemhet said. "Adadni isn't Sargon."

"Their morality is the same," Nefrytatanen said clearly. "Sargon swings his sword, but Adadni is more perverse with words."

Nessumontu stopped walking. "Will we have to fight, do you think?"

"Perhaps."

"For myself, I would go all the way to Shalmanesser's palace and end this thing," Nessumontu said softly. "It's hard to always be on the alert for this serpent to rise again. I'd rather cut off its head and have done with it."

"But then, to keep the Hyksos under control, I would have to rule them." Amenemhet's golden eyes seemed to appraise the future, and he sighed. "Zahi has no treasures to enrich Tamera. Holding them under our dominion would drain the Two Lands."

"Your point is well made," Nessumontu agreed. "But how will you solve the problem?"

"I don't know," Amenemhet replied. He was quiet a moment as he gazed at the delegation still standing on the palace steps. "It must be a long-lasting solution, not one which endures for a year or two."

Nefrytatanen took his arm. "Maybe one day the Hyksos will grow wise enough to realize what one builds for himself is more secure than what one steals from another."

Nessumontu's eyes narrowed. "I won't live in hope that the Hyksos will display that much intelligence."

Amenemhet sighed. "Nor I. One lifetime isn't that long. I'll teach Senwadjet to be as good a ruler as he can, and maybe one day Tamera won't have to hold its own borders by force. Meanwhile, we must be strong."

Having an entire wall open to the jungle with only lattice-work for protection gave Nakht mixed feelings. He wasn't fond of the sight of Kenset's jungles hanging over him, ready to invade his room, but he felt safer to have more than one exit to his chamber. He sat in a chair contemplating the scene, though he longed to see the green expanse of a Tameran field.

"Are you weary?" Bak asked, unfastening Nakht's sandals, "Do you wish some refreshment?"

"A goblet of wine would be welcome," Nakht replied. "But

238

only one goblet, my friend, he added quickly. "Numbing the brain with wine isn't commendable at any time, but I think it can be dangerous in Kenset."

The servant put away Nakht's sandals and busied himself with pouring wine. "Do you expect treachery?" he asked. "I could take some precautions if you do."

"Treachery is always possible." Nakht sighed. "But, I think, unlikely. I just feel uncomfortable in Kenset." Accepting the goblet, he stared out at the jungle. "The tension between Balthazar and Karomana has increased since we were here last. It makes negotiating the treaty that much more difficult."

"Neither of them has reasons to turn venom on you." The servant looked uneasy.

"None I know of," Nakht answered, and sighed again. "I just wish we were back in Ithtawe." He closed his eyes, recalling the view from his own house—the Nile glowing silver in the sunlight, the boatmen's calls as they went by, the north wind coming like a caress through his window opening. "I'm homesick," he said, opening his eyes. He got to his feet. "That isn't a desirable trait in an ambassador."

"Surely it is permitted," Bak said, smiling. "I would be condemned for the same crime."

"Then, we are conspirators," Nakht replied, but the word brought back his uneasiness. He couldn't allow himself to fear shadows which the morning sun would disperse. He stood straighter and sipped his wine. "Go on to bed, Bak," he said. "I'll stay up for a time yet, then manage for myself."

"Won't you need help to close the netting around your bed?"

Nakht laughed. "If there's anything I've learned to do well, it's to be sure the nets are tight. I know of nothing I fear more than the insects in this accursed place—not Balthazar, not Karomana, not assassins or even lions." He shook his head, still smiling. "I'll make sure to fasten the nets so nothing can creep in on me. But I'll lie awake half the night feeling itchy anyway."

"Perhaps your difficulty with sleeping is what makes you nervous," Bak suggested.

"No doubt," Nakht agreed. He watched the servant pull down the window coverings and leave the room, then reflected on his sleeplessness.

There had been many times in the past when successive nights had afforded little rest, but he hadn't been so uneasy.

He wondered at himself for a while, until, disgusted with his depressing thoughts, he put down his goblet and began to undress.

He could think of no good reason to feel threatened. He had taken neither side in the struggle between Karomana and Balthazar. As he got into bed, he reviewed his past actions with them, and could think of no reason for either of them to distrust him.

Nakht struggled with the fastenings of the net, then lay back and stared at the gossamer canopy, which seemed like a shadowy cocoon. He wondered if it would protect him as well as a real cocoon protected infant butterflies.

Finally Nakht fell into so shallow a sleep that he awakened frequently still thinking about his problems. He was exhausted before the goddess of slumber's gentle hand smoothed his brow.

Through the cool veils of sleep, Nakht heard a soft sound. But so immersed was he is a dream recalling a woman he had taken to a sunny meadow near Anu that the sound disturbed him too little to arouse his interest. Moments later, the movement of the netting around his bed registered on his senses, but it didn't awaken him. Neither of those things in themselves were enough to arouse him—but they had made impressions. When the soft feeling on his fingers—as if a hair brushed his skin—was added to the previous sensations, Nakht's eyelashes fluttered at last.

The persistence of the feeling, which moved from his fingertips to the back of his hand, caused him to open his eyes, which fastened on his hand in horror as he stared at a round, black shape with many legs.

He let out a shriek of terror. He tore open the net with his other hand and shook the scorpion, which was momentarily too confused to strike out, onto the floor. Afraid to step out of bed and afraid to stay lest there were other scorpions among the linens, Nakht knelt on the edge of the bed and peered at the shadowy floor.

Bak came racing in, and Nakht shouted, "If you're barefooted, don't come in here! There's a scorpion on the floor!"

Bak's slapping feet halted instantly, then raced out, returning with the sound of heavy boots. He carried a lamp in one hand and a spear in the other.

"Find it!" Nakht ordered. "There may be more of them!" He shuddered, looking at the suspicious shadows of the tangled linens. "Do you think to spear it?" he cried. "Turn

240

the spear around and beat it with the handle! Do you see it? Do you?"

To Nakht's relief, Bak bent and pounded frantically at something on the floor, then announced, "The creature is smashed to pieces."

"Bring the light here," Nakht said, leaping from the bed. "I must be sure there aren't more of them." He took the spear and cautiously lifted a sheet with it. Then he lifted another. Finally, he turned to Bak. "My hair is standing on end," he said shakily, "and my whole body is covered with bumps of fear." He looked around distractedly. "By all the divine beings of Tuat, I swear I'll never sleep again in this place!"

"How could it have gotten up into your bed?" Bak asked in confusion. "I don't understand it. Did you fasten the nets securely? I knew I should have waited and done it myself."

"The nets were fastened," Nakht said weakly. "The fingers that untied the knots I made would have as easily undone yours."

"Do you think, then, the creature was placed in your bed?" Bak stared at Nakht, appalled by the idea.

"It didn't untie the knots itself, nor does it have wings to fly up to my bed," Nakht declared. "But how did my would-be assassin manage to get into my chamber?"

"It would seem a matter to bring before Balthazar and Karomana," Bak declared. "Have no fear for your future safety. I'll take turns watching with Absu to assure no further disturbances."

Nakht took a deep breath. "My head aches," he said softly. "Let me consider this for a moment or two." He was silent as he paced the length of the room and thought about it. He longed to sit down, but he was too afraid of more scorpions. Finally, he stopped walking. "Let us say nothing of this except to Absu tonight. I accept your offer to guard with gratitude, but if I questioned anyone now, it would alert them to my suspicions. It will be better, I think, to observe the expressions that greet me in the morning. Whoever planned my death may be so surprised at my appearance he'll reveal himself." He sighed. "I dislike raising an alarm just as they're preparing to sign the treaty. I'd prefer to get it signed, then just leave Kenset."

"I'll only tell Absu," Bak promised. "No one will be happier to leave this place than I."

"I'll be happier," Nakht vowed. "Any degree of happiness surpassing my own would result in hysteria."

The next day's sun had cast long blue shadows on the polished floor before Nakht marched into Balthazar's private apartments for the personal audience he had requested.

Balthazar looked from a pile of papyrus sheets and nodded dismissal to a thin, restless-looking man who reminded Nakht of a certain small burrowing animal in Tamehu.

After the man left, Balthazar leaned back in his chair and looked expectantly at Nakht. "What urgent business can you possibly have with me, ambassador?" Balthazar asked. "I'm ready to sign the treaty, even if Karomana still has questions."

"This doesn't concern the treaty," Nakht replied, meeting Balthazar's eyes. "It's a more sensitive subject." Balthazar's eyes flickered with interest, but his smile remained unchanged as Nakht told him about the scorpion.

"I came to learn the reason it was done," Nakht said.

Balthazar arose from his chair slowly. "You think the scorpion was placed in your bed?" he asked, looking genuinely surprised.

"It seems unlikely scorpions have learned to untie the knots on the protective nets," Nakht replied.

Balthazar moved slowly around the table toward Nakht. He sat on the edge of the table and faced Nakht. "As you say, this is a sensitive issue," he said. "Do you have any idea who would do such a thing? Perhaps one of your servants with a secret grudge?"

"Not one of my servants," Nakht said promptly. "Not any of those who accompanied me from Tamera." Nakht continued staring at Balthazar and added, "I think I know who it was."

Balthazar said nothing for a moment as he studied the ambassador's dark eyes, which looked steadily at him. Nakht seemed very confident of himself, Balthazar concluded. "You haven't come to accuse me, have you?" Balthazar asked. "I wouldn't send a scorpion into the bed of a man who saved me from a lion."

"I don't accuse you."

"Who is it you suspect?"

"I warned my servants to keep silent, for I had it in mind to surprise my would-be murderer with my appearance this morning," Nakht replied. "When I came down for the morning meal, I watched carefully the eyes of everyone I met. The reaction wasn't obvious, and it was almost instantly hidden, but not quickly enough." Nakht took a deep breath. "Balthazar, why do you think Karomana wants me dead?"

Balthazar's surprise was apparent in his speechlessness. He stood up slowly, then walked a few paces away, poured two goblets of wine and, returning, offered one of them to Nakht. "This wine is my own, which I watch carefully. Drink it with confidence," he said and took several swallows from his own goblet. When Nakht still hesitated, he said, "I'm not the poisoner in this palace. I never poisoned Karomana's wine, although I am often much tempted."

"Then who did it?" Nakht was confused.

"Karomana herself." Balthazar studied Nakht's reaction a moment, then explained. "She knew her slave would die first, so she was safe enough. She wanted the court to think I did it. By making me appear the traitor, she hopes the court won't mourn my demise and turn against her when she kills me. You didn't realize that, did you?" Nakht said nothing, and Balthazar continued, "If you and Lord Kheti hadn't been on the lion hunt, my sister's problems might have been permanently solved. And who would have blamed her or even whispered a question?" Balthazar shook his head slowly. "No one. Not after they witnessed what they thought was my attempt to poison her." Balthazar smiled bitterly. "I can only think she hoped I'd be blamed for putting the scorpion in your bed. Probably she had some plan to accuse me of it, maybe even someone who would say they saw me or my servant enter your room." Aware of Nakht's odd expression, Balthazar asked, "You're shocked?"

"I was surprised to tell a man his sister is a potential murderess and have the news accepted without his raising an eyebrow," Nakht said slowly, "but from what you've told me—"

"She isn't a potential murderess," Balthazar interrupted. "She is a murderess. She killed our father to get the throne while I was out of the country. Don't forget you saw that poor little slave she poisoned." Balthazar paused, then said softly, "There have been others."

"Now I wonder if I should leave Kenset immediately—while I can. It seems there's little chance she'll sign a treaty." Nakht stood up and put his goblet on the table.

"I think not," Balthazar replied, "but I can't advise you on your own business." He stood up and faced Nakht. "I can only tell you her plans won't succeed," he whispered. "She won't kill me, nor will she keep the throne." Nakht stared at Balthazar, who smiled. "Any treaty she signs—if she doesn't

243

kill you instead—won't mean much while she's queen, I can assure you that. It will mean nothing when she's no longer on the throne." Nakht made no comment, and Balthazar put his hand on Nakht's shoulder. "Do what you wish. I've told you frankly what I plan. If you believe I can accomplish my goal, it seems reasonable for you to return to Ithtawe and wait. Whatever your decision, I suggest you begin having someone taste your wine and food, because Karomana doesn't stop trying once she's made a decision to do something."

Nakht walked silently to the door. Before he opened it, Balthazar said, "I wish you continued good health, ambassador."

"Thank you," Nakht replied. "I wish you long life."

"I need all the good wishes I can get," Balthazar answered.

In her chamber, Karomana took a scroll from a courier and ordered, "Leave me!"

She watched the messenger go, then gazed intently at her attendants. They quickly followed the courier.

Karomana sank into a nearby couch. Breaking the seal, she unrolled the papyrus, and read it. Then she lay back more comfortably among the cushions to think about the message she had received which was from Zahi's King Shalmanesser. It contained a report about the many fields in Tamera now infested with the insects and worms which Karomana had supplied to Marmarus in the form of cocoons and eggs for him to distribute to governors who opposed King Amen-emhet. The message requested that more of the pests be given to another agent of Zahi, this one posing as a wine merchant, who, in another month, would arrive at Tamera's south border. She closed her eyes, thinking with satisfaction of King Shalmanesser's report.

Images of Kheti floated through her thoughts. His dark-gray eyes under half-lowered lids glancing at her as he sat next to her at the table. His smooth, long-legged gait. His quick, light leap into his chariot. His half-smile at one of Nakht's remarks, disappearing as quickly as it had formed. Karomana had thought, if Nakht were to die, it might bring Kheti to negotiate the treaty in his place. Now she hoped Nakht was frightened enough that he might ask for a substitute ambassador to Kenset; Kheti would be the logical choice. Karomana was confident that if Kheti came alone, she would win him to her.

In exchange for her cooperation with Zahi in the destruction of Tamera's government, she had been promised the south half of Tamera to be added to Kenset—the half of Tamera that included Kheti's province.

"Shalmanesser can do what he wants with the north," she whispered, "but when I have rid myself of Balthazar and possess not only Kenset but the south part of Tamera, Lord Kheti can have more than a small province to govern. If he is the man I think he is, he will sit at my side as consort." She sighed and sat up to add, "If he is not, I can dispose of him." But she didn't care to contemplate that possibility.

Sarenput opened the door to his apartments and stopped on the threshold to stare in amazement at the confusion that greeted him.

Veils of all colors were strewn around the chamber. Every piece of furniture was heaped with glittering fabrics spilling over and dripping onto the floor, which by some magic had become rivers of crimson, purple and amber silk. Everywhere he looked there were pieces of material, rich orange and shimmering green, gossamer blue and melon. Glittering from folds of riotous colors were silver lights, like stars, running among streams of gold. Over all of it hung the warm spice of a familiar tangy perfume.

"Bring the azure linen!" called a voice in the next room.

"Have my apartments become a harem?" he said loudly.

Two almond-shaped eyes cautiously peered around the corner. Then Taji ran into the room, long black hair tumbling loose around her shoulders, a blaze of fabrics on her arms. She dropped them on a chair already glowing with a rainbow of colors.

"It'll all be finished before nightfall," Taji said apprehensively. When she saw Sarenput's widening smile, she laughed and hurried into his arms. "Queen Nefrytatanen directed her servants to carry my belongings here," she explained. She stepped away, her smile fading. "We will be a little crowded, and if this inconvenience displeases you, I can move back into my chambers until we leave Ithtawe."

Sarenput frowned. "Then I'd have to creep through the palace corridor each night as if I were your lover."

"I'd gladly come here each night," Taji offered.

"I would more gladly hold you in my arms all night. I think I can endure whatever crowding results." He drew her closer. "I think you're so small a creature I can spare the space."

245

"Will we have a room together at your house in Thes-Hertu Province, then?" Taji asked.

"We will," Sarenput assured. "Our house is large and our sleeping chamber spacious." He smoothed a strand of hair that curved along her shoulder. "We also have a beautiful courtyard, which I'm having redone to resemble my favorite section of the garden at my father's palace. There will be a lotus pool and a fountain, and the windows of our sleeping room look upon it. The perfume of the flowers will fill our chamber in the morning."

"I long to see it," Taji whispered.

"We'll stay awhile longer at Ithtawe, if you don't mind too much," Sarenput said.

"I'm happy where you are," Taji replied quickly.

Sarenput kissed her forehead. "You're so eager to please me I sometimes fear you conceal your own wishes."

"Pleasing you pleases me," she murmured. "You are the vessel from which all my desires pour, like golden dust in a shower of wealth. I have no wish other than to make you happy. It's for this purpose I was born."

"That was as your mother taught you, but I would have you do what makes you happy," Sarenput said.

"Giving you my love in this fashion is what truly makes me happy," Taji assured him.

"I'm humbled by your willingness to give love."

"Oh, no!" Taji exclaimed. "You must be proud, not humble. You're my strength. Before you came, life was pleasant, but I wasn't happy. The lack of love in my heart was a thing I felt. When I came to dance at the queen's party, I felt empty. Then I looked up, and you were there. Your presence was so powerful, I was filled with you."

Sarenput laid his cheek on her silky head and closed his eyes. "I thank Hat-Hor for you," he whispered. "We'll stay at Ithtawe for a little longer to see what happens with these latest troubles. Then we'll go home," he promised.

Ilbaya's copper head bent over his task of mending a camel harness. He crouched in a shady corner of the market place near Marmarus' tent, where he could listen to the conversations of the passing crowds without drawing attention.

"That golden-haired Greek girl Marmarus keeps for himself would tempt me greatly," a man nearby remarked.

Ilbaya continued at his task. He had heard many comments about Lyra, but few buyers had come for any of Marmarus' slaves. Marmarus' bad reputation had spread quickly, and Ilbaya had learned the citizens of Tamera didn't buy slaves readily in any event. He had often wondered why Marmarus wasn't more disturbed at his lack of sales. The trader had complained many times, but Ilbaya thought his complaints lacked conviction.

"That Babylonian would charge the king's own treasure for her, I think," another commented.

"She's wasted on Marmarus," declared the first.

Ilbaya glanced up briefly, quickly appraising the speakers. They were prosperous merchants, he judged from their garments.

The man added, "What a pity she's like a flute, while Marmarus seems to be a man who not only cannot play a flute, but is also deaf."

Ilbaya fixed his eyes on the harness. He dared not raise them, because he was angry to hear Lyra spoken of as an object and it wasn't proper for a slave's eyes to heat with anger. He thought of the many times he had wanted to be with Lyra, to love her as a free man. He recalled the few hasty kisses they had exchanged since his beating, and pain filled him. Marmarus watched her too closely to allow Ilbaya and Lyra more than a stolen moment together.

"I wonder why the king allows the Babylonian to stay. Surely he's heard reports not pleasing to him." The merchant's remark regained Ilbaya's attention.

"The king has problems to worry him that are of greater importance than a slave dealer." The other man sighed. "It's whispered at court that his majesty is suspicious of these governors who always have problems at the same time the Hyksos begin stirring."

"It makes me curious that it's the provinces always farthest from the palace that have the worst problems," the first man declared.

Ilbaya managed to control his expression and looked up from his work at last, but the men had strolled on to mingle with the crowd, and he heard no more. As he bent again to his work, he considered their conversation carefully. Marmarus had met a Hyksos messenger and a Tameran nobleman secretly in the night.

Sure that the interlude carried much significance, Ilbaya regretted his limited knowledge of the Tameran language. He could understand enough for a clearly spoken conversation such as the present one between the merchants, but the hur-

247

ried whispers of that nocturnal meeting were only blurred sounds to him. Closing his eyes, he thought about the Tameran's shadowed features. He knew he could easily describe the man, and he wondered if his description would identify the man. Even so, Ilbaya decided, the rest of his story surely would arouse interest, if the king was having trouble with the governors and the Hyksos. Ilbaya considered again how he might speak to someone in the palace. Marmarus no longer shackled him at night, and he wasn't too far from the palace. He continued to plan, still scraping the leather harness.

Marmarus stepped out of his tent, and Lyra was behind him. Ilbaya saw her eyes briefly look in his direction before she followed Marmarus, her golden head drooping.

Ilbaya watched the shine of her hair in the sun until it disappeared in the crowd. Each night he delayed going to the palace was another night Lyra had to endure Marmarus; another night he remained a slave and without his love. He resolved to find a way into the palace if he had to climb the very walls.

Eighteen

"**I do not wish** to sleep," Senwadjet announced. Yazid saw the set of the prince's small chin and knew he wouldn't relent. The servant sighed. He must try anyway.

"If you get no sleep . . ." Yazid began.

"I'll sleep when it pleases me," Senwadjet said. "It doesn't please me now."

Yazid looked helplessly at Dedjet, whose brown eyes flashed with an angry light.

"Go away," Senwadjet ordered. "I command you to leave me."

"You're a little small to give commands," Dedjet said sharply.

"Go," Senwadjet repeated, his face implacable.

Yazid turned to leave, muttering in his own language, which was that of the sand-dwellers.

"I heard you!" Senwadjet leaped out of bed. "I understood what you said. I'll have you punished for it!"

Yazid turned to face the prince. The servant was tired and his patience was gone. "Your father wouldn't permit you to do such a thing," he said quietly, "and your mother would be shamed by your words."

"Get out!" Senwadjet shouted, picking up a jar of costly unguent and raising it threateningly.

"Put that down and go back to bed!" Dedjet snapped.

Senwadjet's golden eyes flickered. Then he threw the jar against the wall, missing Yazid's shoulder by a hair. The two servants stared incredulously at him. The boy watched the oil run down the clean alabaster with a look of dismay, but when he saw the servant's faces, he hid his feelings and ordered, "Go!"

Yazid turned to Dedjet and, taking her arm, propelled her hastily into the hall.

"Close the door!" Senwadjet shouted.

Yazid slammed the door, and the sentry started at the sound. "The prince is getting willful," the guard remarked.

"He's developing the temper of a demon," Yazid muttered. "If he continues in this fashion, in ten years he'll have half the palace servants in chains."

"The princess is little better," Dedjet observed. "Maeti doesn't shout and throw things. She fixes her eyes on you and will not move one finger or say a word until she gets her way. If she has the queen's powers when she gets older, she'll do worse than put us in chains."

"I'll find a way to clip that little hawk's wings yet," Yazid muttered.

Yazid walked stiffly to the royal bedroom and rapped sharply on the door. When he was allowed to enter, he found Amenemhet and Nefrytatanen talking quietly. Amenemhet looked up and, noticing the expression on Yazid's face, was alerted to a coming storm.

"What's wrong?" Amenemhet asked.

Yazid stared at Amenemhet and Nefrytatanen a moment. Embarrassed at what he had come to tell them, he calmed himself and said, "It's too small a matter to trouble you with." He turned to go.

"Wait!" Nefrytatanen called. "Tell us anyway."

Slowly Yazid turned to face them. "The prince has recently been causing us some trouble," he admitted. "Dedjet said the princess has also been a problem."

Amenemhet and Nefrytatanen exchanged glances. The queen asked, "What did Senwadjet do, Yazid? We aren't entirely unaware of some rising tendencies, and we don't look upon them with favor."

Yazid's brown face turned a dusky rose.

"Tell us," Amenemhet urged.

250

Hesitantly, Yazid related the latest difficulty.

Amenemhet said, "Senwadjet is a bit short in stature to make such threats."

"I'll go to him myself," Nefrytatanen declared as she got to her feet. She didn't wait for Amenemhet's comments, but left immediately.

Nefrytatanen found Senwadjet still sitting defiantly up in bed, but there was shame already in his eyes. She sat beside him and patiently explained his present status, which confused him. It was difficult, she knew, for a small boy to be revered like a god, to see his father and mother accept noblemen who prostrated themselves at the foot of the golden thrones, to know he would inherit from them absolute power over the land, and still have to obey servants. But because he was in their care, he had to do so.

When Nefrytatanen finished speaking, she asked, "Do you understand me, Senwadjet?"

He remained silent, embarrassed that after so many explanations he didn't understand. It wasn't logical to him. Her fingers under his chin tilted his face to hers, and wide golden eyes met blue ones, which were warm with humor.

"Senwadjet," Nefrytatanen murmured with a smile, "if you merely repeat words you don't understand, you'll be no wiser than a camel transporting a shipment of scrolls." She rumpled his hair and laughed softly. "Now, Senwadjet, do you understand me?"

Senwadjet smiled sheepishly. "No," he replied.

"Good!" Nefrytatanen declared. "Admitting your ignorance is the first step to knowledge. Now, I'll try a different way to explain."

When Nefrytatanen returned to Amenemhet, she was smiling.

"Did you make any progress?" he asked slowly.

"Beloved, I think we must give the children to Ankhneferu to teach," she replied.

"I thought the time was near. It's sometimes difficult to teach your own children," he admitted. He sighed and added, "I think I'll walk in the garden before I come to bed. Why don't you take your bath?"

Nefrytatanen had been ready to say she would go with him, but she realized he wanted solitude and so she said, "I am a little tired, and a bath will relax me. Will you be long?"

251

Amenemhet shook his head. "I'll return before you sleep. If you fall asleep too quickly, perhaps I'll awaken you."

"I won't sleep until you come," she promised.

Without consciously choosing to, Amenemhet found his feet carrying him toward Senwadjet's room. He opened the door slowly and hesitated to enter. He had no intention of speaking to his son, but he wanted to look at him. Sending the children to study under Ankhneferu was the closing of the chapter of a book, he knew. Senwadjet and Maeti wouldn't be the same after they began such studies. Amenemhet stepped into the chamber, which was lit only by the moon's silver shafts.

Senwadjet's long eyelashes were black fans fitting snugly against his golden cheeks, and Amenemhet gazed at his slumbering child's moonlit face for some time.

"My son, I must open those innocent eyes to such subtle pain as only knowledge can produce," Amenemhet whispered. "With every drop of your blood are you heir to my throne, so I cannot allow you to remain either ignorant or innocent." Amenemhet sighed, and after another moment, he left the room reflecting on Senwadjet's future sorrows.

In the garden Amenemhet paced near the fountain in the dark, staring at the shimmering water of the pool as if he were trying to find answers among the lotuses. The garden's perfume descended on him, soothing his soul. Finally, his burdens slowly lifted one by one, and his heart felt a little lighter.

Because he had heard no footsteps on the paving stones, Amenemhet was startled by the hand on his arm, and he turned quickly to face its owner. Amenemhet stared at a face partially hidden by shadows.

"I don't know you," Amenemhet said, his muscles tensing. "You're dressed like a servant, but I don't recognize you."

"I'm not of the palace," Ilbaya whispered, "but I must speak to someone here."

Amenemhet studied the stranger and saw that he had no weapon. He asked, "Whom do you wish to see?"

"I have important news I must give only to someone in a high place, someone as close to the king as possible," Ilbaya murmured, hesitant to say more. This tall, golden-eyed man wore very simple garments, but his manner told Ilbaya he was no servant.

"You may tell me whatever it is," Amenemhet said quietly. The stranger studied him appraisingly, and Amenemhet realized the man didn't know he was the king. A faint smile touched the corners of Amenemhet's mouth.

"How can I be sure you won't betray me?" Ilbaya asked. "I speak of important matters, I assure you." Ilbaya saw the other man's eyes become topaz as a cloud momentarily darkened the moon. But they looked so steadily at Ilbaya that he found himself wondering if this man could read his mind.

"I won't betray you," Amenemhet said.

"What is your title?" Ilbaya ventured. "Is your place high enough to have influence?"

Amenemhet's smile grew. "It should be," he said.

"What is your title, my lord?" Ilbaya persisted. "Forgive my impertinence, but I must know before I speak."

"No one's place is higher than my own," Amenemhet answered. "I am the king."

Ilbaya stared at Amenemhet in stunned silence. His heart sank. Did he haggle about titles with the king? He decided it wasn't possible. This man who claimed to be king seemed to make less of his supposed royalty than Marmarus made of his ownership of slaves.

"You wear no crown," Ilbaya said suspiciously. "I see no guards."

"If I wore the double crown all the time, my shoulders would be stooped from the weight of it," Amenemhet replied and sat on a bench. "My guards aren't beyond my call," he added, looking up at Ilbaya. "I don't usually require an escort in my private garden just below my chamber's terrace."

Amenemhet glanced up, and Ilbaya followed his gaze to the terrace, where a woman stood watching them. Amenemhet waved to her, then looked at Ilbaya. "The queen waits for me," he noted, then urged, "Tell me your story or leave the way you came, because I intend to return to my chambers soon." Amenemhet looked curiously at Ilbaya and asked, "How did you get into the garden?"

"I climbed the wall," Ilbaya answered, beginning to feel a weakness in his knees. He was rapidly becoming convinced this man really was the king, and he wondered what he should do. "I can't believe a king would stroll around without an escort," he stuttered.

"I can defend myself, if necessary. And it is my own garden." Amenemhet glanced up again at Nefrytatanen, who continued to watch them from the terrace. "I'm really anxious to go inside," he added.

Ilbaya was sure now to whom he spoke, and he didn't

know whether to kneel or prostrate himself full-length at Amenemhet's feet.

"Sit down here," Amenemhet prompted, seeing Ilbaya's expression. "Forgo the formalities for now."

Ilbaya moved to sit beside Amenemhet, grateful for the invitation, because at this point he was sure his shaking legs would collapse.

"I truly didn't recognize you . . ." Ilbaya began.

"I can see you aren't from Tamera," Amenemhet said, then sighed. "Tell me your story."

Suddenly, Ilbaya's throat was dry. "Sire," he croaked, "I don't know where to begin."

"Begin where you intended to had I been a nobleman," Amenemhet suggested, then added, "I must say you have courage to climb my very walls."

Ilbaya smiled in fresh embarrassment and took a deep breath. "Sire, do you know of the Babylonian slave trader, Marmarus?" Observing Amenemhet's frown, Ilbaya decided he did, and continued, "I'm one of his slaves."

"How did you escape him to come here?" Amenemhet asked.

"He thinks I'm simple and will not flee," Ilbaya replied. "He doesn't keep me chained, and that is how I learned what I have to tell you. It was something I thought so valuable I've said nothing of it to anyone until now."

"And what is that?" Amenemhet asked, feeling a sudden foreboding at what the news might be.

"Some slaves would bargain for reward or even freedom for such information," Ilbaya said hopefully.

"And are you such a slave?" Amenemhet asked.

"I would gladly give this information to my owner if he were yourself," Ilbaya said slowly. "How could I refuse if my master is a king, and divine at that?"

"You, of course, wouldn't think of bargaining with a deity." Amenemhet smiled slightly, understanding Ilbaya's unspoken hope of ultimate freedom. "I'll keep that attribute in mind," he said. "Tell me something of what you know so I may decide if you're worth my trouble."

Ilbaya said a quick, silent prayer and began, "On our journey to Ithtawe, I witnessed something that might have to do with your problems with the governors and the Hyksos."

Amenemhet suddenly tensed with interest. "What did you see?"

"A meeting between Marmarus, a messenger from Zahi

254

and a Tameran nobleman—an incident that nearly cost my life," Ilbaya whispered.

"Tell me more," Amenemhet urged.

"Majesty, I would gladly tell you everything, each detail of what I observed and heard, but it would take some time. If I don't return to Marmarus now, I'll be missed and severely punished." Ilbaya didn't breathe, hoping Amenemhet wouldn't have him dragged away.

"You want me to buy you first," Amenemhet concluded.

Ilbaya took a deep breath and whispered, "I beg you to buy me." He was afraid to mention Lyra yet, but he thought that if he could manage to join the king's service, he might later ask about her.

Amenemhet stood up. "Go back to Marmarus," he directed. "I'll do as you've asked."

Ilbaya got to his feet, his eyes wide with disbelief. "You'll let me go after I've told you so little?"

Amenemhet smiled. "I can get you back."

Ilbaya's plan had worked so well he couldn't believe his good fortune, but he decided not to tempt the gods by staying longer. Bowing hastily, he turned away.

"I suggest you leave by the south wall," Amenemhet said. "There's a large tree near the wall, and the area is darker than most."

"That's how I got in," Ilbaya admitted.

"That's what I suspected," Amenemhet murmured, watching Ilbaya melt into the shadows.

The morning sun and the slow rhythm of the horse's pace almost lulled Amenemhet to sleep as he and an escort of guards rode through the marketplace. He thought over what he planned to say to Marmarus and smiled grimly. Today he would play the part of the king who was not above taking a bribe. Amenemhet turned his face to the Nile, inhaling the river's cool scent. Kheti had just finished telling Nessumontu a joke, and their soft laughter took the grimness from Amenemhet's eyes, although he hadn't heard the story.

Amenemhet hunched his shoulders, stretching the muscles of his back like a cat awakening from a nap, to keep himself alert. A few minutes later, Nessumontu touched his arm to indicate they were near their destination.

"There's Marmarus' tent," Nessumontu said. Amenemhet saw a large orange tent looming brassily among the white-

255

plastered shops. "And there's Marmarus," Nessumontu added, pointing to the trader.

"What a nose he has—like the beak of a vulture," Kheti remarked, then added more softly, "a badly formed vulture."

Kheti's description was accurate, and Amenemhet smothered his smile. "We're here on serious business, Kheti," he reminded. "Remove the humor from your face."

Kheti managed a scrowl. "Do I now look sufficiently threatening?" he asked.

Amenemhet glanced at him. "You do."

Kheti studied Nessumontu. "You don't have to make an effort," he observed. Nessumontu's eyes glittered with humor, but that only added to his menacing appearance.

"I have a reputation to uphold," Nessumontu said softly. "It took some effort to regain it after the king beat me so badly at practice."

"I hope that doesn't lie heavily in your mind," Amenemhet remarked.

Nessumontu allowed a wry smile to momentarily soften his features. "It taught me a lesson about being alert to every possibility," he replied. His smile vanished as they stopped before Marmarus, who stared up at them with a frightened expression. Nessumontu's eyes narrowed. "Are you ignorant?" Nessumontu snapped. "Kneel before the son of Ra."

Marmarus threw himself on his knees, pressing his forehead in the dust.

"You may rise," Amenemhet told the slave dealer.

Marmarus got to his feet slowly and looked up. His eyes met those of the king, which were glowing with a strange golden tint in the sun. "Welcome to my humble place," he whispered. "Will you honor me by allowing me to offer a cup of cooling wine?"

Kheti and Nessumontu looked hopefully at Amenemhet, who said softly, "No."

"Complaints have reached the king's ears regarding you," Nessumontu said in a cold voice.

"But I've done nothing, majesty!" Marmarus exclaimed, glancing uneasily at the guards. He wondered if it was the king's intention to pull down his tent and have him dragged away.

"His divine majesty will decide what you've done," Nessumontu replied.

Marmarus shifted his gaze to Amenemhet. A shiver went

through him as he again met those eyes, which seemed shot with sunlight.

"I don't smile on any slave dealers," Amenemhet said, his tone soft with menace.

"Divine one, someone must deal in such matters," Marmarus pleaded.

"Maybe," Amenemhet replied, "but the profession carries little honor in Tamera." He deliberately allowed his eyes to wander past Marmarus to a group of female slaves, who watched and listened intently.

"I beg your compassion, majesty," Marmarus implored, noting the shift of Amenemhet's eyes with hope. The king, Marmarus concluded, seemed to be interested in female slaves, because his gaze had grown a trifle warmer. "Have you no slaves, divine one?" Marmarus risked inquiring.

"A few," Amenemhet replied. "But my slaves are criminals who are paying for their crimes in service. I don't buy slaves who have been kidnapped from their homes or dragged from caravans in bandit raids."

"But I have no slaves who were kidnapped!" Marmarus exclaimed. "Examine them, radiant son of the sun," he begged. "See if they aren't healthy and well treated."

"You'd be a stupid merchant to let them fall ill," Amenemhet remarked. "Unhealthy slaves bring low prices." His eyes again wandered to the female slaves and lingered appreciatively.

Taking courage from this, Marmarus ventured, "Would it please your majesty to enter my humble tent, which would afford you some protection from this fierce sun?"

"I'm not a night-walking creature who fears Ra's light," Amenemhet declared, "but I will step down a moment." He allowed his eyes to shift again to the women as he dismounted.

"A cup of wine? A cool slice of melon?" Marmarus offered.

Amenemhet ignored Marmarus, his eyes moving slowly over all the slaves. He took a step in their direction.

Marmarus tried again. "Divine one, let me show you some gesture of my good intentions."

"Be silent," Amenemhet ordered, brushing past the merchant as he walked slowly toward the slaves. He approached a girl with gray eyes and golden hair, who was more richly dressed than the others. He guessed immediately what she was to Marmarus, and he stopped before her to let his eyes

257

run slowly up and down her form. He smiled faintly and asked, "Are you a slave?"

"Yes, majesty," Lyra murmured, dropping her eyes.

Amenemhet's fingertips under her chin lifted her face to his. "You must be a very special slave," he observed. He could see she was terrified of him and asked softly, "Why do you fear me? Surely your life would be no worse in my hands than in his."

Amenemhet's hand dropped, but he looked at her thoughtfully a moment before strolling on. Disinterestedly, he ran his eyes over the others he passed, until he saw Ilbaya standing a little away from the group. Amenemhet stopped and turned to again look at Lyra, calculating her worth to Marmarus. Then Amenemhet turned to the slave dealer, and asked, "You mentioned a gesture of your goodwill?"

Marmarus looked at Lyra and blanched. He didn't want to give her to Amenemhet if he could avoid it. "Her beauty is deceiving," Marmarus whispered.

"How can such beauty be false?" Amenemhet asked.

"She makes trouble," Marmarus confided. "See how high she holds her head? Note the defiance in her eyes."

"I dislike excessive humility in any servants," Amenemhet said, "and I prefer some spirit in females."

Marmarus took a deep breath as he wondered what he could tell the king to dissuade him. Inspiration flashed, and Marmarus murmured. "I don't like to admit such a thing, for I've already told you about the good health of my merchandise, but the girl is a recent acquisition. I was cheated in the bargain, for she has a certain personal disease not easily cured."

Amenemhet's eyebrows raised. "Are you sure of this?"

"Sire, I am sure," Marmarus lied. "Would I dare present your majesty with such a girl? I would not wish this terrible thing passed to you, son of Ra!"

"Not to any of my people either." Amenemhet's glance turned to Ilbaya. "Where's that one from?"

"Minoa," Marmarus answered promptly, "but—"

"Don't tell me he also has some sort of pestilence," Amenemhet warned, "or I'll begin again to question your methods of treatment."

"No, no!" Marmarus said quickly. "Ilbaya is very healthy." He didn't want to give Ilbaya away either, because he counted on a high profit from his sale. He thought quickly, then

258

added, "But that one may try to escape. He has tried before. Surely you don't want so troublesome a slave."

"Slaves don't escape me," Amenemhet said. "If I cannot find even a decent stableboy among these you have . . ." He let the threat hang ominously over the merchant.

"The Minoan is very strong and healthy!" Marmarus exclaimed. "Look at him. He'd make an excellent stableboy. You can see it in his bearing. His people are good with horses. It's a talent born in them."

Amenemhet met Marmarus' eyes. "Do you expect me to go to him? Bring him here!" he commanded.

"Come here, Ilbaya!" Marmarus said sharply. "Quickly, quickly!"

Ilbaya came to them dragging his feet, his eyes carefully downcast.

"His hair is a strange color," Amenemhet observed.

"It is decorative, is it not?" Marmarus said eagerly. "Look at the set of his eyes, his teeth's health. See his muscles. He's strong. He's not very intelligent, but clever enough to do his work." Marmarus continued extolling Ilbaya's good qualities, weaving into his discourse numerous titles and phrases complimentary to Amenemhet. His ingratiating manner wore on Amenemhet's nerves.

"Yes, yes, yes," Amenemhet finally said abruptly. "Get him ready and be done with it. There's more to running my kingdom than hearing your recital of attributes my own two eyes can see."

"You'll take him, then?" Marmarus said in relief.

Amenemhet inclined his head slightly in agreement and turned away. He gave Kheti and Nessumontu a look of disgust and mounted his horse.

As they rode away, Nessumontu said softly, "It's too bad that girl is infected. She would decorate my house nicely."

"She's as healthy as I am," Amenemhet replied. "That snake keeps her for himself, which is no pleasure for her, I'm sure."

"Perhaps I'll return and buy her when I have time," Nessumontu said thoughtfully.

"He would ask a price that reaches the sky," Kheti noted.

"How can so sick a slave be expensive?" Nessumontu asked reasonably. "I would think he'd be happy to get a diseased slave off his hands. I think I might persuade the old palm beetle." He smiled, his hand touching his sword's handle significantly.

"I thought our lessons would be given in the temple," Senwadjet said, "but you bring us to the garden."

Ankhneferu looked down into the prince's sulky face and smiled. "There are many things, my prince, which can be learned under the roof of the sky better than in the temple."

"We don't mind being in the garden for lessons," Maeti observed, "but it wasn't what we expected."

Ankhneferu stopped to gaze at the sunlit path before them. "Isn't our land beautiful?" he whispered. "Is not all that the One Alone created a marvel?" He knew the children realized why they had been placed in his care and that they would stubbornly resist what they were sure was punishment. Ankhneferu decided his first task would be to erase this idea, because he planned to open a new world to their curious eyes. He glanced at the grass under a nearby tree. "Look at that flower growing in the shade," he said softly, turning to approach the bloom. Carefully brushing his robes out of the way, he knelt before the plant.

Senwadjet and Maeti watched Ankhneferu, amazed that the high priest would kneel before one small flower. They knelt solemnly beside him, wondering if this was some special flower.

"You're surprised that I lower myself to the grass to study a simple flower?" Ankhneferu asked. "It's a creation of the One Alone, and most beautiful. Put your nose to it," he suggested, "and breathe its fragrance."

Hesitantly, they leaned closer to the blossom.

"What do you suppose makes such a scent come from a flower?" Ankhneferu asked.

Never having thought of it, Senwadjet looked up at Ankhneferu in surprise. Maeti continued to contemplate the flower.

"We see nothing rising in the air from this little creature, but it fills the atmosphere with perfume," Ankhneferu said. "Is not such a thing wonderful?"

Maeti smiled faintly, but Senwadjet stared at the flower as if to discern if anything visible did rise from the plant.

Ankhneferu said, "Close your eyes and touch one of the petals. See if it isn't smoother than the finest fabric in your mother's wardrobe. Look closely at the lines in its leaves. Have you not similar lines beneath the skin of your wrists?"

Ankhneferu smiled as he watched them lean closely over

the plant to study its leaves, then examine their own wrists. He watched as their resistance melted.

"What's Tamera's high priest doing kneeling in the grass?" Adadni's voice came from the path.

Ankhneferu's black eyes moved reluctantly from his charges to regard the ambassador from Zahi.

"We are learning," Maeti said sharply. "Ankhneferu is giving us lessons."

"In my land girls don't need priests to teach them to be girls," Adadni said derisively, "and the boys of Zahi learn to fight, not gaze at flowers."

Ankhneferu was ready to answer, but changed his mind when he saw that Senwadjet had gotten to his feet and was facing Adadni with an attitude the priest had often seen in the king. It was difficult to suppress a smile, seeing Amenemhet's golden eyes staring sternly from Senwadjet's small face.

"My lessons in military skills have begun," Senwadjet stated coolly, "but before boys in Tamera learn how to fight, they must learn what they fight for." Senwadjet turned to Ankhneferu. "I wish to continue this lesson in a more private area of the garden," he said, and turned away to walk with great dignity down the path.

"The boy is much like his father," Adadni observed. He reached out, intending to pat Maeti's head, but she stepped away, fixing her eyes on him with an expression that chilled him. "She's much like her mother," Adadni said. "I can see why your people think the queen can work magic when I look into her daughter's eyes."

Ankhneferu slowly rose to face Adadni. "The beliefs of my people mean nothing to you," he said quietly, "but certain sacred truths serve Tamera very well. They're secrets come from a past so remote we believe the divine being Tehuti personally gave them to our ancestors." Seeing Adadni's scornful look, Ankhneferu observed, "You smile at my words, but our wisdom is from the One Alone. The seat of our magic is Noph, city of our queen's birth. Queen Nefrytatanen no longer merely represents Hat-Hor. The queen is Aset, and when she emerged from the pyramid after visiting Tuat, the first thing she said to King Amenemhet was that he is Amen-Ra." Ankhneferu took a breath and added, "That you can dream of overthrowing their rule is witness to your ignorance."

"You speak well, but you won't convert me to your beliefs," Adadni announced.

"You prefer addressing your prayers to empty statues, who have neither ears nor eyes?" Maeti whispered.

Adadni looked down at her. She was studying him with so intense an expression the hairs on the nape of his neck stood up. "I believe in nothing," Adadni said, and turned to leave.

"I think you made him uneasy," Ankhneferu told Maeti as they followed Senwadjet, who had stopped around a bend in the path and was waiting for them.

"If I knew all my mother knows, I'd make him more than uneasy," Maeti said sharply.

"I'm sure you'll learn those things one day." Then, noticing Senwadjet's grim expression, the priest asked, "Why do you look thus? Adadni is merely Zahi's ambassador, not its king."

"Their king, I hear, is worse," Senwadjet replied. He looked up at Ankhneferu. "Would you think me cowardly if I confessed I'm afraid?"

"Many of us are afraid, though not cowards," he replied. "We must look at what we fear to vanquish the darkness of fear. Why are you afraid?"

Senwadjet considered this a moment, then answered, "I'm afraid the Hyksos will overcome us one day. I'm afraid many of our people will be killed and those left alive will suffer greatly."

Ankhneferu looked at the prince a moment, then said, "It's possible, but unlikely. If it does happen, what is there to fear about death, little prince? People of more ignorant lands fear death above all else. We know there is a succession of lives. It's part of what I'll teach you."

Ankhneferu explained, "The Hyksos live in the darkness of ignorance, so it is they who are terrified of death. They hope to gain power over death by killing others. We know better. What we must fear is only that we become evil. That, child of Ra, is a profound waste, which is then what we truly should fear—wasting this life in evil doings which only bring us a debt we must repay in sorrow in this life or some later lifetime." He was silent a moment, listening. Then he said, "Your father has returned. It will soon be time for your midday meal. After you've rested, come to the temple, and I will introduce you to the divine beings."

"We will bring a gift," Maeti promised.

"Bring with you only your desire to know," Ankhneferu said. "It's the gift the divine beings expect from you."

262

Nineteen

Ilbaya told Amenemhet and Nefrytatanen about the night he had seen Marmarus, the nobleman and the messenger from Zahi. He ended by adding, "If you doubt what I've told you, I can show you where I hid the courier's body. I'm truly sorry I didn't know enough of your language to understand what they said."

"That peasant you saw beaten did die, but much later than they expected," Amenemhet muttered. "He clung to life long enough to speak to my minister of crops, but not long enough to name his murderer. Your description of the nobleman could fit any one of several governors—if it was indeed a governor." Amenemhet turned to Nefrytatanen. "I wish Ilbaya could have understood that conversation."

"How well did you hear their whispers?" Nefrytatanen asked.

"Most of it was a murmuring I can almost hear again in my mind, it's so tantalizing," Ilbaya answered regretfully.

"If you had understood the language better, do you really think you would have been able to know the words?"

Ilbaya hesitated while he thought about this. "Yes, I think it would have been possible." He sighed and admitted, "I still find it difficult to understand your language when it's spoken

263

rapidly and carelessly because the words run into each other so easily. When it's spoken in whispers as well, my ignorance triumphs."

Nefrytatanen turned to Amenemhet. "If Ilbaya heard the words, they're in his memory whether he understands them or not. It's possible I could merge my mind with his and not only recognize the Tameran he saw, but also understand the conversation, or at least enough of it to help."

"How would you do that?" Frightening visions filled Ilbaya's imagination.

Nefrytatanen quickly reassured him, "I wouldn't hurt you." She looked at Amenemhet and asked, "Shall I try?"

"Yes, try it," Amenemhet quickly answered. "Whatever you could learn will be more than we know now."

Nefrytatanen arose from her chair. "Sit here, Ilbaya," she said. Ilbaya obeyed, but glanced nervously at her over his shoulder.

"Sit back in the chair and try to relax," she directed him, placing her hands lightly on his temples. They felt strangely cool to Ilbaya. "Close your eyes," she said quietly. As he shut his eyes, the sensation of coolness seemed to vanish. "Don't be afraid. Remember that night. Relive it in your thoughts just as it happened." Ilbaya tried to concentrate, but his nervousness had emptied his mind.

Nefrytatanen leaned closer and prompted, "The forest was dark and cool. They stood in the clearing with the moonlight shining on them." Her perfume drifted over him, and he thought its scent intriguing. She murmured, "Don't think about my perfume." Feeling his muscles tense in surprise, she explained, "That's how it works, Ilbaya. Merely think and I'll experience your thoughts. You needn't speak at all—just remember that night."

As Amenemhet watched them, he could see Nefrytatanen had begun to learn what she sought. Even with her eyes closed in concentration, he could see her tension rising, because anger tightened her features.

Finally, Ilbaya's eyes opened; and he turned to look questioningly at her.

Nefrytatanen opened her eyes and looked down at Ilbaya. "You did well, Ilbaya, but I would have you leave us while we discuss what I've learned."

Ilbaya glanced at Amenemhet, who nodded in agreement. The slave rose slowly, still looking at Amenemhet. Then, as if he had made a difficult decision, he whispered, "Majesty, if the information I have given you is valuable, I would ask one more favor."

"What favor?" Amenemhet said.

"There is another slave in Marmarus' hands I would beg you to purchase," Ilbaya whispered.

"Why do you want me to buy this slave?" he asked.

"Majesty, it is Lyra—the golden-haired woman you looked at when you visited Marmarus," Ilbaya answered. He lowered his eyes and said softly, "I love her, and she is Marmarus' . . ."

"I understand," Amenemhet said at Ilbaya's pause. He looked at Nefrytatanen. "Is Ilbaya's information worth the price of another slave?"

"It is worth every slave Marmarus owns," she said coldly.

"After you show me and my soldiers where the Hyksos' body is, you and Lyra will have each other. I will free you both," Amenemhet promised.

Ilbaya's eyes flooded with tears. "Majesties, I . . ." he whispered.

"You have been helpful. You may go to the bed allotted to you now, and allow us to discuss our problem." Amenemhet's dismissal was kind but firm.

Blinded with tears, Ilbaya bowed low, then left them with his heart pounding, his soul flooded with joy.

Nefrytatanen watched Ilbaya close the door, then turned to Amenemhet with fire in her eyes. "It was Lord Menkara!" she exploded. "There are others whose names were mentioned as well!"

"Tell me all of it," Amenemhet said, his jaw set in anger.

Nefrytatanen began to pace in her fury. "When one scheme doesn't work, the Hyksos merely devise another which is even more evil," she said. "Marmarus is Babylonian, but he is here as an agent of Zahi. He came from the south because he stopped in Kenset to add to his caravan a shipment of cocoons and eggs to be distributed to certain province governors. These governors planted them in our soil like seeds, from which the worms and insects destroying our crops have bloomed."

Amenemhet stared incredulously at her for a moment before he said, "This is the first time I've heard of such a thing, but I suppose it could be done. If the Hyksos would apply their cleverness to running Zahi, they'd be rich without having to steal from others."

"They have it in mind to starve Tamera into weakness,

then attack and overthrow us." Nefrytatanen lowered her voice and said, "The Hyksos promised Menkara a portion of whatever they take from Ithtawe for his part in this—a promise I'm sure they'd never honor. I think they must have made similar promises to the other governors involved in this."

"This is Gobryas' doing. He's evil, more evil than you can conceive," Nefrytatanen declared. Her eyes met Amenemhet's, and the expression in them made a chill run through him. "Let me destroy him," she said softly. "Let me end his existence before he causes us more grief."

Amenemhet understood Nefrytatanen's intention, and despite his own anger, he shook his head. "You cannot kill a man by magic."

"When you come upon a deadly serpent, do you wait for its bite before you crush it?" she demanded. "The serpent is innocent, merely striking out of fear according to its nature, but Gobryas is not innocent."

"Gobryas is a man, and you cannot murder him by magic," Amenemhet replied firmly. "It would bring evil upon your own spirit. You did not receive your wings for this purpose."

"Gobryas will bring evil on our whole land!" she cried. She fell silent a long moment, then finally whispered, "You are right, beloved. I'm ashamed. It would be murder. Your wisdom overcomes my passion and sets my feet on the true path. I won't do it."

"You wouldn't have been able to do it once your passion had calmed and you'd thought it over," Amenemhet said softly.

"I'm not sure," Nefrytatanen murmured. "I know Gobryas will yet give us reason to defend Tamera."

"He and others like him are why Nessumontu keeps the royal army strong." Amenemhet turned Nefrytatanen's face to his. "Don't think I underestimate Gobryas or any of his evil kind," he assured her. "In the morning I'll go with Nessumontu and a patrol to find the Hyksos' body. Then, we'll have enough evidence to send Adadni back to Zahi and punish the guilty governors."

"What of Marmarus?" she asked.

"I'll have him watched until I return," Amenemhet answered. "Then he'll be arrested for dishonest dealing. It won't be mentioned that he's an agent for Zahi until I have already punished the guilty governors."

266

* * *

Later, when the palace was deep in slumber, Nefrytatanen crept carefully from Amenemhet's side and, putting on a white robe, walked quietly from their sleeping chamber to the room where they bathed.

The blueness of the pool's water shimmered translucently in the light of the small lamp she carried. As she sat down next to the edge of the pool, the green streaks in the black marble wall flashed with the dancing flame's gyrations.

When Nefrytatanen was comfortably settled, she stared into the flame for a long time. Finally, the room echoed with the whispers of a strange language as Nefrytatanen spoke to the fire.

Far away in Zahi, Gobryas was suddenly awakened from a deep sleep by a voice that shocked him. He sat up in bed to peer into the blackness of the room's corners with the hairs on his arms rising in fear. A pale light seemed to grow from his mirror, and he stared incredulously at it while Nefrytatanen's glowing form stepped from the copper surface and faced him.

"Gobryas, if you try one more time to take Tamera, you will die. I will see to it," Nefrytatanen threatened. "I'm not a dream from which you can awaken. I am real."

"But you have to be a dream!" Gobryas said hoarsely. "How could you be here?"

"I am the servant of Ptah, who makes things that are," she announced. "I am Aset. Now I go where I wish on Aset's wings." Her smile faded and the white glow surrounding her became fiery red. "I no longer have to beg the forces to favor my requests. I command their obedience, except for the One Alone. In your land the goddess Aset is called Ishtar; but your rituals have brought shame to her temples."

Nefrytatanen took a step closer to Gobryas' bed, and he shrank away in fear. Her eyes were purple in the fierce red glow.

"I can command the forces in whatever language they're named, but so that you'll understand my purpose, I'll use the names you know," Nefrytatanen said. "Shortly your ambassador will be driven from Tamera and you will persuade your king to do nothing in revenge."

Gobryas opened his mouth to speak, and Nefrytatanen lifted her hand to point threateningly at him. He shut his mouth.

She continued in the same cold tone, "If you disobey me,

I'll send Lamashtu, and she will dwell in your house until its destruction is complete." Nefrytatanen paused, rethinking what she had told him, then said, "Or perhaps Pazuzu is better to send swooping from the mountains of your land like a whirlwind." She smiled grimly. "Think about these things, Gobryas. When Adadni returns, remember what I told you and decide carefully how you'll influence King Shalmanesser."

Satisfied by Gobryas' terrified expression, Nefrytatanen laughed softly. Then her crimson figure faded before Gobryas' astonished eyes until it had vanished completely, and he wondered if he had been seeing visions, as he once had during a fever. But Nefrytatanen's familiar perfume floated on the air, denying illusion.

Amenemhet signaled Nessumontu to take the Hyksos messenger's weapons and insignia, then mounted his horse.

"Will you not have him buried?" Sarenput asked, looking at the body's rotting remains, which they had covered with a cloak.

"Let him lie here, as he would have left Ahsen lying," Amenemhet replied bitterly. "There are many creatures who will find him tasty yet." He turned to Nessumontu. "Let us leave this place and return to Ithtawe as quickly as possible."

A short time later, they turned their horses and Nessumontu gave his soldiers a sharp command to speed up, but his words were accompanied by a strange rumbling sound that startled him. He looked at Amenemhet as the noise grew in volume and the ground began to tremble.

"It's an earth tremor," Nessumontu said.

"It sounds like a big one." Sarenput was grim. "We must get out of this mountainous area."

Amenemhet dug his heels into his horses' side, and the animal sprang forward. The men needed no orders. They all knew what the rumbling meant, and they wasted no time following Amenemhet's example.

Sand and small loose stones slid down a bank of soil beside the riders. The bank's surface undulated as it moved, like the waves of the Great Green Sea, making a noise as loud as a sandstorm's blast. The deep-throated growl was broken by the brittle snapping of the earth's crust. Gnarled roots of trees sprang into view like great dusty whorls of serpent coils.

A jagged shadow appeared on the rocky slope, and parallel to it the riders raced on desperately. It was no shadow, but a

268

growing rent in the earth. The crack leaped across the path ahead, and the horrified men saw it widening, forming webs of small cracks as they raced toward it. The terrified horses needed no urging. As they neared the crevice, the animals gathered speed, calculating for themselves what they must do. There was no hesitation in them as their powerful muscles coiled and flung loose like springs to carry them across the opening.

Amenemhet glanced into the crack as he soared over it, seeing below him the place where the two walls ground rocks into powder between them. At the additional roar of falling stones, he glanced over his shoulder to see a ridge collapsing behind them. The sound caused his horse to scream in terror and break into an additional burst of speed. Amenemhet wondered how long the animal could endure such a race, but he couldn't have slowed the terrified horse if he had wanted to.

The riders broke into an open space in their flight from the treacherous mountains. The sharp report of snapping rocks inspired the horses into new life, and they rushed from the cliffs like arrows just released.

The valley roared with echoes, blending the individual sounds into one reverberating flood of chaos. The whole face of a cliff split from its top to the valley floor as a great slab of stone fell slowly at first, gathering momentum, to crumble into a confusion of rubble and dust.

Believing they had reached a relatively safe place, Amenemhet paused to watch the collapsing mountains. Instead he saw a new horror and, spinning his horse around, he raced on.

Nessumontu, who rode a little behind the rest of the group, slapped his horse's rump, and the animal sprang into a frantic pace. Ilbaya, who was the last of them, rode a little behind Nessumontu, desperately urging on his exhausted horse.

A tower of stone shaped like an obelisk trembled, then swayed dizzily, falling with a roar like a monstrous tree on the heels of the fleeing group. Amenemhet grew pale and his heart sank as Nessumontu and Ilbaya both disappeared from view. For a breath-stopping moment, he could discern no sign of them. Then Nessumontu emerged from the dust clouds, coughing violently. When he stopped beside Amenemhet, he shook his head.

"I promised to free Ilbaya," Amenemhet said softly. "It

269

was all he wanted. I was going to do it when we returned to Ithtawe."

Slowly the noise of the earthquake faded, and the dust-covered group stared at the mountains as if they were in a trance. Still overcome with the flood of emotions they had experienced, they felt drained, their senses numbed.

The horses stood on shaking legs, their nostrils distended as they struggled for breath. Their heaving sides were white with foam, and their eyes still rolled white in fear.

Amenemhet slid off his horse to stand on his own trembling legs. "Let us rest the animals for a time," he ordered. "Then we'll try to find Ilbaya's body."

Nessumontu looked suspiciously at a rock, then sat gingerly on it—as if he thought it might yet move—and said, "Let us rest the animals, by all means, me most of all." He wiped his forehead, leaving a grimy smear. "I must sit down," he added. "I cannot stand. I'm too weak with terror."

"I have never been so afraid," Amenemhet confessed.

Sarenput silently watched the settling dust, his gray eyes filled with memories of Atalan's catastrophe. "I have," he finally said. "I surely have."

Neferset watched her child's efforts to stand, her eyes sparkling. "Look, Nefrytatanen!" she exclaimed in delight. "Soon he'll be walking!"

Nefrytatanen smiled at little Nakht, who was standing shakily between Neferset's knees clinging to his mother's fingers. "He certainly will," she agreed. "Although he doesn't yet have enough strength, he has the inclination."

Suddenly Taji leaped from her chair and, laughing, ran to Nakht to sweep him off his trembling legs into her arms. "He's done enough work for today," she declared.

"You spoil him," Neferset chided, but she was smiling.

At Dedjet's entrance, Nefrytatanen turned.

"My lady, Ambassador Nakht has returned and waits downstairs," Dedjet announced.

"Did he mention the treaty?" Nefrytatanen asked, getting to her feet.

"No, my lady."

"I'll go down immediately," Nefrytatanen decided.

"I'll go with you," Neferset said. "Kheti will be there questioning Nakht, I'm sure, and I want to tell him of his son's progress." She took the child from Taji and waved Azza

270

away. Her eyes still lit with pleasure, she said, "I'll carry him down."

From the top of the stairs they could see Nakht in the entrance hall, turned to face the opened doors, where Kheti came hurrying in, asking questions before he even reached the ambassador's side. Nakht was shaking his head in good humor when they heard the women and turned to look up.

"Nakht stood up today," Neferset called down. "He'll walk soon."

"He was a little shaky, but he did stand," Nefrytatanen confirmed, then said more seriously, "Welcome back, Nakht. How did it go?"

"It isn't a thing I can quickly tell," he replied quietly.

"I don't doubt it after what we've learned."

A small, peculiar sound came from Neferset, and Nefrytatanen turned to see Neferset's eyes wide with terror. Neferset was teetering on one foot, struggling to catch her balance. Nerfrytatanen reached for her, but Neferset thrust her child into the queen's arms even as she fell.

"Oh, Ptah, no!" Neferset gasped and slipped beyond Nefrytatanen's reach. Falling first against the wall, then tumbling before their horrified eyes down the stairs in a series of thumps, Neferset rolled off the open side of the staircase to fall with a crash onto the alabaster floor below.

Nefrytatanen stared at Neferset's still body for a moment, then raced after her. At the bottom of the steps she handed the baby to Taji, who had run down the stairs behind her.

Kheti stood, staring at Neferset's crumpled form as if he were paralyzed. Nakht bent over her, and Dedjet ran through the corridor screaming for Horemheb.

Nakht looked up. "Don't try to move her," he said sharply. "Wait for Horemheb." Glancing over his shoulder at Kheti, he added, "She's alive."

Kheti approached slowly, walking like a man in a nightmare, his face blank and uncomprehending, until he knelt beside Neferset. Then grief began to melt the frozen look of his eyes and tears rolled down his cheeks. He touched Neferset's silver hair as if to confirm it was Neferset who lay unmoving on the stone, her blood staining the white alabaster. Wiping his eyes, he looked up at Nefrytatanen, his lips parted to speak, but his numb brain couldn't find words.

Nefrytatanen dropped to her knees beside Kheti and, taking his hands in hers, silently gave him in her touch what her words couldn't give. They waited for Horemheb, the only sounds Taji's soft weeping and Dedjet's calls to the physician, which seemed to echo through a maze of corridors.

They felt as if they were frozen in time while they waited for the physician, staring at Neferset's face, wondering if her life ran from her body as the blood ran from her hair. They were holding her soul present by the might of their combined will, it seemed.

No one heard Horemheb's running feet and they were unaware of his approach until he knelt at Neferset's side. He looked up at their faces and waved them away.

Nefrytatanen rose slowly, drawing Kheti to his feet like a child, because he seemed to have no will of his own. Grasping his hands, Nefrytatanen backed away to a bench and sat down, guiding him to her side. Horemheb arranged for a litter to carry Neferset. They watched while she was carefully placed upon it, and then Nefrytatanen stood up, bringing Kheti also to his feet. Both of them followed the litter to the room of healing.

Even after Neferset's small form was carried into the room and the door closed behind it, they stood in the hall, numbly waiting. Finally, Dedjet arranged for chairs to be brought to them so they could sit until they knew if Neferset lived or died.

When Amenemhet and Nessumontu returned in the evening, they found the palace strangely quiet. Amenemhet was immediately filled with fear. When Nefrytatanen wasn't in the courtyard to greet him, he knew something was wrong. He leaped from his horse and ran through the doors with Nessumontu at his heels to find Yazid sitting on a bench in the entrance hall waiting for them. Amenemhet's heart sank at Yazid's expression.

"What's wrong?" Amenemhet asked quickly.

Yazid stood up, his eyes filled with shadows. "Lady Neferset had an accident this afternoon," he told them. "She fell down the stairs, and they all wait outside the room of healing."

"How badly was she injured?" Nessumontu asked. "Does anyone know?"

The servant shook his head. They followed him to where Nefrytatanen still sat beside Kheti, holding his cold hands in hers. She looked up at Amenemhet, her eyes filled with tears, but said nothing. No one spoke. Kheti stared directly ahead, not recognizing Amenemhet or Nessumontu, unaware of their

272

approach. Chairs were brought for the two men, and they joined the silent vigil.

When Ra rose over the eastern horizon, casting shafts of orange-gold light across the floor, the door opened, and Horemheb came wearily out. Kheti stood up, moving on his own initiative at last, his eyes begging the physician, his lips mute. Horemheb closed the door behind him, and their hearts stopped.

"She will live," he said softly.

Kheti closed his eyes, sinking weakly back into the chair.

"Kheti, there's more I must say," Horemheb added.

Kheti's eyes lifted to the physician's face.

"She is blind," Horemheb said sadly. No one uttered a word or made a sound until Horemheb added, "I don't know why she's blind. I don't know what to do about it. My knowledge isn't enough to help her."

"Is she awake?" Kheti finally whispered. "Can I go to her?"

"You can go to her," Horemheb replied dully. "She slips in and out of sleeping from moment to moment, but you should be with her."

The weary Kheti got to his feet and disappeared into the room.

Lyra followed Marmarus and another merchant through the winding city street, only half-listening to their conversation. She wondered how Ilbaya was faring in the palace. Although she was happy he had found a way to escape Marmarus at last, she felt a terrible emptiness in his absence. In the past Lyra had lived with loneliness until it had become an old acquaintance. But since Ilbaya rode off with the king, loneliness had become a thing gnawing at her insides, mocking her nights until she cried herself to sleep.

"Do you remember that slave you gave the king?" the merchant asked Marmarus, catching Lyra's attention instantly. "I understand he rode somewhere to the north with King Amenemhet," the man said slowly. "I don't know exactly what happened, but I did hear something of his accident."

Lyra's head snapped up, and her heart began to pound as she struggled to hear the merchant through the interfering street noises.

"They were caught in the mountains during that last earthquake," the merchant continued. "The slave was trapped under a fall of rocks." Lyra's heart stopped beating and became a dead thing in her breast as the merchant finished, "I heard that he was killed."

"We felt some of that tremor here, but I understand it was much worse in the south," Marmarus remarked. "We passed through that very area on our journey to Ithtawe. I'm glad the earthquake waited until after we got through."

Lyra's heart started beating again, but it was so filled with pain it felt as if it tore with each beat.

"You say Ilbaya was killed?" Marmarus asked. The merchant nodded. "That's too bad. He was an obedient slave, once he'd learned his proper place," Marmarus said softly.

Lyra took a deep breath and, through blurred vision saw Marmarus' smug smile as he turned to look at her. She lowered her head to hide the tears that trembled on her lashes even while she wanted to scream out her grief. She heard Marmarus' soft chuckle, and her hatred of him was an explosion that blasted away her reason.

Abruptly, she whirled around and ran into the thickest part of the crowd. She didn't notice the ragged burnoose-clad figure, leaning heavily on a walking stick, hobbling after her.

Dashing into the shadows between two buildings, she saw that the narrow passage's end opened onto another street, and she followed it. Hearing shouts in the marketplace behind, Lyra fled without knowing where she was going or even why—she no longer cared about her freedom. Through one crooked lane after another she ran, down a straight paved street and through a fragrant garden, until she was beyond the city's limits. Dragging her feet through a newly harvested field, where the sweet warmth of the earth mingled with the golden light of the falling sun, she hurried on.

She tore off her jewelry, flinging it behind as she walked, leaving a trail of sparkling lights. Finally, she sank to the ground and sat with drooping head, remembering Ilbaya's copper hair shining in the sun, the warmth of his arms, the touch of his lips. A vision flashed through her mind of his body crushed under a pile of rubble, and she stiffened with pain. She lifted her eyes to the golden hills, and in the fading light, they shimmered through her tears.

"Ohhhhh," Lyra moaned and threw herself down, resting her forehead on the warm earth. Her expanding grief was so great she wondered how her body could contain it, but decided that if her heart was overwhelmed with the pain and stopped its beat, she didn't care. She lifted her head and stared helplessly at the sky's implacable silence.

"Gods of Tamera, why have you taken him?" The sobs that tore her breast forced her words out in short gasps. "Knowing Ilbaya walked the earth made my slavery bearable! Loving him gave me hope! Now I'm more a prisoner than Marmarus could ever make of me!"

When she saw the serpent rising from his hiding place a mere cubit away, her sobbing began to lessen. She watched its head grow larger as its hood expanded. It wasn't fear that kept her motionless, for a feeling of peace was replacing her pain. Here was the gods' answer, she thought. Here was her way to be reunited with Ilbaya. The cobra swayed near Lyra's face, staring at her with eyes like jet beads, and she smiled at it.

Suddenly an arm flashed down before her eyes, a hand holding a heavy stick that struck the cobra aside, that raised and struck again and again. Stunned that even her means of escaping life was being taken from her, she leaped to her feet. Her mouth opening to cry out, when she saw the stick fall one final time. She stared angrily at the burnoose-cloaked figure that bent to inspect the dead snake. Then the man pushed back the hood that had concealed his face, revealing hair that gleamed with the same tint as the disappearing sun.

Incredulous, Lyra watched Ilbaya turn toward her. Unable to move but for her trembling, she stood motionless until his arms wrapped around her, and she was drawn into his embrace. She closed her eyes, momentarily unable to speak, hardly able to breathe.

"I followed you from the marketplace," he said softly. "I would have come faster, but I can't walk quickly now."

Lyra clung to Ilbaya, pressing her cheek against his, confirming through her touch what her other senses couldn't believe. She felt his hand at the back of her head, holding her face against his. "I thought you were dead," she finally managed to whisper. "I wanted the snake to kill me."

Ilbaya gently pushed her away. Then his hands framed the sides of her face. He looked at her wonderingly. "You'd rather die than live without me?" he murmured. "You love me that much?"

Unable to speak through her tears, she nodded.

Ilbaya pulled her back into his arms and kissed her tenderly. Then he again pressed his cheek to hers, overwhelmed with gratitude that such a love had come to him. After a time had passed, he murmured, "I suppose the king and his soldiers tried to find me, but had to give up when darkness

275

came. I was hidden under a slab of stone that was propped up by some other rocks. I didn't regain consciousness until nearly dawn. Then I managed to wriggle out. If a farmer hadn't given me a ride to Ithtawe in his cart, I probably would still be hobbling down the road."

Lyra pulled away from him. "Your legs were hurt?" she whispered anxiously.

He nodded. "They'll mend. They've gotten better already. They had some time to start healing while I sat in the marketplace pretending to be a beggar, watching you as I tried to think of how to help you escape Marmarus. I couldn't let him recognize me, though."

"You were within sight of Marmarus' camp?" she breathed.

"For several days," he replied. "I just couldn't think of a way to let you know it."

Fresh tears welled in her eyes, and she put her head against his shoulder to cling to him. "We're free, Ilbaya," she whispered. "At last we're free and together." She paused, remembering Marmarus, who had surely began a search for her. She drew away from Ilbaya. "We must hide ourselves from Marmarus," she said urgently. She bent to pick up his walking stick and put it in his hands. "Oh, my love, we must hurry before they find us."

"The palace isn't too far away. We should be able to get there before Marmarus finds us," Ilbaya said calmly.

"The palace!" Lyra cried. "Would you return to slavery? Let us escape while we can!"

"King Amenemhet promised both of us freedom," Ilbaya soothed.

"How can you know he'll keep his promise? Let's take our freedom while we can," Lyra insisted.

"You haven't met the king. I have, and I know he'll free us," Ilbaya said quietly. "We won't have to begin our life together with deception. We won't have to be afraid someone will one day discover we're runaway slaves." He put his free arm around her waist and squeezed her comfortingly. "Come, Lyra. Trust me."

Lyra sighed and lifted her head to look at him. "Whether we go to freedom or death, I'll come with you," she said softly.

"We'll travel to the temple at Ahbidew," Kheti promised, kissing Neferset's hand. "As soon as you have the strength, we'll visit the sacred place where Asar is buried. Ankhneferu said that wonders have been done there. I've already ordered a prayer tablet carved in your honor. We'll beg for Asar's compassion at his special shrine."

Neferset's eyes stared at unending darkness, but she smiled. "Kheti, we can do this if you wish. Even if my sight doesn't return, I will spend the remainder of my years looking at your face, which is forever engraved on the tablet of my memory." She put her hands on his cheeks, intending to caress him, and whispered, "I feel tears coming from your eyes. It's unnecessary."

Nearby, Nefrytatanen wiped her own eyes. She dared not speak and betray her own weeping as she stood beside Amenemhet, helplessly watching them.

Kheti said brokenly, "When we return from Ahbidew and you again have your eyes, you must be careful never to stumble on staircases."

"I didn't stumble," Neferset said quietly. "I was pushed." She felt Kheti stiffen in surprise and added, "I don't know who did it, for we were just at the top of the stairs. Anyone could have crept around the corner behind me, but I know I was pushed. I felt the hand on my back."

Kheti stared at her in disbelief. "But why?" he whispered. After a moment, his bewilderment drained from his eyes, leaving them looking like two pieces of gray granite. He said quietly, "I'll find who did this and put out his eyes with my own fingers."

Neferset shuddered. "Don't say such a thing! You wouldn't do that!"

"I would! Do you not wish revenge? Are you not afraid of another attempt to kill you?"

Neferset was silent a moment. Then she sighed. "How can you feel bitterness toward the kind of person who did this?" she asked. "I've been thinking about it in my quiet moments, and I've decided that person is so empty, how can I envy him his sight? I'm freer in this prison of darkness than he is outside of it." She took Kheti's hands in hers and laid her cheek against them. "Although my eyes cannot see, my spirit is free," she whispered. "Whoever did this cannot harm my spirit. He could only do that if I allowed him to." She smiled. "I'm wiser for this experience—whether I regain my sight or not. I have been lying here thinking about my life and many other things. If this unknown enemy of mine killed my body, it would be but a dead thing, while what I am will have es-

277

caped my enemy's reach. What, then, can my enemy threaten me with? He sees less than I can see with my blinded eyes."

Neferset's eyes stared straight ahead, and to Azza, they appeared to be looking at her. Azza felt a shiver run through her. Did Neferset somehow know her guilt? Azza wondered if Neferset had somehow been given another form of vision not requiring sight.

Amenemhet, noticing the expression on Nefrytatanen's face, laid his hand on her shoulder and turned her around to lead her to the door and into the hall.

"Let us go downstairs," he said softly. "Crying before them will help no one. I could use a goblet of wine to steady my nerves." They walked in silence until he finally breathed, "How courageous she is!"

Having reached the top of the stairs, Nefrytatanen didn't answer. She stopped, staring down the white expanse before her, again seeing Neferset tumbling off the open side, and she couldn't move. "Beloved," she whispered, "I cannot go down these steps."

Amenemhet looked down at Nefrytatanen. She was pale and trembling. "I'll hold your hand," he said. "You'll feel differently if you go down with me. It won't frighten you then."

Nefrytatanen forced herself to take one step, then another. She felt strangely dizzy on this staircase she had run down so many times. The open side menaced her, and she shrank from it against the wall.

Amenemhet firmly took her arm. "Do you think I'd let you fall?" he asked softly. "I promise I won't allow it."

She looked up at him, thinking of his strength. "I feel so foolish," she whispered. "I cannot bear to look at that open side. It makes me dizzy." She glanced briefly at the staircase and returned her eyes to his face as if his being were a refuge. "I'm foolish," she said weakly.

"No," Amenemhet said quietly. "I don't like to see it either, and I wasn't here to watch Neferset fall." He put one arm around Nefrytatanen's shoulders and, sliding his other arm around her waist, promised, "I'll have a low wall added to the open side so you won't have to worry any more. Lean on me, and don't feel foolish," he urged. "Whenever you wish to come down these stairs until the open side is closed off, I'll come with you."

"I feel like a child afraid of shadows," Nefrytatanen murmured, taking another shaky step, "but I can't explain the terror that fills me. There seems to be no reasoning it away."

"Lean on me," Amenemhet whispered. "It isn't necessary to explain your fear. Only trust me enough to lean on me."

Nefrytatanen looked up into the golden eyes that gazed on her and murmured, "I trust you."

Twenty

Shortly after Neferset's accident, Nefrytatanen had asked her to temporarily exchange Azza for Dedjet. Although Nefrytatanen still knew of no real reason to distrust Azza, the uneasiness she had felt about the slave from the beginning hadn't diminished. It reassured her to have her own fiercely loyal servant at Neferset's side, in any case. But during the several weeks Azza acted as Nefrytatanen's personal attendant, Nefrytatanen wished many times that Dedjet could be returned to her.

Looking in the sheet of polished copper that served as her mirror, Nefrytatanen was critical of the way Azza was trying to arrange her hair. Azza seemed not to realize, although Nefrytatanen had hinted many times, that her implacably straight hair resisted being brushed into curls even when they were tightly fastened with pins.

"I don't like that," Nefrytatanen said. Azza quickly pulled out several pins and combed the resulting tangle into a smooth length of black silk. Nefrytatanen added meaningfully, "I think it can only be worn hanging straight under that coronet."

"Be glad you don't have to endure this," Amenemhet complained as Yazid applied fixative to his chin in preparation to

281

attach his ceremonial beard. Wearing the beard was an ancient custom Amenemhet obeyed only on the most solemn occasions. A tap on the door made him sigh in disgust. "Now what is it?"

Amenemhet didn't look forward to revealing to the court the names of the traitorous governors, or sentencing them—especially when Ilbaya, his sole real witness, had been killed. Amenemhet's temper had already been shortened by worry as well as sundry annoyances that morning, and every delay irritated him more. He kicked aside the trailing hem of his formal robe and turned to face the messenger who had entered. Accepting the scroll the courier handed him, he impatiently waved the messenger away and tore open the seals.

At Amenemhet's continued silence, Nefrytatanen turned in her chair to look questioningly at him, and she found him so engrossed in his reading that she was doubly curious. She watched his eyes move down the papyrus, observing the expressions that traveled fleetingly over his face, until she no longer could endure the suspense.

"What is it?" she asked, waving away Azza, who was trying to place her coronet in her hair.

Amenemhet's golden eyes lifted from the papyrus. "King Balthazar is inviting Nakht to return to Kenset. He wants to seal a treaty with us."

"King Balthazar?" Nefrytatanen, surprised that Balthazar alone had dispatched this invitation, took a moment to consider this news. She was too absorbed in her thoughts to notice Azza's increased tension. Finally, she asked, "What happened to Queen Karomana?"

Amenemhet shrugged, replying, "Karomana was asked by Kenset's high council to leave the throne after Balthazar intercepted her message to King Shalmanesser agreeing to send another shipment of insects to plant in Tamera's fields. Balthazar says Karomana admitted that she was to receive a portion of Tamera as her reward for helping Zahi. Balthazar begs our forgiveness."

"Obviously, while she was waiting for Zahi to conquer us, she planned to kill Balthazar," Nefrytatanen remarked.

Amenemhet rerolled the papyrus thoughtfully. "It was convenient that Balthazar could rid himself of Karomana and regain our favor at the same time."

"I wonder what was done with her," Nefrytatanen mused.

"Maybe he finally fed her to a lion as she had tried to do him," Amenemhet replied.

282

Nefrytatanen grimaced. "That's an ignominious way to end a reign."

Amenemhet again presented his chin to Yazid, commenting, "Hers was an ignominious reign, but we don't know if she's been executed or even exiled."

Azza had listened to this news with mixed feelings. At first, she reacted with a gladness she struggled to hide from the others, but after hearing that Karomana was probably alive, her old fears returned. Karomana's agents knew, just as surely as she, that if Karomana wasn't dead, she would try to regain her throne, and they would continue to follow Karomana's orders. Just as Urum, Karomana's sorcerer, wouldn't hesitate to level a curse at Azza if she didn't succeed. Failing in her mission to kill Neferset would bring the same penalties as before, and she must find another way to kill Neferset, although she couldn't think of how she would accomplish it now that Nefrytatanen kept her so occupied. Her attention returned to Nefrytatanen, who signaled Azza to put her coronet in place.

Amenemhet turned to Yazid to allow the servant to apply the ceremonial beard. "Accusing so many governors of being traitors fills me with dread," he said solemnly. "Not only will the shame of it dishearten many of the other governors and noblemen, but it's a grave charge to make without having even a witness."

Again there was a tap on the door, and Amenemhet lowered his head in disgust. "This session of court will begin at midnight if we continue to have so many interruptions," he muttered. He nodded to Yazid, and the servant hurried to the door.

Amenemhet was stunned to see Nessumontu enter the room followed by Ilbaya and Lyra. He got to his feet and stared speechlessly at Ilbaya.

"The guards at the palace gates brought Ilbaya and Lyra to me because they didn't know their identity or purpose," Nessumontu explained. "I knew you'd want to see them without delay."

Ilbaya and Lyra immediately sank to their knees. When Amenemhet signaled for them to rise, Ilbaya had to use his walking stick to get to his feet.

"Majesties, I've returned to be your witness, as I promised," he said quietly.

Amenemhet sank into a chair and, noticing Ilbaya's awkwardness, waved for them both to sit down. "How did you

283

escape death?" he managed to whisper. "We searched for you until it was too dark to see what we were doing."

"Sire, I was unconscious, trapped under a slab of stone that was held just high enough by some others to prevent my being crushed. I made my way back to Ithtawe as quickly as I could, but I delayed coming back to the palace to get Lyra," Ilbaya explained.

Amenemhet wondered how Ilbaya had managed to wrest Lyra away from Marmarus, but said only, "I'm most grateful you returned instead of simply taking flight, which must have been tempting."

"Majesty, Lyra and I wanted our legal freedom, so we wouldn't have to live with fear for the rest of our lives," Ilbaya reminded the king hopefully.

"I promised you freedom, and it will be legal as soon as my scribe can write the necessary documents," Amenemhet answered. Satisfaction filled him as he watched the joy that lit their faces. Then, realizing freedom was only what he intended for all of Marmarus' slaves, he wondered what more he could do to reward Ilbaya. "Have you made any plans for your future?" he asked.

Ilbaya couldn't conceal the excitement in his voice when he answered, "Although I can't return to Minoa, Lyra can go back to Thessalia, her homeland—"

Lyra couldn't contain her happiness and interrupted, "My father is a merchant, just as Ilbaya's father was. I know he'd accept Ilbaya as a son." Suddenly realizing to whom she was speaking, she fell silent.

Ilbaya flashed her a smile, then explained, "Lyra became a slave when she was stolen from one of her father's caravans and her brother was killed trying to defend her. Her father had no other children and so now is alone."

"I can imagine the joy you'll give him when you return with the daughter he thought he'd lost," Nefrytatanen commented softly.

"Ilbaya was trained to run his father's business, so he'll do very well with my father's," Lyra said excitedly. Realizing that she had addressed the queen without using even the most informal title, she blushed and lowered her eyes. "Forgive me, divine lady," she whispered.

Nefrytatanen smiled at Lyra's penitence and said, "I assume you intend to be married. Will you do so here in Tamera?"

"Majesty, my father has been cheated of his daughter for

several years and I thought we would first travel to Thessalia so he can share that happy moment with us," Lyra murmured.

"Divine lady, Thessalia and Minoa are similar in their customs and beliefs, and I would feel almost as if I were home again if we could begin our life together there," Ilbaya said.

"I would offer you a position in my palace as reward for your services, but I can understand your desire to go home with Lyra," Amenemhet said. "It is a long voyage to Thessalia, and you'll need passage on a ship. Would you like that passage to be arranged on a ship of the royal fleet?"

Stunned by a vision of their arrival in Thessalia in so sumptuous a fashion, Ilbaya imagined escorting Lyra to her father accompanied by a contingent of royal guards, and he breathed, "Sire, are you offering to send us to Thessalia on one of your personal vessels?"

Nefrytatanen stood up. "We will, of course, make sure we send a few wedding presents as well," she reminded Amenemhet. He nodded in agreement.

Ilbaya and Lyra glanced at each other, too awed to speak. Gifts from such a king and queen would undoubtedly be treasures.

Amenemhet smiled and got to his feet. "It wouldn't do for you to go to your prospective father-in-law empty-handed, Ilbaya. You have earned something for all your trouble." He paused and sighed, remembering how late they were to begin court. "Such delightful plans are a pleasure to make, and we will speak further about them, but at the moment, we all have a less pleasant task to perform." He turned to Yazid, and the servant handed him his scepters.

When Yazid opened the door, Meri was standing outside with fist poised ready to knock.

"Forgive my intrusion," the prime minister said quickly. "I came to see if something is wrong. What delays your coming to court?"

"What is wrong will be set right in the throne room," Amenemhet answered. He hurried past Meri and walked with long swift strides toward the private corridor that led to the throne room. Nefrytatanen followed, trying to keep pace with him.

In the past Amenemhet had often felt bowed under the awesome weight of having to enter the throne room holding the sweet promise of life in one hand and the power of ending life in the other. But to have to proclaim the treason of

285

the heads of several noble families and sentence them to death was a chore he would gladly have passed to another.

When the door to the private royal entrance opened, those waiting in the throne room turned expectantly to watch their rulers enter. Amenemhet took Nefrytatenen's arm and with a purposeful step, they entered the room together.

Amenemhet looked at the faces uplifted toward him, mouths slightly parted in awe of him, faces filled with hope and those merely curious, the guilty eyes of those he would soon condemn, and he wondered what they would do if he announced, "I am a man. I would be a carver of statues, a scribe, an architect—but for my birth." He knew they'd be shocked that their divine king confessed his humanity. Yet, Amenemhet thought, humanity was the real crown, and those awaiting his commands possessed it the same as he. The scepters in his hands were symbols of his authority, but they felt cold and lifeless to him. Life, he mused, was warmth and light and movement.

Amenemhet stood before the dais with the golden seat of Heru on it and wondered why his body didn't become lost in so exalted a place. He glanced again at the swarm of faces waiting for him to offer mercy or give punishment, and he was amazed that any people could expect such things from a mortal man. No one was that wise. But they considered their king not a mortal like themselves, he reminded himself. Perhaps that was the answer, he decided. The king held such power his subjects dared not think him an ordinary human being. They elevated him to godhood. He sighed. It wasn't easy to be a god, but he straightened his shoulders and lifted his head as he stepped upon the dais.

The vast expanse of the throne room was awesome in its magnificence. Amenemhet wondered if those standing at the opposite end could hear his voice when he spoke. The columns cast shadows on some of the throng—just as shadows fell over some men's lives, he reflected.

Meri struck the golden hawk inlaid in the floor, and the gong of the seal sent its mellow voice across the blue air in signal. The people sank to their knees before the thrones.

The warmth of Nefrytatenen's hand left Amenemhet's arm, and he glanced at her quickly, wondering why she had let go of him. He saw her step off the dais and face him, her eyes a glow of lapis. How small in stature she seemed when she stood below the thrones, he thought, but why did she do this when her place was beside him?

Nefrytatanen took off her crown and put it in Amen-emhet's hands. She smiled as she sank to her knees before him as the others had. "King Amenemhet," she said, her voice carrying clear and sweet through the gold-flecked air, "though my station is as high as your own . . ."

Then Amenemhet knew she had read his thoughts of self-doubt, and he whispered, "Higher, winged one, than mine."

"I bow to you," she continued, "not because I must, but from love do I prostrate myself at your feet." Nefrytatanen touched her forehead to the floor, then lifted her eyes to his and declared, "Amen-Ra, Heru, and Amenemhet are three names for the same being!"

Amazed at the queen's act of obeisance, the crowd stared at her for a moment, then quickly decided to follow her example and three hundred foreheads touched the floor.

Amenemhet started to shake his head at her, but she smiled and whispered, "You are not merely a man. You're our king."

Amenemhet replaced her crown on her head and took her hands in his. "Rise, Aset-Nefrytatanen," he said softly.

Nefrytatanen stood up, a satisfied look on her face, and stepped onto the dais, returning to Amenemhet's side.

After they had settled themselves on their thrones, Meri's staff again struck the seal, and only when the gong sounded did Amenemhet and Nefrytatanen's subjects dare lift their faces.

"Commander Nessumontu!" Amenemhet called. Nessumon-tu came forward. "Give Ambassador Adadni the objects I had saved for him," Amenemhet commanded.

Adadni watched curiously as Nessumontu went to a wait-ing guard, who gave him a bundle. Then Nessumontu ap-proached Adadni and dropped the armful at his feet with a crash that echoed through the silence. The bundle split, and Adadni stared in surprise at the assortment of weapons and insignia at his feet.

"Those belonged to a courier from Zahi," Amenemhet said coldly. "That courier and others like him visited a number of my governors persuading them to ruin Tamera's crops by planting insects in our fields. After we had been starved into weakness, Zahi would then conquer us. The governors were to receive portions of my kingdom as reward for their be-trayal."

At Amenemhet's words, several noblemen rushed noisily to

the doors, but finding themselves facing a line of leveled spears, they stopped.

Amenemhet's attention had shifted to this flurry of activity, but his narrowed eyes quickly returned to Adadni. "The delegation from Zahi will leave Tamera immediately and never return."

"Will you give me no chance to speak?" Adadni asked. "This is a mistake!"

"You're a liar," Amenemhet declared, "and I have no time to waste hearing lies."

"How can you say that without letting me speak?" Adadni cried.

"Why should I expect a dishonorable man to speak honorably?" Amenemhet said contemptuously. He was growing dangerously angry and had little patience to control his temper. He stood up and said, "Take this bundle back to your treacherous king and inform him that I want no ambassador from Zahi, not even a trader from your land, ever to cross our border again. If another Hyksos is seen in Tamera, whatever his purpose, he will be executed as a spy!"

Adadni's eyes became angry slits. "King Shalmanesser will send Commander Sargon to answer this insult," he spat.

Amenemhet replied disdainfully, "Tell your king to make sure to send enough archers to drive Sargon to our gates."

At this, Nessumontu laughed softly in derision.

Adadni turned on his heel and walked out quickly, the others of his delegation hurrying behind him. After the doors had been closed, Amenemhet and Nefrytatanen again sat on their thrones.

Meri approached them to whisper, "And the guilty governors?"

Amenemhet's eyes traveled over the crowd, resting angrily for a moment on the noblemen who were circled by spears. "I see they're all present," he observed. His eyes returned to Meri. "You will now announce the names of the traitors to the court."

Turning to Lakma, Amenemhet's scribe, Meri received the list of names. Then he faced the court and read the list aloud in a voice that made each governor feel as if the sound of his name were the striking of a funeral gong.

Lord Menkara, who had not tried to escape with the others lest his own fear announce his guilt, heard his name, and putting an outraged expression on his face, he stalked brazenly

288

to the foot of the thrones. Nessumontu stepped forward alertly, but Menkara didn't even glance at him.

"Majesties—" he began.

"You must kneel before you address the king and queen," Meri reminded sharply.

Menkara's frown deepened, but he obeyed. After Amenemhet had gestured for him to rise, he got to his feet and faced them without wavering. "Your majesties, my name was included on that list, and I am innocent of any wrongdoing," he said loudly.

"It was in your province the Hyksos courier was found," Amenemhet said sarcastically.

"That proves nothing," Menkara replied sharply. "Sire, more proof than this must be presented to the court for so severe an accusation!"

Amenemhet nodded to the guard who stood by the doorway into the corridor of the royal chambers. The guard opened the door and admitted Ilbaya.

"I have a witness who heard your conversation with the Hyksos courier," Amenemhet said coldly. "Ilbaya, can you identify this man?"

Ilbaya slowly came closer, staring intently at Menkara a moment before he turned to Amenemhet and knelt. After Amenemhet had given him permission to rise, Ilbaya said clearly, "Your majesties, this is the man I saw with the courier from Zahi."

Menkara took a step backward in fright. "Sire, who is this man that accuses me? How can you believe him, a stranger to our land, before me, the son of a loyal noble family?"

Nefrytatanen said coolly, "His majesty can believe Ilbaya before you because I have searched Ilbaya's thoughts and know their truth. While I waited for you to finish speaking, I reached into your mind and confirmed your deceits."

Menkara knew that winged priestesses were supposed to be able to read the thoughts of others at will but was never sure he believed such a thing. Still, he knew her saying that aloud in court sealed his fate. He could think of nothing to say.

Nessumontu gestured for a nearby soldier to escort Menkara to join the other guilty governors.

Meanwhile, Amenemhet arose to address the court. "Lord Menkara demanded more proof than my word, but he forgets that I am your king and he could demand nothing from me, that I need give proof to no one for my decisions but Asar," he said sternly. "There is only one sentence for treason.

289

These men will be sent to the executioner and their penalty exacted tomorrow morning. Their successors will be named within the decan."

Nessumontu signaled the guards, and they prodded the guilty noblemen with the tips of their spears. The prisoners left with fearful and hesitant steps. Only Menkara dared to glance angrily back at the thrones, while the others fixed their eyes on the floor.

Meri returned to his place and struck the seal with his staff, once for each condemned nobleman. When the last echoes of the reverberating gong had faded, Amenemhet again sat on his throne.

"Now you will bring before me the slave dealer, Marmarus of Babylonia, whose caravan distributed the insects as he traveled through our provinces," Amenemhet said coldly.

Marmarus had been arrested early that morning, and he had assumed that the charges being brought against him were the relatively minor ones associated with his slave trade. But after hearing Amenemhet's words through the half-closed door of the antechamber where he stood waiting, he was frozen with fear. The door opened wide and the pair of soldiers guarding him looked at him expectantly. He didn't move, and they gave him a sharp order. Still he didn't move. The soldiers, realizing he was paralyzed with fear, took him by his arms and half-carried him into the throne room. Marmarus was puzzled by Ilbaya's presence, but he was too afraid to even think about it.

Nefrytatanen watched Marmarus' humiliating entrance and whispered to Amenemhet, "His very person is disagreeable to look upon."

When the soldiers released Marmarus, he fell like a rag doll at the foot of the thrones and cried, "Mercy, majesties, mercy! The Hyksos forced me to do it. I have no interest or knowledge of politics! They forced me!" He followed this with a half-sobbing, hysterical account of how the Hyksos had threatened him.

Tiring of his cries, Amenemhet looked down at Marmarus and said, "The sound of your voice annoys my ears, and the unpleasant odor rising from you affronts my nose."

Nefrytatanen said, "His story is a lie. He was being paid well."

Amenemhet signaled to Meri, who came forward, carefully stepping around Marmarus' prostrate form. "Announce to the

290

court that, since this man isn't of our land, he hasn't betrayed us. I cannot sentence him to death."

Marmarus looked up, surprised. "You won't kill me?" he asked in an anxious whine.

At this possibility, Ilbaya took a step forward, his eyes filled with glowing green flecks of anger.

Amenemhet looked at Marmarus with disgust. "His slaves will be freed and all his possessions will be divided among them," he announced. Noting Marmarus' steadily growing relief he added, "To assure that no other merchants will consider working for Zahi while they're in Tamera, I must make certain that Marmarus doesn't enjoy whatever payment he received from the Hyksos."

At this announcement, Marmarus slowly got to his feet, his eyes refilling with fear.

Amenemhet signaled to Nessumontu, who came forward. "Have this creature escorted to our northeast border and expel him from Tamera. Supply him with enough food and water to reach Zahi."

Ilbaya rushed to the foot of the thrones and knelt clumsily. "Your majesty, will nothing more be done to him?" he whispered incredulously.

Amenemhet looked down at Ilbaya. "You didn't wait for me to finish," he said softly. He raised his eyes to Marmarus, and they hardened until their surface resembled the metal their color was named after. He said coldly, "Commander Nessumontu, you will make sure that before he leaves Ithtawe, every bone in his hands and feet is crushed. Henceforth he will do nothing more harmful than beg coins for his living."

A scream rose from Marmarus' throat, but Nessumontu, looking as if the task pleased him, ordered Marmarus dragged away.

Amenemhet waved Meri to come closer. When Meri approached, Amenemhet said quietly, "Now that Marmarus has been disposed of, you will have incense burned in this room tonight, so its fragrance will be improved for tomorrow's audience."

Twenty-One

Nessumontu stood aside and opened the palace door for the king. After the heat of the day, the early-evening breeze was a gentle breath on Amenemhet's skin as if, with the sinking of the sun, the air's weight had been lessened. He took Nefrytatanen's arm and they stepped outside to follow Nessumontu across the courtyard toward the gates opening onto the palace's private quay. The sky of orange and lavender was washed with gilt, drawing a sheer golden veil over Ithtawe. The Nile was a ribbon of black satin reflecting the lights in the sky.

Although Ilbaya and Lyra, who followed Amenemhet and Nefrytatanen, didn't speak even to whisper to each other, Amenemhet sensed their self-consciousness at being escorted to the ship by a king and queen as well as a half-dozen royal guards. He wondered what he could say or do to put them more at ease. It was, he thought, a small enough favor to bestow when Ilbaya's courage had saved Tamera from famine and invasion. Amenemhet reflected for a moment on how one slave's hunger for freedom had influenced the course of an entire kingdom, how the love of this one man and woman had changed tens of thousands of other lives.

When Amenemhet and Nefrytatanen stopped at the foot of

293

the causeway leading onto the ship and turned to face Ilbaya and Lyra, Amenemhet smiled at the expression on their faces. They were staring at the ship's graceful silhouette against the orchid sky as if they still couldn't believe it was real.

"The ship is amply stocked with foodstuffs from the royal stores, and Sepu assured me that the private cabins have been comfortably prepared," Nessumontu told Amenemhet. "I've placed a squad of palace guards aboard as well as enough soldiers to provide protection should any Hyksos vessel sight a royal ship of Tamera and be too tempted—though it would be unlikely with Ilbaya and Lyra sailing northwest, farther away from Zahi than Tamera."

Ilbaya tore his eyes from the vessel, whose gold trim was catching fire from the sun's declining rays. "Majesties, Lyra and I haven't the wit to express our thanks," he whispered.

"To give us our freedom was wonderful enough, but to send us home in one of your own ships loaded with presents and soldiers to guard our well-being is . . ." Lyra paused, like Ilbaya not knowing what else to say.

"Because of you the damage in the infected provinces has been contained and stopped," Nefrytatenen said. "It will take a little time to repair the fields, but that will be a relatively easy task. A few presents and the use of one ship is small enough reward for the suffering you prevented."

"Your freedom is something you always possessed. We didn't give it to you. The divine beings only arranged for it to be restored to you," Amenemhet reminded them.

"Majesties, though we'll live in Thessalia and aren't citizens of Tamera, we always will be two of your most loyal subjects," Ilbaya promised. "I only hope my sisters may somehow find that destiny leads them to Tamera, because here they would find justice."

Nefrytatenen took Ilbaya's hand and whispered, "I'll offer prayers for them."

Ilbaya nodded, his eyes filled with tears of gratitude. He knew the requests of a winged priestess weren't taken lightly by the gods. "High One, I too will offer prayers each day for the strength and prosperity of Tamera, for you and your family's health and happiness."

"If you would do me a favor, I ask that you pray for Lady Neferset's sight to be restored at Asar's shrine in Ahbidew. We're beginning the pilgrimage tomorrow morning, and the ceremony will take place in five days. Even though you don't know her, such fervent prayers as you promise will surely aid in her healing," Nefrytatanen said.

"Divine lady, we will pray together for her cause on every one of those days," Lyra vowed.

Nefrytatanen took their hands and held them both between hers, then said, "During your voyage, may Ra warm your days and Aset's sphere silver cloudless nights. May Shu's breath fill your sails to speed you safely home. After you've reached your destination, may Heru be a friendly spirit to guard your house and Hat-Hor bless your love with children to give you joy."

"Divine lady, that your lips have given us this blessing assures the happiness of our future," Lyra whispered gratefully as Nefrytatanen stepped away.

"And Montu's protection goes with the guards accompanying you," Amenemhet said.

"Montu will make certain this flower reaches her own garden safely," Nessumontu promised.

Lyra was startled at Nessumontu's remark, and she quickly glanced up to find his eyes regarding her warmly. She blushed and lowered her eyes, realizing that she didn't know how to gracefully reply to a compliment. She had received none during the years of her slavery other than having her desirability reflected by her price's increasing.

Ilbaya had not missed the admiration in the commander's gaze, and he was seized by a sudden impulse to remove Lyra from Nessumontu's sight. Hastily, he turned to Amenemhet and Nefrytatanen. "Majesties, I think the ship's captain is waiting, so, if you'll allow us, we must leave," he said.

Amenemhet granted permission, and Ilbaya and Lyra boarded the vessel. The lines that bound the ship to the dock were untied, and it immediately began to move toward the middle of the Nile.

Ilbaya took Lyra's hand, and they stood at the rail silently watching Ithtawe's great walls recede until they became mere shadows in the distance. As Ilbaya gazed at the shore silhouetted against the amber sky rapidly sliding past, he thought wistfully of the coming night.

"We're finally alone and free to do as we wish," he said softly.

Lyra's eyes lowered to gaze at the water slipping by. Sensing Ilbaya's desire to spend the night together, she suddenly felt shy with him—shy and eager and confused about how to

295

behave. Wanting to buy a little time to sort out her feelings, she said, "My father will be so happy to see me again. I'll be proud to introduce you to him." Ilbaya put his arm around her waist, and she chattered nervously, "His business is so much like what you told me of your father's, I know you'll do well. I'm sure you'll feel at home in Thessalia."

"I will be home, if your father approves of me," Ilbaya replied. Aware of her tension, he asked quietly, "What's wrong Lyra?"

She raised her eyes to meet his and whispered, "I've been a slave since I was twelve. During those seven years I wanted so badly to be free every moment I was awake that I dreamed of it while sleeping. Now that I am, I'm not sure how to behave. I told you once that I was a thing to Marmarus. I find I'll have to learn how to be a woman."

"I noticed how surprised you were at Nessumontu's compliment, and I saw the uncertainty you felt about replying to him. It has reminded you of less happy days," Ilbaya said. He put his hands on her shoulders and turned her to him. "I can understand why you feel differently now from the way you felt on that hillside when we first kissed. You were an innocent child when you were taken as a slave, and you've had no experience with men that wasn't forced on you. You've never been courted, but you've been taken. You've never even been caressed by a hand you could refuse."

"None but your own, Ilbaya," she said softly.

"It's very strange to have been forced to live as I have these many long years, yet to know as little about love as if I were yet untouched. To be faced with its reality is a little frightening to me. I don't know what to do," she admitted.

"You never have been touched by love, only by lust. You'll have to learn about it like a maiden," Ilbaya said softly. "Although my emotions are anxious for physical expression, love—unlike lust—can be patient until you've learned how to accept it."

"I want to learn quickly, Ilbaya," she breathed.

One of the sailors lit a lamp in the cabin behind them, and the sudden glow made streaks of copper fire in Ilbaya's hair. She remembered how he had looked in the sunlight on the hill. She wished she could see if his eyes now held the same green lights as they had then, but a shadow over his face hid his features. He bent to kiss her forehead. When she put her hands on his waist, she felt the shiver that ran through him,

296

and she put her face against his cheek, silently thanking the gods for having given her such a man.

"I think," she whispered in his ear, "I begin to learn already."

Twenty-Two

Kheti and Neferset were well liked, so a large number of court officials insisted on accompanying them on the pilgrimage to Ahbidew to add their prayers to Neferset's cause. After three days of living with the complications involved in sailing with all these officials and their families and servants as well as a large contingent of palace guards, Amenemhet ordered an overnight pause in their journey before they turned west and continued overland to the temple of Asar. It wasn't easy to organize so large a group for an early start the next day, and the caravan didn't set out until late in the morning.

Most of the ride from the river was over fertile land, but in the afternoon when the sun was hottest, the caravan reached the limit of the cultivated land and had to continue over a long barren stretch. There were few trees; only patches of sparse, scrubby yellow grass grew in the powdery soil. There was no shelter from the sun's heat, and the wind was hot and dry, giving no relief. Because so many children were traveling with the pilgrims and many peasants from the area followed on foot, Amenemhet called for several rests, and progress was slow.

When Amenemhet finally saw the temple in the distance,

he turned to Nefrytatanen, who rode beside him, and suggested, "Neferset might like to know Asar's temple is in view."

"I'll tell her," Nefrytatanen offered and turned her horse to ride back in the column to where Neferset's litter was being carried.

Nefrytatanen drew back the shielding curtains to find Neferset reclining on the cushions, eyes closed. Nefrytatanen whispered, "Neferset?"

"Yes?" she answered. Her eyes opened to stare blankly in the direction of Nefrytatanen's voice, and Nefrytatanen could see from their greenness that Neferset had been weeping.

"The temple's in sight," Nefrytatanen said gently. "We'll reach it well before dark."

Neferset smiled wistfully and said, "I wish I could see it. I've never visited Asar's shrine."

"You'll see it," Nefrytatanen firmly replied.

"I don't want to set my heart on it," Neferset said. "If my sight isn't restored, I'll be too disappointed."

"You won't be disappointed," Nefrytatanen assured her.

Neferset struggled to keep down the excitement that rose in her each time Nefrytatanen promised that. With an edge to her voice, she asked, "How can you be so certain?"

"I'm certain because I know," Nefrytatanen answered. "I'll rejoin Amenemhet now, but remember what I've told you. I know you'll return to Ithtawe able again to see the faces of your children."

"I hope so," Neferset said in a small voice that made Nefrytatanen smile.

Nefrytatanen knew how much Neferset wanted to believe she would recover her sight, and she happily anticipated Neferset's joy when she opened her eyes to discover her miracle had been accomplished. Nefrytatanen turned and rode back to the front of the line.

Azza, walking beside Neferset's litter, had overheard their conversation, and she looked into the curtains to enquire, "My lady, is everything all right?"

"It goes as well as can be expected," Neferset answered. "The queen merely wanted to encourage me."

"I realize the king has promised you'll regain your sight," Azza said, thinking she might discourage Neferset, "but perhaps the queen shouldn't be so positive on only his word. She might find it difficult to forgive him if we're disappointed."

Neferset smiled at that idea. "The queen has her own reason to believe I'll be able to see again. And Nefrytatanen would forgive the king just about anything, I think."

"That's a great deal of faith to have in any man, even a king," Azza remarked.

"Maybe so, but she believes in him as I believe in Lord Kheti," Neferset said. "You too will love one day. Then you'll understand the full meaning of trust."

"Perhaps," Azza replied.

Azza let the curtain fall back into place, thinking she had a lover of her own she would soon return to. She stared down at the sandy soil she trod, which was alien to her, and longed for green jungle paths, for the familiar sounds and scents of home.

Queen Nefrytatanen had reclaimed her servant, Dedjet, for the trip, and Azza anticipated at last having an opportunity to kill Neferset. She resolved to do her best to carry out Karomana's order before Neferset's sight was restored, if it ever would be. Then she could return to her village, confident that Karomana's agents wouldn't bother her, that Urum's curse would never be leveled on her. Even if Karomana were dead, Azza would have been afraid not to fulfill the orders she had been given. But Azza was sure Karomana was in hiding and planning a way to regain her crown.

When Nefrytatanen rejoined Amenemhet, he was staring straight ahead, paying no attention to Kheti and Nessumontu, who rode just ahead of him.

"What are you looking at?" Nefrytatanen asked softly.

Amenemhet turned to her and smiled. "I was watching the wind build cities from the sand, then, like a dissatisfied artist, sweep them away."

Realizing that Nefrytatanen had returned, Kheti turned and asked, "How is Neferset? Should I go back to her? She was sleeping the last time I looked."

"She's awake now," the queen answered. "She's trying not to hope too much, but it's a struggle she's losing."

"I'll go back to her," Kheti decided. "Maybe I can cheer her."

"I think so," Nefrytatanen agreed.

Kheti promptly turned his horse to fall back in the line.

By the time the travelers reached the temple's walls, the sun had sunk low. It wasn't possible to set up a camp beyond the temple's first pylon, so they stopped just outside the tall copper doors, which glowed warmly in the sunset.

After Amenemhet and Nefrytatanen dismounted, they

301

stood together for a moment, silently gazing at the soaring walls before them, which reflected the gold tint of the sky. The carvings and hieroglyphs on the outside walls were unpainted, and their sunken lines made purple shadows, while the raised areas reflected pale gold.

Nefrytatanen turned to Amenemhet. "Beloved, while the camp is being prepared, will you come with me into the temple?" she asked.

"Yes," Amenemhet answered. "We're very dusty from the journey," he said slowly. "Should we not cleanse ourselves first?"

"We'll shake as much of the dust from our garments as we can out here," she replied. "We can rinse our faces and hands in the pool inside."

Amenemhet signaled to the keeper of the gates to open them, and the great copper doors swung inward slowly on their bronze hinges.

Amenemhet felt dwarfed by the walls as he walked through the entrance, and he looked up in awe at the carved figures of kings and queens who had long ago passed into Tuat.

The carvings on the inside walls were painted in brilliant colors lavished with gold leaf, and among the fading light's shadows, the figures seemed almost ready to move. The place was silent. Even Amenemhet's and Nefrytatanen's footsteps made no noise. He decided it must be because the place was so immense sounds were dissipated into nothing.

After they had washed their faces, arms and legs in the pool provided for this purpose, Amenemhet turned to examine the walls surrounding them. "It's a strange thing," he murmured.

"What is strange?" Nefrytatanen asked as she wiped her face.

"As awesome and sacred, as immense and silent, as this temple is, I'm not uneasy in any way," he said softly. "When I enter a temple dedicated to Anpu, I feel uncomfortable. But here, in this place where Asar's mortal body is buried—a place more holy than any other—I feel at ease, serene and safe."

"Why shouldn't you feel safe?" Nefrytatanen asked. "You come to this temple to do honor to Asar, and your soul is pure."

Amenemhet smiled. "I'm not so pure," he said, "but I do
302

feel at peace here. I feel comforted within these walls, as if all the turmoil in the outside world could pound against those doors, but could never enter."

Nefrytatanen took his hand. "If this outer court is beautiful, imagine how much more beautiful it is beyond the next gateway and the next. Let us go deeper into the temple," she suggested.

"How far may I go?" Amenemhet asked. He knew he could enter deeper into the inner chambers than a commoner or a nobleman, but there were some areas where none but the high priest was allowed.

"You can go as far as I," Nefrytatanen answered.

"How far is that?" he asked.

"I can go into the inner sanctuary itself, for no priest is elevated higher than I am," Nefrytatanen said, smiling.

"I didn't pass the test in the pyramid," Amenemhet protested. "I'm not a high priest. Only Ankhneferu can go with you."

Although Nefrytatanen said nothing more, she continued walking deeper into the temple. Amenemhet followed her through more silent chambers lined with colossal limestone statues of unsmiling divine beings, until outside the room preceding the inner sanctuary, he stopped.

"Are you sure I may enter this chamber?" he asked.

"We will go together into this room and the final one beyond it," she answered.

"I think I cannot," Amenemhet protested.

Nefrytatanen pointed to a door in one of the outside walls. "There is the door to the garden," she said. "We will first choose bouquets. Then we'll take them into the inner sanctuary—together." A smile escaped her. "Your education lacks something," she remarked.

Amenemhet said nothing.

"As king, you're supreme high priest of the land," she reminded him.

"The title of Lord of Rites is a courtesy," he said.

Nefrytatanen shook her head. "You are divine by birth, elevated even above Ankhneferu. It is by this right I enter the innermost holy place—not only because I received my wings in the pyramid." She sighed at his lingering doubt and said, "Let us go into the garden. While we choose our offering bouquets, reflect on my words, and you'll realize their truth."

Amenemhet and Nefrytatanen again approached the doorway to the inner sanctuary, but he still seemed unconvinced. Taking his arm firmly in hers, she pushed open the gold door to the chamber.

"Would I encourage you to commit sacrilege?" she asked. "Come," she urged and drew him into the room.

It was smaller than the others they had walked through because the outermost courtyard was the largest in length and width and height and each chamber they had passed through was by tradition a little smaller. This, the most sacred of all the rooms, was not one-quarter the size of the first. Its diminished area was meant to concentrate the power of the rituals conducted here.

The chamber was hushed except for the gentle whisper of the oil burning in the lamps. The dim light made sparks of the gold flecks in the lapis lazuli panels lining the walls. The statue of Asar at the far end of the room was lit by lamps placed at its base, which made the gold image a blaze of splendor. A layer of myrrh incense veiled the ceiling in blue haze, and in the closeness of the room, the perfume was compelling.

Amenemhet stood just inside the doorway, still hesitant to go closer, awed at the idea of being in this most holy of shrines.

"You're inside now, and you might as well come farther," Nefrytatanen said. "We must, at least, approach the offering table."

Amenemhet and Nefrytatanen took the few steps toward the low, glistening stone table, that stood midway to Asar's statue. As Amenemhet placed his flowers on the table, his golden eyes, glowing in the light, fastened on Asar's face.

Nefrytatanen placed her flowers beside Amenemhet's and sank to her knees, touching her forehead to the black stone floor. Although he never had so prostrated himself in his life, Amenemhet did so now, because he felt humble there. He heard Nefrytatanen speak to Asar, and his soul silently echoed her words.

"We have come, O merciful Asar, Lord of Eterity, to pay homage," she prayed. The chamber absorbed the sound of her voice as if her prayer disappeared into Asar's ears. "We are yet dusty from our journey, but I wished to see you before all else—so we may ask a special favor." Nefrytatanen paused a moment, listening to the lamps' whisper, as she considered her request. "I know Neferset's sight will be restored, and my heart is filled with gratitude, but what I request is a different thing."

Amenemhet glanced up at Nefrytatanen in surprise. She had lifted her head from the floor and was gazing at the statue's face. He watched her carefully, wondering what she would request.

"For Tamera I beg protection from the Hyksos, who would invade our land," Nefrytatanen said clearly. "I ask for wisdom and strength for my beloved, Amenemhet, and for the next king, our son Senwadjet. I ask your favor for those of our blood who will follow, so our land will survive and the truths taught us by Tehuti will remain untarnished. May justice always stand beside us and the powers coming from Aset to certain ones of us turn away the evil which will always, it seems, be part of mankind's struggle."

Again Nefrytatanen bent to touch her forehead to the floor, and she remained silently in this posture for some time.

Amenemhet lifted his eyes to the face of Asar in wonder that the previous misgivings he had had to enter this chamber had vanished. He decided Nefrytatanen had been right. He was glad he had come.

Long after the camp had fallen into slumber, Azza lay awake remembering the day's events and reviewing the plans she had made.

After the tents had been set up, Kheti had taken Neferset to the temple. In the outer courtyard, the priests had placed a prayer tablet dedicated to Neferset's cause, and Kheti, Neferset and their friends had prayed with the priests. As they left the courtyard, Azza, pretending with the other servants to pray, studied the prayer tablet. It was a slab of limestone on which a prayer had been carved for Neferset's health. At the top of the tablet Neferset's likeness had been carved in bas-relief. An ancient belief of Tamera shared by the people of Kenset was the basis for Azza's plan. If she destroyed the carving of Neferset's face, it would put a curse on Neferset, who wouldn't be able to see, hear, speak or even breathe. If Azza chiseled away the hands and feet of the relief, Neferset herself wouldn't be able to use her limbs. If Azza obliterated Neferset's name in each place it was mentioned in the prayer, the gods would forget Neferset and not only ignore Kheti's request to restore Neferset's sight, but destroy Neferset completely. Azza managed to steal a small chisel and hammer after she left the temple, and she hid them carefully.

Azza was doubly grateful for the talisman Karomana had given her before she had left Kenset, because its protection would conceal her plans even from Queen Nefrytatanen. Azza knew Nefrytatanen was disturbed by her own presence, and she knew this was because Nefrytatanen's powers as a priestess were so strong she sensed Azza's danger, though the talisman prevented the queen from discerning exactly why Azza caused her tension. But for the talisman, Azza was convinced she would be undone.

At dawn Kheti and Neferset planned to lead the members of the pilgrimage into the temple to again ask Asar's compassion. While they prayed, the high priest, Ankhneferu, was to pray in the inner sanctuary, including in his sunrise rites for Amen-Ra a plea for Neferset's recovery. Then they all would go to the sacred pond at the west side of the temple, which was fed by a hidden spring, where Neferset would bathe her eyes in the water. Wouldn't they be surprised, Azza thought smugly, when all their careful rituals had no effect on Neferset. Wouldn't they be surprised that Neferset would rapidly sicken and die. Everyone would surely accept Neferset's death as divine decision, and not look for her murderer.

Wondering if enough time had passed, Azza turned her attention from her thoughts of triumph to listen to the camp. The only sounds were those of the pacing guards, and she decided it was time to enter the temple and destroy the prayer tablet. She got up from her mat and slipped out of the tent with the stealth of a night-prowling cat, then crept silently through the darkness between the tents to the shadow of the temple's wall. Ordinarily, the copper doors were closed during the night, but in honor of the king and queen, the doors had been left open. Azza slipped through the opening under cover of its heaviest shadows and sought the corner where Kheti's prayer tablet had been set.

Azza crouched beside the limestone table and examined the stela carefully. Although she was unable to read the hieroglyphs, she was familiar with the picture-symbols representing Neferset's name, and she located each place the name was written. The portrait of Neferset's delicate features at the stela's top was beautifully accurate. Azza took out her chisel and hammer, wrapped several layers of heavy linen around the top of the chisel, and began to destroy Neferset's carved face. It seemed to Azza the chisel's noise echoed off the walls and the whole camp would be awakened. But, in reality, the sound was muffled by the linen wrappings as well as the courtyard's space, just as Amenemhet's voice had been muffled earlier.

Once the chisel slipped, and the top of Azza's hand was torn by its point. She stopped and held the wound tightly with her other hand. Tears came to her eyes from the pain, but she resumed her work, leaving blood smears on the stone. Almost finished with her destruction, Azza paused to examine the results. A soft step, directly behind her, made her spin around, and she looked up to see Lady Taji, Lord Sarenput's wife, watching her.

Taji's almond eyes were narrowed, and their slanted depths held black fire. Before Azza could move, Taji leaned down and examined the tablet more closely. Her eyes widened with horror.

"How dare you do such a thing?" Taji demanded, anger making her voice brittle. "You would kill Lady Neferset? Even destroy her soul?" Taji's hand swiftly grasped Azza's wrist, and her long nails pressed painfully in Azza's flesh. "I heard of such practices in Retenu!" Taji declared. "I know what this means. Don't try to lie to me, you little spider! How could you do such a thing to Neferset? You're evil. Evil, evil, evil!"

Azza was surprised by Taji's aggressiveness and astounded by her strength. Azza stood up and twisted her arm to free herself, but Taji spun her around, folding her arm behind her back in such a way that Azza dared not move, for fear her arm would be torn from her shoulder.

"You will come with me to Lord Kheti," Taji said coolly. "He'll know how to deal with you." Taji pulled from her hair an ornament with a long pointed shaft and reached up to hold its point close to Azza's ear. She almost had to stand on her toes to accomplish this, but her training as a dancer kept her perfectly balanced. "Make one move, you wicked creature, and you'll die," Taji warned the slave. "This point driven through your ear and into your brain is simple and silent, an exceedingly neat way to kill an enemy." Azza shuddered and Taji added smugly, "Move nothing, you little spider, but your legs, and let them propel you to Lord Kheti. But walk carefully," she warned, "for if you stumble, I may kill you accidently."

Azza made a slight move as if to resist, but she felt the cold point of the ornament's shaft brush her ear threateningly, and she knew that Taji would kill her if she disobeyed. At Taji's nudge, Azza began forward, wondering what she could do to save herself. She decided to behave in a docile fashion until she found an opportunity to escape this strong little creature.

Unresisting, Azza plodded slowly ahead of Taji, who continued to grasp Azza's arm firmly behind her and hold the ornament to Azza's ear. They crossed the courtyard and continued toward the great copper doors in this fashion.

Just inside the gateway, tall floor lamps stood, one on each side, and seeing the open orange flames as they approached, Azza had an idea. When Azza passed the closest lamp, she kicked one of the legs of its pedestal, which, as she had calculated, fell toward Taji.

Taji freed her hold on Azza to leap out of the fire's path, but the lamp's dish fell with a crash, spreading flames in a pool of oil at Taji's feet. The flames caught on Taji's skirt hem, and she threw herself to the paving stones, rolling quickly away from the fire. Then she leaped to her feet and raced to the pool, where Amenemhet and Nefrytatanen had earlier washed themselves, and dove into the water.

As Taji stood up in the pool, she saw Azza's shadowy figure running toward the temple's inner recesses. She heard the feet of the sentry racing from the door across the courtyard.

"Guard! Get that woman in the temple!" Taji shouted.

The guard paused to see who was in the pool calling orders. Recognizing Taji, he turned to run after Azza. Taji quickly climbed out of the pool and, with her dripping garments slapping her legs with each step, ran after the guard.

"Forgive me, Asar," the guard muttered as he followed Azza into the temple, anticipating that the slave would run straight through to the inner sanctuary. To his relief, he saw the dark figure veer to a side door. He heard the sound of feet running up a stairway, and reaching the door, he saw a winding stone staircase disappearing into darkness. He unsheathed his sword and ran up the steps, which were worn and slippery with age. He could hear Taji's bare feet running up behind him.

When he reached the top of the stairs, he found himself on the temple's roof. He could see clearly in the full moon's light that Azza was running around the perimeter of the roof frantically searching for another way down.

"There is no other way!" the guard called. "Surrender and come with me!"

Seeing the gleam of metal in the soldier's hand, Azza turned and ran farther along the roof's edge, then stopped. Beyond the place where she stood, she could see another roof of the temple complex; she calculated the gap between. She heard the guard shout again to surrender herself, and she ran back from the roof's edge a few paces. Then she turned and raced toward the opening. With a supreme effort, she sprang into space.

In the instant she knew she couldn't make it, she flung herself forward to reach for the roof with her hands, but her injured hand hadn't sufficient strength to cling to the stone. She felt her fingers slipping as she clawed frantically at the edge. Black eyes wide with disbelief, she fell to the stones below.

The dull thud of her body announced her soul's release.

The guard ran to the roof's edge to gaze down at Azza's broken body, then stepped back as Taji reached his side.

"Why did she try so foolish a leap?" he asked. "What did she do that she so feared being caught?"

"Evil," Taji murmured, looking over the edge. She straightened to look at the guard, her eyes glittering with triumph. "Terrible evil."

Neferset clung to Kheti's arm as he led her from the temple toward the sacred pool. She could hear the footsteps of their friends slowly following, and she wondered at their thoughts. Kheti was silent as they walked, and she perceived from the sound of his steps that he was stiff with tension. His arm was warm, and she held it gratefully, not only because he guided her feet, but because even his arm held the touch of love and gave her courage.

Neferset lifted her head. She could hear the whispers of palm fronds above and knew they walked beneath the trees that ringed the sacred pond. Kheti stopped walking.

"Directly in front of you is the water," he said softly. "All you have to do is kneel where you are and reach forward."

"How does the place look?" she asked.

"We have walked about thirty cubits from the temple door," Kheti replied. "The sacred pool is surrounded by palm trees and low shrubs, and we now stand on a soft carpet of thick moss. The pond is shaped as a rectangle and the water is very clear. I'd judge it will be cold, as it comes from a spring somewhere deep in the earth." He paused, then added in a soft voice, "The water is as green as an emerald—as green as your eyes when we love."

Neferset smiled, then whispered, "And how does the sunrise look?"

"Ra is filling the sky with a splendor I cannot describe," Kheti answered. She heard the emotion in his voice, and her hand crept slowly to his face, but Kheti took her searching fingers in his hand and kissed them, whispering, "You will see the sunrise for yourself. Ra has given us this magnificent dawn so its beauty will be the first thing to greet your vision."

"No," Neferset said. "If my sight is restored, it will be your face I'll look at first." She lowered herself to her knees, and poised with her hands over the water she could sense below her fingers, she paused.

Behind her Neferset heard Nefrytatanen's urgent whisper. "Do it, Neferset. Don't be afraid."

The water was surprisingly warm in Neferset's cupped hands. She opened her eyes wide to receive the moisture, but it escaped through the crevices between her fingers. Neferset rearranged herself to lie on her stomach, and she held her breath to dip her whole face in the water. Only when she had to breathe did she withdraw, but she continued staring sightlessly at the pond's surface. Tears filled her stinging eyes. It was useless she thought. She would be blind forever.

Neferset dipped her face again into the water, knowing all the others held their breath with her. She stayed in the water until she thought her lungs must burst, staring at the hazy green light. Then she raised her face and turned toward Kheti. She couldn't see him. All that came to her view was the same green blur. She began to weep.

"It's no use," she whispered through her tears. "Only a green blur replaces my darkness."

"Wait a moment more," Neferset heard Nefrytatanen say.

The green shadow became a veil, and behind the veil, which seemed to grow transparent, Neferset saw the blur of a shape. It was not one veil she peered through, but many, and one by one they were drawn aside. The shapes beyond the veils slowly became clearer, until the last veil was lifted from her wondering eyes, and she looked into Kheti's tear-streaked face. Wordlessly, she stared at him.

When Kheti saw Neferset's eyes gradually losing their blank look, he took her hands in his. Soon her eyes focused into an expression meant only for himself, and he knew. He remained unmoving a moment, staring at her in wonder, allowing her the time to look at him, knowing the discovery she made.

Finally, Kheti smiled through his tears and stood up, drawing Neferset to her feet with him.

"There's Ra's smile celebrating your triumph," he whispered.

Neferset silently gazed at the shimmering gold of the sky, her eyes speaking for her, shining with gratitude at the rising orange disk of the sun's face.

Nefrytatanen awoke with a jerk. Beside her, Amenemhet turned and sat up. "Is something wrong?" he asked sleepily.

She took a deep, shuddering breath of the cool night air and expelled it slowly. "I was dreaming," she finally said.

"Was it an evil dream?" he asked. He pulled her closer and put an arm warmly around her waist.

She peered into the darkness, as if trying to penetrate its secrets, while she struggled to remember the dream. "I don't think it was evil, but it was strange," she said slowly. She put her arms around him, anchoring herself to reality. "The dream is coming clearer now," she whispered.

Amenemhet became aware of her trembling, and he put his other arm around her. "How was it strange?" he asked.

"Where I was in the dream was chill and damp," she said softly. "There were mountains in the distance—strange, forbidding mountains with jagged peaks, not like our mountains."

"The dream wasn't of Tamera?"

"No," she answered, then was silent. Memory of the dream suddenly had returned. "You were there," she whispered, "but we were in a place I have never seen."

"What was the dream about?" he coaxed, thinking the telling of it would drive away its effect on her.

In Amenemhet's arms, Nefrytatanen slowly relaxed. "The skies weren't blue like ours, but gray with clouds, and the wind chilled me. There was mist hanging in the air that smelled like Retenu's forest. I walked on a street lined with strange-looking buildings, and the people I passed had features of other lands. They were dressed in peculiar garments, many garments protecting them from the cool air. I was dressed like them."

"That does not sound like an evil dream, yet you leaped

311

from your slumber as if you were afraid," Amenemhet remarked. "What frightened you?"

Nefrytatanen discovered she didn't want to remember, but finally she whispered, "It was an alien place, and I was lonely." Again she was silent, thinking, until she said hesitantly, "I looked up at your face and you looked at me, but it was as if we didn't know each other and were afraid to speak. We stared at each other and said nothing."

Amenemhet didn't comment. He couldn't imagine a time when he wouldn't speak to her, even in a dream. Suddenly the dream was frightening even to him. He held her closer, comforting them both.

Against his shoulder she whispered. "When I looked into your face, it was as if we were strangers knowing we weren't strangers. Your eyes gazed into mine, and a force poured out of them that filled me with such emotion I couldn't speak or think. You smiled at me, and I wanted to smile back—I tried desperately to smile—but I couldn't make my lips obey me. I stared at you like a numb thing, but I was anything but numb. Such powerful sensations were building in me I could hardly endure them. Finally, I couldn't bear them, and I lowered my eyes. You walked so close I felt the warmth of your body, but you didn't touch me. Instead, you passed by."

"See how foolish that dream was," he whispered. "I could never pass without even touching you."

"I turned to look at you, as a flower follows the sun." She sighed. "It was as if we were so surprised by each other's existence the world stopped in its course."

"I hope that dream isn't prophecy," Amenemhet murmured. "I wouldn't care to live in a world where we'd be surprised by each other's existence, a world where I'd walk past you."

"But you stopped and turned," she said softly. She leaned away and looked at him. "Each time your eyes rose to look at me, my heart stopped beating. I waited for you. I stood like a fearful child in that place, unable to move, waiting for you to come to me." She took a deep breath, and he knew she was filled with emotion and near to weeping. She whispered, "If you only had taken my hand, I would have been able to move, to go with you."

"What did I do?" he asked softly.

"You were with other people and I was with other people and they took us away." She paused for a moment, thinking about the dream, then said brokenly, "I almost wept. I have never been so lonely as I was in that dream. I never knew such loneliness was possible until that moment. I was afraid that once you were out of my sight, there would be no way I could find you again, no way for you to find me." Her voice faded to a whisper. "That's why I leaped out of my slumber and awakened you. That was why the dream was so terrible. I couldn't endure the loneliness."

Amenemhet again drew Nefrytatanen close, to rest her cheek against his. "Perhaps it was the prophecy of a lifetime to come," he whispered. "But it would have no meaning unless, after the dream ended, we didn't meet again. You probably awakened too soon. The dream, I'm sure, would have continued to reveal how the gods would have allowed us to find each other again."

Nefrytatanen considered this possibility for a moment. "It could have been a beautiful place if the sun had been shining," she conceded. She shivered at her still-vivid memory and whispered, "Without Ra, it was an alien place. Without you, it was empty and cold."

"In that future lifetime, as in this, I'll put my arms around you and make you warm," he murmured.

Nefrytatanen smiled against his cheek. "Then Ra would appear from behind those gray clouds and I'd fear nothing," she whispered. The warmth of him was what she needed. He was her reality. His lips brushed her shoulder and lingered, his warm breath becoming a caress. She tilted her head to feel the soft texture of his hair against her forehead and, in her movement, made a hollow at the base of her neck his lips slid into, where the tip of his tongue explored, causing shivers to run over her back like warm waves. Without her knowing it, her arms tightened around him.

Against her skin he said softly, "Do not hold me, beloved." Surprise instantly loosened her grasp. "I must be free to come to you as I will," he added, and at his words, a new tremor flowed through her. With his lips so close the words trembled in her ear he whispered, "I would warm you in my own way."

His mouth moved along her cheek to the corner of her lips, and she felt his teeth lightly travel the perimeter of her mouth with soft little bites. When his lips met hers, their touch was carefully soft, but his hands left her back and his fingers sensitively explored the rounded sides of her breasts. Beginning under her arm, he deliberately caressed her sides,

313

tracing paths like wavering fires over the curves of her hips. Then, he moved away.

She opened her eyes to see him kneeling beside her, an enigmatic smile on his lips.

"Has your appetite awakened?" he asked softly.

"Come to me," she whispered.

"In a moment," he promised.

She didn't question him, but watched until he leaned nearer to kiss her eyes closed. Her lips received his as a flower receives the sun. He kissed her with unhurried delicacy, even while her mouth reached encouragingly toward him and he leaned away to just elude her. His tongue's tip traced the outline of her lips like an artist's brush. Then, touching the corners of her mouth, he followed its opening before he allowed her to part her lips. But when she would have kissed him, he again withdrew just enough so she could not, and again he carefully explored the roundness of her lips, until the craving for him was an aching like a pleasant wound.

Nefrytatanen's arms lifted to embrace Amenemhet, but his hands on her wrists held them firmly against the bed. She opened her eyes to look at his face coming closer, to watch his mouth settle on hers, filling her with so intense a pleasure her breath was taken away. This kiss no longer held the measured teasing of before, but was a kiss that possessed her. She lay still, looking at his face through blurring vision.

His mouth held her captive, commanding in that kiss a surrender she would have gladly given if she had been able to speak, but she could do nothing except breathe like a small animal after a long run. She closed her eyes.

Amenemhet withdrew, and her eyes flew open to see that he smiled down on her. "I enjoy the way you breathe when I kiss you that way."

Nefrytatanen waited, wondering what he would do next, not caring. She was beyond questions. Again her eyes slipped closed.

His hands touched her, his fingers sensitively caressing her body, sure of what aroused her. With deliberate restraint he evoked fires that sprang from her very core. With his lips he caressed her until she wondered if she could endure the sensations that grew to impossible intensity. When she had become a gasping, mindless, writhing thing, he stopped.

Heart pounding as if it would burst from her breast, inflamed beyond thought, she opened her eyes and looked at him through a web of her own exquisitely ignited nerves. He was kneeling over her hips, motionless, looking at her with eyes streaked by golden flames. She reached up toward him as if she reached for a life that was slipping away, put her hands on his narrow waist and, with strength she didn't know she yet possessed, pulled him down to her. She moaned in the torment of the need he had so carefully built in her, but he didn't move. She turned her face to the side, helplessly drawing ragged breaths.

"It will never be cold where you are," he whispered.

His hands turned her face to his. He brought his mouth to hers—their lips' meeting poured burning honey through her. She could no longer wait. Her body demanded release and began its own irrevocable course, a primitive instinct in her suddenly knowing it was what he waited for.

She clung to him as if he were the only reality in the universe. Eternities flared with brilliance and passed, until he returned her to tranquil pools of shimmering light.

As he touched his lips to her eyelids, her temples, her shoulders, she was silent and motionless, unable to speak or move. She had just the strength to breathe, and her breath was filled with the scent of him.

Amenemhet looked at Nefrytatanen a long moment, his eyes still glowing from the remnants of his passion. Then he lowered his head to her breast to listen to her pounding heart slow, her breath become regular.

He wondered if she realized that when the moment came to her, she had cried out his name; she had murmured, again and again, through her rapture calling him her beloved. He sighed and kissed her shoulder, and even in her exhausted slumber, she nestled closer.

He smiled and whispered to her unhearing ears, "I have, as you asked before, put my seal upon you. But your love has stamped my soul forever."

As drained as Amenemhet's body was, his mind had no need for sleeping. He lay awake, thinking of Nefrytatanen and all that the gods had arranged for them. He was profoundly grateful, and his sleeplessness was a mutely eloquent prayer.

When the darkness in the tent had begun to lighten, Amenemhet arose from the warmth of Nefrytatanen's body. His movements, as he pulled on a tunic, made no more sound than the withdrawing moon. As the sun began to send streaks of pale gold into the indigo of the sky, he stepped from their tent.

Waving to a sentry, Amenemhet walked quietly through the shadows of an earth yet clinging to the night. At the temple's threshold, he paused to watch a hawk glide in a graceful arc on the blue-tinted air over the wall's crest. The towers of the temple stood over him like silent, lonely sentries watching as he turned and entered the courtyard.

The stones were cold under Amenemhet's feet, but he walked with long, swift strides to the courtyard's center, where again he paused and turned to look at the walls.

The painted figures of kings and divine beings seemed not so solemn in expression as they had before. Now Amenemhet noticed a gleam of humor in Tehuti's eye, the lips of the goddess Aset tilted with the hint of a beginning smile. Ra gazed from beneath his golden headpiece at Heru, who with outstretched arms expressed joy at some triumph. Amenemhet wondered if his triumph was life itself.

Ptah bent over his potter's wheel, engrossed in the task of fashioning from human clay a new prince, while the child's soul in the form of the royal hawk hovered nearby waiting to inhabit the small body. A king stood close, smiling proudly, his arm gently around his queen's softly swollen waist; a line of servants marched around a wall carrying gifts to lay on an offering table already adorned with garlands of lotuses. At each corner of the courtyard stood colossal statues of Asar, watching in silent approval.

Suddenly Amenemhet realized the scene didn't depict a mortal king and queen awaiting their child. This king was Asar. This queen was Aset. The child being made by the divine beings was Heru. Here, in Asar's burial place, was the story of his final triumph over death. Here was the legend unfolded of his son's conception and birth even after Asar had been killed. Here was the result of Aset's magic—Asar giving her their son even after his death. Love triumphant over eternity.

Amenemhet continued across the courtyard to enter the whispering corridors and move through shadowed chambers and still another sun-warming courtyard, until, at last, he approached the sacred pond.

It was an island of lush green against the golden brown of the landscape; and there, on the emerald moss, did Amenemhet kneel.

A bird called faintly to the sun, which now climbed rapidly

316

from behind the mountain's black silhouette accompanied by a host of flaming clouds.

Amenemhet picked up a handful of earth and bent his head to inhale the sweet fragrance of its promise, then lifted golden eyes to the soaring sun disk and whispered, "This soil, so small a part of my land, O Asar, I love! Is there any land holding magic and life like Tamera?" he asked. He shook his head in answer to his own question. "I need not your wisdom to know that answer. And my people know the truth of this as well as I—and they are grateful, Asar. They are grateful, even as I am."

Amenemhet paused, thinking of the reasons for his gratitude, not noticing the shadowy figure that stood behind him watching and listening to his words.

Raising his head proudly to the open sky, Amenemhet recalled Nefrytatanen's prostrating herself at his feet before all the court, and he asked, "What more of life could I want? Although I sometimes complain of my burdens, wishing I were but an architect who might watch a royal procession pass and turn back to my instruments and drawings, I know it's a foolish wish; for were I to see Nefrytatanen go by sitting beside another king, I would then long for royalty, that I might be at her side in his place."

Amenemhet was silent a moment. Finally, he whispered, "The first time my eyes rested on her, I thought I perceived a vision—as he who wanders in the desert sees visions born of his water madness. And when she smiled at me, I who had but moments before anticipated her arrival with dread was transformed into a state of wonder speculating on what would ruin this dream, which was too perfect to be reality. I thought something must be amiss and I merely had yet to discover it. Perhaps she would have a harsh voice, I thought, or a sharp tongue—but the sound of her voice was the serene melody of a lyre and the words she spoke were honey. There was nothing about her person in which I found offense or even a hint of disfavor. When she laid her hand so sweetly on my arm and I felt her warmth, I knew her finally to be real and not a vision. And when we kissed, our lips spoke the words which the Invisible One uttered to create the universe. The sky wheeled over my head, the earth shivered under my feet, and I stood trembling like a bird on a waving papyrus stem."

"When I stood in the meadow of Tuat before Amen-Ra himself," Nefrytatanen's voice came softly from behind him,

"I looked into the face of the divine being, and my heart whispered, 'It is my beloved.'"

Amenemhet turned and lifted golden eyes to hers.

"Yes," Nefrytatanen said quietly, "those are his eyes looking at me now."

MASTER NOVELISTS

CHESAPEAKE
CB 24163 $3.95
by James A. Michener

An enthralling historical saga. It gives the account of different generations and races of American families who struggled, invented, endured and triumphed on Maryland's Chesapeake Bay. It is the first work of fiction in ten years to be first on *The New York Times Best Seller List*.

THE BEST PLACE TO BE
PB 04024 $2.50
by Helen Van Slyke

Sheila Callaghan's husband suddenly died, her children are grown, independent and troubled, the men she meets expect an easy kind of woman. Is there a place of comfort? a place for strength against an aching void? A novel for every woman who has ever loved.

ONE FEARFUL YELLOW EYE
GB 14146 $1.95
by John D. MacDonald

Dr. Fortner Geis relinquishes $600,000 to someone that no one knows. Who knows his reasons? There is a history of threats which Travis McGee exposes. But why does the full explanation live behind the eerie yellow eye of a mutilated corpse?

8002

GREAT ROMANTIC NOVELS

SISTERS AND STRANGERS PB 04445 $2.50
by Helen Van Slyke

Three women—three sisters each grown into an independent lifestyle—now are three strangers who reunite to find that their intimate feelings and perilous fates are entwined.

THE SUMMER OF THE SPANISH WOMAN
CB 23809 $2.50

by Catherine Gaskin

A young, fervent Irish beauty is alone. The only man she ever loved is lost as is the ancient family estate. She flees to Spain. There she unexpectedly discovers the simmering secrets of her wretched past . . . meets the Spanish Woman . . . and plots revenge.

THE CURSE OF THE KINGS CB 23284 $1.95
by Victoria Holt

This is Victoria Holt's most exotic novel! It is a story of romance when Judith marries Tybalt, the young archeologist, and they set out to explore the Pharaohs' tombs on their honeymoon. But the tombs are cursed . . . two archeologists have already died mysteriously.

8000